LIBRARIES NI
WITHDRAWN FROM STOCK

"You will be haunted by three spirits."

A Christmas Carol, Charles Dickens

PROLOGUE

January 2018

DI Jimmy Stewart (retired) stood by the side of the Finglas Road, his umbrella one amongst many. The crowd was two to three people deep on both sides, as far as the eye could see. The rain had been coming down steadily all morning. Small patches of snow lay about the place, fading to nothing, a memory of another world; one that had been covered in white and full of the joys of Christmas. Not that he had particularly enjoyed Christmas. Behind him, in Glasnevin Cemetery, a snowman leaned sadly, shrinking to nothing.

Stewart had been unable to get into the church. In hindsight, maybe they should have put a PA system outside, but nobody had known how big an event this would be. It wasn't a state funeral or a celebrity, after all, it was just an ordinary man. No, that wasn't right. He was a lot of things, but you probably couldn't hang ordinary on him.

You wouldn't have said he was popular, as such, though everyone certainly knew who he was. He lived in that space between legend, cautionary tale and bogeyman. A man out of time. A man in possession of his own moral code, one that put him out of step with the world around him. He had also been a world-class pain in the

1

arse, which shouldn't be forgotten. He hadn't been a member of An Garda Síochána for a couple of years now, having retired not long after Stewart, so the top brass were spared from putting in an appearance. Stewart had rung Wilson, his former protégé from his time in the National Bureau of Criminal Investigation, to see if he wanted to come, but unusually there'd been no answer. Since Stewart's retirement, he and Wilson had become good friends, though neither of them dared call it that. Wilson would come around for regular chats and Stewart would give him the benefit of his forty years of law enforcement experience. God, he missed the job. More than anything, although he would be loath to admit it, he missed the people. In that regard, today had been a trip down memory lane. As he'd walked along the road, he'd seen a lot of familiar faces. The rank and file had turned out in great numbers, because they remembered this man for exactly the reasons that the top brass wanted to forget him. Everybody had a story.

Not that it was mainly Gardaí. The numbers from the force were dwarfed by the ordinary people. There were other faces Stewart recognised amongst the crowd. The Dublin criminal fraternity had come to pay their respects too. Stewart had passed a couple of faces he was sure had spent several years up in Mountjoy Prison thanks to the man's efforts. Still, they looked solemn. Not a hint of a smirk to be seen.

The parade came around the corner, for that is what it surely was. It wasn't official, but somebody somewhere must have been watching, or one of those who were there in an unofficial capacity had made a call. Uniforms had hurriedly closed off the road. The parade was coming regardless and the sheer weight of numbers meant it wouldn't be stopped. Like the man himself, an unstoppable force.

Behind the hearse, they came in red line after red line, some of them wearing the jerseys of Saint Jude's hurling team, most of them older, just wearing whatever red they had. The current team, then the ones past. They seemed to be walking in rough age groups. Someone might have suggested it, or maybe it had just happened, those who had played together standing side by side as they followed him one last time.

As the hearse passed him, Stewart lowered his head. He wasn't a religious man, but still – respect was respect, and this man had truly earned it.

Alongside the coffin, which was draped in a jersey with a hurley lying across it, a massive wreath of flowers spelt out his name.

Bunny.

CHAPTER ONE

12 December 2017

Detective Superintendent Susan Burns stepped out of the car and straight into a puddle. "Arse biscuits!"

"Everything alright, chief?"

"Yeah, fine," she said, looking down at her sodden left shoe. "It'd just be nice if, every now and then, somebody dug up a body in a nice clean hole on Grafton Street, with mud-free paving stones and decent coffee in close proximity."

"Yes, chief."

"Speaking of my shoes, are you going to be alright with this?"

"Absolutely," said Detective Donnacha Wilson, failing to hide his annoyance at the question. The first time they had met, Wilson had lost his breakfast at the sight of a dead body, destroying her brand new pair of Louboutins in the process and cementing himself in the minds of his Garda colleagues as "Chucker" Wilson for evermore. The year before that, he had similarly tossed his salad over the remains of a man he had just shot. The fact that the dead guy was a highly trained assassin who had been milliseconds away from killing two innocent members of the public, and in all probability Wilson's partner, was never remembered. The vomiting, however, much to Detective Wilson's chagrin, had proven unforgettable.

Burns started walking up the slope towards the building site, ignoring the squelching noise that greeted every other step. Wilson followed in her wake. Today had started badly and was only going to get worse. Her days of visiting gravesites should really be over, but what the Gardaí called "historic deaths" were a politically charged issue due to the amount of IRA victims who had been "disappeared" over the years, their bodies never recovered. As far as DSI Burns was concerned, this was either going to be the resolution of a missing person case – for which her team would receive no credit – or a murder that they would have virtually no chance of clearing. Half the time when long-dead bodies were recovered, it wasn't possible to even identify the murderee, thus making any hope of nabbing the murderer a pipe dream. She was aware thinking in such terms would be considered heartless by many people, but those people didn't have to sit in budget meetings with accountants who had calculated the cost per murder solved.

It was still only 2pm on a crappy winter's day, but what little light there had been was fading fast. The location for this new Environment Appreciation Centre had been picked for the magnificent vista of the Wicklow Mountains it offered. It would no doubt provide a delightful backdrop when the Minister for Tourism came to cut the ribbon in May, but nearing the end of a dreary December day that never got going, the effect was somewhat lost. The builders had only got as far as digging the foundations and they were about to be thrown way off schedule. They had already faced delays of a few weeks thanks to the time it took to get hippies out of trees. As the national newspaper coverage could attest, quite a lot of people thought the environment was best appreciated by not being dug up, chopped down or paved over.

About half a dozen workmen sat around outside a Portakabin, supping tea and enjoying being paid for doing nothing. There was an unmistakable air of celebration. If this really kicked off, there could be overtime somewhere down the line. Fingers crossed the Minister for Tourism had a holiday booked.

As Burns and Wilson walked past, a voice rose up to follow them. "Alright, sweetheart, give us a wave."

"You heard the man, Wilson."

"Very funny, chief."

"That's a fine ass. I'd throw it into that. Hard!"

DSI Burns executed an about turn in one fluid motion, complete with squelch. Her bad mood had just met someone utterly deserving of it.

As she walked towards the men, there was a mix of facial expressions ranging from embarrassment to the giddy excitement of schoolboys. She'd not seen who the comment had come from, but she didn't need to. He was about six stone overweight and two turns over ugly, with a bulbous nose, ratty eyes and impressive collection of chins. He was the only one dumb enough to be looking at her defiantly, a sneer across his face – a face that only a mother could love, though Burns would have laid good money she hadn't.

"What was that you said?"

"Just a bit a banter, darling."

"I see. And was there something in the way I was walking by, going about my job, that made you think I'd be up for some of your top-notch sexually explicit banter?"

The ratty eyes looked past her to Wilson. "Jesus, fella, is she always this much of a moody bitch?"

A couple of his co-workers laughed, though Burns was pleased to see a couple of more looked embarrassed.

"I am always this much of a moody bitch. Yes. You see, it's the pressures of the job. Us silly little women aren't built to cope with the stresses of the really important work, y'know, like digging holes. Instead we have to stick to the simpler things, like... " She allowed herself a little flash of showmanship as she pulled out her ID and snapped it open in one fluid motion "Detective Superintendent in the Garda Síochána."

The king of banter's grin froze into an enjoyable rigor mortis impression of itself, his eyes having registered the change in the wind but the message not reaching all of his face yet. In his defence, he had a lot of face to reach.

"You see, unfortunately, I'm an officer of the law and you've committed an offence as laid out in the Non-Fatal Offences Against the Person Act, 1997, subsection ten dash one: harassment. As I'm sure you know, being such an intelligent man, you can face a fine of five thousand euros and up to twelve months imprisonment for said offence."

"It was just a bit of—"

"Banter," finished Burns. "Yes, you said. Do you want to know how many times in my career in law enforcement I've charged and brought someone before the courts and not gotten a conviction?"

"Alright, look, I—"

"None. Zero. Zip. I'm guessing the same amount of women who you have satisfied sexually in your sorry existence. You see, unlike you, I'm incredible at screwing people – and when I screw someone, they stay screwed. I've had more convictions than you've had hot dinners, and by the look of you, that's a lot. So, in summary, you've lost your job, you're looking at twelve months in prison and you'd be amazed how many favours people who're locked up owe a DSI in the Gardaí. Wilson, do you remember Gary Abbot?"

"Yes, boss. Drug dealer that we got last year for killing his supplier with a baseball bat."

"Do you remember how happy he was when I didn't prosecute his ma, even though he'd been storing his stash in her garage?"

"I do, boss. He cried like a baby."

"Do you think he'd be happy to arrange a little date for our friend here?"

"I'm sure he would."

DSI Burns gave the delightfully mute moron her most winning of smiles. "So, at least you'll finally have sex with someone you didn't have to pay for it. Now, two choices: one, point me in the direction of your boss so we can get the ball rolling on your new life..."

"Please don't—"

"Or..." She left a deliberately long pause, which remained unfilled. Neither the king of banter nor any of his supporting cast were feeling chatty anymore. "Or," she repeated, "'Macarena'."

"What?"

"I'd like to see you shaking that fine ass."

"Ehm, but how can I..."

"Oh, don't worry," she said, pointing at the other men, "they'll all sing the song for you. Unless they'd like me to go and talk to the boss about how they facilitated the antisocial behaviour of a co-worker?"

Five minutes later, Detective Wilson and DSI Burns had signed in on the crime scene log and were standing outside the flaps of the tent that the Technical Bureau had erected. Burns leaned on Wilson as she pulled on the foot coverings that went with the mandatory plastic overalls.

"I was surprised he knew all the words," said Wilson. "I mean, the 'Macarena' is quite old now, isn't it?"

"Are you making a crack about my age, Wilson?"

"Oh, God no, boss."

Burns sighed. This was the problem with being intimidating: it made jokes a lot harder. Sometimes she considered holding up a sign.

"Remind me to never piss you off, chief."

"We've been working together for over a year now, Wilson, I'd have thought you would no longer need reminding. Speaking of which..." Burns nodded towards the tent flaps. "Last chance. You can stay outside if you like?"

"Absolutely not, boss."

"Fair enough. Be it on your own head – or at least somebody else's shoes." DSI Burns glanced at her watch – 3:12pm – then pulled open the flap of the tent and walked inside.

Inside the tent were six people in Technical Bureau overalls, two of whom were down in the hole, taking photographs, while the others stood around watching them. There were two tables, each containing remains covered by white sheets.

"Hello, all," said Burns, "is Dr Devane about?"

Devane was the state pathologist, and she and Burns, while not exactly friends, had at least a very good working relationship.

"I'm afraid not," came the voice from down in the hole. "She's in the UK on a course until tomorrow. You're stuck with me."

Burns faked a smile and swore internally; her day wasn't set to improve anytime soon. Phillips was Devane's second-in-command. He was decent at the job but he did have a love of technical jargon and a bedside manner that made pathology a logical career choice, the dead being rarely inclined to complain.

Phillips climbed up a stepladder to get out of the eight-foot-deep section of trench. He was a tall, thin man. Burns didn't know if pathology attracted people who didn't eat much, or if being around bodies so often permanently dampened the appetite, but the result was always the same. Identifying members of the Tech Bureau team was tricky: every last one of them was a stick-thin figure wearing a face mask and identical overalls.

"So, what do we have?"

"A mass grave."

Burns felt Wilson stiffen beside her, probably because he was less familiar with Isaac Phillip's irritating manner than she was. "By which you mean two or more bodies." She indicated the two tables to the left of the hole. "I assume it is just the two?"

Phillips shrugged. "For the moment. We might need to check the surrounding area." Somewhere, the Minister for Tourism had just felt somebody walk across his grave.

"Still, I think we'll stay away from using the term 'mass grave' anywhere near the press."

"Well, if people will overreact to the use of the correct terminology." Phillips pulled the sheet back on one of the tables to reveal skeletal remains. "Subject number one, male, middle-aged. Cause of death is yet to be officially determined but there is evidence of a stab wound to the chest, judging by the blood found on the clothing."

"Clothing?" asked Burns.

Phillips indicated a clear plastic bag at the bottom of the table, containing what looked like not much more than dirty rags. "Yes, most of the clothing survived. This is a moorland burial site with a highly acidic nature to the soil, meaning there is far less microbial activity related to decomposition. The flesh has all been eaten away but the clothing is remarkably intact."

"I don't suppose any ID survived?"

"No."

Burns nodded. "It didn't feel like that lucky a day. How long have these bodies been down there do we think?"

"Well, to determine that, you'd need an expert in the field of taphonomy."

"The science of how bodies decompose," interjected Wilson. He did this on a semi-regular basis, invariably just before the point that Burns was about to start actually liking him. It was an ego-based form of Tourette's, stemming from a deep-seated need for people to know he was clever. Burns guessed he'd been hugged either too much or not enough as a child – she didn't really care to find out which.

"Yes," said Burns, "well done, Wilson. Ten points to Gryffindor." She turned back to Phillips. "By any chance, would you happen to be such an expert?"

"Oh, I dabble."

"And?"

"Well," said Phillips, giving the bodies the same look she'd got the last time she'd brought her car into the garage for a service, "it's very tricky to say. There are a lot of factors to consider and tests to be run – now, don't hold me to this – but I'd say they've been in the ground for between fifteen and twenty-five years."

"And cause of death on the second one?"

"Ah," said Phillips, excited that his audience had finally asked the right question, "now that's where it becomes interesting."

He waved them over towards the second body and pulled the sheet away with a flourish. "Victim number two, male, between thirty-five and fifty, with non-standard dental work." Burns had noticed the two gold-capped teeth. The first thing anyone notices about a skull is the smile, especially when it contains a bit of bling.

"If you look here, you'll notice a nice round hole in the bone at the back of the eye socket, with some evidence of radiating fractures through the frontal bone as well."

"I see," said Burns. "Stabbed in the eye?"

Phillips shook his head. "No, there's internal beveling, which would indicate a gunshot."

Burns moved around to look at the back of the skull to confirm her suspicions. "But there's no exit wound."

"Exactly," confirmed Phillips, nodding his head. "We'll have to take it back to the lab for tests, but the wound appears to have been inflicted by a non-standard weapon. There is something wedged in the rear of the skull but we can't dissect it here. Most interesting though."

Burns looked down at the body again. "Not for this guy."

Phillips picked up the tweezers from beside the table. "Oh, excuse me a moment."

He looked into the eye socket of the skull. "We seem to have picked up a passenger." He nabbed something with the tweezers and slowly drew out a long, fat earthworm. "Out you come, little fella."

It was at this point that Wilson cracked, sprinting for the tent's exit with his hand over his mouth.

One of the techs held up his watch triumphantly. "YES! Under five minutes, everyone owes me a fiver!" His beaming smile froze when it met DSI Burns's glare.

"Really?" She pointed in the direction of the door. "Detective Wilson is a highly decorated officer, who has put his life on the line in the service of justice in this country, and you idiots are taking bets on how long before you can make him feel unwell?"

Phillips looked uncomfortable. "Well, no. I, we—"

Burns put her hand up. "Save it. You can all explain this ghoulish and unprofessional behaviour to Dr Devane when she returns. Believe me, it will get mentioned. In the meantime, for future reference, I expect all of my officers to be treated with respect and dignity in the workplace."

She didn't bother waiting for an answer, turning on her heel and departing the tent with a pleasing sense of drama. Once outside, she saw Wilson hunched over, leaning with one hand on the back of a JCB digger while spitting in an effort to remove the nasty aftertaste from his mouth.

Burns rolled out her lesser-used softer tone. "Donnacha, are you OK?"

He didn't look up, just waved her away furiously with his free hand.

She turned and walked back towards the car, fishing her phone out of her jacket pocket. She speed-dialled the incident room, where Sergeant Moira Clarke picked up on the second ring.

"Moira, it's Burns. Looks like these two bodies up in Wicklow are going to be ours."

"Yes, boss. And about the other thing?"

Burns glanced back to make sure she was unobserved and then lowered her voice. "He made it to four minutes thirty-seven by my count."

She could hear Moira open her drawer and consult a sheet of paper.

"Congratulations, boss, you won the sweepstake."

Burns allowed herself a mini fist pump. At least something had gone her way today.

CHAPTER TWO

Brigit stared up at the ceiling. There was a picture of a kitten stuck to it that she found irrationally irritating, quite possibly because she associated it with the voice of Dr Megan Wright, and she found that intensely irritating.

"Would you like to discuss your hands?" Her voice sounded nice the first time you heard it, but that's because you hadn't yet noticed the little nasal whine that sat just below the surface.

"No, I absolutely would not." Brigit's hands were stuck inside her hoodie and that was where they were staying.

"I really think we should."

"Well, I don't."

"Why don't you want to discuss your hands?"

Brigit looked back from the couch at Dr Wright, sitting behind her, fingers steepled together in a contemplative pose. Brigit bet she practiced that in the mirror, trying to look as psychiatristy as possible. "Oh no you don't. If we're discussing why I'm not discussing it, then we're actually discussing it and I don't want to discuss it."

Dr Wright sighed in that annoying way she had, like Brigit had somehow disappointed her.

"Has anyone ever told you that you have a very angry energy, Brigit?"

"Not in those words, no, but then, I don't know anyone who is American enough to carry that kind of bullshitty language off."

"I'm actually Canadian."

Brigit knew that. She also knew that getting it wrong really irritated Dr Wright, which was why she did it.

Brigit considered herself in most ways to be a people person. She liked to get on well with everyone; she tried to find something in everyone to like. Dr Wright was a notable exception. Brigit hadn't even tried to like her. That, in fact, was Dr Wright's value – she was someone in her life who Brigit could properly dislike without feeling any sense of guilt.

"I have to be honest, Brigit, I worry that our sessions aren't proving of benefit to you."

"Don't even think about it. I've got twenty sessions, that's the deal. Every Tuesday at 3pm, come hell or high water, I'm going to be here."

"But why are you here?"

"I'm here because, as part of your divorce settlement, you agreed to give me twenty therapy sessions to cover the bill your now ex-husband owed MCM Investigations."

"Yes, I know that. I meant—"

"Because," continued Brigit, "we caught you having an affair with the last investigator he hired to follow you."

"There's no need to—"

"Not to mention the personal trainer you were also banging, and that TV producer—"

"Yes, OK."

"And your ex-husband before the current ex-husband, who you were also stumping."

"Stumping? Really?"

"I'm trying to not use the F-word so much in conversation. I'm worried it is stunting my vocabulary. I mean though, who has an affair with their ex-husband?"

"Judge not, lest you be judged." Dr Wright sounded really irritated now.

"Judge away. To be honest, you were having that many affairs, it is frankly massively impressive just from a time management point of view. How did you fit them all in? No pun intended."

"Oh!" Dr Wright's clipboard hit the opposite wall, taking down a framed picture of a kitten in the process. For a medical professional, she really had an unnerving belief in the healing power of a cat picture. "Fine. Fuck you. Don't tell me about your hands. See if I give a crap."

Brigit turned to look at Dr Megan Wright, serial philanderer and former TV advice-giver, sitting with her arms folded, having properly taken whatever Canadians called the hump.

"Well, that's not very professional."

Dr Wright threw her leg over the side of her chair and took out an e-cigarette. "Screw this, I'm having a vape. I'm done pretending this is a normal doctor-patient thing. This is the most dysfunctional relationship I've ever been in."

"And coming from a two-timing two-time divorcée, that is really saying something."

"Amen, sister."

Brigit put her hand into her bag and took out her own e-cigarette. It was supposed to be her stepping stone to giving up the fags entirely, but so far that plan was proving less than successful. As she placed it to her lips, she could sense Dr Wright's eyes on her, specifically on her hands. To be fair, they were rather eye-catching, seeing as they were more or less entirely covered in yellow paint.

"C'mon, tell me!" She said it in a distinctly whiny tone that Brigit guessed they didn't teach you in whatever the psychiatrist version of medical school was.

"Fine." To be honest she had actually wanted to talk about the morning's latest incident, but she didn't want Dr Wright thinking she was setting the agenda. "So, Paul—"

"Which one is he?"

"Really? Paul? I've talked about him in every session."

"Sorry, but I see a lot of people and your notes are now on the far side of the room because you're so goddamn irritating."

"Are you supposed to say that?"

"I'm trying something new. Anyway, Paul – is he the one you were engaged to who cheated on you?"

"No. He's the one after that prince."

"I've got it!" said Dr Wright, clapping her hands together. "He's the one you thought screwed around on you, but he didn't – your ex, that first guy, set him up. Drugged him and took a bunch of compromising pictures of him with a hooker. See, I remember stuff."

"Like that would be hard to forget." Brigit blew out a long curl of artificially flavoured smoke. "How did you ever get on telly doing this?"

Dr Wright shrugged. "Teeth and tits, sweetheart. And these baby blues really pop on screen."

"You're a terrible human being, you know that?"

"Yeah, well, that may be, but good people give terrible advice. So Paul is the guy you still work with in your marriage-wrecking business."

Brigit laughed. "Oh please, we did you a favour. You go through men so fast, eventually you'd have banged your own husband by accident."

"I've got a lock-up full of furniture I can't fit into my tiny rented flat that says otherwise." Dr Wright didn't say it in a particularly angry way, more as a statement of fact. "So, the guy you wrongly accused, who you still work with – that's Paul?"

"Yes."

"And now you've got this will they, won't they, Ross and Rachel thing going on."

"Since the whole big thing last year it's just been... complicated."

"What big thing?"

Brigit looked back at Dr Wright in honest surprise. "Really? The Skylark Affair?"

Wright gave her a blank expression.

"Somebody started killing property developers, claiming they were doing it as revenge on behalf of the Irish people. Turned out it was just a particularly psycho developer trying to cover his tracks and pin it on my friend Bunny McGarry. We solved the whole thing. It made the papers?"

It had actually made the papers worldwide, and they'd had their full fifteen minutes of fame. That was sixteen months ago now, but it was the reason that the fledgling MCM Investigations had developed such a large client list. It was also the reason Bunny now walked with a limp, as well as God knows whatever else was going on there.

Dr Wright shrugged. "I'm not much of a reader. So what's that got to do with your ex not screwing around on you?"

"It's all... it's complicated."

Dr Wright blew out some more artificial smoke, this time forming it into an impressive smoke ring. "So you keep saying. Anyway, long story short, you and this Paul guy had your moment where it could've been a big, romantic, back-together type thing and you blew it."

"That's a rather harsh assessment coming from you."

"Well, yeah, but say what you want about my car crash of a private life, nobody can accuse me of turning down opportunities."

"True enough. Well, anyway, about three months ago, Paul is on this private investigator training course and this guy, another investigator called Kevin Kelleher, just comes right out and says it was him and his brothers that my ex hired to do it – to drug Paul and help with taking the compromising pictures. Just comes right out and tells him, like it's a funny thing."

"Why would he do that?"

"Ah." Brigit shrugged. "Men."

"Fair enough."

"So now Paul is on the warpath, wanting to bring the Kellehers up on charges. He's gone to the Gardaí about it, only Duncan—"

"The ex?"

"Yeah, him. He's left the country and the 'lady' involved is nowhere to be found either, so Paul can't press charges."

"Bummer."

"So, instead, we're basically at war with another detective agency now."

"I see."

"And it is a nightmare. I mean..." Brigit held her hands up.

"I don't get it."

"So, Paul, to get his own back on the Kelleher brothers, sent them a package laced with itching powder in the post."

"And they covered your hands in yellow paint?"

"No, they broke into our offices and stuck a dead fish in the air vent."

"Oh."

"Yeah. So Paul set their offices up as a brothel. He put cards all over Dublin. They got a lot of callers and then they were raided by the Gardaí."

"And then they—"

"Then they smashed in the windows of Paul's car."

"That's not exactly imaginative."

"I thought that too. Credit to Paul, he then built a wall in front of their offices. Now that was at least a bit more imaginative."

"How...?"

"He hired a couple of brickies. Did it at night."

"I see. So, after that with the yellow paint?"

"No. Then they had us listed as giving out free winter flu jabs."

"How did...?"

"Four hundred angry pensioners. It was almost a very slow riot. So after that..." Brigit paused to make sure she had things in the right order. "Yeah, after that, Paul superglued their office."

Dr Wright paused. "Like the locks?"

"No." Brigit sighed. "Everything. He broke in and glued everything in there to everything else. You could turn the entire office upside down and it'd all stay perfectly in place. He got hold of some Chinese glue that's banned in this county for being too powerful. This was two days ago."

"So today..."

Brigit nodded. "I made the mistake of opening the post..." She held her bright yellow hands up. "Ruined my pantsuit too, not to mention the whole office looking like – well, like a yellow paint bomb hit it." Brigit didn't want to say, but she had deliberately worn her best suit into work today, as Dr Wright always made her feel underdressed. The doctor dressed like a runway fashion show might break out at any time. This was yet another reason why Brigit found her so deeply annoying.

"Can you not wash the paint off?"

"Obviously not!" She had spent an hour trying to do so. She'd had to go way over the top on the perfume just to get rid of the stench of turpentine. She was now wearing a pair of raggedy jeans and a hoodie she had stashed in a cupboard from when they'd painted the office, which, come to think of it, they'd have to do again now.

"So, let me get this straight. You're in this messed-up Dennis the Menace-style nasty prank war with another detective agency…"

Brigit nodded again. "And because the incident that started the whole thing was the start of me not believing Paul, which led to us breaking up…"

Dr Wright mirrored Brigit's nod. "You can't stop the damn thing."

Brigit flopped back onto the couch and sighed. "Exactly. It feels like because I didn't believe him then, I can't not support him now, even though it is seriously screwing up our business."

"That is messed up."

"Thank you for that brilliant insight, doc."

"What do you want from me? You're my patient and – I'm going to say what I don't think I've ever said before – I think you're the sane one and everyone else is friggin' crazy."

"I know. That's why I have so much pent-up anger."

"And why you are so aggressive towards me?"

"Well, you are also intensely annoying."

"Right backatcha, sister. Y'know, this could be a whole new branch of therapy – rage therapy! Catchy title. I might write a book about this." Dr Wright stood up, walked over to her desk and wrote down the name.

"At the rate you're going through divorces, I hope it is a big success."

Dr Wright opened a drawer and pulled out a bottle of red wine and two plastic cups. "From your lips to God's ears." She held up the bottle and Brigit nodded. "So you and Paul own the private dick business together?" Brigit noted the emphasis on the word dick.

"Well, me, Paul and Bunny."

"WTF is a Bunny?"

Brigit also hated people who talked in text speak. "Bunny McGarry. He's our third partner. Not that he's been around much. He came out of Skylark a physical wreck." And a mental one, thought Brigit, although it felt too disloyal to say it out loud. She hadn't known Bunny that well beforehand, but she still knew him enough to realise he'd come out of the whole thing more broken than he'd gone in. He'd spent ten days chained to a wall in utter darkness, all alone save for the daily savage beatings. Then he'd been shot in the foot for good measure. Most people wouldn't have come back from half of that. Bunny wasn't most people, but that didn't mean he was invulnerable. These days, on the rare occasions she saw him, he seemed distant and different. He also didn't have much interest in the day-to-day business of a private detective agency.

Dr Wright handed a plastic cup of wine to Brigit. "Earth to Conroy, you just stopped talking and started staring off into the distance there."

"Sorry."

Wright slipped her shoes off and curled up in her armchair, glass of wine in hand. "OK, so, hypothetically, do you actually want to get back together with this Paul guy?"

"I honestly don't know. I mean..." Brigit picked nervously at the paint on her wine-holding hand. "I've not exactly had the best of luck with relationships. I almost married a man who it turned out was screwing everything that could move. I was then with a guy who not only wasn't screwing around on me, when I thought he was, but who then went and saved my life."

"Really?!"

"Well, yeah, but then I also saved his. Actually, I think it's about two-all now. That's not including how we first properly met."

"What happened then?"

"I asked him to do me a favour and an old man stabbed him."

Brigit drained her cup and Dr Wright leaned over to refill it. "Meh, I've had worse dates."

"And, I mean, look what I do for a living now. I'm a private investigator. I thought it'd be all finding lost loved ones and bringing arseholes to justice, but it isn't. It's all dodgy insurance claims and people screwing around behind their partner's back – no offence."

"Taken."

"It makes you despair about humanity, it really does."

Dr Megan Wright blew a long and loud raspberry.

Brigit turned to look at her. "Excuse me?"

"Oh, I'm sorry." Dr Megan Wright blew another long and loud raspberry.

"I can't believe people pay you for this."

"For the love of God, listen to yourself. You sound like some soft-in-the-head giggly girl who just found out life isn't fair. What age are you, thirty-eight?"

"Thirty-two!"

"Exactly, and you're not getting any younger." A little slosh of red wine splashed onto the doctor's carpet as she gesticulated. "Let me tell you what love is – it's the war on terror."

"OK."

"Shut up, I'm going somewhere with this. I knew this anti-terrorism guy in London."

"...i.e. were banging."

"Actually, no!" Dr Wright looked triumphant for a minute, then her facial expression changed. "Oh wait, come to think of it, just that one time."

"Seriously?"

Dr Wright ignored her. "He told me that the problem is the security services have to get it right every time and the terrorists just have to get it right once."

"You've lost me."

"Life is the security services, and we" – another slosh of wine hit the carpet – "are the terrorists. We just have to be right once! Then *kaboom* – happy ever after."

"This feels like a particularly disturbing reworking of that whole 'you've got to kiss a lot of frogs' idea."

"Shut up! I'm a medical professional and I'm telling you. Fire him, fuck him, in whatever order you want, but that's your solution right there."

"I can't fire him."

"Sure you can. This third partner, Rabbit?"

"Bunny."

"Yeah, get him to do it."

Brigit shook her head. "I'm afraid, doc, that is a whole other world of crazy."

CHAPTER THREE

Paul made his way back from the toilets carefully. Phelan's was not a pub where you wanted to accidentally collide with anyone's drinking elbow. Most pubs prided themselves on having ambience or an atmosphere, but not Phelan's. Phelan's had an insinuation – if not an outright threat – of violence. It was where you drank if you'd been banned from a lot of other places, or if your dog had.

People sat scattered in ones, twos and threes around the bar. There was a low murmur of conversation over an old Johnny Cash record. Jacinta, the owner, would not countenance the playing of anything but Cash and Elvis. The complaints procedure about this policy was famously brief and painful.

They were in the corner booth, which had probably seen more crimes planned than anywhere else in Ireland, with the possible exception of the bar in Government Buildings. As he sat down, Paul glanced around; some of the twos and threes sat in huddled conversations, others in silence. At least one of the ones was holding an animated conversation with himself, which appeared to be getting heated. To the left of their booth, half the tattoos in Dublin were spread across a trio of big lads in too-tight vests, playing pool.

Paul softly banged his half-full pint glass on the table three times.

"Right, I call this meeting of the MCM Investigations defence committee to order."

Phil Nellis took a slurp of his pint of Guinness, belched and wiped the back of the hand holding his phone across his lips. "I've not joined any committee."

"As your employer, I've put you on the committee."

"I'm not even a proper employee."

Paul rolled his eyes. "We've been through this. Brigit said that because of your criminal record, we can't officially get you licensed as a private investigator."

Phil shook his head. "It's a disgrace. I'm putting me life in order. I'm a married man with a baby on the way, for God's sake. The showers that be are preventing me from having full-time gainful employment because of one mistake."

"Phil, you've got fourteen convictions."

"Fourteen teeny-tiny mistakes."

To be fair to Phil, it wasn't a record to strike fear into anyone. He had been a strictly petty criminal and a tremendously inept one at that. He had once been caught trying to break into Pearse Street Garda Station after he'd left his bag behind while being interviewed and didn't want the embarrassment of having to ask for it at reception. His retirement had been no great loss to the criminal world. Paul had to admit, however, that he was a remarkably good private detective. Paul, like almost everybody else, found surveillance mind-numbingly boring, but Phil could happily sit there and watch paint dry. He had a gift for doing absolutely nothing and had quickly become MCM Investigations' secret weapon.

"Who else is on this committee?" asked Phil.

"It's you and me."

Phil pointed below the table at Maggie, who was methodically demolishing a large bone, having already enthusiastically slurped her way through two pints of Guinness. "Is Maggie on the committee?"

"No, Phil, we cannot have a German Shepherd on the committee."

"No offence, but of the three of us, who would you back in a fight?"

"Fine. Maggie is on the committee."

"Grand. How does it work with the voting?"

"We're not having votes. I make all the decisions."

"Very democratic."

Beneath the table, Maggie farted loudly, adding her objection to proceedings.

"Jaysus," said Phil, wafting his hand in front of his face, "she's getting worse."

Paul nodded. The flatulence issue was frankly getting out of hand, but despite all the best advice, trying to get Maggie to eat proper dog food was proving to be a nightmare. "Don't worry about it," he said, opening up his notepad. "Now, our company has been the victim of an unprovoked attacked from the bastard Kellehers. This cannot be allowed to stand."

"When you say unprovoked, we did attack them first."

"Well, yes, but that was only retaliation for what they did before that."

"But before that again, we attacked them."

"Only because they'd attacked us. Let's not forget how this started. We were on your stag do when they—"

"I know, but—"

"Those bastards ruined my life, Phil!"

Phil put his hands up in surrender. Neither of them liked reliving that occasion, not that Paul could actually recall most of it. Being spiked with enough Rohypnol to stagger an elephant will do that to a man. Phil felt guilty, because he'd stormed out and left Paul on his own in the first place.

"I'm not saying you're wrong to be angry. Their actions were completely highness—"

"I think you mean heinous."

"That's what I said. Anyway, my point is, why don't we use the element of surprise?"

Paul drummed his fingers on the table excitedly. "I like how you're thinking. Go on."

"The Kellehers expect us to respond, right?"

"Right."

"So..." said Phil, spreading his hands out dramatically, "we don't."

Paul waited. Phil looked at him expectantly. At the nearby pool table, someone potted a ball.

"And?"

"That's it."

"Phil, how does us doing nothing help us win this war?"

"Because they'll always be thinking, 'When's it going to happen? When's it going to happen?' And it never does. It'll drive them mental."

"That's a terrible idea. You see, this is why we can't have votes."

"I'm sick of this, Paul. I want to go back to just doing work. We've a backlog of cases."

"But we're winning!"

"Are we?" said Phil, looking pointedly at the mobile phone in his left hand. It had been in his left hand for two days now. Paul's plan for breaking into the offices of Kelleher Brothers Investigations had been a two-man job and, as always, Phil had been the second man. While in the midst of gluing everything to everything else, Phil's overriding concern as a father-to-be with a wife ten days from her due date had surpassed all other concerns. He'd answered his ringing phone to a wrong number from a cab company and had it firmly glued to his hand ever since.

"Da Xin made me sleep in the spare room last night. She read somewhere that the radiation from phones can disturb the baby."

"I told you," said Paul, "it'll wear off naturally in a couple of days. Or put it in hot water."

"Yeah," said Phil, "phones love hot water, well known for it." He picked up his pint with his free hand and took another gulp. "Da Xin says I should, y'know, concentrate on working."

"This is work. It's for the company."

"Da Xin says that the stuff Brigit tells me to do, that's for the company. This is your own personal stuff, that's what Da Xin says."

"And does Da Xin tell you what to do?"

"Yes."

"So... wait, what?"

"Course she tells me what to do. She's a lot smarter than me." Phil looked at Paul like he was mad. Paul had forgotten the golden rule: you had to talk to Phil in Nellisian logic. Normal rules did not apply.

"I'm your oldest friend."

"I know that."

"And I need help."

"You're dead right."

"Not like that. I need your help. Who else am I going to ask?"

Phil considered this. "Bunny?"

Paul nearly choked on his pint. "Bunny? Are you mad? Do you want this thing to have an actual body count?"

"No, fair point. It's just... alright, I'll help you—"

"Brilliant."

"One last time," continued Phil, "and then I'm out."

"Of course."

"I mean it this time."

"Absolutely." Paul opened his pad. "Right, we need a plan. I've got some ideas. Now, hear me out here, One-Eyed Barry says he can get hold of some... ehm, kinda like fireworks."

"No, Paulie – hell no. Have you forgotten the reason he only has one eye?"

"Alright," said Paul, crossing something off his list.

"In fact, let me save you some time here." Phil pointed at Paul's pad. "I'm doing nothing that involves the words explosives..."

Paul crossed off two more ideas.

"Kidnapping..."

Another three.

"Or any form of chemical warfare."

Two more. Below the table, Maggie farted again.

"Jesus," said Paul. "Speaking of chemical warfare. Alright, how's about this... we put a badger into their office overnight. I mean, we'd have to get it in and then make sure when they turned up in the morning, it'd be angry. Like really angry."

"Well," said Phil, "seeing as you've taken a woodland creature out of its natural habitat and put it into an office on Leeson Street, I'd imagine that wouldn't be a problem. Please remove any ideas that involve animals too."

"Ah, for..." Paul crossed off four more ideas. "You're giving me very little to work with here, Phil. Alright, how's about we get their offices registered as an ISIS training camp?"

"Who's Isis?"

"Do you not watch the news, Phil?"

"I've read nothing but baby books for six months."

"Well—"

A large hand slammed down in the middle of their table, causing Paul to jump in shock. It was attached to the tattoo-covered arm of one of the pool players. He had a ring through his nose that, from this angle, made Paul think of a bull. A very angry bull.

"What the fuck is that smell?"

"Ehm," said Paul.

"His dog has a bit of a flatulence problem." A large part of what made Phil such an awful petty criminal was that he was unhelpfully honest.

"Well, get the smelly bitch out of here then."

Paul smiled nervously. "She's actually allowed to be here."

"My hole." Raging Bull leaned down so that his face was inches from Paul's. It was noticeable that his zero-tolerance approach to unpleasant odours didn't extend to his own breath. "Get her out of here, or I'll chuck you both out the bleedin' window."

"I really wouldn't do that," said Phil. "She doesn't like to be touched."

Raging Bull looked at Phil and then noticed the phone in his hand. "Are you recording me?"

"No. It's a long story."

"Lads, this chancer is recording me on his phone."

Raging Bull's two pals now stood over the table. If anything, they were even bigger. What little light there was in Phelan's was now being almost entirely blocked out, as though by a really angry eclipse.

A warning growl came from below the table.

"Alright, lads, relax," said Paul. "We're leaving."

A voice came from behind Raging Bull. "Somebody is leaving, but it's not you."

Raging Bull turned around and looked down. Five-foot-nothing, Jacinta Phelan looked up at him with a face filled with defiance. She'd run this pub for forty years and three husbands. She was a legend, not to mention on at least three occasions, an alibi. She was especially known for her uncompromising attitude towards people "acting the maggot" – as was evidenced by the large machete she held in her hand, the tip of which currently hovered an inch away from Raging Bull's prospects of reproduction.

"That dog is on the VIP list. None of you are."

Jacinta had initially not been keen on Maggie at all, but an incident over the summer had dramatically changed her opinion. A junkie with more craving than sense had got hold of a gun and a truly terrible idea. Just before last orders, he'd come in and demanded the register. The Dubs had played earlier that day, so the takings were plentiful. Jacinta would have rather died than give it up – not that this was the likely outcome. Whatever happened, though, it would have been messy. Maggie had resolved the situation before anyone got hurt – at least, anyone who wasn't the junkie. The junkie may not have known it, but Maggie had probably saved his life. After that, she had enjoyed pints for life. That had lasted all of two weeks, once Maggie had figured out how to pick up her bowl and bring it to the bar and Jacinta had realised how much this new policy was costing. Still, there was always a bone ready for her arrival and Jacinta showed her more affection than she had to the establishment's entire clientele in the pub's inglorious history.

"Are you threatening me?" asked Raging Bull, his tone of incredulousness showing how dangerously uninformed he was.

Jacinta gave him a winning smile. "Yes, I am."

"There's three of us."

"Is there?" said Jacinta, in a casual way that would have set alarm bells ringing for a smarter man. "You lads aren't from around here, are ye?"

"No," said Raging Bull.

"I thought not, because ye see, everyone else is."

As one, the rest of the pub stood up. About fifteen or so patrons had been watching this little drama unfold. Some of them were drawing a pension, but they were counterbalanced by those who had their hands on coats, pockets or bags, indicating they were willing to draw something else. This wasn't a pub where you started trouble; this was a pub where trouble came for a quiet drink.

"You'll be leaving," said Jacinta, "but first you'll be apologising."

Raging Bull was suddenly much more of a pussycat. "Yeah, sorry about—"

"Not to me," interrupted Jacinta.

"What?"

She looked down at Maggie.

"Sorry about... good doggie."

"And you'll buy her a pint."

Raging Bull looked around and then begrudgingly took his wallet out of his pocket. Jacinta snatched it from his hands. "That'll cover it. Now feck off, there's a good lad."

"But..." His two friends pushed him towards the door before he could protest any further.

As the door slammed closed behind them, Jacinta reached down and petted Maggie. "Who's a good girl? Yes, you are! I'll get you that drink."

"Thanks, Jacinta," said Paul.

"All part of the service." She turned back to the bar, Raging Bull's wallet held aloft. "Drinks for everybody."

The whole pub cheered.

"Draught only, don't take the piss."

Paul sat back down.

"Jesus," said Phil, "I don't suppose she'd be interested in joining your committee?"

"She doesn't strike me as being much of a joiner."

"Yeah. Oh, I meant to ask, did Brigit mind taking over the surveillance on that Harrison dipshit this evening?"

"I didn't ask her."

Phil looked horrified. "But tonight is Wednesday, that means he's—"

"Relax, I've got my best man on the case."

Phil looked only slightly less horrified. "Oh God, are ye sure that's a good idea?"

"It'll be fine. She's always saying how we need to get him involved in things. He just needs to take a couple of pictures. What's the worst that could happen?"

CHAPTER FOUR

This must be what it felt like to be God.

Jacob Harrison stretched out his arms and yawned expansively. He was standing on the balcony, with the Christmas lights of Dublin twinkling below him, the world at his feet. He enjoyed the feeling of the cold night air on his skin as the wind tugged gently at his dressing gown. In the background, he could hear the shower running. He'd let Samantha go first, ever the gentleman. Having said that, he'd give it a minute and then, if the beast began to stir again, he might join her. A man of forty-five years of age being able to go again after the previous couple of hours, that truly was impressive. He bet she'd giggle about that with her friends. Mind you, Samantha was quite the muse – twenty-eight and flexible, oh so flexible. The Regency Hotel wasn't cheap but it was worth it. The dressing gown felt soft and fluffy against his skin and the view was something else. A canal meandered by directly below the window. Yes, this was what it felt like to be God.

Jacob turned at a knock on the door. Room service. "Just leave it outside, thank you."

He had worked up quite an appetite; they'd ordered oysters.

There was a louder knock. He raised his voice again. "It's fine, just leave it outside!"

A third knock. Oh, for Christ's sake, somebody wasn't getting a tip. Jacob stepped back inside and moved towards the door, past the bed with its tangled sheets. He looked at it and grinned – the scene of his greatest victory.

Then the door came crashing in.

Jacob staggered backwards, shocked, and saw the face of hell heading right for him – a blotchy, bearded face, filled with the mixed reds of anger and alcohol, with a lazy left eye that would have made it look demented even if it hadn't just kicked in the door of his hotel room. In Jacob's scattered mind, still buzzing from the champagne he'd consumed earlier, the thought skipped through that room service seemed inexplicably angry.

Then hands were on him, pushing him backwards.

"Howerya, Jacob boy."

"What are... who are... get off... let me..."

The warmth of the room gave way to the cool air of the balcony. All thoughts fell out of Jacob's head as his body and his world were tipped upside down. He screamed. The metal bars of the balcony appeared before him and he grabbed on to them for dear life. Strong arms wrapped around his legs. He looked down – the view wasn't anywhere near as relaxing now. He screamed again.

"Shut up, ye gobshite, or I'll drop you right now."

The voice had a Cork accent and sounded remarkably calm given the actions of its owner.

"OhGodOhGodOhGodOhGod!"

"You're about to die. Your life is over. What do you regret?"

Jacob's mind raced. "What?"

"What. Do. You. Regret?"

"I regret... I'm sorry, I'm sorry for whatever I did to you." Jacob screamed again as the hands on his legs dipped him down slightly lower.

"Wrong answer. We've never met."

"I'm... oh God, I'm... I have money, please, I—"

"I'm not interested in your fecking money. What do you regret?"

"I, I regret everything." A foot kicked at Jacob's knuckles, clenched around the bar. "Ouch!"

"Try again."

Jacob's mind raced through possibilities before it settled on the memory of a picture in his wallet. "Deirdre."

"Who is Deirdre?"

"My wife."

"Is that her in the shower?"

"No."

"That's right, you dozy prick. You have it all. Wife, two kids and here you are, fucking around like a randy dog with a bag full of mickeys. You had what everybody wants and you pissed it away, because you wanted to get yourself a bit on the side. Well I hope you enjoyed it – because you're royally fucked now."

"I'm sorry, I'm sorry, I'm sorry."

"So you should be. You've—"

The voice from above was interrupted by a scream.

Jacob looked through the bars of the balcony to see Samantha, one towel wrapped around her head and another around her body.

"What the fuck?"

"Stay back, love," said the voice. "I'm just engaged in some marriage counselling."

"Oh my God, who are— Wait, what?"

"Call the police, Samantha. This guy is insane."

It was hard to read her facial expression upside down, but she seemed to be standing unexpectedly still, given the circumstances.

"Jacob, what is he talking about? You're married?"

"I can... can you... for God's sake, get me up!"

Samantha took another step forward. "Is he married? You're married? Oh my God, I'm such an idiot. He said he had an ex and he had to be discreet. Oh, for..."

"I can explain everything."

The voice from above spoke again. "Be really quick, my arms are getting tired."

Jacob's whole body screamed in panic.

"Seriously, he's married?"

"I'm afraid so, love."

"But he told me..."

"It's not what you think," pleaded Jacob, "we barely even talk."

His stomach lurched as the arms dipped him again. "The missus is pregnant with your third child, so you're doing a damn sight more than talking."

"You utter bastard."

"Please, I can explain."

"All the bullshit. He was always away on... Oh Christ, I am such an idiot. I can't believe... Oh God, I'm going to be sick."

"Baby, listen – I'm getting a divorce."

"He wasn't," said the voice, "but I'm guessing he is now."

"Will you stay out of this?"

"I can leave if you want."

"NO!" Jacob looked down at the water below him. He was nine storeys up. Blood had rushed to his head and he was feeling very woozy. "Oh God, please don't. Just pull me up. You wouldn't drop a man off a balcony."

"If history proves anything, it's that I definitely would."

"I can pay."

"Oh, you will. Have no doubt about that, ye waste of space," said the voice. "Well, I think we've all learned a lot this evening. My arms are getting tired, but lucky for you, I don't want to give the council a messy clean-up job this close to Christmas."

Relief surged through Jacob's body as he felt the arms start to drag him back up and over the balcony.

"Drop him."

The voice was Samantha's but it didn't sound like her. That giddy, higher pitch was gone, leaving only cold, hard hate. It sent a shiver down Jacob's spine.

"'Tis tempting, love, but I'm not actually going to..."

Jacob felt the arms start to pull him back up.

"No!" screamed Samantha. "My whole life, I've fallen for arseholes and now when I thought I'd finally... DROP THE PRICK!"

Samantha threw herself at the man, who – Jacob was now fairly certain – wasn't from room service. Jacob's stomach lurched as he jerked suddenly downwards again.

"Get off me!"

"Drop him!"

"Samantha, please! Baby!"

Jacob could feel Samantha's fingernails tearing at the flesh of his thighs as she tried to rip away the hands that were holding him back from gravity's sweet embrace. He swung to the left as the man tried to fend her off. He tried to scream again but he couldn't find the air.

"Get off me, ye mad bitch."

"Drop him."

"Don't!"

Jacob could feel the arms holding him begin to shake.

"Ah Jesus, stop tickling me, stop tickling me, stop tickling me!"

Jacob screamed.

Samantha howled.

The man giggled.

Then the canal suddenly pulled away from Jacob's view as the man heaved him backwards in one violent motion – Jacob's face whacking the metal railing on the way by. All three of them tumbled messily to the ground, half in and half out of the hotel room.

Samantha was crying, the man panting heavily. Jacob was hyperventilating while watching drops of blood from his nose splash down onto the balcony's floor. Despite the pain, he was enjoying the incredible feeling of solid concrete beneath him again. He was alive.

He turned over, his back against the bars, suddenly concerned that the maniac might attack him again. The man was lying on the ground, looking at Jacob, his rage seemingly spent. In the background, Samantha was hastily grabbing her stuff in a flurry of movement.

Jacob spoke between gasping breaths. "Who... the fuck... are you?"

"I'm Santa Claus, happy fecking Christmas – you're on my naughty list."

"I'm going to... you'll be hearing from my lawyer."

The man shrugged. "Ah, big whoop. I'll never understand fellas like you."

"Oh, piss off." Jacob was too flooded with relief to be afraid of this man anymore. "Who are you to judge me?"

"Good point." The man took a camera out of his pocket and took a picture of Jacob. "Smile." Then he kept taking pictures. He took pictures of Jacob as he stood up; he took pictures as he moved back into the room; he took pictures as he tried to explain himself to Samantha as she hastily dressed; and he took pictures as Samantha opened her arms to hug Jacob and then kneed him viciously in the testicles.

Jacob tasted the thick carpet in his mouth as he lay crumpled on the floor, watching Samantha storm out of the door and out of his life.

The screen of the digital camera appeared before his face. "That's a particularly good one of you getting booted in the bollocks, don't you think? I'm beginning to think I've a future as a photographer."

CHAPTER FIVE

"I'm here to see Dr Devane."

The secretary looked up at Detective Wilson with sympathy. "Aren't you the throwing-up fella?"

"No. My name is Detective Wilson."

The woman was in her late fifties and had a matronly air to her, despite the purple bob she sported. "Are you sure? I thought you were the fella who's always vomiting at crime scenes?"

"Is Dr Devane around?"

"I don't blame you, personally – all that death. I have to type up the reports. Some of the things I've seen, I could tell you."

"The message said to get here before lunch."

"There was one from Kildare, death by misadventure." She leaned forward with a conspiratorial air. "It involved a sex toy – three, in fact."

"Right," said Wilson, struggling to find a way to get the conversation heading in the direction he wanted it to go. "Is she in her office?"

"You know how some people," she continued, as if he hadn't said anything, "are always trying to cram far too much into a case when they're going on holidays? Trying to do two weeks with just carry-on luggage?"

"So is her office just down this way?" said Wilson, determined to have the conversation he wanted to have.

"Well, it was like that, cramming far too much in – only, y'know, with sex toys. It happened in *Kildare!*" Oddly, she said the word Kildare in a stage whisper, like that was the shocking part of the story. "I mean, you expect that kind of thing to happen in Dublin, perhaps, but not Kildare."

"I guess."

"Or America. I mean anything can be shoved anywhere in America. It's the land of opportunity and all that."

Wilson started walking down the hallway.

"So her office is down this way?"

"Yes."

"Thank you."

Wilson started hurrying down the hall.

After a few seconds, her voice carried down the hallway after him. "She's not there though."

Wilson stopped and turned around. "What?"

"She's down in the mortuary. Will be for the rest of the day."

"But the message said to come and see her before lunch." Wilson pointed at his watch. "It's eleven thirty."

"She has her lunch at ten thirty."

"But... that's not lunchtime!"

"It is if you start work at 6am, which Dr Devane does."

Wilson trudged over to the lift and pressed the down button. "How am I supposed to know that?"

"I thought everyone did. She is a famously early riser."

"I mean," said Wilson, "ask anybody, eleven thirty is in the morning."

"Not for the doctor."

"I mean, it's AM – AM is the morning. That's not a matter of conjecture, that's just fact. Lunch happens after the morning." The lift doors opened and Wilson stepped in.

"Nowt so strange as folk, as they say, even in Kildare."

Wilson pressed the buzzer. Dr Devane looked up and noticed him at the far side of the glass. Her hands were inside the body on the slab in front of her. She was surrounded by three people – Wilson guessed medical students, but it was hard to tell behind the surgical masks and overalls. She nodded in his direction and then lifted what Wilson assumed was one of the more crucial organs from the body and placed it on the scales. He turned away and sat down on the one chair in the room. A long metal sink stretched beneath the window and a monitor sat on a table in the corner.

After a couple of minutes, Dr Devane pushed backwards through the door, her hands held out in front of her, smeared red with blood. She nodded in Wilson's direction before peeling off her gloves and throwing them into a medical waste bin. He stood awkwardly as she spent a minute thoroughly washing her hands in the stainless steel sink. Once done, she turned to him.

"I was expecting you earlier."

"Yes," said Wilson, who hesitated before adding "sorry", despite his fundamental disagreement about her definition of lunchtime. Dr Devane was the state pathologist, a position of importance that commanded respect. It didn't mean she could change when lunchtime was though.

"No problem," said Devane. "And apologies for the behaviour of Phillips and the others at your crime scene. I have had a stern word. I'm afraid being around so many dead people has a tendency to cause some of my staff to forget the proper respect that should be afforded to live ones."

Wilson shrugged.

Devane looked suddenly embarrassed as she looked behind her, as if remembering where they were. "Speaking of which, are you alright here?"

"I'm fine, doctor."

She leaned back against the sink. "If it helps, it does get easier the more you see. You're no different to anyone else. In fact, Phillips lost several pounds on his first couple of weeks in the job, from not eating. You get over it. You're welcome to shadow me for a day if you'd like to just get it out of your system – sorry, bad choice of words."

Wilson shook his head.

"OK, well let me know if you change your mind. I have a compelling example of the dangers of drink-driving inside if you fancy it." She paused. "It is rather difficult to get into the festive spirit around here."

"I'll pass, thank you, doc."

Devane's facial expression indicated that "doc" was not a welcome step into familiarity.

"Anyway," she said, "your mountain men. Subject A – the taller, younger one – hasn't produced much bar a confirmation that death was by a single powerful stab wound to the heart. Dental work indicated probability of the subject being British or Irish. Subject B, on the other hand…"

Dr Devane walked across to a pile of folders on the metal table in the corner and selected one. "Much more revealing." She flipped it open. "The gold filling and other dental work are indicative of a North American. The cause of death is where it gets interesting though. As you know, there was a large entry wound in the back of the eye but no exit wound, indicating it was a low-velocity projectile. We have now recovered it – only it isn't a bullet, at least in the modern sense." Devane held up a picture for Wilson to see. It looked like a misshapen ball bearing. "It is a shot, most likely having come from a derringer or similar type of weapon."

"You're kidding?"

"I am not known for my sense of humour, Detective."

"Have you ever seen that kind of weapon used before?"

Devane looked as if she were about to say something, but instead she turned back to the file and pulled out another picture. "Fitting with the dental work, we have recovered a ring from Subject B's finger, which appears to be American – military, in fact. It has

'Semper Fi' inscribed on the inside of it with an as-yet unidentified symbol above it – it looks like some form of hammer."

"So this guy was a US Marine?"

"That's speculation. What I can tell you is that he was wearing a ring that may be related to the US Marines – not the same thing. We have, however, sent detailed pictures of the ring and a DNA sample to our American colleagues to see if the body matches up with any missing persons they have. Obviously the twenty-year or so potential gap makes it tricky, but the FBI typically have very good records."

"I see. How long until they come back to us?"

Devane shrugged. "The Yanks are always a tad unpredictable. It really comes down to what they decide to care about. It could be only a week or two, could be months. It depends whose desk it lands on, I should imagine."

"Right. Can you give us a steer on the murder weapon?"

"You're looking for a derringer or derringer-like weapon, Detective, that's all the help we can give you. Despite what you've seen on TV, we can't CSI you up a magic solution."

Wilson nodded, taken aback by her suddenly abrupt tone. "Sure, sorry."

Devane quickly turned and headed back through the swing doors. "Now, if you'll excuse me. My office will be in touch as and when."

"OK, well, thank you for your..." Wilson stopped talking as he realised he was speaking to an empty room. He would spend the drive back to HQ trying to figure out exactly what he'd said to annoy Dr Devane, before determining that eating lunch when it wasn't lunchtime probably put the body in a bad mood for the rest of the day.

CHAPTER SIX

"It's awful cold out, isn't it?"

Bunny's thoughts came back from where they'd been, visiting old friends. He looked at the barman, currently in the process of pulling him a pint. "What?"

"I said, it's awful cold, isn't it?"

"I suppose so. Y'know, it's December and all."

"That's true. I've not seen you in here before?"

"No."

Bunny had never drank in this pub before. It was one of those big soulless barns up on The Quays, somewhere he'd not have been caught dead in normally. He didn't even know its name; it had just been the nearest one to him when he'd noticed the headline in the newspaper that he now held under his arm.

"Can I ask if you were enticed in by our Christmas decorations?"

"No."

The barman looked disappointed. Clearly this wasn't the answer he'd been hoping for. He lowered his voice slightly. "The manager and I had a bit of a ruck about it. She said she didn't want them, but I think they give the place a bit of ambience."

Bunny looked around. There was some anaemic tinsel and a few cheap-looking angels scattered around the place. A memory floated into his head of his schooldays back in Cork. One of the lads had managed to get Sister Morgan, the young nun tasked with teaching God to gurriers, into a discussion about heaven. If angels lived on clouds, he said, where did they go wee-wee? Did they just do it over the side? Sister Morgan had panicked, said that angels didn't wee or poo. He could still remember the look on her face when she realised the hole she was getting herself into. A bunch of ten-year-old boys were always going to have further questions. Trying to dig her way out, she had explained that angels were smooth all over down there and didn't do any of that stuff. None of this explained the nappies though, sister. It was at that point she had just started singing "O Come, All Ye Faithful" loudly and waving for the class to join in. She was out of teaching and off to Ethiopia within a year. It said something that bringing Jesus to people in the middle of a warzone was considered a softer option than a class of ten-year-olds in Cork. Bunny thought of all this while looking at the dismal angel sitting at the end of the bar. It had an unfortunate constipated expression, poor little sod – holding it in for all eternity.

"So, d'ye like them?"

"What?"

"The decorations?"

"No."

"Oh," said the barman, once again getting the answer he didn't want. He tried to rally. "Did ye see the snowman down there at the end of the bar?"

"Any sign of that drink?" said Bunny, ignoring the question.

The barman topped up his pint of Guinness and placed it on the bar. "Four euros eighty please. You're not much of a talker, are ye?"

"No." Bunny handed him a five-euro note.

"I'm the same myself. Some people would talk the arse off you."

Bunny took his change and his pint and started heading down the bar, angling for the far corner. The entire place was deserted. It'd no doubt pick up when the after-work crowd arrived later, drawn in by the excess of ambience.

As he passed by it, the motion caused the snowman on the bar to leap into song. A backhand return with the *Herald* sent it somersaulting off the bar.

"Ah for... you've no Christmas spirit, ye old scrooge."

Bunny said nothing, taking up position at a table in the furthest corner, his back to the wall. He looked around again, confirming that the place was deserted aside from the barman, who was dusting off his snowman and looking all hurt about it.

Bunny unfolded the newspaper and looked down at the headline. It hadn't changed since he'd bought it.

TWO BODIES FOUND IN THE WICKLOW MOUNTAINS

Two sets of human remains have been found by builders digging the foundations for the new Environmental Appreciation Centre in the Wicklow Mountains. Dubbed 'The Bill on the Hill', construction on the controversial project has been delayed three times as protestors objected to it through the courts, before occupying trees on the site to prevent building work from starting. The remains, which Gardaí have yet to identify, are said to be two adult males and are estimated to have been in the ground for around twenty years. The Wicklow Mountains has long been a popular dumping ground for bodies amongst the Dublin criminal fraternity, although the Gardaí have emphasised that it is too early to speculate. The Minister for Tourism, who is, of course, also the local TD for the area, was unavailable to comment at the time of going to press.

Below the article, there was a graphic that showed the approximate location of the site. Bunny looked long and hard at it. Truth to be told, he had no idea where to find the location on a map.

"Oh dear, oh dear."

Bunny looked up with a start. Sitting opposite him, in a white suit, sunglasses and fedora hat, was a man he'd shot, killed and buried in the Wicklow Mountains eighteen years previously.

"I know what you are thinking, Detective. Maybe it is not me?"

"You're dead." Bunny tried to concentrate on the paper.

"Yes, I am dead, but it seems I am no longer buried."

Bunny lifted his pint halfway to his lips and then put it down again. "Could be anything, doesn't mean it is..."

The man smiled. His dark skin crinkled. "It's almost eighteen years to the exact day, is it not? How poetic."

"You deserved to die, I've no guilt about that."

"Clearly." The man shrugged. Bunny had initially known him as Lopez, only finding out after the fact that his name was Daniel Zayas. "Still, though, do the police normally bury the bodies of people they have legitimately killed? You are nothing but a common criminal."

Bunny stabbed a finger in Zayas's direction. "You were a shower of shite who had kidnapped..." Bunny stopped and looked down at the table.

"After all this time, you still can't say her name, can you? Simone. The murderer that shared your bed, albeit briefly."

"Shut up. You're not real."

Zayas took off his glasses, revealing the bullet hole where his right eye had been. "I might not be real, but that doesn't mean you can ignore me, Detective." Zayas nodded down at the newspaper. "Like it or not, your sins are no longer buried and, seeing as we're talking, it seems like your mind is not exactly your own. Just because you're done with the past, doesn't mean the past is done with you."

"Feck off." Bunny hurled the paper across the table, at a man that wasn't there. The sheets divided and fluttered to the ground.

He looked up and noticed the barman, who had been joined by a younger woman. They were both standing behind the bar, looking over at him nervously. The woman nudged the barman, who gave her an annoyed glance before raising his voice. "Are you alright there, sir? Everything OK?"

Bunny gave them an embarrassed wave and then stood up. He grabbed his coat then clumsily starting to pick up the paper. He tossed it onto the table beside his untouched pint and headed for the door.

Behind him, he could hear the laughter of a dead man following in his wake.

CHAPTER SEVEN

Brigit cleared her throat and shuffled the pieces of paper around on the table in front of her, like a nervous three-card monte dealer. "Right," she said, "I call this meeting of the MCM Investigations Board of Directors to order."

She looked up to see Paul sitting on the opposite side of her desk, smirking at her. "That's very formal."

"We're doing this properly."

"Alright, Madam Chairman, calm down."

Brigit looked down at the agenda again. "Attendance: present, Brigit Conroy, acting as chairperson for the meeting. Also present, Paul Mulchrone. Absent with apologies, Bernard McGarry."

"Since when has Bunny apologised for anything?" said Paul.

Brigit ignored him. This was going to be hard enough as it was. Her hands still stung from the soaking in turpentine that had been required to get that damned paint off, then, following the phone call she had received at midnight, she had been way too angry to sleep.

"Mr McGarry, as always, has assigned his proxy to me," she said. "First item on the agenda, the ongoing situation with Kelleher Brothers Investigations."

"OK," interrupted Paul, "before you say anything, what happened yesterday was ridiculous. Paint flying everywhere like that, you could have been blinded."

"I could have," agreed Brigit.

"This is getting completely out of hand."

Brigit felt a wave of relief flow through her. "Exactly, I'm glad you've seen that."

"Don't worry, the situation is going to be sorted – once and for all. Have you ever seen the Michael Douglas film *The Game*?"

Brigit looked at Paul in confusion. "What's that got to do with anything?"

"It was on telly last night. Michael Douglas' brother buys him this, like, immersive adventure thing, where all these actors are involving him in this game where he falls in love with this hot woman. And then somebody gets murdered, and he has to prove it's all a conspiracy – only somebody really does get murdered and Michael Douglas doesn't know what's real and what isn't. I don't know either to be honest, I fell asleep halfway through. But then this morning I made some calls. I'm going to make Kevin Kelleher think he really has killed someone. I think I can get a bunch of actors from this school and..." Paul opened his bag and produced several pages of scribble-filled foolscap. "I've worked out a basic story and, I mean, it won't be cheap, although luckily actors will work for not much money, but there'll be some special effects required and—"

"SHUT UP!"

Paul looked up in shock. Brigit was a little taken aback herself – she hadn't quite meant to shout it quite so loud. It had come from a place deeper than logic. It had erupted from a place of deep frustration.

"Have you actually read the agenda for this meeting, Paul?"

"Ehm, well, I... I had a brief look but not in detail. I scanned it."

"Did you?" asked Brigit, holding up the piece of paper and pointing at the first item. "Item number one, seen here in bold print, is the situation with the Kellehers. Either this ridiculous feud stops immediately or drastic action will be taken."

"What do you mean 'drastic action'?"

"You will be removed from the board of this company."

"You can't do that."

"I bloody well can. I control the majority of votes and I have ample evidence of gross negligence."

"What? Are ye mad? What evidence?"

"How did the Harrison surveillance go last night, Paul?"

Paul pulled at his ear nervously and Brigit felt herself sag. He didn't realise it, but this was his tell when he was about to lie.

"Yeah, y'know, generally alright. Nothing too out of the ordinary."

"Really?"

Brigit could actually see the moment Paul realised he was screwed but still decided to brazen it out.

"Well, y'know, these things are always a bit 'hurry up and wait', mostly dull."

"Sure. Well, I got a phone call from a rather upset Mrs Harrison last night. She'd just received a call from her sleazebag of a husband, who admitted to having an affair while simultaneously accusing her of hiring a man to try and kill him."

"What?"

"Yes," said Brigit, "apparently the man from MCM Investigations burst into his room and tried to throw him off a balcony. Did you do that?"

Brigit could see Paul furiously thinking, trying to decide which path was worse.

"Yes?" He said it tentatively, like even he was surprised that he was attempting this lie.

"My arse you did. You couldn't dangle somebody off a balcony if you tried."

"What do you mean by that? That's a very unkind thing to say."

"Oh no you don't. Do not try and throw this conversation off topic. Did you or did you not send Bunny to do a surveillance that had been assigned to you and Phil?"

"You said you wanted to get him more involved in things."

Brigit would've thrown something if anything had been handy. "Involved, yes, but not dealing with stuff like this. You better than anyone know what he's like. That was like sending a sledgehammer to scramble an egg."

Paul held his hands up. "OK, that was a bit of a mistake on my part."

"A mistake?" Brigit couldn't believe that he still didn't seem to get it. "Do you have any idea how much trouble we could be in? Bunny doing stuff like that, we could lose our licence. What the hell were you thinking?"

"Alright, look—"

"Then there's the matter of all those boxes in reception."

"We need a bit of security equipment to protect the office. There's a lot of gurriers about."

"Any gurrier that breaks in here will only be coming to steal our new security system, seeing as we apparently spent..." Brigit held up another piece of paper. "Six grand to protect an office that holds three second-hand PCs, a couple of filing cabinets and the second-cheapest self-assembly desks from IKEA, one of which still wobbles every time someone closes a door."

"I said I was going to fix that."

"You said you were going to do a lot of things, Paul, and frankly I'm tired of waiting for you to grow up and do them. We're supposed to be running a business here." Brigit took a deep breath. "As I see it, we've got two options: either you abandon this nonsense feud with the Kellehers once and for all—"

"Never!"

"Or you leave the company."

Brigit had sat up all night, debating how she could approach this. She had wanted it to be a calm and reasoned discussion. So much for that plan.

"You can't get rid of me, I own part of this company."

Brigit looked down at the three pieces of paper in front of her again. She couldn't bring herself to look at him as she said it. "You own a third of it, as do I, as does Bunny. I have Bunny's proxy, which gives me the two-thirds majority. You have to either agree to end this nonsense and concentrate on what we're supposed to be doing, or else I'm going to have to ask you to leave. In the long run, you can either retain your shares and get a fair share of the profits, assuming we have profits after the recent 'setbacks', or we can discuss buying you out for a reasonable price."

She looked up to see Paul staring at her, his eyes filled with outrage and hurt. "You can't do this."

"I can." She took a deep breath. "Do you agree to stop all this nonsense with the Kellehers?"

"No." He said it in a quiet voice.

"OK then, I have no choice but to put this to a vote. All those in favour of Paul Mulchrone being removed from the day-to-day operations of MCM Investigations?" She raised her hand. "Aye, and Bunny's votes go with me. Those against?"

Paul stood up. "Nay."

Brigit picked up her pen and started writing. "So by majority vote, the motion has been carried and the..."

Her office door slammed, followed a few seconds later by the front door as Paul stormed out.

CHAPTER EIGHT

"Mickey, what are you doing? Don't do that! For God's sake, fella, use the stick or catch it!"

Johnny Canning turned away from the field in disgust and looked at the St Jude's under-12s coach, to whom he was the assistant, despite knowing little about hurling.

"Bunny?"

He looked into the face of the man he'd known now for seventeen years, and what he saw looking back worried him. It wasn't the splotchy red of burst capillaries that indicated 'an over-fondness for the drink. That did worry him, but only on the same low level it always had. Bunny and drink had been bedfellows for as long as Johnny had known him. Johnny did try and bring it up every so often, but that conversation rarely went well. Since the Skylark incident last year, Bunny had maybe been leaning on the bottle a little heavier, but even a twelve-step fundamentalist like Johnny couldn't hold that against him. Held prisoner and tortured by a true psychopath for ten days, it had been an ordeal that would have broken a lesser man. Physically, Bunny had recovered remarkably quickly, but Johnny was perhaps one of the very few people close enough to catch a whiff of the battles that still raged. He was back bigger and badder than ever as far as most were concerned, the same foul-mouthed tornado of fury he'd always been. The indestructible, irrepressible Bunny McGarry. But Johnny knew better. What didn't kill you didn't always make you stronger. There'd long been that sadness at the eye of the storm, but these days there seemed to be more of it. Still, this, today, whatever it may be, was something very different. He'd never seen him like this.

Johnny tossed the sponge he'd been holding into the red bucket that handled ninety per cent of all medical scenarios the team encountered.

"Alright, that's it."

Bunny's gaze pulled back from the middle distance and he looked at Johnny as if seeing him for the first time.

"What's up?"

Bunny shrugged. "What the feck are you talking about? Nothing's up."

"Really?" said Johnny. "We're into the second half of our worst performance of the season – by some considerable distance, which is really saying something – and there's barely been a peep out of you."

"You told me last week to be more constructive in my criticism!"

"That's not what I said. I said maybe avoid things like telling Daz his aim was so bad, he'd end up staying a virgin until he was forty."

"Well alright," said Bunny, "and I'm taking your advice on board."

"Exactly!" said Johnny, "And when have you ever done that? Your half-time team talk was basically 'enjoy yourselves'. You're taking my advice. Jesus, Bunny, you've barely even swore."

"I'm controlling myself."

"Mickey Marsh just tried to head the ball. A sliotar, a leather ball hurtling at about forty miles an hour, and he tried to head it. And you. Said. Nothing. Now seriously" – Johnny lowered his voice – "what is up with you? Is everything alright?"

"I'm fine, it's just... It's been a rough couple of days."

"Do you want to talk about it?"

"Jesus, Johnny, if you're hitting on me, I'm flattered and all, but that's not the way my flag flies."

"Don't flatter yourself. If all men were you, I'd be chasing vagina like it was the last chopper out of Saigon."

"I'm alright, just... TERRY FRANCIS, GET STUCK IN!!"

Bunny bellowed so loudly that Johnny felt sure he'd temporarily lost hearing in his left ear.

"OK, well, someone's back."

Johnny turned back to the game just in time to see the centre forward from St Mary's add what might be his tenth point of the match, sending the ball hurtling into the nettles beside the back wall in the process.

"Rambo, get that back, will ye, please?"

The tubby kid who was theoretically the St Jude's goalkeeper gave Johnny a smile and a thumbs up before running off – the first indication all game that he was in fact aware of his surroundings in any way, shape or form.

"Who's that?" asked Bunny.

"Who?"

"Over there."

Johnny looked in the direction Bunny had nodded. "The woman with the pram? I dunno. Do you want me to see if her kid wants to play midfield for us? Can't do worse than Ciaran."

"Nah, it's just I've not seen her around. She's not a mother of any of the boys or anything."

Johnny looked in the direction of the skinny blonde woman pushing the expensive-looking buggy. "So? I mean, I'm no expert, but maybe she fancied some fresh air. This is the only bit of green for several blocks. Maybe she's just a big hurling fan?"

"What the feck would she be doing coming to watch us then?"

"Yeah," nodded Johnny, "fair point."

"She looks familiar."

"Well, you do know almost everybody around here."

"That's it, ye see, she's not from around here and I – I was sure I saw her earlier today as well."

Johnny looked at Bunny again. "What, like somewhere else?"

"Yeah, only she didn't have the baby, and she was brunette."

"What?"

"Don't mind me. Just a coincidence."

"OK."

Whatever was bothering Bunny now seemed to be getting into Johnny's head too, as he could have sworn she was now surreptitiously looking at them. Having caught him looking back, she bent and fussed about the baby before turning and heading back towards the gates.

"C'mon, lads, let's up our game here. You're playing like a bunch of—"

"Bunny!" They had previously had a long and detailed discussion/argument about words Bunny was not allowed to use to finish that sentence.

"One-eyed sons of a cock-eyed Suzie."

"Oh, alright." After all these years, Johnny still wasn't entirely sure what that actually meant, but it seemed OK.

"What score is it?" shouted Padraig Dawson.

"Don't you worry about the fecking score," replied Bunny, "'tis all about the performance!"

"Oh," said Padraig, kicking disconsolately at his hurley, "we're losing by that much already?"

The game restarted and Saint Jude's sprung into life, immediately giving away two frees, which at least showed more effort than their previous attempts at tackling.

"That's it, lads, get stuck in! They don't like it up 'em!"

Johnny rolled his eyes.

"Johnny?"

"Yes, Bunny?"

"If anything ever happened to me, you'd take care of the club, wouldn't ye?"

Johnny turned around again. "Alright, seriously, have you been to the doctor's or something?"

"No," said Bunny, shooing him away with his hand, "don't be daft. I'm just saying. You would, wouldn't ye?"

"God help me, I'd try my best, but what has you in this mood?"

"Nothing, just— REF!"

A collection of twelve-year-olds from both sides clattered into each other, causing a pile-up in midfield with a fair share of hurt feelings and unhappy parents. The ref blew so hard the pea came out of his whistle.

Without a word, Johnny snatched up the bucket and ran onto the field to make everything alright again.

"Why don't you tell him?"

Bunny turned at the voice. A man eighteen years dead sat behind him, on the cooler box for the halftime drinks.

"Why don't you tell him that, soon, you may be going away for a *looong* time," he said, mockingly drawing it out. "After all these years, telling generations of kids to stay on the straight and narrow. How d'you think they'll feel?"

"Ara, fecking shut up."

Daniel Zayas smiled up at him, his left eye sitting incongruously beside the cavity where his other one should be. "Talk to your friend. Tell him you are going crazy. The ghost of a man you murdered eighteen years ago is chasing you. Maybe you should have gone to see that shrink. Maybe you should have taken the tablets. Maybe you should not have killed me in the first place?"

"I never regretted that for a second, ye one-eyed wank stain."

"Oh, I know I was not your first. I'm just the one who will be your downfall."

"They've nothing to link—"

"Oh please, we both know that isn't true. They'll be looking now, now they have the bodies. You can hear the footsteps. They are coming. It might take a little time, but they are coming. That's why I'm here."

Bunny swung the hurley in his hand at a man that wasn't there – knocking the drinks cooler on its side and sending its contents sprawling across the ground.

Then he found himself alone again. He turned back to the field to see Padraig Dawson looking back at him, his twelve-year-old eyes filled with a new kind of fear. Everyone was scared of Bunny, but it was the right kind of scared. At least it had been.

"There was a wasp. Buzzy little fecker."

Padraig nodded and moved away.

Bunny ran his free hand up and down his face. Get it together. He glanced over to see the mother pushing her buggy out of the gates.

CHAPTER NINE

"I can't believe it," said Paul. "The whole thing is ridiculous."

"Yeah," agreed Phil. "I mean, it's not my job to go telling people bad news. I've enough stress in my life."

"What? What are you talking about?"

Phil removed his eye from behind the telephoto lens and looked at Paul. "I'm talking about how when this idiot is having his end away, Brigit agreed that I would ring the client, his missus, and tell her. I mean, I've enough stress in my life!"

"That's not what I was talking about," said Paul. "I was talking about how Brigit has removed me from my position in this company."

Phil tutted and resumed looking through his camera lens. "Oh, that. You were going on about that an hour ago. I thought you'd finished."

"Finished? I've lost my job for absolutely no reason. I'd have thought you'd be a lot more sympathetic, Phil."

"Well..."

Paul's eyes narrowed. "Well what?"

"Nothing, only, you've not been doing any work for the last few weeks and you've been spending a lot of money and the office is now covered in yellow paint."

"Exactly, and whose fault is that?"

Phil pulled his head back and looked up at the ceiling of the van. Paul could see he was thinking this through. "Yours?"

"No! The Kellehers!"

"Alright," said Phil, flinching back from Paul. "Fine, it's all their fault. Only..."

"Only what?"

Phil looked back into the camera again. "Nothing."

"Jesus, Phil, would it kill you to back me up just this once?"

Phil didn't even look up from the camera this time; he just raised his bandaged hand. His wife, Da Xin, sick of her husband having his phone actually physically glued to his hand, had insisted he go to Casualty and get it removed. "Six hours in Casualty and the doctor insisted on bringing lots of people in to see it. I was a laughing stock, so I was."

Paul rubbed the back of his neck. "Yeah, alright, sorry." The thought crept into Paul's head that he might just be being a tad self-centred. "How's Da Xin doing?"

"Well, she's as big as a Ford Cortina now so the poor girl can't do much. The baby keeps kicking every time she hears my voice too."

"Isn't that a good thing?"

Phil gave Paul a sideways glance.

Paul lowered his voice. "Are you still having the dreams?"

"The nightmares, you mean? Yeah."

Phil had been having a recurring dream where he awoke to find that his unborn daughter had snuck out of her mother and was strangling him with the umbilical cord.

"I told you, you're being daft."

"Am I?" said Phil, "D'ye know how many people have liked me in my life?"

"Ah, you're being crazy." He wasn't being crazy. Paul, more than anyone, knew what Phil meant. As his best friend in the world, he could categorically confirm that Phil Nellis was an acquired taste. Their schooldays hadn't been massively fun for anyone, but other kids went home at night thinking, well, at least I'm not Phil Nellis. He was cursed with his own Nellisian logic that looked a lot like stupidity if you didn't catch it from the right angle, and few did. He also had a stubborn stick-to-it attitude, which meant that if he didn't understand something, he asked questions, a lot of questions, and for the worst reason imaginable – a genuine thirst for knowledge. Other students hated that, as did the teachers, although you could see them trying to hide it. Nobody could forget their science teacher, Mr Lawrence, having a breakdown, prompted by Phil's honest question, "Sir, Einstein or Newton, sir, who was better?" After a few minutes of floundering, the teacher had gone for the "That question is impossible to answer" option. Phil had sympathised and said not to worry about it, he'd ask one of the other teachers who would know. Mr Lawrence had gone into the storeroom and not come out for twenty minutes. Someone had eventually gone and got the headmaster.

"Of course your daughter is going to love you," said Paul.

"That has not been my experience of people. I mean, statistically, the odds are against it, aren't they?"

A thought struck Paul. "But her ma, your wife, she loves you, doesn't she?"

"Well, yeah."

"There you go. Love is hereditary."

Phil looked away from the camera again. "Is it?"

"Yeah, course it is. Same way that your daughter is going to look Chinese."

"Is she?" Phil seemed genuinely surprised. Paul gave him a long look.

"Obviously. I mean, her mother is Chinese. She's going to be a mix of you and her, isn't she?"

"Is she? I thought that, like, babies born in China would be Chinese and, like, babies born in Ireland, would look, y'know, Irish."

"Ehm, no, Phil. That's not how it works."

"Really?"

There was a knock on the window. Paul was relieved – he was skating dangerously close to having to have the birds and the bees talk with Phil. He would rather sit in a van filled with actual bees than do that.

"Go away," said Paul in a loud voice.

A voice responded from outside. "I'd like a 99, please."

Paul shook his head. "People are daft."

"Yeah," agreed Phil, "people."

The MCM Investigations van had been Paul's idea. Well, their obvious need for one had been Brigit's suggestion, but Paul had been put in charge of acquiring it. He had a love of a bargain. Actually, from years of living off virtually no money, he had a need for a bargain verging on the pathological. He was starting to realise that this was becoming a problem. Case in point: the van. He had acquired it off One-Eyed Barry, who had acquired it from somebody who had shown far too much faith in the invincibility of a full house, kings over nines. The van did have a lot going for it: it had been going very cheap; it was a good size; it had just passed its NCT; and it had a nice big side window that they could replace with one-way tinted glass – perfect for surveillance. In fact, there was only one problem with the van.

A fist hammered on the window. "Here, give us a 99, ye lazy bollocks."

It didn't matter that they'd painted it black and removed all of the signage. Something deep down in the Irish psyche recognised the shape, and an ice cream van was still, and would forever be, an ice cream van.

"Alright, keep your bleedin' hair on," responded Phil. He reached behind him and pulled a cone out from under the machine that they'd never bothered to remove. He then flipped the handle down and started assembling a 99 cone.

"What the?"

Phil looked across at him. "It happens so much, I figured this'd just be easier. I got some stuff from the cash'n'carry." He shoved a flake in the ice cream and slid the window across. "Two euros."

A small hand reached through and handed Phil a couple of coins in exchange for the ice cream. "Here, I wanted raspberry sauce."

"We're out." Phil slid the window closed again and picked up the camera.

"No raspberry sauce? You're a fucking disgrace, mister. I'm never coming back here again!"

"Good," shouted Phil.

Paul looked on in disbelief. "You're selling ice creams now?"

"It's easier than dealing with all the angry people demanding ice creams. I got the idea after them kids tried to turn the van over in Ballymun that time."

"But," said Paul, "you're supposed to be doing surveillance."

"Exactly," said Phil. "And nobody is going to suspect a van that's selling ice creams of being a surveillance vehicle. It's the perfect cover."

Paul stopped to think about this. He was in all too familiar territory. Nellisian logic on some intrinsic level felt like it didn't make sense, but it was always incredibly hard to actually find fault with it. Before Paul could attempt to do so, Phil sprang into action, the camera clicking rapidly.

"Here's our boy – and he's got a woman with him."

Paul picked up the binoculars from the bench. He saw a middle-aged couple – a portly man and a skinny woman with caramel-coloured hair – entering the Philbert Street apartment block opposite. The man held open the door for his companion. She looked around, scanning the street before entering.

"That was weird," said Paul. "She seemed to take a hard look at the van."

"Maybe she fancied an ice cream?"

The couple disappeared inside.

"See now," said Phil, "as far as I'm concerned, this is all the proof we should be providing. People going in, people coming back out again, maybe a bit of a snog."

"Why, what have you been told to do?"

Phil shot an irritated look in Paul's direction. "Have you not been listening to me at all?"

Paul didn't say anything, but he did feel slightly embarrassed. He may have been slightly too wrapped up in his own outrage at being fired to pay a great deal of attention to the other half of the conversation.

Phil shook his head in disappointment and went back to looking through the camera. "Apparently they're going to be in the second-floor apartment there on the far left."

Sure enough, as soon as Phil said it, a light came on at the indicated window.

"Now, get this, not only do I have to take pictures of them, y'know…"

"Right."

"Knobbing," said Phil, who had never quite mastered the art of implication in conversation, "but I've to ring this prick's missus and tell her when they're at it."

"Oh."

"Yeah," said Phil. "I don't want to be giving some poor lady a play-by-play on her other half being a cheating scumbag."

As they watched, the curtains of the window were thrown open by the woman they had seen earlier. The portly man came up behind her and put his arms around her. He then proceeded to push her up against the window and conduct what a customs officer would consider a highly comprehensive full-body search.

Phil sighed. "I hate people. Right, here we go…"

Using his bandaged hand, Phil placed his phone on the counter and dialled the number he had written on a piece of paper. Then he picked it up and cradled it between his ear and shoulder. "Fingers crossed she's not—" He didn't get to the final word in the sentence – probably "in" – as the call was answered on the second ring.

"Hello, Mrs Kilfeather, it's Phil Nellis here from MCM Investigations. Are you alright? You sound a bit out of breath?"

From where Paul sat, he couldn't make out the other half of the conversation beyond the low burble of a female voice.

"Yes," said Phil. "I'm outside the Philbert Street apartments right now and I'm afraid your husband is inside."

Pause.

"Yes, he is with a woman."

Pause.

"Ehm, yes, the other woman. I suppose you could say she is that."

Pause.

"Well..." Phil squirmed uncomfortably. "I suppose you could say she is a dirty girl."

Pause.

"Ehm... I personally wouldn't use that language, but I know you're upset."

Pause.

Phil grimaced. "Alright, if you insist. Yes, I supposed she is a dirty girl. She is a dirty, dirty girl."

A thought struck Paul. He picked up the binoculars again. The full-body customs search in the window had now very definitely passed beyond standard practices.

"Phil, hang up the phone."

Phil ignored him. "Alright. She's a wanton floozy, so she is, a hussy. She is a wicked woman."

"Phil," said Paul more loudly. "Hang up the phone."

Phil was now looking incredibly uncomfortable, as if he were in physical pain. "Ah please, I don't want to say that."

Paul reached across, snatched the phone from Phil's shoulder and disconnected the call.

"What the feck are you doing, Paulie? I had to tell the woman, it was part of the instructions. She wanted to know. We can't keep losing customers like this! Brigit will bleedin' kill me!"

"Are you finished?" asked Paul. "If you want, you can ring Mrs Kilfeather back. Look, she has her phone handy."

Phil gave Paul a confused look, then he looked through the camera again.

The woman had her phone in her hand and she was still talking into it, looking directly at the van.

"Oh..." Phil sounded slightly confused. "Ohhhhhh." Realisation hit. "Ughhh, I bleedin' hate people."

"Yep," said Paul, handing Phil his phone back. "I'm going home to bed. Wake me up when the world has come to its senses."

CHAPTER TEN

Brigit sat nursing her glass of white wine and trying hard not to look like she was being stood up on a date. She wasn't. She was meeting a friend, and that friend, while late, had sent fourteen text messages to assure her that she was still coming. The large glass of wine in her hand was almost empty and she had started looking at the one sitting opposite her on the table, bought in anticipation of her friend's arrival. She had also put it there as a way of fending off any of the sleazoid men that wine bars seemed to attract. This was what the job was doing to her, making her cynical about the rest of humanity. The stocky guy at the bar had slipped off his wedding ring on his way in. The woman at the corner table had sent a text from one phone and then slipped away from her date to answer a call on another. The guy with the ponytail sitting near the door had, well, he had a ponytail. Brigit considered ponytails to be unacceptable, frankly – even on ponies.

It had been a long day, she was exhausted and not in the mood for this, but a promise was a promise. She didn't have enough friends that she could afford to let a good one down. Still, three more minutes and she was having that glass of wine.

The honk of a car horn drew Brigit's attention. Nora Stokes, barrister, mother of one and stressed-out force of nature, was making her way across the street outside. She was rummaging in her bag while simultaneously offering a half-arsed attempt at an apologetic wave to the driver who had just slammed on the brakes to avoid giving her some much-needed time off in hospital. She blew strands of her blonde hair out of her face and then spotted Brigit through the window – managing to cram hello, sorry and oops all into the same smile. Nora was too busy for facial expressions to have just one meaning. She bundled herself through the door and hurried across the bar, sweeping the glass of wine and Brigit up into a hug.

"Sorry, sorry, sorry, sorry. Sorry."

"It's fine," Brigit assured her.

"No, it isn't. You were nice enough to come out with me and I left you sitting here alone amongst all these dreadful people."

She said it slightly too loudly and Brigit could feel the eyes of the aforementioned "dreadful people" burning into them as they sat down. Not that Nora cared, she was too busy knocking a large white wine back in one to register anyone's disapproval.

Brigit had first met Nora about two years ago when, as Paul's barrister at the time, she'd been dragged into the Rapunzel affair. Brigit still felt guilty, as their actions had accidentally led to Nora, then heavily pregnant, receiving a visit from a thug who had tried to intimidate her into giving up Paul and Brigit's location. This had led to Nora Stokes first macing and then tasering the aforementioned scumbag, a fact that even now made her something of a legend in the otherwise stuffy and male-dominated world of the Irish legal profession.

Since then, she and Brigit had become friends in a rather haphazard manner. After the Rapunzel affair, Nora had struck out on her own, and when Brigit, Paul and Bunny had set up MCM Investigations, Nora had been the natural choice for their lawyer. Since then, they had sent each other work on a few occasions, and when it had come time for MCM Investigations to move offices, Nora had tipped them off to a suitable place that was becoming available around the corner from hers, near Christ Church Cathedral. The two women had bonded over the challenges of running their own businesses. Brigit was aware she wasn't supposed to actually be the boss of her business partnership, but it had become quickly apparent that she was the only fully-functioning adult in the building, which she deeply resented. It must be great to be the flaky one; she was always secretly jealous of people who somehow managed to bumble through life on luck and other people's kindness. To be fair, Nora worked alone, save for an incompetent assistant she fired three times a week, which meant she was both the boss and the flaky one. She had a two-year-old kid and hadn't slept more than five continuous hours since giving birth. In short, they both found themselves in the position of being the closest thing the other had to a female work colleague, even though they didn't actually work together.

Nora finished the wine and sat down. "Christ, I needed that." She held the glass up and whistled loudly, attracting the attention of the sour-faced, stick-thin brunette behind the bar, who glared at her. Nora tapped the glass. "Two more of these bad boys, please, barkeep." She turned back to Brigit before the barmaid could protest that they didn't offer table service.

"So yes, sorry, sorry, sorry – his highness shat in my handbag."

"Is that a figure of speech?"

"Nope. Got into the taxi and I thought, Christ, this guy has a serious BO problem. Then I tried to get my phone out and realised that himself had found a new place to exercise his latest hobby of random defecation."

"Oh."

"Oh indeed."

The shitter in question was Dan, Nora's two-year-old son. There were a lot of euphemisms people had for his behaviour – "he's a bit of a handful", "rambunctious", "emotional". The reality, however...

"I swear he is possessed by the Devil."

"Oh, you don't mean that."

"The hell I don't. The Devil! Did I tell you about this morning?"

Brigit shook her head.

"So I get a call from the nanny. The playgroup he's in, they've banned him."

"What?"

"Banned him!"

"Is this because of the biting?"

"Surprisingly, no. Poo throwing."

Brigit grimaced. "He's started throwing poo?"

"No, he's started encouraging other kids to do so. They hospitalised one of the other mothers. Hit her right in the eye with her own kid's turd. Had to get it washed out and all."

Brigit laughed and then clamped her hand over her mouth. "Well, it shows good leadership skills."

"Shut up. It is not funny."

"Sorry," said Brigit "It is though. It is a little bit funny."

It was at this point that the brunette from behind the bar appeared with two large glasses of wine and a face that seemed utterly appalled at what her body was doing. "Just so you know..."

Nora cut her off by handing her a twenty-euro note. "Keep the change."

The brunette seemed suddenly happier about life.

"Question for you," said Nora. "How would you feel if you got a poo in the eye?"

The barmaid shrugged and pocketed the twenty. "I've had worse. Guys are into all kinds of weird stuff." She turned and walked back towards the bar.

Nora watched her go. "She's had worse. That's the modern dating scene summed up right there." Nora took a large swig then sighed. "Speaking of dating and unruly children, how'd it go with Paul?"

It was Brigit's turn to take a large swig of wine. From a distance, they must've looked like a pair of alcoholics who'd just been rescued from a desert island.

She wiped her mouth and took a deep breath. "I fired him."

"Fuck off!"

Brigit nodded. "I did it."

Nora put her hand up for a high five.

Brigit looked embarrassed. "I don't think this is really a high-five moment."

"The fuck it isn't. This right here is a Beyoncé track. Throw it up, girlfriend, or I'm going to start singing."

Reluctantly Brigit put her hand up to receive a rambunctious high five.

"How did he take it?"

"Well, it's not like I wanted to do it. I mean, I just wanted him to start taking the job seriously and not turn it into this never-ending quest for vengeance."

"More power to you."

"I feel awful."

"Do you know what you need?" Brigit was all too aware of what Nora felt she needed, but it wasn't like that would stop her saying it. "Cock. A bit of meaningless, degrading, sweaty rumpy pumpy."

"Thank you, Dr Freud."

"How long has it been?"

"You know how long it's been."

"Too long."

"You're one to talk."

"Oh stop," said Nora. "It's been that long, I'm not sure everything still works down there."

"I take it things haven't improved with Donnacha then?"

Nora pulled a face. She and Detective Donnacha Wilson had an on-again off-again romance that was mostly off again, and had been since they'd met. Wilson had been assigned to protect Nora after the incident with the thug. This had led to him unexpectedly delivering her baby on her kitchen floor.

"Long story short, two things are wrong there. First off, he's eight years younger than me and frankly I spend enough time being mummy as it is."

Brigit shrugged. "That's not much of a gap."

"And secondly," continued Nora, "never try to date a man who has pulled a tiny human being out of you. Every time we got anywhere near anything involving my fufu, he'd go this funny colour and make an excuse. I'm telling you, once they've pulled a baby out of it, they have a very hard time seeing it as the tunnel of love anymore. Now it's like the Channel Tunnel with tiny nappy-clad refugees running through."

"Well, time to move on then."

Nora locked eyes with her. "Who are you and what have you done with Brigit Conroy?"

"Well yeah, but my situation is different, isn't it?"

"Is it? You're more of a babysitter than a partner."

"Oh please, let's talk about something else. Who's taking care of Dan the Man tonight?"

"The service said, and I quote, 'they had nobody available'. This was nearly two weeks ago I rang them, mind. Nobody available, my arse: we've been blackballed. Honestly, one teeny tiny fire and they all bottle it. I offered to pay double, too. This is just like that scene in *Pretty Woman* where the fancy shops won't take Julia Roberts's money to make her look less like a hooker – only, y'know, it's a toddler who doesn't look like a thingie but does have an alarming tendency towards physical and psychological torture. OK, that wasn't a great metaphor, but... What the hell was I talking about? Oh yeah, so, I took the nuclear option. My mam has come up for a couple of days."

"Wow, but you said after last time—"

"I know what I said. Don't quote me to me. She can be as interfering and judgy as she likes, let's see how she copes with the demon child for a night. Oh God, I don't mean that." Nora blessed herself and took a gulp of wine. "I'm a terrible mother."

Brigit shook her head emphatically. "Bollocks to that, you're like bloody Wonder Woman. It's the terrible twos, that's all."

"Should I ring home? I mean, I said I wasn't going to, but maybe I should just check. Should I check?" Nora started rummaging through her bag. "I'm just going to..."

Brigit reached across and snatched Nora's handbag away from her. "Relax. Dan will be absolutely fine."

"It's actually more Mam I'm worried about."

"Seriously, calm down. What's the worst that could happen?"

Nora fixed her with a stare. "You're kidding, right?"

"Well, I mean..."

"D'you know what I miss most?"

"Sex?"

"Silence! You've no idea how rare silence is in my house. And d'you know what scares me the most?"

Brigit shook her head.

"Silence. At least when he's making noise, I know where he is and what he's doing. It's when he goes quiet that I'm truly terrified. Last week, I found myself on the sofa, nodding off, then I heard it – silence! Do you know where he was? In the bathroom, flushing my rabbit down the loo."

"Oh my God, the poor... Wait, you don't mean the fluffy-eared kind of rabbit do you?"

Nora shook her head slowly.

"How did you explain that to him?"

"Never mind him, it was explaining it to the emergency plumber that was the tricky bit."

Brigit howled with laughter.

"It's not funny!" pleaded Nora, laughter rippling through her voice despite herself.

"It bloody well is," said Brigit, wiping a tear from her eye.

"Shut up, ye bitch."

Brigit raised her glass and clinked it against Nora's. "To independence."

"Independence." Nora clinked her glass but didn't drink. She was looking over Brigit's shoulder. "Don't look now, but you've got yourself an admirer."

Brigit began to turn her head.

"I said don't look!"

Brigit sighed exasperatedly. "How am I supposed to see then?"

"Just... hold on." Nora swirled the remains of her wine around her glass as she looked over Brigit's shoulder through narrowed eyes. "Do you know anybody who's about six-foot-two, leather jacket, long black hair, with a bushy beard that, despite how hipster it sounds, he is making work. He looks like a beast of a man but with dancing eyes. The 'read you poetry after he ravishes you' type."

"OK," said Brigit, "you're making this up."

"I'm not. If he was looking at me like that, I'd be over there humping his leg right now. He is definitely looking at you though."

"He's looking at the back of me, apparently."

Nora pursed her lips. "That's a good point."

The whole bar turned to gawp at them after Nora's remarkably loud wolf whistle. Brigit could feel herself turning bright red. "Oh Jesus, ye mad bitch!"

Nora pointed at her. "She's single, in case you were wondering."

Brigit put her head in her hands and looked at the tabletop with the kind of intensity associated with death matches. Her voice came out in an urgent whisper. "I am going to fecking kill you."

Nora looked around her, seemingly oblivious. "It's alright, everyone. Sorry, I was just moving things along. I'm on a schedule here, gotta be home by midnight. I wasn't talking to you, Ponytail, turn around."

Brigit sensed someone standing beside their table, but she was too mortified to look up.

"Hello, I'm Nora, the slightly demented friend."

"Hi. I'm Anthony."

"Anthony, hello. This is my friend Brigit."

Nora got a kick under the table.

"Ouch," she said, looking across at Brigit. "That really hurt. She's sensitive, that's one of her many fine qualities. She's also not normally this red in the face. She's caught a bit of sun."

"Don't mind her," said Brigit, actually looking at their visitor for the first time. She had to admit, he was as advertised. He had piercing blue eyes and a pretty damn cute embarrassed smile. "She's not had a proper night's sleep in about two years."

"I haven't had a proper a lot of things in that time, but we're not here to talk about me."

Nora's bag started playing the *Jaws* theme tune. "Oh Christ." She dived into it, fishing her mobile out. "Hi, Mam, is everything OK?"

She listened for a moment. "No, no problem. What's up?" Nora shot a look at Brigit. "He's chased the cat up onto the top of the wardrobe? Right – biggest thing here, Mam, we don't actually own a cat. Hang on a sec, I'll go outside where it's easier to hear you." Nora put her hand over the phone and stood up. "Sorry, it appears we have a hostage situation. Speaking of which" – Nora nodded at Anthony – "you, sit here, be charming." And she strode off towards the door.

Anthony smiled awkwardly. "She's quite something."

"You can say that again. You don't have to..." Brigit looked at the other chair.

"Well, actually, if it's OK with you?"

"Yeah. Sure. Fine. I mean... Christ we're starting to sound like a Hugh Grant movie, just sit down."

Anthony nodded and did so, giving Brigit an adorably embarrassed smile. He shifted nervously. "So, this is awkward."

"You're only noticing that now?"

"Yeah, I mean beyond the obvious."

"And the fact that everyone in this bar is now watching us?"

"There's that too, of course."

"Well, everyone except for my soon-to-be-dead friend, who, from the mime I can see through the window, appears to be instructing a woman in her sixties on how to get a cat off a wardrobe with a mop."

"Yeah. Look, could you stop talking for one sec."

Brigit sat back in her chair. "Are you new to this? Because I'm pretty sure that's a flirting no-no."

He shifted nervously again. "I'm sorry, I just... I kind of followed you here."

Brigit gave him a hard look. "Right. Again, bit of a flirting no-no there. I'm kinda glad people are watching us now."

"No, you see, I'm Anto. Anthony Kelleher."

Brigit thrust her hand into her bag. "I've got mace!"

Anto held his hands up. "Relax, I come in peace, I promise."

"Oh yeah, you and your brothers are very peaceful – I've got an office covered in yellow paint to prove it."

"Not my idea, I promise. None of it was my idea, and I'm fairly sure none of it was yours either."

"Let's not forget who started this whole thing – and how, you disgraceful shower of scumbags."

Anto nodded. "That's fair. For what it's worth, that wasn't me, and to be honest, I agree with you entirely. What they did to your friend was appalling and, believe me, if I'd known about it, I would have done everything in my power to stop it. I mean, drugging a man and then taking those pictures, that is absolutely disgusting. I'm here to apologise first and foremost, so if you just give me two minutes and take your hand off what I'm fairly sure is a can of deodorant, then I'll be on my way."

Brigit didn't even look down. "Deodorant, yeah, and I've got a lighter too. You look rather flammable, ye big hairy lummocks. What are you doing following me?"

"I didn't mean to... Look, I couldn't come into your offices for obvious reasons, and over the phone this would sound like just another ploy in the never-ending cycle. Just give me sixty seconds. After that, if you still want to, feel free to set me on fire."

"Don't think I won't."

"I don't doubt it. I'm going to take my hands down now, OK?"

Brigit nodded. As she did so, she glanced around the bar. Every last pair of eyes was on them. "D'ye mind? This is a private conversation."

Everyone looked away for a fraction of a second and then resumed staring at them. Whatever this was, it had the distinct possibility of becoming a story.

"OK," said Anto. "Again, let me reiterate, I'm sincerely sorry."

"For which bit?"

"All of it. It's childish nonsense. We both know how it started but, the reality is, if my brothers and your boyfriend—"

"He's not my boyfriend." Brigit felt herself blush again. Why on earth had she felt the need to point that out?

"Fair enough. Still though, this thing is ruining our business and I'm guessing yours too. I just wanted to approach you and see if we could talk about it like adults. If it'd be possible to get some kind of a truce so, y'know, I could flush the toilet in our office without checking for explosive ordnance first."

As Nora made her way back into the bar, she passed Anthony on his way out. She hurried over to the table and sat down. "So, what happened there?"

"He's Anthony Kelleher."

"And?"

Brigit gave Nora a long look.

"Oh shit, right – sorry, mummy brain. As in, the other side in your little war. Did you tell him to bugger off?"

"Sort of."

"Sort of? Why am I getting a whole Romeo and Juliet vibe here?"

"Don't be daft. I threatened to set him on fire."

"Men go for mad women. Fact!"

"Well," said Brigit, casually holding up a piece of paper with a mobile number on it, "he did give me his number."

"Dinner and dancing?"

"More like truce talks with him and his brothers."

"Damn," said Nora, snatching up her empty wine glass. "First date and already meeting the family, this is serious." She held her glass above her head again. "Garçon, same again, we're celebrating!"

CHAPTER ELEVEN

"I'm telling ye, lads, she was all over me. It was embarrassing. She was like a dog in heat."

Horse leaned over the handlebars of his bike and favoured his audience with his most suggestive of wide grins. Tommy and Daz were loving it, but Karl, always fecking Karl, was pulling that face he did – smirking lanky bollocks.

"She didn't seem that keen down the park," said Karl.

"Yeah, well, she warmed up."

"She told Janice that nothing happened."

Horse flicked his long fringe out of his eyes. "That's bullshit, right. We did it all – kinky stuff, the lot. Course she's not saying, a gentleman doesn't kiss and tell."

"You're supposed to be the one who doesn't tell, in that case."

"Shut up, Karl. I was a lot of things, but I wasn't gentle."

Daz guffawed as Karl rolled his eyes. He was fast coming due a slap. Horse wasn't going to take this kind of disrespect.

"Howerya, lads!"

Horse's heart jumped into his throat, but he didn't turn around. He didn't need to in order to recognise the voice. He hadn't done anything wrong, had he? At least nothing anybody would know about. His body made a decision before his mind got involved, and he hit the pedals of his bike hard, trying for a sprint start. He got up just enough momentum in the first couple of feet that when the hurling stick was jammed into the front wheel, he was sent hurtling over the handlebars.

The air expelled from his lungs with a whoof as he landed on the ground in front of the big wheelie bins that served the whole of the Dolphin House flats. Horse looked up into the mid-morning Dublin sky. There presumably was a sun up there somewhere, buried between the thick dark clouds, but it was unlikely to be putting in an appearance anytime soon. Certainly Horse's future wasn't looking sunny.

"Jesus, Horse, sorry about that. It appears that my hurley got tangled up in the spokes of your wheel there."

Horse turned his head to the side. He could see Tommy and Karl legging it back into the flats for all they were worth, bleedin' cowards – not that he could blame them. He didn't want to be here either. He looked upwards again as the distinctive head of Bunny McGarry hove into view, looking down at him with mock concern.

"Ye don't look well, Horse. Are ye off your feed?"

Horse liked to pretend that his nickname was due to his endowment in certain areas, but the reality was that it had started back in his schooldays. Horse was called Horse because, well, he resembled a horse. His teeth looked way too big for his head, giving him an unfortunate overbite. He had been a half back for the St Jude's hurling team, if not exactly by choice. Bunny didn't give you a choice.

"Who the fuck is this mad old prick?"

Horse winced at the sound of Daz's voice. Daz had just moved into the area last year, which explained, if not excused, the error he was making. With a groan, Horse started to stand up. He noticed the wide smile on Bunny's face as he favoured Daz with that patented McGarry stare. This was nothing but bad news.

"Shut up, Daz," said Horse.

"Is this dude the feds?"

"The feds?" repeated Bunny. "Was this lad dropped as a baby or something? You're in Ireland son, speak proper."

"Not exactly," said Horse, which was true. Bunny was not technically the Gardaí any more; he was, however, still very much Bunny. "Daz, you should head off, alright?"

Daz looked at Horse in disbelief. "What? I'm not having some mad old fart coming into my manor, disrespecting my crew."

"Crew?" said Bunny. "Crew, is it? Are youse rowing the coxless fours now or something, Horse? This fella does look a tad on the cock-less side alright." Bunny turned to face Daz. "Bunny McGarry at your service, sunshine. Now do yourself a favour and toddle off, I'd like a private word with the man called Horse."

"And who's gonna make me, ye wonky-eyed Cork prick?"

Thirty seconds later, Horse had his back to one of the large bins, with Bunny McGarry standing uncomfortably close to him. "Now, Horse, can you guess what my little visit is about?"

"It fecking stinks in here, let me out," Daz shouted from inside the bin. Some people just didn't know when to shut up.

"Keep it shut, ye donkey gobbler, and be thankful I put you in the food bin and not the one full of all the broken bottles."

There was a moment's silence, followed by another one. Apparently even Daz could learn his lesson if it was explained in clear enough terms. You could accuse Bunny of a lot of things, but understatement was not one of them.

"Now, do you know why I'm here, Horse?"

"Is this about Sharon? Because I didn't say nothing. She's lying."

Bunny pursed his lips. Horse felt like an idiot. He'd forgotten one of the golden rules: never guess why Bunny might be angry. If you were wrong, he now had two reasons to be angry.

"No, this is not about Sharon, although..." He clattered Horse on the ear.

"Jesus, Bunny, what was that for?"

"I don't know, but I'm guessing Sharon does. Do I need to repeat the little talk I gave you about respecting women?"

Horse looked downwards. "No, Bunny."

"Good. No, I'm here because there's a very nice lady up on the third floor there called Mrs Aweyeme. Nigerian lady. Got three kids, very well behaved. They seem to be getting an awful lot of hassle for some reason. Apparently one of the main villains of the piece has one of them floppy fringes and an equestrian bent to his facial features. You wouldn't know anything about that, would you, Horse?"

"They're moving in here, Bunny. Taking over. This is our manor."

"Yeah," agreed Daz, from inside the bin.

Bunny booted the side of the bin – hard. "Ouch."

"You shut up. And as for you..." Bunny moved in close enough that Horse could smell the Monster Munch on his breath. "Jesus, Horse, are you that stupid? They're poor people, moving here looking for a better chance at life. The sheer stupidity of people who have feck all attacking other people who have feck all – it makes me want to scream."

"They're not from round here but."

Bunny pointed at the bin. "Neither is that sack of shite. What's the difference?"

"Well he's, I mean..."

"I'm Irish."

Bunny booted the bin again.

"I'm Irish," Bunny repeated in a mocking voice. "Irish, as in the people who had feck all for generations and went to America, Australia, England, Canada – anywhere that'd have us, and a few places that wouldn't, all because we wanted a better life. Are those the people of whom you speak?"

"That's different."

Bunny booted the bin so hard this time that he left a distinct imprint of his boot in it. "It's the exact fecking same!" His roar had an edge of the really unhinged to it. Horse prayed that Daz had the sense to shut up, or else he'd soon be looking back on his time in the bin as the good old days.

Bunny looked directly into Horse's eyes, giving him the full McGarry wonky-eyed stare. "You were a decent kid, Horse. Don't grow up to be a pathetic excuse for a man, blaming your lot on everything and everybody but yourself. There are many reasons you might not get the life you hoped for, but believe you me, none of those reasons will be because a widow and her three kids moved into a flat on the third floor. Be a man, for Christ's sake. Make something of yourself. You can start by hanging around with a better class of humanity that Captain Dim-in-the-Bin here, and apologising to this girl Sharon for whatever the hell you said, did or whatever. You're one of my boys, Horse. I'd like to be proud of ye."

Horse looked down at the ground, unable to make eye contact with Bunny.

"All you're doing is fearing the different. Remember this – some day, you might meet the right woman or piss off the wrong man, and you'll find yourself somewhere else in the world, and you'll be the different. Remember how you treated these people now, because that'll be how you or your kids or your kid's kids will be treated. It's a small world, and what goes around comes around."

Horse remained staring at his feet. He rubbed a finger in his eye. "Yes, Bunny."

"What was that? I'm going a bit deaf in my old age."

Horse cleared his throat and spoke a little louder. "Yes, Bunny."

"Good lad. Now, I've a question for you. Look at me."

Horse looked up.

"Over my left shoulder there, do you know who that bloke in the baseball cap is?"

Horse glanced over Bunny's shoulder. He'd no idea how Bunny had seen him, but there was a tall fella in a baseball cap leaning casually against the railings down by the shops.

"I don't know him, Bunny."

"He's been watching us for the last few minutes."

"Well, I mean, no offence, Bunny, but ye did just bung a lad into a bin. That's the kinda thing that draws people's attention."

Bunny pursed his lips. "Yeah, I suppose."

Horse looked over again. "He's disappeared now, where'd he go?"

Bunny stepped back and glanced around. The man was nowhere to be seen. He shrugged and bent down to pick up his hurley, extracting it from the mangled remains of Horse's front wheel.

"Right so, Horse, are we clear?"

"Yes, Bunny."

"Good. I'll be checking back in. Tell your ma I was asking for her."

Horse nodded.

Bunny walloped the side of the bin with his hurley. "And as for you, welcome to the neighbourhood. We welcome any and all people who behave themselves and treat others with respect. What's your name?"

"Daz."

Bunny walloped the bin with the hurley again. "Proper name. What does your ma call ye?"

"Darren. Darren Yates."

"Well, Mr Yates, I'll be taking a personal interest in you from now on. I hope this little meeting has been of use to you as well."

"You're mental."

Horse watched as Bunny stared over to his right, like he was looking at someone or something – but when he turned his head, there was nothing there.

"You might be right."

Horse stood in silence as Bunny strode off, a slight limp to his gait.

"Can I get out yet?"

Saying nothing, Horse picked up his bike and walked away.

CHAPTER TWELVE

Detective Superintendent Susan Burns hated swing doors. After the meeting she had just had, she really wanted to enter the office of the National Bureau of Criminal Investigations with a proper good slam, but the bloody swing doors made it impossible. She held in her hand the cup of coffee she'd brought into the meeting upstairs, now stone cold and still untouched. She'd been too busy fire-fighting to pause for a drink. The problem with dead coffee is that it's hard to find somewhere to dispose of it. Facilities had removed all of the potted plants from this floor of the building, quite possibly for this very reason.

"Where the hell is Rowe?"

Sergeant Moira Clarke looked up from her desk, like a woodland creature sensing that a bear was on the prowl. "He's out at the Ranelagh thing, guv. Do you want him now?"

"Look at my face, Moira."

Clarke snatched for her phone with a speed normally reserved for catching babies who had been accidentally dropped into volcanoes.

"And as for the rest of you" – DSI Burns raised her voice, so that every pair of eyes in the room were fixed on her – "Tinder, speed dating, websites, being introduced by friends, out drinking in a bar, in the supermarket – hell, even writing your phone number up on a toilet door – all of these are ways I am perfectly fine with you trying to acquire new romantic partners. Witnesses in one of my murder investigations, however, are entirely off limits. I would have thought that went without saying, but apparently not. If any of the rest of you fancy being Romeo and Juliet, do remember, they both die in the end."

"Eh, boss?"

"Yes, Moira?"

"He says—"

"I have no interest in what Rowe has to say, I only want him here to shout at. This isn't one of those times where avoiding the boss until she calms down is the smart play, this is one of those incidents where the longer I have to think about it, the worse it'll get."

"Right, just he says—"

Burns grabbed the receiver out of Clarke's hand. "I'll make it very simple, Alan. Either you're standing in front of my desk in an hour or you're cleaning out yours."

She slammed the phone down before the voice at the end of the line could say anything else. She felt better for finally getting to slam something. "Thank you, Moira." DSI Burns realised as she said the words that her angry tone didn't match them at all. She was conscious that Clarke hadn't done anything wrong, so tried to belatedly soften her delivery with a smile, but she hadn't got it in her.

"Ehm, guv, on another front—"

DSI Burns turned on her heels and headed for her office. "Not now, Moira. I've got a fun phone call with HR coming up."

"But—"

"Later."

Burns slammed the door of her office.

"Shower of penis-wielding wankers! Like I've not enough shit to be..."

It was only as she sat down that DSI Burns noticed the red-headed woman sitting on the other side of her desk. This at least solved the problem of what to do with the cold coffee, as DSI Burns promptly spilled it all over herself. "Christ."

"Oh deary, are you alright?"

"Ahhh, yeah, fine – I mean, it's cold."

Burns pulled her sodden and severely stained blouse away from her skin. It was only new on today too.

Burns looked up to see Moira Clarke's head sticking in the door. "I tried to tell you."

Burns took a deep breath and looked down at the front of her blouse. "You did, Moira. Sorry, I'm having a bit of a day here."

The last bit was delivered as a general apology to the world.

"Sure sounds like it," said the redhead. "Some vinegar will lift that right out."

"Yeah."

Moira tossed a box of tissues through the door and beat a hasty retreat. DSI Burns pulled out a couple and patted down the front of her blouse, to at least stop herself from dripping onto the desk. Then she tossed the sodden wad of tissue into the bin while taking a first proper look at her guest. The woman had a large perm of red hair on top of a wide face, heavy with make-up. Her accent was American, and it had an incongruous Tinkerbell tinkle to it.

"Sorry, forgive my manners." DSI Burns stood and extended her right hand across the table. "DSI Susan Burns, and you are?"

"FBI Special Agent Alana Dove."

With a soft whirr of mechanics, the other woman extended her hand. DSI Burns pulled hers back reflexively and then remembered herself. "Oh God, sorry," she said, shaking hands. "How rude of me. You caught me a bit off guard there, is all."

"That's quite alright, throws everybody for a loop the first time." She patted her right arm under her cream jacket. "This here is the catchily-titled GL480. It's a prototype designed by the boys over at DARPA. I've had targeted muscle reinnervation surgery that allows me to control this modular prosthetic limb. It's a really high-tech piece of machinery."

"Right, wow. Very impressive."

DSI Burns tried to look as natural as she could while shaking hands with a robotic hand, which was surprisingly warm. As they shook, the metal fingers tightened around hers.

"Oh sorry, I'm still breaking it in. It goes a little power-shake crazy from time to time."

Agent Dove spent the next minute prising the prosthetic hand's iron grasp from around Burns's fingers, as both women smiling politely. Once done, Burns sat back down, stretching her fingers out under the desk. "So, Agent Dove, you're a long way from home. What can I help you with?"

"I'm hoping we can help each other. We got a DNA match. One of the bodies you recently recovered is one of ours."

"Ah, we thought it might be an American."

"No, I mean FBI. Special Agent Daniel Zayas."

Agent Dove took a headshot photograph from her bag and slid it across the table. It showed the smiling face of a Latino man in his forties with a receding hairline.

"I see. When did he disappear?"

"About eighteen years ago."

"That fits the timeline we've established. Do you have any idea of the identity of the second individual?"

"No clue, I'm afraid."

"Was your agent here on some form of official business?" Burns asked the question more to see Dove's reaction than in the expectation of a meaningful answer. If an FBI agent had disappeared in Ireland while on official business, she would undoubtedly have already known about it.

"Holidays. We think he may've been trying to trace his family roots."

Burns gave her a quizzical look and then looked at the picture again. "Really? What was the second name again?"

"Zayas. The Irish is on his mother's side."

"Yes, I'm sure," said Burns, who would've bet her fully functioning right arm that this was bullshit too. "Was there an investigation at the time?"

"Yes. The last trace we had of Agent Zayas was him getting on a ferry from here to Britain. Liverpool, I believe. He was never heard from again."

"I see."

Burns looked down at the photograph again, as much to have something to look at other than Agent Dove. She was trying not to stare. The woman's face didn't appear to move. It had either been Botoxed to within an inch of its life or she'd had something else done. Her skin had an unnatural smoothness to it. When Dove blinked, it happened unusually slowly, like she was taking a second-long nap. She reminded her of the make-up dummy her sister had had as a child – and it was not a flattering comparison. The overall effect made it feel like she was having a conversation with an animatronic robot.

"Can I be honest with you, Inspector?" Though they were alone, Dove leaned in and lowered her voice. "Off the record, we had believed that Agent Zayas was going through some personal issues at the time. There was a theory that he may have..." She walked two of her fingers along the edge of Burn's desk and then jumped them off. "Either on the ferry or soon after."

"I see. Any revised theories now that he's turned up buried in the Wicklow Mountains?"

Agent Dove shrugged, the smile remaining fixed on her face. "Robbery homicide? Despite the best advice, a lot of tourists do travel with a great deal of cash on them. You know what people are like."

"Yes," agreed Burns, "but I'm afraid robbery homicide, while not entirely unprecedented, is extremely rare in this part of the world. Nobody is snatching a tourist's wallet and then burying them up in the mountains."

"I believe neither body was found with a wallet."

"Yes, but they were found buried with two fully loaded handguns, which doesn't really mesh with your hypothesis."

"Well," said Dove, with that same smile fixed to her face, "I guess that's what I'm here to find out. I am hoping for your full cooperation with my investigation."

Burns gave her own tight smile in response. "I think you'll find this is my investigation. The FBI has no jurisdiction here, obviously, though I will be happy to keep you fully up to speed."

"We always have a full investigation into the death of any American citizen in suspicious circumstances."

"Yes, but this is still a matter for Irish law enforcement. As I said, we will be happy to keep you informed of any—"

"I expect to be fully involved in any investigation."

"I'm afraid that's not possible."

"He's our guy."

"It's our country."

"I had hoped we'd be able to get along."

"So had I, Agent Dove, but you can't just come marching in here—"

The phone on DSI Burn's desk started to ring.

"You should get that. It will be your commissioner."

Burns looked at the display on the phone and recognised the number. She gave Dove a long, hard look. Dove gave her the same frozen smile and then blinked, unnervingly slowly.

CHAPTER THIRTEEN

Bunny leaned on his hurley and looked up at the crucifix hanging high on the wall, and in particular at the figure nailed to it. Something about it bothered him. He'd seen thousands of them over the years, of course – it wasn't that long ago that no house in Ireland was complete without having Our Lord and Saviour nailed to a piece of wood somewhere on the walls. That and the pictures of Pope John Paul II and John F. Kennedy were very much the holy trinity of twentieth-century Irish interior design. Fashions had changed over time and IKEA had gradually replaced icons. Still, this crucifix wasn't right. It was the face. Normally Jesus wore an expression of angst appropriate to having nails stuck in you. On this one, he looked positively cheerful. Bunny had an inkling this was by design, like even the pain of crucifixion couldn't stop the son of God from being impressed at the bargains on offer.

Bunny turned at the sound of a throat being cleared politely behind him. Jerry Malone stood there, all five-foot-nothing of him, his wide smile leaving barely enough room on his face for other features. He wore a golden crucifix around his neck too. Subtle. Jesus Malone, as everyone called him, should probably be in line for some form of entrepreneurial award. Not that he would accept it, of course, as that would mean admitting something he had always ferociously denied.

Ten years ago, his second-hand car dealership and repair business had been on the verge of bankruptcy when he had a divine moment of inspiration. He'd been passing a skip when he saw a battered, framed picture of the Virgin Mary. He had retrieved it and placed it on the wall of his garage. Suddenly, clapped-out bangers that he couldn't convince even joyriders to steal for the insurance pay-out started selling. Malone Motors went from a wasteland to the busiest dealership in Dublin. Jerry put it down to the good Lord smiling down upon him. Most of those in the know put it down to Jerry realising a fundamental truth: nobody, but nobody, trusted a mechanic or a second-hand car dealer. A born-again, hallelujah, happy-clappy car dealer on the other hand... You couldn't fault the logic. If someone lived in fear of burning in eternal hell, they'd probably not weld two lemons together and sell it to you. Even atheists believed in Jesus Malone. The walls of this branch of Malone Motors, now one of four in the Greater Dublin Area, were festooned with religious paraphernalia. As well as the crucifix, there were framed portraits of the Virgin Mary, St Jude, St Augustus, Mother Theresa and Pope John Paul II. There was also a portrait that someone with even fewer scruples than Jesus Malone had managed to convince him was of the latest Pope. Despite every member of staff wearing a crucifix and liberally smattering "God bless" and "Praise the Lord" into conversations with customers, none of them appeared to know that the picture was in fact the comedian George Carlin. They did all agree that the Pope was a good-looking man, however.

In short, Jesus Malone was one of the most untrustworthy people on the planet and Bunny trusted him completely to fix his car. That was because, while he may or may not have found God, Malone had no great desire to meet him again soon, so Bunny's car would be dealt with lovingly and cheaply.

"Bunny. How are you? Great to see you. God bless."

"Yeah. Just thought I'd pop in and see how me car was getting along?"

Bunny casually rested his hurley against his shoulder. It was something of a leading question, given that Bunny's beloved Porsche 928S, the finest vehicle the 1980s had to offer in Bunny's admittedly biased opinion, lay behind Jesus with its innards spread out beside it.

"Honestly, it's not going great. Like I told you last time, this car is really more hassle to you than it's worth."

"Just fix it."

"Well, I can order the parts in again from Britain if you want, but honestly, I could do you a great deal on a new—"

"How long will it take?"

"It's hard to say for sure."

"Try." Bunny casually rested the head of the hurley on Jesus' shoulder.

"I do wish you wouldn't do that."

"What? Do you not like Mabel?"

"Mabel? I thought it was called Susan."

"That was the last one. She got broken dealing with—"

Jesus threw his hands up. "I don't want to know. We go back a long way, Bunny. I'm hurt that you think intimidation is necessary. I run an honest business here."

Bunny nodded. "There's a couple of lads over behind you with a drill that appear to be 'fixing' the mileage on that Ford Focus."

"I resent the implications of that statement, Bunny. Next time, could you not bring the hurley with you, it makes my staff very nervous."

"What? It's just a bit of sporting equipment."

"Yeah, so is a baseball bat. My brother is the manager up at that big sports store on Henry Street, says they sell hundreds of baseball bats every year."

"Is that so?"

"Yeah. And they've had the same three baseballs in stock since 2007."

"Speaking of which, any chance I'll get my car back for Christmas?"

Jesus Malone sighed. "Hang on, I'll go check."

"Wonderful. Thanks be to Jesus."

As Jesus scurried away, Bunny walked over to look at his car. It looked so sad and vulnerable.

"She looks bad, Detective, but then don't we all?"

Zayas sat on a pile of tyres beside the wall. Bunny ignored him.

"Do you think you'll get a chance to drive her again before..."

Bunny spoke in a whisper. "Would you piss off and mind your own business." He turned around. Zayas was now leaning up against the wall beneath the crucifix.

"But you are my business, Detective. We are joined at the hip now, don't you think?"

"Just feck off and leave me alone."

Bunny was disturbed by the sound of a throat being politely cleared. Jesus Malone was looking at him, his previously ubiquitous smile noticeable for its absence. "Everything OK, Bunny?"

"You tell me. The parts?"

"First week of January, I'm afraid. It's a nightmare to get anything at this time of year. Seriously, are you alright, Bunny? You don't look well."

"Sorry, I think I'm going down with something."

Bunny tried to ignore the figure in the white suit now leaning on his car's bonnet, laughing at his choice of words.

"Are you alright with the loaner in the meantime?"

Bunny didn't answer.

"Bunny?"

"What? Sorry. Yeah, it'll be grand. Thanks, Jerry. Have a Merry Christmas and all that."

Malone looked up at Bunny, his face a picture of worry, and not the normal kind of worry that being face-to-face with Bunny McGarry typically inspired in people. "Cheers. You should seriously get yourself checked out though – you're white as a sheet. It's like you've seen a ghost."

Bunny walked out of the gates of Malone Motors and stopped, trying to remember where he had parked Jesus's "loaner", a 1995 Fiat Uno. Nobody would steal it, but they might accidentally step on it. Bunny felt ridiculous crammed into the thing, but it was all that was available. To be fair, he didn't have much more room when driving his own car, but he happily put up with that.

He remembered that he had parked it up around the corner. The streets round here were a chaotic free-for-all due to a lack of parking restrictions, so office workers anywhere within a mile competed to be the first here in the morning. It was a sneaky oasis in the sea of parking meters that Dublin had become.

As Bunny headed off to his left, he passed the smirking figure of Zayas leaning against the wall of the garage.

"Excellent work, Detective. It is good to keep up the pretence of normality. Try to remain calm."

Bunny ignored him, tried to get his mind to focus on something else. Sunday. Who would he pick in the St Jude's team for Sunday? Invariably, it would be whoever turned up, but still.

Zayas fell into step behind him.

"Do you think they will have identified the bodies by now? It has been a couple of days."

"You're not real." Bunny hissed it through gritted teeth as he quickened his pace.

"No. I'm your mind losing its grip under justifiable stress. And just because I'm not real, it doesn't mean I'm not a problem."

"Stop following me."

"I'm not the one following you."

Bunny stopped and turned around. Zayas was nowhere to be seen, but Bunny did clock a man with lank red hair walking a collie dog on the far side of the road. He glanced at Bunny and then looked away. Bunny turned around and started walking again.

"Oh dear, Detective, I do hope you're not getting paranoid."

Bunny turned the corner; the loaner was parked up across the street. Every time Bunny saw it, his heart sank a little further. As metaphors went for how his life was heading, it was a little on the nose.

Further down the street, Bunny heard a car door open as he fumbled with the keys. The button to disarm the alarm only worked about one time in six, and even then it didn't open the door. He thumbed it repeatedly until the front lights flashed and then put the key in and heaved the door handle upwards to disengage the lock. It would actually be easier to smash the window in and rob the damn thing – if you could even call it robbing. The object had to have some form of value to someone for it to be considered theft.

"Mister McGa—"

Bunny felt the presence of the man behind him just before he began to speak. On instinct, he swung around and grabbed the stranger's hand as he reached up to tap him on the shoulder, twisting his arm around and slamming the man into the side of the car.

Five-foot-eight or so, the man was wearing a suit and far too much aftershave. He had a recent holiday tan and was wearing a gold bracelet that fell to the ground as Bunny twisted his hand into his back. He yelped in pain.

"Who the fuck are you?"

"Get off me!"

Bunny shoved his face beside the man's ear. "Answer the fecking question!"

"Doesn't matter who I am."

Bunny grabbed the man's fingers and squeezed. "I'll decide what matters. Who sent you?"

"Agh... inside pocket."

Bunny shoved his hand inside the man's jacket and pulled out a white envelope. "What the hell is this?"

"In accordance with the powers given to me by the Private Security Services Act 2004, you've been served with a summons. Have a nice day, you fucking prick."

Bunny squeezed the man's fingers – a little harder than he meant to – and heard a cracking noise.

"Agghhhhhh."

Bunny released him and stepped back. He still held the unopened envelope. The man in the suit cupped his right hand. "You fucking lunatic, you broke my bleedin' finger."

Bunny looked down at the man. "Ye... ye shouldn't sneak up on people."

"Sneak up? In broad daylight on a public street? You're a lunatic. Smile for the camera, dickhead."

With his good hand, the man pointed down the street, where a much larger man in a suit was holding up an iPhone and recording them.

Bunny looked around. A couple of office workers had stopped down the street, one of whom had her phone out, clearly debating whether to call the Gardaí. On the opposite corner, the dog walker with the lank red hair watched on, before dragging his dog away.

CHAPTER FOURTEEN

Not a date.

Brigit kept repeating those three words in her head as the taxi nudged its way through the afternoon traffic on O'Connell Street.

Not a date.

Not a date.

Not a date.

And it wasn't. She was going for a meeting with Anto Kelleher and his brothers in the Gresham Hotel. It had been agreed in a series of texts between herself and Anto over the weekend. The texts had perhaps been a little flirtier than was entirely appropriate in the business environment, but, still, she was on her way to a meeting. Had she told Paul about it? No. But they weren't talking at all, seeing as she had removed him from the company. He would no doubt hit the roof if he found out she was talking to the Kellehers, but that was exactly the problem. She was trying to run a business here, whereas Paul was trying to run a bloody guerrilla war.

Alright, she had made a bit of time yesterday to get some shopping done, but she'd been needing some new work clothes for a while. Admittedly, she had spent so much on the blue Ted Baker pencil dress that she was going to be returning it tomorrow at lunchtime, but it was important to look nice for meetings. She had also splurged on a taxi rather than walk the fifteen minutes down from the office, as it was a fairly rotten day weather-wise and she didn't want to run the risk of trying to return a rain-soaked dress.

She was annoyed with herself too. Paul and she hadn't been an item for eighteen months, so why exactly would her exchanging texts with another man be a problem? He had no right to think that. Not that he knew but, in her head, he thought that. The version of him she carried around with her was saying so right now. She didn't owe him anything. Alright, maybe she did. But she didn't owe him idiotic blind loyalty. If he wanted something, be it her or the company, then he needed to damn well put the work in. Destiny was a speeding train, not a taxi – you either caught it or you missed it. She'd read that in one of her self-help books, of which she had started to acquire an alarmingly large collection.

The taxi pulled up outside the Gresham Hotel and Brigit paid the driver. Before she could touch the handle, the taxi's door swung open. Anto Kelleher stood there smiling, an open umbrella held out.

"Well," said Brigit with a nervous smile, "aren't you full service."

"Ah," said Anto, "it's a thoroughly miserable day. Didn't want you turning up looking like a drowned rat."

"Charming!"

Brigit slid out of the taxi and under the umbrella. Anto grinned at her. "That dress deserves to be kept dry and, if at all possible, preserved for posterity."

"Cheeky. Keep your eyes off my posterity."

Brigit took the proffered umbrella and strode forward, turning her head to hide the smile playing across her lips. Anthony slammed the car door and hurried after her. A concierge in faintly ridiculous top and tails opened the door for her with a bow. She nodded her thanks and walked in, collapsing the umbrella and placing it in a nearby stand. It had been a while since Brigit had been in the Gresham. The last time had been at the works do of a guy she'd been seeing very briefly several years ago. She remembered the meal being lovely – considerably nicer, in fact, than the guy had turned out to be.

"Where do we..."

Anthony indicated a set of double doors on the far side of the reception area. "We've got a meeting room booked. I even splurged for the tea- and coffee-making facilities."

"Wow," said Brigit. "You really know how to show a girl a good time."

Kevin and Vincent Kelleher were Anthony's brothers, that was obvious. You could see that the same essential ingredients had gone into the recipe, it was just that the other two had come out of the oven considerably less hot. Kevin was about eight inches shorter than Anto, whereas Vincent was about the same amount taller. Both of them were bulky, leaning towards fat but not actually there yet. All three of them had blue eyes. Kevin's glowered out at the world in a squint while Vincent's sat under an unfortunate monobrow that gave him the air of a caveman who'd been squeezed into a shiny suit. In contrast, what hair Kevin had on his head had been very well maintained, primarily in an attempt to de-emphasise the lack of it. Brigit would've bet that the excess was on his back. Both of the older brothers had that gorilla feel to them. She imagined Anthony's body was very smooth, not that she had spent any time at all thinking about Anthony's body – which she very definitely, absolutely had not.

"Kevin, Vinny – this is Brigit Conroy."

"Hello," said Brigit.

"Nice to meet you." Kevin smiled from across the far side of the mahogany table but he didn't get up. Vincent nodded from his position holding up the wall behind him. Anthony had clearly got all of the charm in the family. The room smelled of polish and carpeting that had been recently hoovered. It looked like every other hotel meeting room she'd ever been in. There was a framed picture of James Joyce on the wall.

"Take a seat. I'd offer to shake your hand, only..." Kevin held up his right hand; he had a couple of fingers taped together.

"Oh dear," said Brigit, sitting down opposite him. "What did you do to yourself?"

"Oh, I didn't do it to myself. It's been quite the morning."

Anthony clapped his hands together. "Right. Tea, coffee?"

"Tea would be lovely, one sugar."

"I'm fine," said Kevin. "I see you've not brought either of your partners with you?"

He said the word "partners" with a tone Brigit didn't like.

"No, I thought it best if we try and clear this up between us first, before involving anyone else."

Anthony was busy over at the tea and coffee station. "We've a few biscuits here as well. Proper ones too, none of that Rich Tea nonsense."

He was trying to force the mood towards jovial without a great deal of success. Brigit was now a whole different kind of nervous. Coming here had seemed like a good idea, but as she looked across at Kevin and Vinny Kelleher, she wasn't so sure. She couldn't read what was going on. Kevin had an odd smirk about him that didn't ring true to what the purpose of this meeting was supposed to be. If he was building up towards an apology, he was going an odd way about it.

Anthony placed a cup of tea on a saucer in front of Brigit. "Enjoy."

"I'm not sure she will."

"Kevin?"

Brigit could feel the tension as Anthony looked across the table at his older brother.

Kevin smiled back at him. "You see, we've just taken on a new client." He took an envelope out of the inside pocket of his suit and tossed it towards Brigit. It landed halfway across the table and skidded to a halt in front of her fingers.

"Kev, what is this?"

Kevin didn't look at his brother. "Shut up, Anthony, grown-ups are talking."

"What the fuck are you playing at? This isn't what we—"

"Shut. Up."

Brigit picked up the envelope and slowly opened it.

"His name is Jacob Harrison, I believe you're familiar with him?"

Brigit unfolded the piece of paper and glanced at it. "I see. And this is your idea of a truce meeting, is it?"

"Truce?" laughed Kevin. "I don't want a truce. Consider yourself duly served with a summons on behalf of Doherty's Solicitors, representing Jacob Harrison. He is suing MCM Investigations for loss of income and emotional distress arising from your partner's assault on him. I served Mr McGarry with his summons personally this morning." He held his hand up again. "He didn't exactly take it well. Still, it was a great bit of video. It'll do wonders in the trial towards proving his proclivity for violence."

"This is crap," said Brigit.

"Is it?" said Kevin. "Let's see what the courts make of a private investigator dangling someone off a tenth-storey balcony. He's also filed a complaint with the Private Security Authority by the way, so you can expect to be hearing from them."

Brigit stood up. "You dragged me here for this?"

Anthony's face held a look of undisguised horror. "I didn't know. Hang on, just take a seat and we'll..."

Brigit looked across at Kevin. "I don't think we've much more to discuss."

Kevin grinned. "Not unless you'd like to sell your business to us right now? I mean, it's just lost a whole lot of value, but we need a photocopier if you've got one."

"Go fuck yourself."

"You'd want to control that temper, Miss Conroy. Look how much trouble it got your friend Bunny into."

Brigit pushed the chair way and turned towards the door.

"Kevin? What the fuck, man? This isn't what we agreed."

"Shut up, Anthony. You sound like an idiot."

"Screw you. We had an agreement. You said..."

The rest of it was lost to Brigit as she slammed the door and started marching purposefully down the hall. Shit. Shit. Shit. How could she have been so stupid? All this had been was a set-up, designed to humiliate her. She still held the summons clenched in her hand but she was too angry to read it. She was so angry she couldn't even tell who she was most angry at. The Harrison thing had been a straightforward follow-and-record job until Paul fobbed it off on Bunny. Then Bunny, had... well, he had been Bunny. It wasn't like it was unprecedented behaviour. He had a very black and white view of the world. Unfortunately, that had now landed their company in all kinds of crap.

She stomped across reception and pushed open the outer doors. The concierge was distracted with helping some old dear up the steps. She heard Anthony calling after her but she didn't turn around. The cold December air hit her like a slap across the face after the centrally-heated comfort of the hotel. She hurried down the pavement, not even sure where she was heading, just knowing she had to get as far away as she could. She needed to think. First, though, she would need to calm down, and that might take a hell of a long time.

The number 70 rushed by, the rarity of an unobstructed bus lane allowing it to build up a bit of momentum. The driver either didn't notice the puddle or didn't care. The bus hit it hard, sending an arch of dirty water onto the pavement and adding the cherry atop a truly shitty day by leaving Brigit standing there soaked through, in a dress she now owned, clutching a summons for a company that, legal proceedings pending, she soon might not.

CHAPTER FIFTEEN

Detective Donnacha Wilson took a deep breath and watched as the lift hit B for basement. This was his second trip to the mortuary in a week and he was a long way from happy about it. He'd received a message that DSI Burns wanted to see him here immediately, and was a little suspicious that it could be a set-up, perhaps orchestrated by DS Rowe, a well-known prankster – at least in his own head. In reality, he was a grown man who spent an inordinate amount of time trying to bully and annoy his co-workers. As far as Wilson was concerned, Rowe was single-handedly responsible for the dissemination of the "Chucker" nickname that he so detested. He went to great lengths to see if he could make Wilson throw up; Halloween had been a particularly fun week. Wilson doubted this was Rowe's work, though, seeing as the last he had heard, he was up to his neck in it with DSI Burns. Even he would have the sense to keep his head down in those circumstances, wouldn't he? Still, Wilson had triple-checked the message with DS Moira Clarke before coming down to the mortuary.

The doors pinged open and Wilson stepped out, looking for any possible sources of "shenanigans". There was a large green bin, marked "Medical Waste", beside the door leading into the mortuary itself. Wilson kept his eyes on it as he walked by, fully prepared to punch anyone who popped out of it and put it down to "impulse reactions". The bin lid remained resolutely closed as Wilson pushed through the door.

He was greeted by the sight of DSI Burns and Dr Devane standing side by side, watching something on a monitor. Wilson politely cleared his throat and Burns glanced over her shoulder. "Ah, Wilson, good of you to join us."

"Sorry, guv, I was heading straight out to the Ranelagh thing when I got the message."

"Why were you—" Burns stopped herself. "Oh right, yes. I suspended Rowe." Wilson smiled and then quickly hid the reaction before it could be noted. Burns kept her eyes on the monitor. "You may not get much daylight down here, Denise, but you at least don't have to deal with your team developing romantic attachments to their work."

Devane shook her head. "No, thankfully."

Wilson hovered behind the two women, unsure what to do next. "You wanted to see me, guv?"

"I've got a job uniquely suited to your skill set."

"You do?" Wilson was unaware that he had a skill set, at least not one that his boss had shown an appreciation for.

"Yes, you're a devious little sod and I want to put that politician's mind of yours to work for me."

Wilson sagged. He came from a family of politicians, and while he tried to put that firmly behind him, everyone kept bringing it back up. That and the fact that he had the unfortunate habit of literally bringing stuff back up were becoming the two recurring themes of his career, and he was becoming royally sick of hearing about both of them.

"Don't pull that face," said Burns – much to Wilson's consternation, as she wasn't actually looking at him. "This is a good job. I think you'll actually like it. It's a bit glamorous."

"Really?"

DSI Burns shrugged. "Well, it's at least different. An FBI agent rocked up in my office yesterday evening…"

"Yes boss, Special Agent Dove."

Burns glanced at him. "How did you… never mind." She tapped her forehead with a finger. "An FBI agent with a metal arm, I imagine that got the gossip wires buzzing. Rory Trainer still excitedly remembers that time Moira brought her dog in, I'd imagine this blew his tiny mind."

Annoyingly, it was Detective Rory Trainer who had found some excuse to ring Wilson yesterday, basically to tell him this bit of news. DSI Burns had an unnervingly accurate instinct about people.

"Anyway," continued Burns, "one of those two bodies from the Wicklow Mountains is an FBI agent called Daniel Zayas who disappeared eighteen years ago. We have been instructed to cooperate fully with Agent Dove in her investigation."

"But isn't it—"

"Our investigation? Yes," interrupted Burns. "It is supposed to be her helping us. Believe me, I have had this conversation quite a few times. The Americans have brought some heavy pressure to bear and our bosses have heroically folded like a shitty tent in a thunderstorm. So you are my liaison."

"Yes, boss."

"Because, as mentioned, you're a devious little sod and I really think I should start making use of that more. I want to know everything she does, everything she knows and everything she thinks she knows. And I want her to only know what I want her to know."

"Yes, boss."

"The woman is a bit…"

"Odd," finished Dr Devane.

"That's a kind way of putting it. She asked for a moment alone with the body to pay her respects. She has now been standing inside looking at Zayas's remains for…" Burns glanced at Devane.

"Eleven minutes."

"Eleven minutes," repeated Burns. "Just standing there, staring at it. We think she's got a funny look on her face but it's hard to tell as the picture on the monitor isn't great and, to be honest, neither is the face."

Dr Devane made a noise. It could have been a suppressed laugh but it was impossible to tell with any certainty.

Wilson stepped forward to stand beside Burns, peering at the screen. A redheaded woman was leaning against the autopsy table, looking down at the skeletal remains.

"What do you think she's actually doing?" asked Burns.

"I have no idea," replied Devane. "Those remains have been examined for everything I can think of, so it's not like she'll be able to ascertain anything further from this. Do you think she knew the man?"

Burns shrugged. "She said she never met him, but then, she also told me a lot of other lies so I wouldn't take much from that. In the version that the Yanks are pushing, Agent Zayas was here to trace his roots."

"Really?"

"I double-checked with a friend I have at the embassy, and he clearly doesn't have any. Family are all from Cuba or Mexico."

Wilson felt he should say something. "Have we confronted Agent Dove with that?"

Burns shook her head. "No, no – we've been told to play nice. Can't go calling our American friends liars. We have to pretend to go along with that story, while you find out what's really going on here."

"Yes, guv."

Clearly Dr Devane was starting to get a little annoyed. "I mean, does she think she's communing with the spirit of the dead man or something? How much longer is she going to be?"

"You can ask her if you like, Denise, but I've been officially told to let her do as she likes."

"Well, I haven't and I have work to do. She can't stand around in there all day." Devane reached forward to press a button beside the monitor. "Is everything OK, Agent Dove? Can I assist with anything?"

Dove looked up as if she were coming out of a trance. "Sorry, I'll be right out."

They watched her take one last look at the remains, and she appeared to say something before she turned to go. At least, most of her turned to go. Her right arm remained resolutely gripping the edge of the metal examination table.

Burns, Devane and Wilson watched in awkward silence for the next minute as Dove failed to prise the metal fingers off the table. She even swung her leg over the metal arm and attempted to heave it off between her legs.

Devane looked at Burns, who shrugged.

She leaned forward and pressed the intercom again. "I have a screwdriver if that would be of assistance?"

CHAPTER SIXTEEN

Brigit was looking straight into the face of terror. Wide-eyed, sweaty, breathless terror.

"For God's sake, Phil, would you relax."

Phil Nellis swallowed hard, as if trying to summon up words. "You said you needed me here for an important meeting?"

Brigit nodded. "I do. Seeing as you and Paul decided to let Bunny loose on the Harrison job, this company is now getting sued, so I need to talk to Nora to find out quite how much shite we're in."

"Am I being punished?"

"No. I am fully aware who was the brains behind that particular disaster. I know you'd always do what I ask you to do if left to your own devices."

"So why are you making me do this?"

"Jesus, Phil, I'm asking you to keep an eye on a two-year-old boy for an hour. Nora couldn't sort a sitter on such short notice. You'd swear I was ordering you into a cage full of lions."

"Yeah boss, only..."

"I'm not your boss right now, Phil. I'm just a friend asking another friend for a favour."

"Right. In that case, no."

"No?"

"Kids terrify me."

"You're about to become a dad, Phil."

"Yeah, I'm aware of that."

"This'll be good training for you."

"No, thanks."

Brigit sighed. "OK, I am your boss now. Keep an eye on the damn kid. How hard can it be?"

Phil looked up nervously from his desk. "Oh God."

"Now what?"

"Just, in my experience, every time somebody says 'How hard can it be?' the answer always ends up being 'Really, really hard'."

"Has anyone ever told you that you're one of life's great pessimists, Phil?"

"Yeah. Usually right before something really bad happens."

The intercom buzzed and Brigit picked up the phone. "Hiya, c'mon up." She hit the button and turned to look at Phil. How could one man sweat so much, so quickly? He looked like he had just been dragged ashore.

"Will you relax? You'll be absolutely fine. If you're calm, he'll be calm. Kids can smell fear."

Phil looked even more stressed out by this. "Oh Jesus, can they?"

The reception area of MCM Investigations wasn't exactly the biggest. It held a two-person sofa and Phil's desk – not that Phil spent much time at it. They had never got around to hiring a receptionist and Phil had sort of become an unofficial permanent member of staff, even though he wasn't strictly on the books. Brigit shared an office with Paul, and Bunny had his own office, which he'd only been in about half a dozen times, and even then only for a kip. They'd moved the printer in there a couple of months ago.

Nora arrived with Dan in tow, looking like an adorable child straight out of a catalogue advert. Nora had two big bags of supplies with her. Maybe it was just Brigit's nostalgic memory, but she had a sneaking suspicion that when you went somewhere when she was a kid, it hadn't been quite such a logistical feat.

Nora and Brigit exchanged hellos and then Brigit kneeled down so she was eye to eye with Dan. "Hello, Dan, thank you for coming to visit us."

"Hello, Auntie Bridge!" He said it with a heart-melting smile and a flash of those adorable dimples that could send any woman's biological clock into overdrive.

"This is Phil. He's going to take care of you while Mummy and I have a little chat in my office."

Dan smiled up at Phil, who regarded him with the kind of look normally associated with the phrase 'he doesn't bite unless provoked, just don't hold eye-contact for too long'.

Nora took a colouring book and some crayons out of one of her bags and placed them on the coffee table in front of the sofa. "Now, angel, listen to Mummy. Here are some crayons and your book. Remember this book? You like this book."

Dan nodded excitedly.

"Now I want you to sit here and do me a lovely picture, ok?"

Dan nodded again.

"And this is important, sweetie – no drawing on the walls or the table or the sofa, OK? Or else Auntie Brigit will be very cross with you. Alright?"

This time Dan looked up at Brigit directly and beamed the kind of wholesome innocence that an ad agency would spend a fortune to acquire. "I'll be good, Auntie Bridge."

"Ah, I'm sure you will be, sweetheart."

Brigit closed her office door softly behind them as Nora took a seat. "He seems absolutely lovely."

"Yeah. I'm sure the iceberg looked lovely out of the portholes of the *Titanic* too."

Brigit sat down at her side of the desk and then made to get back up again. "Sorry, where are my manners? Tea? Coffee?"

Nora waved her away. "I've had so much coffee, I think it's lost all effect on me. Let's get down to business."

"OK."

Nora pulled a file out of her bag. "Do you want the good news or the bad news? Actually, forget that, I'm afraid it's all bad."

"How bad?"

Nora looked across and met Brigit's eye. "Bad."

Brigit placed her head down onto the desk. "I can't sodding believe this. We get things moving in the right direction and these idiots screw the whole thing up!"

"Yep. Look, this Jacob Harrison guy, he's laying it on thick, but he does have a case here. I mean, your associate did dangle him off a balcony."

Brigit started softly thumping her head against whatever IKEA used instead of wood. It felt unexpectedly satisfying.

"He's claiming that since the incident that he is suffering from vertigo, aquaphobia…"

Brigit looked up and raised an eyebrow at Nora. "Is that…?"

"Fear of water, yes. He's also claiming genophobia."

Brigit sat upright. "Wait a second, I read about that in a magazine I found on the bus a couple of weeks ago. Fear of sex?"

Nora nodded.

"Fuck off!"

"He says the incident, which took place immediately after he got his end away, has led to him being unable to perform sexually."

"This happened eight days ago, at which point his wife announced she was going to divorce him and the woman he was having an affair with literally assaulted him. I'd imagine both those facts put a rather big dent in his love life too."

"And we'll make that case, but he's also lost his job."

"His job? At the company owned by his soon-to-be-ex-wife's daddy? Can he really pin that on us?"

"He said the incident has left him so bereft of confidence that he is unable to contemplate applying for another position."

Brigit started thumping her head slightly harder against the table.

"OK, stop that. We need to plan here. The first thing they'll do is try and prove that Bunny has a history of violence. How can I phrase this...?"

"He does," said Brigit, "I mean, he's not some nutter going around and starting fights in bars but he... well, I suppose you could say he is a tad old-school in his approach to problem-solving."

Nora scribbled something on her foolscap pad. "Yeah, I think dogs in the street may know that."

"To be fair, he only, y'know, does it when it's deserved. He's not a monster."

"That's not how it's going to look. I know the barrister that Harrison has hired. Her name is Siobhan Doherty and believe me when I tell you, he will be when she is done with him. She is going to try and prove a pattern of behaviour, and she'll say that you, i.e. the company, knew about it."

"Oh God."

"Yes. Now, first off, the incident a few years ago when he threw a senior Garda off his balcony."

"Allegedly!"

"Excellent. Did he not do it?"

"Oh. No. He did it alright."

The Garda in question was Assistant Commissioner Fintan O'Rourke. He and Bunny went back a long way, although Brigit, like almost everyone else, was sketchy on the details. To be fair, O'Rourke could and should have gone to jail once evidence of his corrupt partnership with the gangster Gerry Fallon had come to light. He was only saved by the fact that Fallon had been in a coma for two years and counting, meaning the state's case had stalled. Instead, O'Rourke got to retire while pleading his innocence and lawyering up to the hilt. The papers had tried to get into an uproar about it but had been slapped down as, technically, a court case was still pending and they couldn't taint the jury pool on the off-chance Gerry Fallon ever woke up and started talking.

"Well," said Nora, "this O'Rourke guy might be unwilling to testify due to his legal position, so it'll make it tricky to bring it up. I suppose it depends on how much the guy wants to get his revenge on Bunny."

Brigit shrugged. She had never met O'Rourke and could only guess. Being dropped off a three-storey building and then disgraced in the eyes of a nation was probably the kind of thing people didn't get over easily, but that was merely speculation on her part.

"OK, look. I'm not going to lie, this is going to be tricky. What we have in our favour is that Harrison isn't exactly the most likeable guy. With the right judge, who knows? There are a couple of things you need to do for me, though. These Kelleher guys…"

"Arseholes."

"Yeah and, by the way, bit of a side question, but what is happening with you and the hairy hunky one?"

"They're trying to destroy us."

"It would make for some intense, angry sex alright."

"Nora!"

Nora put her hands up. "I'm just saying… OK look, here's what's going to be happening. They're going to be on Bunny, trying to get evidence of his violent nature."

Brigit flashed back to the meeting and Kevin Kelleher's damaged fingers. "I think they might already have some."

Nora threw her hands up in exasperation. "Well, you need to make sure that they don't get any more. You've got to warn Bunny to be on his best behaviour."

"That's easier said than done. He hasn't answered his phone in a few days. I've left about a dozen voicemails."

Nora pointed across the table with her pen. "You need to find him and get him to play nice. I also need to sit down with him ASAP. And finally… you need to suspend him from the company."

Brigit rubbed her temples. She could feel a doozy of a migraine building. "I can't do that."

"You have to."

"Jesus, Nora, the man basically saved my life."

"And now you need to save his arse. This is for his own good. The Kelleher brothers are going to be on him and digging around into his past. It could get nasty. Step one is him being whiter than white, and step two is getting some dirt on Jacob Harrison. You are now your own most important client. You need to follow him and get me some evidence of him being full of shit that I can use in court."

"Won't they expect us to try that?"

"Yep, but you've got no choice. Fingers crossed, this idiot has even less self-control than we think he has."

"OK," said Brigit. "You to me, unofficially, how good are our odds here?"

Nora tossed her pad onto Brigit's desk. "Honestly, hon, not great. I assume the Kellehers will have let the Private Security Authority know about this, so you might be in danger of losing your private investigation licence. Is there anything else you need to tell me on that score? Anything dodgy, now is the time – I can't protect you from things I don't know about."

"Oh crap," said Brigit. "There's Phil."

"As in?" Nora pointed back towards reception.

"Yes, that Phil. He's working for us but it's not official. His criminal record means we can't technically get him licensed for investigation work."

Brigit noticed the alarm on Nora's face. "Oh, no, he's just – he was a petty criminal is all. Nothing bad, honest. He's just..."

"Right," said Nora. "Maybe next time, tell me that before I leave him in charge of my kid."

"Oh relax. He's two weeks off becoming a dad himself."

Nora picked up her pad again. "Can you get rid of him?"

"He's our only decent employee. I need him to get the evidence on Harrison."

"I'm telling you, the PSA are going to come looking."

Brigit looked towards the door. "I can't. I... I'll give him a warning, how's that?"

Nora sighed and shook her head. "You're way too soft for your own good, do you know that?"

Brigit opened the door and she and Nora stepped out. She didn't want to look at Phil, already dreading the chat they were about to have.

"And how did you two..." Nora stopped talking.

Dan was sitting in the exact same position he had been in when they'd left him, smiling up at them with full-on dimpled sweetness. Phil on the other hand, had a rather shell-shocked expression. It was hard to judge it below the pink, purple and red crayon that now covered much of his face, but it was definitely there.

"Oh, sweet Jesus," said Brigit.

"Well," said Nora, "I can see you two hit it off." She gathered up Dan and all his stuff before heading for the stairs. "Bridge, I'll ring you later."

"Right."

"Bye bye, Uncle Phil!" Dan waved enthusiastically as he went out the door. Phil flinched.

When they'd gone, Phil turned to Brigit. "This day cannot get any worse."

Brigit took a deep breath and attempted a reassuring smile. "Can you step inside my office for a sec, please?"

CHAPTER SEVENTEEN

If Paul were being honest, he would have to say that he had always had a bit of a thing for Phil's Auntie Lynn. To be fair, it's not like he was alone in that. Lynn Nellis had always been a highly desirable woman: flaming red hair, green eyes and a figure that in less enlightened times would have been called "bombshell-esque". Out of respect for Phil, who had lived with Lynn and her now departed husband, Paddy, since the age of eleven, Paul had of course never expressed this opinion. He was aware Phil was very sensitive about it, not least because the other boys at school had *not* been very sensitive about it. Lynn Nellis's regular trips into school to discuss Phil had meant that she was a hot topic of conversation. Phil got into fights for a lot of reasons as a kid, but defending Lynn was certainly one of the main ones. That said, calling them fights was a bit of a misnomer. Phil always knew he wasn't going to win, but he would still feel duty bound to put himself in the way of a beating when somebody made what he deemed an inappropriate remark. Paul, for his part, got into a lot of fights while trying to get Phil out of them. It wasn't that Lynn was in any way seeking attention, she was just a damn good-looking woman. She had never shown any interest in another man while her Paddy had still been around. A bloke in their local pub had once decided to show his appreciation for her arse by giving it an appreciative pat. The hand had been in a cast for six weeks after. Lynn was a charming woman, but woe betide the idiot who got on the wrong side of her, or indeed put his hands on any side of her.

Still, as a young boy making the awkward leap into manhood, Paul had been aware of Lynn Nellis. Paul may have, in private moments, been very aware of Lynn Nellis.

Now, as a man knocking on the door of thirty, he had, of course, grown out of any childish infatuation, but that wasn't to say that deep down, in some dusty filing cabinet of memory, there wasn't still an extensive collection of impure thoughts and confused feelings. That may have been a small part of the confusion when Paul had woken up to find Lynn Nellis on top of him in bed. What further added to this confusion was that she was slapping him around the head.

"You. Stupid. Little. Bastard!"

Paul wrapped his arms around his head to fend off the blows that punctuated each word. "What the fuck?"

In the four days since he had been fired from the company he had set up, Paul had spent a lot of time moping in bed. He'd punctuated this with moping on the sofa and moping around the nearby park, because an existential crisis is an existential crisis but dogs still need to take a dump and Maggie had no interest in Paul's resentment of the world.

It wasn't a very big flat but then he didn't have an awful lot to compare it to. For most of his adult life he'd lived alone in the house owned by his not dear but definitely departed Great-Aunt Fidelma. He had then briefly lived in Brigit's flat, with Brigit, which had been great, followed by a period sleeping in the old offices of MCM Investigations, which had not. He now rented a bedsit in Rathmines that gave him an excellent view of a lot of other bedsits in Rathmines. The fact that he shared it with a German Shepherd who had, at best, inconsistent standards of personal hygiene was unfortunate. The one upside of having Maggie there would surely have been security, but Lynn seemed to have broken in without any trouble.

In between fending off blows from Lynn, Paul glanced to the side to see Maggie sitting there, watching proceedings with what appeared to be a keen interest and no intention of intervening. That was it; they were going back to store-brand dog food after this.

"For fuck's sake, Lynn, get off me!"

"Get off me, he says, get off me! I'll get off you alright. Anything you say, Your Highness."

But the fact that she continued to wallop Paul's arms as he shielded his head rather undermined the sentiment. Even so, the little idiot in the back of Paul's mind noted that she had changed her hair. The long red mane was gone, replaced by a short auburn bob. It worked for her.

"Jesus, Lynn, have you lost your mind?"

The blows stopped raining down suddenly.

"Ah crap."

Paul dared to peek out.

"I broke a bastard nail."

"Sorry for your trouble." As soon as he said it, he regretted it. Lynn's fist was cocked back. "Sorry, sorry, sorry. Just... what the hell are you doing here?"

"What the hell am I doing?" Lynn sat back. "That's rich."

Paul tried to sit upright. Conscious that he was sleeping naked, he gathered the duvet to cover himself. "I don't understand why you're angry," he said. It sounded pathetic but it had the advantage of being true.

"Yeah, you wouldn't, you selfish bastard."

She was no longer shouting at him while hitting him, which had the odd effect of making the words hurt more.

"I don't..."

"Thanks to your idiotic behaviour, your company is getting sued and Phil is going to lose his bleedin' job."

"What?"

"Yes, did you not realise your actions might have consequences?"

"But..."

Lynn turned around and sat on the edge of the bed. "He's two weeks away from becoming a dad. He'd got himself a job he was actually good at and now look – look what you did. Jesus, Paul, you were supposed to be his friend."

"I don't understand, we're being sued?"

"Bunny threatened to chuck some bloke out of a window. Phil says you sent him there instead of doing it yourself."

"Oh God."

"Yeah. You've royally messed this up."

"Me? It's those bastard Kellehers!"

Lynn looked at him and shook her head. "Oh, for God's sake, Paul, when are you going to grow up? Brigit, Phil – they were doing fine until you went off to wage your little war."

"But the Kellehers..."

"The Kellehers, the Kellehers. For God's sake. Listen to yourself, would ye? Everything is someone else's fault, isn't it? Phil said he's been trying to ring you, but you've not been answering."

"I was..." Paul stopped talking. What he had been doing was wallowing. He'd not answered the phone to Phil. In his head, it was dramatic. In his head, Phil was reporting it back to Brigit. In his head, she'd realise she was way out of line and come crawling over to apologise.

"Oh Christ, I'm an idiot."

Lynn nodded. "You'll get no disagreement from me."

"I thought you'd gone to Spain?"

"I had. I flew back, didn't I? So much for my plans. Abdul had asked me to move there, for good, with him. There's too much of my Paddy in this town. Too many memories. Over there, fresh start." She glared at Paul. "Can't do that now, can I? I've got to sort Phil out. He loved that job, y'know. First thing he'd been good at."

"Look, I'm going to..."

"Oh shut up." She didn't even sound angry now, just disappointed. Somehow that was much worse. "D'ye know something, you were a good kid, Paul. God knows you had it tough with your ma and everything, but I really thought you'd turn out to be a better man than this. I always felt bad that I didn't help you more

– then and, y'know, with that thing a couple of years ago. Maybe this is on me. Karma's a bitch."

"I'll sort this, Lynn, I promise."

Lynn stood up. "Sure you will." Her voice was edged with bitterness. "Just do me a favour and keep Phil out of any more of your bright ideas. Knowing you, you'll get him sent down. That baby of his needs a da and we both know how important that is."

She looked around. "And for God's sake, clean up your flat. It's a pigsty."

She had a fair point.

"How did you even get in here?"

Lynn glanced back at him. "Do you think you spend twenty years married to the finest burglar in the country without picking up a few things? I got through your locks with a hairpin."

"Oh. Right." Then, for the want of something to say, he added, "I like your new hair, by the way."

"Yeah, it was all part of the new Spanish me." Lynn gave Paul a long look. "Why do you think it is, that when someone else messes up, Phil is the one who always suffers?" She turned towards the door. "And it stinks in here."

"It's the dog."

She walked out of the bedroom. "Sure it is. Sort your life out."

Paul sat there in silence as, a second later, the front door slammed. He looked down at Maggie, who'd sat there calmly watching the whole thing.

"Well, you were a massive help."

She responded by farting loudly.

CHAPTER EIGHTEEN

"Yada, bollocks." Noel took off his glasses, wiped the lenses and then put them back on his face. Sadly, it did nothing to improve the state of the spreadsheet he was looking at. He could see it fine; he just didn't like what he was seeing.

Thankfully, he didn't need Charlie's jazz bar to make a profit due to his savings, but it still couldn't keep losing money quite this fast. The speed it could lose money was entirely dependent on how long Noel was going to live for. He had kept it to himself, but he was turning eighty on Christmas Eve. He was in reasonably good nick, considering. Tourette's was not known to be fatal and his blood pressure was high, but he had a pill for that along with every other damn thing. It seemed he couldn't go to the doctor without coming out with another new prescription. He was surprised he didn't rattle when he walked. The GP seemed determined that Noel was going to live forever, regardless of whether he could afford it or not. The rheumatism now meant that he didn't play piano in front of people anymore, which he missed. He had never liked performing, but he did like sharing. It wasn't like he'd ever been great at it, but sometimes, just sometimes, he'd touched good. That had always been more than enough. His life was the music. For all the regrets he'd stored up, he had never regretted that. He still played in private, and on a good day his fingering was still there. On a bad day, well, he just had to try and remember the good days.

He hated this time of year. The birthday made him feel old and then Christmas made him feel lonely. All those ghosts of Christmas past swirled around him and brushed against his bruised soul.

The office door behind him burst open.

"There is crazy man in bar."

"Remember how we talked about knocking, Svetlana?"

She walloped the open door twice. "Is crazy man in bar."

"When you say 'crazy', it isn't my friend Peter again, is it? As discussed, having Tourette's does not mean you are crazy."

"No, is different kind of crazy. Talking to himself."

Noel sighed. Svetlana was a good barmaid, and in five years she had never missed a day's work. He appreciated her reliability, because he certainly wasn't keeping her around for the sense of joy and frivolity she brought to the place.

"OK, ask Joey to have a quiet word with him then."

"Is no Joey. Is Wednesday night."

Noel looked across at the calendar. Was it really Wednesday already? Where did the time go?

"I said we needed Joey," continued Svetlana, "but you say we no can afford. I suggest we fire Hugo and put on record instead, but you say we cannot do. Now crazy people taking over bar."

Noel pushed his fingers up underneath his glasses and rubbed his eyes. He wasn't going to have this argument again. Hugo might be flaky, and a tad too fond of a vodka martini, but he could play and without someone on the piano they were a jazz bar in name only, in which case he might as well accept one of the offers to sell. Svetlana didn't agree with this, or indeed understand that, as an employee, she didn't actually have a say in it.

"Alright," said Noel. "I'll be right out."

With a wince, he stood and straightened his back out as best he could. Maybe he'd head home early tonight, stick on some Miles

Davis and soak in the bath. If he was going to live forever, he might as well try and enjoy it a little.

He didn't know what he'd been expecting, but it hadn't been this. As the man turned his head slightly, Noel could see that he had a beard now, but even from the back, he was unmistakable.

Noel glanced up at the collage of pictures above the bar and saw her smiling down at him from the past. It was one of only two pictures he had of her. It was what? Good God, eighteen years since Simone had disappeared from his life. Noel still didn't know the how or why of it. He'd only been assured by the Sisters of the Saint that she was fine, that she'd had to go home suddenly, and, while it was never said in so many words, she wouldn't be coming back. He'd always known she was running from something – he just hoped she was alright. Well that, and hoped against hope that someday, maybe, she might come back. On the few occasions Bunny had dropped back in, he'd had no other information. In truth, Noel felt like he was intruding and tended to leave Bunny to himself. He better than anyone knew why Bunny was here. It was a pilgrimage. This was where her memory was strongest. In a quiet moment, Noel could close his eyes and still remember what it had been like to hear that voice swirl around this room. It had been beautiful. So much so, that the memory hurt. They had both loved her, in different ways, of course, but each man with all his heart. Noel didn't like to look into Bunny's eyes, where he only saw his pain reflected back at him.

"See," said Svetlana, slightly too loudly, "crazy man. Sit there, talking to himself."

Noel watched for a few moments. "Leave him be."

"What?"

"And his drinks are on the house."

Svetlana looked appalled. "Crazy men drink for free now?"

"That one does."

Bunny sat on the stool and moved his glass of whiskey around on the pockmarked surface of the table. What was unsettling were the changes – mainly the fact that there weren't any. Charlie's looked exactly the same as it had all those years ago. Like time had stopped on the day she left.

"D'ye remember that first night we came in here?"

From across the table, a dead man, a different dead man, smiled back at him. This one he wasn't trying to avoid; this one he had come here to see.

"I do indeed, amigo. I had to drag you in here kicking and screaming."

Bunny smiled back at Gringo. "I wasn't exactly keen on the jazz at the time."

"Yeah, but by the end of the evening, you were hauled out of here, smacking together the heads of a few boys who wouldn't keep the noise down."

"Talk about an inauspicious start."

"You always had an admirably low tolerance for bad manners."

"I'll drink to that." Bunny raised his glass and took a sip of his whiskey. He placed it down and then ran his hand over the table's surface again, like a blind man reading braille.

"So, are we going to talk about it?" said Gringo.

"What?"

"You know what. You're sitting in the corner of a bar, talking to yourself. Not good, amigo."

Bunny shrugged. "Ah sure, I'm just taking a wander down memory lane."

"This is happening more and more now though, isn't it?" Gringo gave him that look that Bunny remembered all too well and lowered his voice in that way he had. "I'm all for sentimentality, but... after the thing last year, remember how that doctor said you should go talk to somebody?"

"Ah, what good would that do?"

"You could get some more of those tablets."

Bunny blew a raspberry. "They made me feel funny."

"That's an ironic thing to say to an hallucination of your long-dead best friend."

"Sure, if I know it's an hallucination, what's the harm in it? Besides, it's not like I've got the time to be waiting around for doctor's appointments, or that I could even explain the situation to them anyway."

Gringo nodded. "You might have a point there."

Bunny had seen the headline earlier, but this time he'd not bothered to buy the paper. Big splash across the front of the *Herald*: "Dead Body is FBI Agent".

"They know who he is," said Gringo, "and they'll figure out why he was here soon enough, if they don't already know. Sooner or later, it'll lead back to you."

"Ah," said Bunny, "maybe it will and maybe it won't."

"We both know it will, and even if it doesn't, there's the other shoe waiting to drop."

Bunny shrugged and ran his fingers through his hair. By definition, it wasn't as if Gringo was telling him something he didn't already know. Eighteen years it had been, but the memory was still fresh. Gringo, his best friend – and despite everything that had gone on, still his best friend – had helped him rescue Simone. It had been the right thing to do, but it had left two men dead. They'd buried them under the moonlight. It was Bunny who had found the wallet and passed it to Gringo, and they'd realised that the man who had been calling himself Lopez was in fact an FBI agent called Daniel Zayas. The next time Bunny had seen Gringo, he'd been dying in his arms on that beach, having got too deep into a stupid scheme to rob the robbers. He and the other two Gardaí involved had been buried as heroes, the higher-ups not wanting to ask any questions that they might not like the answers to. As they'd waited for the ambulance, Bunny, drenched in his own shame and his best friend's blood, had checked to see if Gringo had Zayas's wallet, but he hadn't. Which led to the question, who did? He'd waited and worried, but it hadn't turned up. Bunny had tried to convince himself that perhaps Gringo really had just got rid of it, but the idea had never really stuck.

"You need to get out ahead of this, amigo."

"How?" said Bunny. "We did bury those bodies."

"For good reasons."

"Sure, but those reasons are long gone. Everyone who knows the why and wherefore is either dead or…"

Simone. Who knew where she was now? Eighteen years and not so much as a postcard.

"You could leave?"

"And go where? Fecking move to the Costa del Sol with all the gone-to-seed gangster gobshites? No, thank you."

"You'll end up going to jail if you're not careful."

"Ah well, I've always fancied having a shot of them weights they seem to spend all their time doing in prison movies, see how buff I could get."

"For Christ's sake, Bunny. You up in Mountjoy? Can you imagine how many nutters with a grudge you'll be surrounded by?"

Bunny picked up his drink and shot the rest of it back in one fluid motion. "That's the problem with living too long. When all your friends are dead, all that's left are the enemies."

"Not all your friends are dead."

"No," said Bunny, loud enough for the man from the couple at the far side of the room to look in his direction. "Whatever happens, I've to keep this away from them. I won't be taking them down with me."

When Bunny raised his head again, Gringo was gone. Replaced with the smiling face of Zayas – his left eye sparkling beside the open wound where the other one should be.

"Don't worry, Detective, I think there will be plenty of pain to go around."

CHAPTER NINETEEN

Detective Donnacha Wilson tried hard to keep his eyes on the road, which was a little tricky as the woman in the passenger seat of his car was currently taking her arm apart.

"Damn thing. The guy from DARPA said I must have a screw loose."

Wilson did not know what the socially optimal response was in this scenario, or indeed, what the hell a DARPA was. He remained silent but, despite himself, glanced downwards. The arm was sitting on her lap as she turned it around, flipping open panels and tightening screws. Unnervingly, the hand occasionally clenched and unclenched as she did so.

"He said it was something to do with the whatchamacallit receiving confused signals down from the, y'know."

"Right, yeah." You couldn't go wrong with agreeing with somebody, could you? Not unless she was being sarcastic. He didn't think she was, but it was hard to tell. From his limited experience with American accents, she spoke in what he guessed was a sort of West Coast whine. Her freakishly smooth and tight skin made her hard to read. It felt rude to look at her face too long, but then every time he averted his eyes, he seemed to end up looking at the arm. At least he knew he could look at the road without getting into trouble. Right now, he was really trying not to think about what remained up Agent Dove's right sleeve. It was nearly rubbing up against him. Could he use the word stump? That definitely sounded rude. Oh God, this whole thing was a bloody nightmare.

They'd spent the morning working through what leads they had, which weren't many. The problem with a body that was eighteen years dead was that there were very limited leads. When the body in question wasn't even supposed to be in the country where it was found, the leads were scarcer still.

In six hours, he had yet to see Dove eat anything. She seemed to live off coffee and an alarming collection of pills, which she stopped to pop about once an hour. He didn't know what they were for, and he wasn't going to ask. The woman was a conversation-killing machine. Oh God, he shouldn't think of her as a machine, that would definitely be offensive, at least to the ninety-three or so per cent of her that was human. God, now he thought of it, were there any other bits of her that were mechanical? How much until you were technically a cyborg? Another for the list of questions he couldn't ask. It wasn't that the woman was unfriendly – if anything, it was the opposite. She smiled a lot, in fact, frankly, far too much. There was a certain level of cheerfulness that was downright creepy, and she had exceeded it. Nobody was that happy, and anyone who pretended otherwise was either secretly miserable, completely unhinged from reality, or both.

He turned onto Promenade Road and looked down again. He just realised what this reminded him of – *Star Wars*! Wasn't there a scene where Luke Skywalker was tinkering with his own hand like that? Wilson looked up and slammed the brakes on – just in time to stop them slamming into the back of a cement truck whose driver had stopped to contemplate a road sign.

"Woah!"

"Oh God, sorry!"

Agent Dove looked around on the floor. "I think I lost a screw there."

"Ehm, I can pull over if you like. See if we can find it?"

"It's a sweet offer but I never pull over for a screw while I'm working."

In a part of Wilson's brain, he was aware that she had probably just made a joke. Unfortunately, she made it as the same time as she did one of those weird slow blinks, which freaked him out. The correct human response required of him in this situation was at least a courtesy laugh. Instead, he just gave her an open-mouthed look. Someone behind them honked their horn and, cheeks burning, Wilson turned his attention back to the road.

A BMW pulled around them, its driver unable to waste another valuable second in his incredibly important day waiting for Wilson to start moving. The red-faced man behind the wheel was so busy that he held the phone he was talking into in one hand while flipping them the bird with the other. Wilson watched him drive off and hit the speed bump slightly too fast, resulting in the satisfying scraping of expensive suspension coming off the worse with karma.

"You want to pull that a-hole over?" asked Dove.

"Nah, we've got somewhere to be."

"Back home, we'd be shooting his tyres out."

Wilson laughed too hard at this. He was only sixty per cent certain it was a joke, but he was overcompensating having let the last one sail by without taking a whack at it.

He pulled out past the cement truck and continued driving.

"So, what are you packing?" she asked.

"Excuse me?"

"Hardware-wise?"

"Oh right," said Wilson. "We don't actually carry weapons most of the time."

"You are kidding me? What do you do when you need to shoot somebody?"

Wilson shifted in his seat. He was aware that he was obliged to defend the honour of the Gardaí, but he wasn't sure from what.

"I mean, we have access to guns. We can carry them if we're

apprehending a suspect, or if we're dealing with gangs, terrorism, that kind of thing."

He could feel Dove shaking her head. Then he heard a clicking noise as she reattached her arm.

"That dude in the Beemer that just went by – what'd you do if he pulled a gun on you?"

"Well, duck, for a start."

"And then?"

That had been Wilson's attempt at a joke. Clearly the humour barrier went both ways.

"I can put in a call, get an armed response."

"So you ring somebody, and they send you a gun?" Her tone was incredulous.

"No. They send out a team of people, all with guns."

"To what? Protect our dead bodies? I mean, no offense, but you guys are insane."

"Well, we feel the same about the American attitude to guns."

"Yeah, I bet. Everybody hates a gun until they need a gun. I'm glad I'm packing."

Wilson glanced over at her. "You don't mean now?"

There was a second of a delay. "No."

Wilson took the third exit on the roundabout and then looked over at her again. "Seriously, I mean, you're in Ireland. You've got no right to carry a firearm here."

"Sure."

"So you aren't?"

"I said no, didn't I?"

Wilson pulled the car into a parking space in front of the offices of Sláinte Ferries. He put on the handbrake and turned to look properly at Dove. "Seriously like, my boss would freak out if she found out you had a gun."

"Are you saying you want to frisk me, Detective?"

As she said it, she gave him the biggest of her smiles and her left eye winked. He wasn't sure it was a movement that had been entirely intentional. The eye may have been going solo. Was it a nervous tic, or was she hitting on him? His brain froze in terror and he gawped at her open-mouthed, unable to think of a single thing to say.

After a moment, she grabbed her handbag from the footwell and exited the car.

This was going really well.

CHAPTER TWENTY

Brigit checked, double-checked and triple-checked the door of the office to make sure it was locked.

She could still remember her excitement when MCM Investigations had first moved here. Their first office, a single room over the Oriental Garden restaurant, had only lasted for four months. They had outgrown it in many ways, not to mention the fact that the torture of smelling Chinese food for twelve hours a day had meant she'd put on half a stone. She'd heard that story about employees in a chocolate factory being allowed to eat as much as they liked in the first month, but it had never made much sense to her. The theory was they would soon get sick of chocolate. That had not been her experience with food. She would have been dead within a fortnight, being rolled out by Oompa Loompas singing a valuable lesson.

This office was decidedly fancier. She'd had to talk Paul into it, back in the days when they were still talking. It was just off Christchurch, which, while not exactly Grafton Street, was a pretty serious real estate neighbourhood all the same. To be fair, it had been a sound business decision at the time. The increase in their workload had more than justified the higher rent. After the Skylark Affair, as the press had dubbed it, the phone at MCM Investigations had been ringing off the hook. They had needed somewhere to meet clients, because they actually had clients – lots of them. In fact, they had the weird problem of having too many. Brigit had perhaps been overly keen to start, accepting anyone who required their services and was willing to pay. She learned her lesson after the infamous "Mrs Geoghan's Cat" incident, which had resulted in Phil being accused of catnapping twice, not to mention having to get rescued from a tree by the fire brigade. It had finally emerged after a chat with a neighbour that the reason the cat was so hard to find was that Mrs Geoghan had reversed over it in her car and nobody had the heart to tell her. After that, MCM had tried to stick to finding humans or, at least, finding out what certain humans were doing, which invariably turned out to be other humans they weren't married to.

Brigit stood back and quickly scanned the windows. They were locked, for all the good that would do in the "war of the eejits", as she had taken to calling the on-going situation with the Kellehers. The meeting with Paul had not gone well. She had hoped that a kick up the arse might have made him cop himself on, but if anything, it had had the opposite effect. The meeting with the Kellehers had gone even worse, and MCM Investigations was now staring down the barrel of oblivion via litigation. Despite it essentially being his fault, she was having a hard time getting angry at Bunny. He hadn't been himself over the last few months, although, to be fair, dangling someone off a balcony – that had been very Bunny.

She turned and walked around to the back, where the only vehicle present was her own car. It looked rather pathetic, battered and scraped as it was, sitting in a puddle that reflected neon flashes from the taxi company and takeaways on Thomas Street. She'd been meaning to get a new one, but she couldn't quite bring herself to do it. This car had great sentimental value, and it was also free of that guilty feeling from picking up the monthly scrapes, scratches and prangs that came from driving in Dublin. She wouldn't be able to relax driving a new car; she had no idea how everyone else kept them looking so neat.

Since the incident last year, one of the few things Brigit had made time for was self-defence classes. Every Monday night without fail she was down at the dojang on Harcourt Street. She had taken to taekwondo like a duck to water. They'd had to move her up two ranks. Most women were nervous of hurting someone, but not Brigit. As a nurse, she'd seen plenty of pain and, thanks to her less than stellar career in romance, there were more than a few people she didn't mind the idea of inflicting it on.

As she neared her car, she heard sudden footsteps behind her and an unexpected voice.

"Brigit?"

Her instructor, Sharon, would have been proud. She reacted fast. The leg sweep took her assailant clean off his feet before he knew what hit him. It felt different when it wasn't somebody slapping down onto a crash mat. A satisfying woof of wind came out of him as he hit the tarmac.

She stood over him, gripping her keys between her knuckles, ready to permanently ruin his enjoyment of 3D movies.

Anto Kelleher lay there with his hands out. "I surrender! I surrender!"

Brigit let out the breath she realised she had been holding in. "Jesus, Anto. What the hell are you doing sneaking up behind a woman in a car park?"

"I wasn't sneaking. I saw you coming out and I ran up to try and catch you. You're not answering my calls."

"Yeah, because you tricked me into coming to a meeting where I got served with a summons."

"I swear I didn't know about that. I know how it looks, but honestly, I didn't."

"Yeah, well, I'm pretty sure my lawyer would suggest not talking to someone who is currently suing me."

"Good news on that front, I'm not suing you. I have left the employ of Kelleher Brothers Investigations. Permanently."

Now that her heart rate was slowing from the high-speed techno beat it had been keeping, she was able to take a better look at him. He had a split on the left side of his bottom lip and bruising around his right eye. "What the hell happened to you?"

"I've just come from a family meeting. Put it this way: my brothers weren't wild about my decision to leave the company. The family Christmas is going to be fun this year. If I promise not to do anything as aggressive as saying your name again, can I get up?"

Brigit nodded and Anto pulled himself to his feet.

"Let me have a look at you." She put her hands gently on the side of his face and then turned it so it could catch the light. "Jesus, they did a bit of a number on you."

"Ah, you should see the other guy."

"Got a few good shots in yourself, did you?"

"Actually, no. And the one I did get in might have actually improved Vinny's ugly mug. It'd be hard not to."

Brigit had never been a fan of beards, but his did feel very nice in her hands. It was very soft. She wondered if he used some kind of conditioner on it.

She quickly pulled her hands away. "You need to put something on that lip."

"What did you have in mind?" He said it with a twinkle in his eye.

"Behave yourself. I know three other moves I've not used yet."

"I'm sure all your moves are impressive."

"Shut up and come inside."

She started to walk back towards the office with Anto following behind her.

CHAPTER TWENTY-ONE

Brigit cradled the phone against her shoulder as she rummaged through her bag. She had definitely had tissues earlier. She was pretty sure she was coming down with the cold she seemed to get every Christmas.

"So," continued Nora Stokes, "I had a chat with Siobhan Doherty, Harrison's barrister."

"Right," said Brigit, "and how was that?"

"As expected, is probably the best way of putting it."

"What's the second-best way of putting it?"

"She wants everything. She reckons they've got a bulletproof case and that if this goes to court, they'll win."

Brigit didn't find tissues but she did find the two Christmas cards she'd been carrying around for a week that she still hadn't managed to put a stamp on and send. "Is she right about that?"

"This thing is a process and we need to see things through. It's important that we stay calm."

"Oh fuck."

"What?"

Brigit dumped her bag on the floor. "You don't sugarcoat

anything, Nora, and you're sugarcoating this. That's a really bad sign. How screwed are we?"

"As things stand? Totally. Look – they've made a proposal. It's a terrible proposal. I don't want you to take this deal but I'm legally obliged to at least explain it to you."

"OK."

"They've said that they'll take the whole company – lock, stock and barrel. Name. Client list. Everything."

"Harrison wants to own the company? Why the hell would he want to own the company?"

"I don't know, but he seems serious about it. Maybe he figures that he's already a dick, so he might as well be a private one. You would also not be allowed to set up in business against it for ten years. All that, plus eighty grand."

"Christ."

"I told you, they're just trying to scare you."

"It's working."

"How are things going with trying to get evidence on this creep?"

Brigit pushed a few strands of her hair back out of her eyes. She was going to need a haircut soon, if she could ever find the time. "I've got Phil exclusively doing surveillance on Harrison, while I'm trying to cover the rest of the cases we have single-handed."

"Any luck?"

"Nah. Last I heard from Phil, there was nothing new to report."

"I see."

"Ehm..." Brigit hesitated. She knew she was going to have to give this update, but she had been kind of dreading it. "Now, I don't want you to overreact, but Anto Kelleher came to see me last night."

"The big hairy bastard. How did that go?"

"Well, I sort of leg-swept him."

"Oh my God, you mad bitch. I think I might be in love with you."

"Stop it. He surprised me and I..."

"Kicked his arse!"

"It wasn't like that. He'd come to apologise. He said he'd had no idea his brother was going to pull that stunt at the meeting. He has left the company – in fact, they literally came to blows. He had a black eye and stuff."

"Ohhhhhh, interesting."

"I'm only telling you this because he doesn't agree with all that's going on. He wants to help us."

"He wants to help *you*."

"Would you stop. I'm telling you this as my lawyer."

"And as your lawyer, I am telling you to slap a saddle on that bronco and ride him off into the sunset."

"Seriously, Nora, stop it! You're being unprofessional."

"Says you. Your detective agency throws people off balconies. I wouldn't go casting stones. So where did all this happen?"

"In the car park out back." Nora gave a dirty laugh so loud, Brigit had to pull the phone away from her ear for a second. "It wasn't like that. We went back into the office."

"Oh, did you?"

"Just so I could put some ice on his swelling." Brigit instantly regretted her choice of words. She had to shout over the "awooga" siren noise Nora was making down the line. "On his eye. On. His. Eye!"

"Sure," said Nora. "You swept him off his feet and then you did a bit of Florence Nightingale while you tended to his wounds."

"I *was* a nurse, you know."

"I do. Did you keep the uniform? Some men go mad for that."

"You've got a one-track mind, d'ye know that?"

"I don't, actually. I am just tragically fascinated by your love life because, anaemic though it is, it is still infinitely more interesting than my own – which currently consists of the thirty-four minutes I get on the bus into the office every morning with whatever steamy e-book I have on the go. By the way, side note – have your bosoms ever heaved?"

"What?"

"In all these books, there's a crap-ton of heaving bosoms. Do they just mean breathing, d'ye think? I mean, I've occasionally had to heave one of them out of the way while I'm sorting the washing, but

I'm pretty sure that's not what they've meant. Anyway, sorry, back to you."

"It's alright, I am finished."

"Oh no you're not."

"What's that supposed to mean?"

"Tell your extremely young and attractive Auntie Nora the other bit."

"What other bit?"

"You are a dreadful liar, Conroy. You know what other bit."

Brigit went silent for a minute. "Alright, well, just so we can, y'know, work out our next move and all that, I am meeting him for lunch on Thursday."

After about thirty seconds of sound effects intermixed with frankly shocking language from the very best legal representation she could afford, Brigit hung up the phone. She guessed it might well be several minutes before Nora noticed.

CHAPTER TWENTY-TWO

Bunny opened the door and stepped inside, kicking a couple of pieces of post on the carpet to the side as he did so. He threw his keys down on the side table, on top of a neat pile of unopened correspondence. He didn't remember doing that. It wasn't the fact the letters were unopened that was strange – he generally only opened the post when someone banged on the door or the lights went out – but since when had he started to pile anything up neatly?

He moved down the hall into the front room, the plastic bag containing milk, a Pot Noodle and a packet of chocolate Hobnobs bouncing against his thigh as he did so. Everything looked much the same as it always did. Not for the first time, he thought about getting himself another cleaner. Ever since Mrs Byrne's back had started to act up, he'd been without one. Initially, it'd felt rude to go looking for somebody else. She had assured him she'd be right as rain in a week. Always in a week. That was a good six months ago now, and the place could do with a serious dusting. He could do that himself, of course. But he wouldn't.

He stopped in the middle of the room and looked around. Something was off. Nothing was missing or anything, but still... The place felt strange, like everything had been shifted a millimetre. He wasn't one for any of that feng shui bollocks, but the air felt different.

He had only been gone a few hours. He'd gone up to the Liberties to deal with that thing, then he'd dropped into O'Hagan's for a couple, then he'd walked back out to Cabra. It was a fairly long walk – a couple of hours with his gammy foot – but he still liked to do it. He liked to feel the city around him. After all these years, there was a comfort in that. Plus, he needed the exercise. Those were the two reasons he'd give if anyone asked, but there was another one too. He had nowhere else to be, nothing else to do. That was the truth of it. Private detective work didn't interest him; he'd no stomach for following randy little shites about while they were trying to get their holes, or proving somebody was actually able to walk fine since falling off a ladder. He was a copper, same as he'd always been. When they'd taken the badge away from him, they'd taken his purpose too. He still handled things that needed to be handled, like the thing with Horse, but it wasn't the same.

All the way home, the feeling had been there, gnawing at him. The feeling that eyes were on him. He kept noticing people noticing him. And he was sure he was seeing motorbikes more often than usual. It didn't help that Zayas kept trying to engage him in conversation. He tried to ignore him, push it away. It was all in his head. He just needed to calm himself down and everything would be fine.

He walked a couple more steps towards the kitchen and stopped again. He looked at the shelves containing his videotape library. Every All-Ireland since 1982 and every Cork match from the Munster final onwards. He'd been at most of those games in person, but he'd always paid one of the lads from the team to come in and record it for him. He'd never trusted the timer on the video. Of course, these days, they didn't want you to have a video any more. It was an outdated technology, a bit like himself. He'd had to haul it to three different places to get it fixed the last time it had died on him. He didn't trust some digital box to store his matches. One day the thing could just forget everything on ye; he'd seen something in the paper.

He looked at the tapes again. They were out of order. They were never out of order. The football and the hurling were mixed together – he never did that.

He dropped the shopping bag and started pulling out tapes at random. They were all still there, but where was all the dust? Someone had touched his stuff.

He turned and ran out into the hall and up the stairs, grabbing the hurley that'd been sitting beside the door. His heart was pounding. He looked at the clock on the wall as he climbed the stairs: 9:22. His watch said the same. The clock was always slow. He hadn't fixed it, had he? It didn't seem like... He wasn't sure.

Zayas sat at the stop of the stairs, smiling down at him. "Are you OK, Detective? You look a little pale."

"Shut the feck up, you!"

He swung his hurley at the space where nobody was, walloping the side of the bannister and knocking a chunk off of it for his troubles. He slowed his breathing and walked into the bedroom. Everything looked as he had left it. A pair of his Y-fronts lay in the middle of the floor, looking in need of a wash – or better yet, burning. They'd seen better decades. The bed was unmade, as it should be. One of the wardrobe doors was open. Had he left it like that? He probably had. C'mon now, he told himself. Get it together.

He looked over at the far side of the bed. That's where she had slept.

His heart caught in his throat.

The picture was gone. It had been on the bedside cabinet.

He moved around the bed, his grip tightening on the hurley.

As he passed the corner of the bed, he saw it, lying face down on the floor. It could have just fallen over, he supposed. He leaned down and picked it up. A crack now ran down the front of the glass – snaking between himself and Simone. He sat down heavily on the bed and ran his finger up and down the broken glass. Then he looked at her, smiling back at him from the past.

Bunny drew in a deep breath and let it out again, a hitch catching in his throat. "I think I'm fucking losing it, love."

In the background, he heard a dead man laugh.

CHAPTER TWENTY-THREE

Paul opened the passenger door of the Ford Fiesta and got in.

"I got you a tea."

Phil Nellis looked confused. "What are you doing here?"

"Maggie was missing you."

"What do you mean, Maggie was— Agh!"

Phil jumped in shock as he glanced in the rear-view mirror and noticed a German Shepherd smiling back at him from the back seat.

"How did she get there?"

Paul gave him a confused look. "What do you mean? I opened the back door like three seconds ago and she hopped in."

"Right. Yeah. Sorry. I was focused on my surveillance." That was the freakish thing about Phil's unnerving ability to focus – you could ask him to watch a door and that's exactly what he would do, even if the building fell down around it.

"Seriously though, you can't be here. Brigit said you can't be here. Why are you here?"

"I told you. The dog missed you and I brought you a tea." Paul held out a cardboard tray containing two takeaway cups of tea. "It's still relatively hot. The bloke in front of me was having an argument about the correct temperature for coffee. The fella behind the counter said that it couldn't be actually boiling for health and safety reasons and the dude said it was 'political correctness gone mad'. Said it was the logical conclusion of the country having a gay Taoiseach. Then a woman threw a cup of tea over him. Lucky for him it wasn't boiling. People get very angry in queues, don't they?"

"Yeah, well..." Phil stopped himself. "Ah no, you're doing that thing where if you talk about something long enough, I forget the thing I was going to talk about. What are you doing here? And don't go into another long story about tea."

Paul took his disposable cup out of the cardboard carrying tray and placed it carefully on the dashboard. Phil was very particular about his Auntie Lynn's car remaining clean. "Alright, look – I came here to apologise."

"I knew it," said Phil. "Cats and dogs *can* have babies."

"What? No. We had that discussion months ago. How are you still on about that?"

Phil Nellis, as well as being possessed of his own Nellisian brand of logic, had a freakish memory. He seemed to remember everything, just not in a useful way.

"I'm telling you, I saw a thing on the Internet."

Paul removed the lid to blow on his tea, effectively having an exasperated sigh without being rude. "No, it's not about the cat and dog thing. Remember we googled that?"

"Pah. Ye can't go trusting the Internet."

"But that's where you said you saw this thing about—"

"A kippy. Cross between a kitten and a puppy. I came up with the name myself."

"You've not figured out a name for your own baby yet, but you've come up with a name for a non-existent animal?"

"Says you."

"Says Google."

"Ye can't trust them. It's all run by the Russian mafia now."

Paul was getting that feeling he knew all too well, like he was falling down a bottomless pit of sheer Philness. Time to redirect.

"No, I'm not here to apologise about the cat and dog thing. You're still wrong about that."

"Panda on the moon?"

"Again, there's no evidence."

"I've seen a picture."

Paul took a long drink of reasonably warm tea. Phil looked suspiciously at his and did the same.

"Right, let's try this again. I'm here to apologise about getting you involved in the thing with the Kelleher brothers, and also for shirking my responsibilities, and sending Bunny to take care of the Harrison job as well…"

"Yeah, that screw-up looks like it's going to destroy the company and put me out of a job, right before I'm about to become father to a baby that I'm pretty sure hates me."

"Right," said Paul. "Although not the last bit. The baby doesn't hate you. Babies don't hate people, they're babies."

"Every time she hears my voice, she kicks. I'm going to have to buy a helmet if she keeps doing that when she's out of there."

"Phil, I'm telling ye, your baby does not hate you. You're just nervous is all, because it's your first one."

"Christ," said Phil, looking up at the roof.

"What?"

"D'ye think she'll want to have another one? Will we have to keep going until we get a good one?"

"Phil, have you been sleeping much?"

"Not really. I mean, the last three days, I've been following this Harrison fella eighteen hours a day, and then when we're in bed, I spend a lot of time looking at Da Xin's belly, trying to think of nice things to say to it so it won't hate me."

Now that Paul took a good look at him, Phil did look more than a little wired.

"How are you staying awake?"

Phil picked up a can from the compartment in the door. It was yellow and green. "I got a load of this East German energy drink from One-Eyed Barry. Very good for focus."

Paul looked at the can. The product appeared to be called Yackbac and all the other writing was in foreign. Paul hadn't done much languages in school. "Ehm, Phil... East Germany isn't a country any more."

"Ah yeah, where'd you find that out? Google?"

"How many of these have you had?"

"About a dozen."

"Right."

"Today."

"Today?! Holy shit, Phil."

"They're fine. I mean, they make your wizz smell like petrol, but apart from that. You soon get used to the taste."

"What does it taste like?"

Phil gave Paul a confused look. "Well, petrol, obviously."

"Right," said Paul, "I'm going to split duty of following Harrison with you."

"Oh no, Brigit said you were under no circumstances to be involved in this."

"Look, I already apologised, didn't I? And you do need the help."

Phil seemed to consider this. "Well, Da Xin does have a doctor's appointment this afternoon. Auntie Lynn said she'd take her, but—"

"Go," said Paul. "I've got this. Now, what's Harrison been up to?"

"Nothing much, to be honest. He's been staying in those apartments over there since the wife kicked him out."

"How did you find him?"

"I watched his old house. I figured he'd turn up and beg the wife to take him back. Sure enough, he did."

Paul nodded. "That was pretty clever."

"Not on his part. She turned the hose on him. Then I followed him back here. He's also been sacked of course; her da owns the company he worked for."

"What an idiot."

"Hang on a sec," said Phil. "Come to think of it, how did you find me?"

Paul pointed into the back seat. "Maggie."

"Really?! Wow!"

Paul sighed. "No, Phil, not really. We set up that Find My Friends app on our phones, remember?"

"Oh yeah. Anyway, I'm not sure how much good it's going to do us, following Harrison. I think he expects it. I've hung back but he's looking around a lot."

Paul nodded. "Yeah. I'd imagine his lawyers and those Kelleher pricks have told him to be squeaky clean."

"Yep. Pretty hard to catch somebody being a dick if they know you're trying to. Thing is, though, if we don't get proof that this fella isn't really afraid of water and heights and shagging and all of that, then it'll be us who are totally screwed."

Paul looked out the window towards the apartment again. "Yeah. How the hell are we going to do that?"

"I dunno," said Phil, "but we'd better think of something pretty damn fast."

CHAPTER TWENTY-FOUR

Donal Martyn threw back a couple of tablets, chased them with a gulp of water, then slammed his palm into his chest and belched loudly.

"Forgive me. We had the work Christmas do last night, feeling a bit worse for wear. There were a lot of drinks. Some of them were on fire."

Detective Wilson nodded. Sitting beside him, Agent Dove just smiled and blinked slowly. Wilson didn't see her do it, but he saw the slightly disconcerted look on Martyn's face. He was fast realising that everyone found her alarming.

They had spent most of the morning in the offices of Sláinte Ferries, chasing down the one lead they had. Wilson didn't need Martyn to tell him it had been their office Christmas party the night before; the evidence was ample. The staff that had made it in had spent the morning moving around Wilson and Dove like zombies – albeit zombies who smelled like a wino's arse and looked like they might break into tears at any point. Wilson couldn't help but feel that it unfortunately confirmed every stereotype of the Irish that Agent Dove probably had. At one point, a woman called Sophie who had been helping them check back through records, had picked up a bin and thrown up into it, before finishing the sentence she had been in the middle of. The conversational vomit was a new one on Wilson, although he had to admit it certainly served to accentuate whatever point you were making.

"So," said Martyn, as he wiped a hanky around his rather large, sweaty face, "how can I help you?"

Normally, the interviewee sweating was a sure sign of heightened nerves. In Martyn's case, however, Wilson felt pretty sure he would be sweating regardless of them being here or not. He was a touch on the morbidly obese side; his massive gut strained against his shirt and the arms of his office chair. It also appeared now, as Wilson looked more closely at him, that he'd only shaved the left side of his face. Like he'd started and then forgotten to finish, or just couldn't be arsed.

"We're looking into a case from 1999," said Wilson. "We were told that you might be the one to talk to."

"Right, how so?"

Wilson took out the photocopy of the sailing manifest that they'd found. "This is from the 1am boat on the tenth of December 1999 from Dublin to Liverpool. It lists a Daniel Zayas." Wilson pointed at the line that had been highlighted. Martyn leaned forward to look at it, his office chair groaning in agony as he did so.

"Right, yeah."

"The problem we have is, Mr Zayas was found buried in the Wicklow Mountains last week, so we're rather confused as to how he ended up on that ferry?"

Martyn leaned back. "I've no clue. It's a long time ago now. To be honest, I'm having a hard time remembering me own name after last night." He gave a half-hearted laugh that quickly died when he realised nobody was joining in.

"At the time, you were working as the head bursar on the Saint Joseph ferry," continued Wilson, "before you moved into your current role in the office."

"Yeah, I mean, I swapped about. I couldn't tell you exactly when."

Wilson gave him a thin smile. "If you look, you signed off on the manifest at the bottom there."

Martyn leaned forward again and the office chair once again groaned in protest. "Right, yeah. That's me." A drop of sweat from his brow plopped onto the paper.

"We were just wondering, how do you think a dead man could end up on a manifest like that?"

Martyn looked up and licked his lips. "I dunno. I mean, let's be honest, the ferries aren't exactly the most secure mode of transport in the world. With the free travel between here and Britain, it's not like we have big passport checks and all, like at the airport. Although with the Brexit, who knows? That's going to cause all kinds of hassle, let me tell ye. It's going to be an absolute nightmare, the Brexit."

"It's just Brexit."

"What?"

Wilson shifted in his seat, aware he was doing it again. "It's just 'Brexit', not 'the Brexit'. Not that it matters."

"It does matter. It's going to cause no end of hassle. Nightmare."

"Anyway," said Wilson, trying to pull them out of this diversion of his own creation. "What worries us is that adding somebody onto a ferry's manifest would be an excellent way of pretending that they had left the country when they hadn't."

Martyn sat back. "I'm not sure I like what you're implying, Detective."

"I'm not implying anything, Mr Martyn, I'm just asking. With your experience, help us understand how this could happen."

"Well, there's lots of ways. Maybe somebody else travelled on this fella's passport. Or maybe it was him, and then he came back? I mean, maybe the paperwork is missing on him coming back over on another ferry. Or he could've come into Belfast and come down. We're not responsible for border security, y'know, although Lord knows, after the Brexit..."

"Yes," said Wilson, "but could it be possible, theoretically, for a member of staff to add someone to a manifest?"

Martyn's collection of chins wobbled as he emphatically shook his head. "Absolutely not, that'd be a firing offence."

"Actually, it would be fraud. But if somebody wanted people to think that Mr Zayas had left the country, that's the kind of thing they might do, isn't it?"

"I suppose, but... if that man is listed on the manifest, then he was on the ferry, or at least someone with his ID was."

Wilson lowered his voice. "Look, Donal – sorry, can I call you Donal?"

He nodded.

"Donal. We're not bothered about who might or might not have added a name, OK? What we want to know is who asked them to do it. That is the person we'd really like to talk to. Do you see what I'm saying here?"

"I'm telling you, I've no idea how that name got there."

He leaned forward and pounded his chubby finger on the sheet of paper for emphasis. Wilson could have sworn that there was a cracking noise in the chair's groan this time, like it couldn't take it anymore.

"OK," said Wilson, "fair enough. I just want you to do me a favour, Donal, and take a long, hard think about this. You" – Wilson stopped himself and rephrased – "a person, at the time, wouldn't have known what they were doing, or why, when they added that name to the manifest. We can look past that. But now it's a murder investigation and this is serious stuff. The penalties for holding stuff back from a murder investigation..." Wilson sucked air in through his teeth and shook his head, in the 'well, it's the parts' way that mechanics have before dropping a massive bill in someone's lap.

"Look," said Martyn, "I can't help you here. It was eighteen years ago. If that piece of paper says he was on the ship, he was on the ship. If you need anything else, you're going to have to take it up with the company's lawyers."

Wilson put his hand into his inside pocket and pulled out one of his business cards. "OK, well, if you think of anything, anything at all—"

"You have a lovely family, Mr Martyn."

Wilson and Martyn both turned to look at Agent Dove. It was an odd non-sequitur. The small-talk section of the interview had been about five minutes ago; Wilson had been all set to leave. Agent Dove had a broad smile on her face again. She pointed at the picture sitting on the shelf behind Martyn's desk. In it, Martyn stood with his tiny wife and three obese children. They collectively looked like they could make an all-you-can-eat buffet's owner break into tears just by walking in.

Martyn turned to look at it, as if his family being considered lovely was news to him. The chair made a different, if equally pained squeal as he did so. "Well, yes, of course. I mean, thanks. That's a couple of years old now. John is off to university this year and Sharon is doing the Leaving Cert."

"Really? Wow."

Wilson was fairly certain Dove didn't even know what the Leaving Cert was, but she still acted massively impressed. "You have a sister too, don't you?"

Martyn turned to look at Dove again, suspicion now writ large across his face. "I... yes, I... how do you know that?"

Dove blew right by the question. "She lives in Sunriver, Oregon, doesn't she? An absolutely beautiful part of the world. Have you visited? I hear the fishing is to die for."

Martyn held his mouth open for a second, his large tongue washing around his teeth. "No," he said. "Kathy comes home every few years but we've not been over yet."

"Right. Well, I guess her and Pete are kept pretty busy with the landscaping business and all. She does the books for him, I saw on their website. Their son Fiachra helps out at the weekends too – a real family business."

Martyn looked at Wilson, who shrugged. He was none the wiser on where this was heading.

The smile remained fixed on Dove's face as she reached down and pulled a can of Diet Coke from her bag with her prosthetic arm. "Do you mind if I have a drink before we go? I'm parched."

"Sure." Martyn sounded like he hadn't been less sure of anything in his life. He was looking at the metallic hand now; you couldn't not. It just drew your basic human curiosity. Agent Dove cracked the can open, produced a straw from inside her jacket and placed it in.

"I knew a guy once. He had a landscaping business, a lot like the one Kathy and Paul have. It was going great until one day – BAM – the IRS took an interest." Dove carefully took a sip of her drink. "Full audit. Sorry, do you know who the IRS are? They're our tax people in the States – mean SOBs." She said it with a smile and then took another sip and blinked one of those slow blinks. "Caught him doing a couple of jobs cash in hand, fucked him royally in the ass. I mean hard. He ended up going to prison."

Martyn looked at Wilson again, his eyes wide. "Is she trying to intimidate me?"

"Oh heavens, no," said Dove, the smile still unmoving on her face. "Just a little chit chat. His wife got deported – back to, y'know, wherever. Daughter ended up turning tricks on street corners, last I heard. Real shame, she was a sweet kid."

Martyn stood up. "I'd like you to leave."

"And I'd like you to sit down and tell us the truth right fucking now." Dove's tone didn't change; it was the same as when she had asked about his family.

Marty rubbed his hand across his chest again. "I can't be dealing with this. You can call our lawyers if you want to—"

"Oh, I won't call anyone's lawyers. But I will walk out that door and make a phone call. One phone call. That's all it'll take. Hey, don't worry about it. Maybe your brother-in-law is the only landscape gardener on the planet to put everything through the books. He probably doesn't have a team of dirt-cheap Mexicans working for him illegally. Maybe it is just him, with little Fiachra at the weekends. ICE will find out. You know the ICE, right? Immigration and Customs Enforcement. They make the IRS look like the fucking Smurfs. They skull-fuck people just for fun."

Dove was the most unnerving swearer Wilson had ever seen. It was like hearing Mary Poppins threatening to stab some toerag.

Martyn leaned heavily against the desk, rubbing his hand up and down his sweaty face. He looked like he was about to be sick.

"Your sister, her husband, little Fiachra, they could all go to prison. Fiachra probably wouldn't get much time, but it depends where they put him. One call and he's in with some of the worst scum on earth. I mean real trash. Imagine how sweet little Fiachra will be when he comes out of there? Assuming he does."

Dove turned to Wilson. "Am I saying that right? Fee-ca-ra?"

Wilson nodded.

"Such a beautiful language you have. It has a wonderful lilting quality, doesn't it?" She looked back to Martyn. "I want to know who asked you to put a dead man on your manifest. I also want to know if they asked you to help sneak a woman out of the country. She'd have been thirty-one at the time, African American, about five-foot-three. Her name was Simone Delamere but I'm sure she would have been travelling under something else. I want to know all of this, and I want to know it now – or else I go out that door and make the one and only phone call it'll take. So, Mr Martyn, I want you to think long and hard about the next words that come out of your mouth, as they will have a significant effect on lots of people's lives."

Martyn said nothing. His face appeared to have gone even redder and his lips were clenched together so tightly that the skin around his mouth was turning white. He leaned on the desk and looked across at Dove like he was building up to saying something momentous.

As it turned out, the momentous thing could best be described as "Annnggghhh".

He clutched at his chest and fell backwards, causing his long-suffering office chair to collapse under him, sending him sprawling onto the floor.

CHAPTER TWENTY-FIVE

"Here, mister. Excuse me, mister."

"Phil, don't!"

Paul and Phil had been watching Jacob Harrison for four days. Four uneventful, extremely dull days. They had split shifts to keep an eye on him pretty much around the clock, Paul taking 6pm to 6am and Phil the early shift. That afternoon, Paul had shown up a few hours early, mainly because all he had in the flat for company was the dog, and Maggie wasn't much of a talker. The heating was also rubbish and, combined with the need to keep windows open due to Maggie's vicious canine farts, it meant it was permanently freezing. To be fair, her presence meant that the MCM Investigations surveillance truck was now also freezing, but on the upside, the smell wafting out of the back window did put people off trying to buy an ice cream. It turns out a big sign saying "Go away, we do not sell ice cream" was utterly ineffectual, if not actually counterproductive in stopping people asking, but nobody wanted to buy an ice cream off a truck that smelled like a bad case of the trots.

"Here, mister," repeated Phil.

"Oh, for God's sake."

Phil, between his permanent state of pre-fatherhood stress and his comedown from going cold turkey from energy drinks from a country that hadn't existed for thirty years, wasn't sleeping much. Instead, he was watching an awful lot of late-night TV. He'd seen one programme where a supposedly smart professor fella from Oxford or some such had talked about how we might all see colours entirely differently. It was called *Is My Blue Your Blue?* Phil had been outraged – blue was blue. Paul had made the mistake of trying to explain what the professor had presumably meant, namely that each individual's perception of the colour spectrum could be entirely different.

The man walking by the van pulled out his earphones. "What?"

"What colour is that postbox?"

"What?"

"What colour is that postbox?"

"What does it look like? It's green, ye dozy prick!"

Phil turned triumphantly to Paul. "See, it's green. You and your 'It might look blue to that fella.'"

"I was speaking hypothetically."

"Well, I was just speaking to the actual bloke, and he said it was green. That's because it is green. Green is green. My great-grandad didn't fight in the War of Independence so that a hundred years later, some Open University spanner from Oxford could start telling us that green isn't green."

Luckily for the state of Paul's mental health, Jacob Harrison chose this moment to emerge from the doors of his apartment building.

"Hello," said Paul. "Old 'Shagger' Harrison is on the move!"

"Yeah. That's a nice, definitely green blazer he's got on there too."

It was. For the past few days, on those rare occasions when Harrison had put in an appearance at all, he'd been wearing sweatpants and a hoodie. They'd observed him answering the door to a pizza delivery, two Chinese deliveries and an Indian. He had disappointingly failed to even attempt to have sex with any of those people. He'd been unshaven and, on at least one occasion, his clothing had shown evidence of the last takeaway while he had been paying for the next one. So it was with some excitement that Paul noted that he was now freshly shaved, smartly dressed and walking with a sense of purpose. In other words...

"He's looking like a man looking to get laid!"

Normally, following a suspect who was on foot while you were in a vehicle would be a problem, but luckily the traffic was just warming up for rush hour so it rarely moved much faster than walking pace. They followed him down the Adelaide Road until he eventually took a right into a pedestrianised shopping area. Wordlessly, Phil hopped out of the van and continued the follow on foot, while Paul turned the corner and, after a frustrating ten minutes of circling, managed to nab a space just as a Tesco delivery van was pulling out.

He was about to text Phil his location when the passenger door opened and Phil got back in.

"Well?"

Phil shook his head. "Nah, he's not up to anything."

"Shit."

"He's just gone for a massage."

Paul's head snapped around. "Really?"

"Yeah."

"Grab the camera bag. Which building is it? If we're lucky there might be a window we can get an angle on."

"What are ye talking about?"

"Phil, it might be a 'massage' massage."

Phil gave Paul a blank expression, a look he had entirely mastered.

"Y'know, it might have 'a happy ending'."

"What? Like when the boy gets the girl?"

"Yeah, something like that. Let's go."

"What about Maggie?"

Paul looked into the back of the van. Maggie was fast asleep, doing that weird twitching thing she did. In normal circumstances, people say it looks like a dog is chasing cars in their sleep. In Maggie's case, it could be anything. From what little Paul knew of her past, Maggie had been a police drugs dog until she had somehow consumed some LSD. Her behaviour since, if one was being really diplomatic, could be described as 'erratic'. Paul had made the mistake of buying a lava lamp for his new apartment; she had stared at it for three days solid and growled every time he tried to turn it off. Then she'd smashed it and drank the contents.

"Probably best to leave her," Paul said. "She doesn't like being woken up." This was true, it being one of the many things that could put Maggie in one of her moods. One of these moods could often result in nightmares, mostly for whoever was unlucky enough to have put her in the mood in the first place.

Paul and Phil weaved through cars to get to the far side of the street. Paul could feel the adrenaline surging through him. "This could be it, Phil, we might finally have the bastard. We catch him at it, the case collapses, the Kelleher brothers are vanquished and Brigit will see that I was right."

"Don't get excited, Paulie."

"Why not?"

"Well, things just never work out that well for us."

"You're such a pessimist. I'm telling you, after wading through all this shit, I think we've finally got to the gold!"

"Ah, but what if what you think is gold is actually only your perception of the colour gold and it's actually an entirely different colour?"

"Shut up, Phil."

CHAPTER TWENTY-SIX

Twenty-four minutes later...

Paul limped as quickly down the alleyway as he could, with Phil walking alongside, keeping an eagle eye out behind them for any signs of pursuit.

"All, I was saying was..."

"Phil, I don't want to talk about it." Paul winced. His hip was bloody killing him.

"I'm just saying..."

"What did I just say?"

"Where we went wrong..."

"Didn't I just say I don't want to talk about it?"

"You stink, by the way."

"Likewise." Paul looked at his watch. The last twenty-four minutes had not gone well...

Manny's Massage was on the second floor of a building, above a shop called Eclectica, part of a relatively small shopping complex. There was also a convenience store, a chemist, a couple of clothing stores, a German restaurant, an interior designer and a chandelier shop.

Beside the chandelier shop was a unit to rent. Paul wondered what had been there that had proven less popular than chandeliers, German cuisine and whatever it was Eclectica sold.

They scouted around but quickly determined that the only entrance to Manny's Massage appeared to be through the shop.

They huddled quickly.

"Right," said Paul, "leave this to me. We need to get up there, and then I can bust in and get a picture of Harrison in the act."

"What act?"

Paul ignored the question. He didn't have time to explain to Phil the different interpretations of what a massage could consist of, particularly pertaining to which body parts were being "relaxed".

The bell above the door of Eclectica tinkled as Paul entered. After a moment, he heard it tinkle again. He winced internally. He hadn't told Phil specifically not to come in with him, which meant he had.

As he walked towards the counter, Paul noticed a beaded curtain to the right, behind which was a flight of stairs. This meant that the woman behind the counter, who had long white hair and an unnerving, spacey grin, must be some kind of receptionist. Her facial expression put Paul in mind of someone who had been constipated for a week and for whom the levee had just blissfully broken. She gave off a vibe of exhausted ecstasy. Eclectica was unlike any shop Paul had ever been in, mainly because it seemed to specialise in selling stuff that no other shop would sell. It had a lot of things made out of beads or bamboo, and some pottery that had that authentic, not-quite-able-to-sit-flat-on-a-table look to it. It was an artisan shop, according to the sign on the wall, although that sign appeared to also be for sale, so it was hard to trust. They also sold incense, pebbles and wind chimes. As far as Paul could figure out, the wind chime had been invented specifically for deaf people who really hated their neighbours. In that regard, it was also the most useful thing in the shop. What do you get the person who has everything? Pebbles, apparently.

"Hello," said Paul.

"Greetings," said the woman, with hands placed together and a bow. She was speaking in that sort of posh, stoned voice that only exists in films for women who appear out of nowhere to pass on expository information.

"Lovely place you have here."

"Blessings on you."

"Yeah. Likewise. I was wondering, can I get up to the massage place through here?"

"You may, yes. If you have an appointment."

"Ah, I don't. Could I go up and make one?"

The woman shook her head. "No. You have to ring to get one."

"I see. Have you got the number?"

The woman took a card from beside the register and, with her head bowed, held it out to him in both palms.

Paul took it, throwing in a bow in return, as he felt it was expected. "And is it, y'know, full service?"

"Oh yes."

Paul looked at the woman closely. It was hard to judge much from her face. He guessed she might maintain the same contented expression if she was on fire.

Behind him, Paul could hear Phil colliding with something. If he broke it, Paul was not paying for it.

"OK, so I'll ring up and make an appointment then," said Paul.

"Namaste."

"Yeah. Thanks."

Paul then went outside, closely followed by Phil.

"Do you reckon it's money laundering?"

"It must be," said Paul. "Nothing else makes sense."

"They've got a bottle of water in there that contains essence of rocks. Is that not just sand?"

"I dunno," said Paul, who had fished out his mobile and was dialling the number on the card.

On the third ring, someone answered. "Greetings, Manny's Massage."

He recognised the voice and turned to look in the window of the shop. The white-haired woman behind the counter was now on the phone.

"Hi, I'm the guy who was just in your shop."

"Oh. Hello."

She gave him a happy wave through the window.

"Yes. Hi. I was wondering if it would be possible to book myself in for a massage?"

"I'm afraid we're very booked up. The only gaps in the diary are for emergency massages."

"But this is an emergency."

"Oh dear, I see. We only really provide that service for customers of the shop."

"Right," said Paul, opening the door and re-entering. "So, if I bought something, then I would be a customer."

"Yes." The woman was still talking into the phone, despite the fact Paul was now standing in front of her.

"Right." Paul hung up the phone and looked around the shop. "Well then, I think I'll get..." He picked up a smooth blue pebble from the display beside the counter. "I'd like to buy this."

"Ah, an excellent choice. That will be sixty euros."

"Sixty!?" Paul tried to keep the shock from his voice, but it was impossible. Not that long ago, he'd have lived happily for a fortnight on that much money. Now he was spending it on a pebble.

"This is very powerful. It can be used to realign a person's chakras."

"Oh, that's good. I do feel like me chakras are properly ballsed up," said Paul, as he handed over all of the money he currently had in his wallet.

"Would you like a bag?"

"Sure."

"That's another three euros."

"What? Is it a bag for life or something?"

The woman gave him that smile again. "Better than that. It is a bag for many lives. It has been woven by hand and blessed in a Hindu temple by a blind woman called Sharona, who many believe to be a prophet." As she said this, the woman popped the stone into a bag that was just big enough to carry a reasonably sized pebble. Resisting any and all ripostes about prophets and profits, Paul fished three euros out of his pocket and handed them over.

"Gracias," said the woman, who appeared to be fluent in bullshit in several languages.

"So," said Paul, taking the proffered bag, "can I make an emergency appointment now?"

"Oh no, I'm afraid Manny is seeing the last client of the day now. You'll have to ring back tomorrow."

Paul gave the woman a long, hard look. "Really?"

"Yes, but do come back." The woman reached across and placed her hand on Paul's chest. "I can sense you have a lot of tension."

Plan B, which Paul had quickly decided on, involving finding their way around to the back of the shops. There was a large metal gate on which was hung a rather stern 'keep out' sign, leading into a back yard where four cars were parked alongside a couple of dumpsters.

Paul and Phil looked up at the windows.

"How do we figure out which one it is?" said Phil.

"Hmmm."

"You could try chucking your pebble up at the windows, see who looks out?"

"Don't be daft, Phil, that would give us away." Plus, Paul was hoping that he could possibly return the pebble and get his money back. Sixty euros was, after all, sixty euros, and blue wasn't even his favourite colour.

Paul looked at the windows again. "That one!" It wasn't the most Sherlockian of deductions, but he was quite proud of it. Five windows on the second floor had lights on, but only one of the rooms appeared to be illuminated by a soft diffuse light with a pink glow to it. He'd never been in anything that could be termed a boudoir, but he'd seen them in films, and he was pretty sure they were big into mood lighting.

They moved one of the dumpsters to below the window and clambered on top of it, but even with Phil's six-foot-six height, they couldn't reach the window. Paul had then managed to convince Phil to boost him up. They needed to do it quickly. Paul was aware they were somewhere they weren't supposed to be, with no good reason to be there and that the clock was against them. Paul didn't want Harrison to get away due to him being "prompt" in the activity he was hopefully currently engaged in.

Paul took his phone out and then put his foot into Phil's cupped hand.

"One, two, three!"

In one fluid motion, Phil lifted Paul skyward, and he was able to grab onto the window ledge with his free hand.

"Wait, wait, wait," said Paul in an urgent whisper, as he thumbed his phone to open the camera. "Take your time."

"That's easy for you to say. You've not got a face full of crotch."

"Wait!" Paul looked at his phone to confirm the camera was working. "OK, go!"

With Phil boosting him up fully, Paul was able to get his head and chest above the windowsill. What he saw was a muscular man in a T-shirt two sizes too small for him – Manny, presumably – performing acupuncture on a naked man lying face down. There was no sign of any hanky-panky.

While what Paul saw was disappointingly mundane, the same couldn't be said for Manny. From his perspective, a man had just appeared outside his second-floor window. This caused him to scream in shock.

And this caused Jacob Harrison to scream, as the man who had been carefully sticking needles into him for twenty minutes suddenly stuck one in very un-carefully.

All of this screaming caused Paul to scream – and to press the photo button on his camera. The flash went off, reflecting against the window glass and blinding him slightly. This caused him to wobble.

This wobbling and the chain reaction of screaming caused Phil Nellis to scream and wobble. Phil was a man who constantly believed that the sky was about to fall, and for once he was proven correct. Paul started to fall sideways. Phil followed after him, trying to somehow regain control, before gravity got the best of them both. All this resulted in was Phil effectively launching Paul into the open dumpster beside them, which belonged to the restaurant. Apparently the sauerkraut was not selling as well as hoped.

Phil had then fished Paul out of the dumpster and they had beaten a very hasty retreat. Luckily, Manny must have been too distracted dealing with his bleeding client to give chase. Paul was only able to hobble, as his hip was killing him. He had landed hard on the pebble in his pocket.

As Phil and Paul came around the corner to where the van was parked, they were confronted by an unwelcome sight. Kevin Kelleher, his hand in a bandage and a smug grin across his face, was leaning on the bonnet of the van.

"Howerya, lads? Any chance of a 99?"

"Not for you," said Paul.

"Yeah," added Phil, "the machine broke yesterday."

Paul looked at Phil, who shrugged. "Well, it did."

"So," continued Kelleher, "did you have fun following Mr Harrison while he was getting acupuncture? He's trying to deal with some issues he's been having with his back, stemming from being dangled off a balcony."

Kelleher pushed himself off the bonnet, exaggeratedly dusting himself down. "You lot are a joke. Do you really think Harrison can't keep it in his pants for a few weeks?"

"Well," said Paul, "he doesn't have the greatest of track records in that area."

"Still, though, you're following him, we're following you. What a fun little game we're playing. By the way, I have an agreement with Mr Harrison and his solicitors that when he eventually owns your sorry business – as scant consolation for the mental hardship you've caused him – I'm going to buy it off him, for a very fair price. The reason I bring that up is that I'm a bit concerned with the sorry state of this vehicle I'm about to own."

Kevin Kelleher ran his finger along the side of the van and tutted. "Filthy. I think it needs a thorough clean, inside and out. Luckily for you, my brother Vincent and I are also shareholders in a mobile car valeting business."

As he said this, Vincent, the monobrowed monolith of the Kelleher clan, appeared from behind the van, holding a hose. Paul moved a couple of steps to the right, and saw that the hose was running from the back of a blue van parked behind theirs.

"Complimentary jet wash. Just to show there are no hard feelings." Vincent gave what Paul could only assume he considered a smile as he pushed the hose in the gap of the partially open van window. "By the way, you should really close your windows properly. There's a lot of nefarious characters around."

"I wouldn't do that if I was you," said Phil.

"Wouldn't ye? What are you going to do about it? Call the cops? What with one of you very closely resembling a peeping Tom spotted in the area? Or are you going to resort to physical violence? Go right ahead, you've not got your psycho partner with you now."

Paul noticed that Kevin reflexively cradled his bandaged fingers.

"Actually—" began Phil, before being interrupted as Paul put a warning hand across him.

"No," said Paul, "just let the man get on with it, Phil. We deserve this."

Kevin laughed. "Too fecking right, and I'm going to enjoy it."

"Not as much as I am."

"Yeah, we'll see. Vinny!"

"What?" responded Vinny.

Kevin Kelleher looked slightly exasperated. "What do you mean *what*? Turn on the damn hose."

"Oh. Right."

Vinny then duly turned a knob on the hose, and Paul could clearly hear water whooshing through it, into the MCM surveillance van.

There were quite a few things in this world that Maggie did not enjoy. She didn't like being woken up. She didn't healthy food. As the last local election had proven, she really didn't like politicians – their building, indeed their whole street, was very possibly going to be free from people trying to shake your hand and give you a sticker for at least the next decade, if not longer. The refusal to eat healthy food had of course resulted in her monumental flatulence problem, which was why the window had been open a crack. Paul would have left it open wider, but Maggie also didn't like the cold.

But more than any of this, as Paul had found to his cost, Maggie hated bath time.

A blood-curdling yowl issued from the back of the van and it started to rock violently.

Paul and Phil each took a couple of steps back. This was definitely a situation where distance was preferable.

Kevin Kelleher suddenly looked a lot less pleased with himself. It was a credit to his rat-like survival instincts that he was halfway through shouting the word "run" when the window of the van exploded outwards and a mass of very wet and extremely unhappy dog landed on the pavement.

What happened next was like a scene from a bad horror movie, with the Kelleher brothers running as fast as their legs could carry them, which was nowhere near fast enough. As they ran, Maggie bit at their heels. She leaped up and took down Vinny, before continuing after Kevin.

"Should we stop her?" asked Phil.

"How?" said Paul.

They watched in silence as the Kelleher brothers screamed and yelped their way around the corner.

Paul moved over and pulled the hose out of the window. "Right, wait for her to come back and see if you can dry this thing out a bit."

"And where are you going?"

Paul pointed at the van belonging to "Kelleher Valet Services". "I'm going to get the Kellehers some free advertising by parking that little beauty in a bus lane."

CHAPTER TWENTY-SEVEN

DSI Burns was aware that, at times, she came to conclusions about people too quickly. It was a flaw she had identified in herself while reading a management book called *How to be a People Person*. It had been an interesting discovery, not least because she was so rigorous about assembling all the facts in a case before coming to a conclusion. She was a big believer that instinct was a word lazy people had come up with to make guessing sound like something more impressive.

It was with some considerable effort that she had, until this point, tried not to form a hard and fast opinion of FBI Special Agent Alana Dove. Yes, as soon as she had met her, DSI Burns had received a call from the commissioner, who'd told her that instructions had come from what he called "the highest level" to give her any and all assistance requested. That had pissed Burns off. She didn't like anyone messing with her investigations, especially a foreign agency, but Dove was only the tip of that spear. She would have been sent here by her bosses and any copper knew that part and parcel of the job was being put in positions you didn't want to be in. Burns still remembered the day, as a young Garda on the beat, when she had been forced to put the cuffs on a young woman who had fought back against her abuser. The job defined you, but at the same time, at certain points, you and the job could vehemently disagree. As old Sergeant Murphy had said at the time, we can't just enforce the laws we agree with.

So no, DSI Burns didn't dislike Dove because of the job she had been sent here to do. The prosthetic arm was disconcerting, but it was, of course, not a reason to dislike someone. In fact, when she thought about it, it was pretty impressive that Dove had managed to succeed in her career despite such an obstacle. She didn't even dislike her for the fact that, at any given time, Dove appeared to be wearing more make-up than Burns owned. She did wonder if the creepy slow blink thing was because of the sheer weight of mascara her eyelids were required to lift. But no, DSI Burns was not going to hate someone for shallow aesthetic reasons. Now, though, she had a damn good reason to hate FBI Special Agent Alana Dove and she was going to embrace it with all her heart.

She opened the door to her office. "Agent Dove, please come in."

Dove had been waiting outside for twenty minutes while Wilson gave Burns a full debrief on what had happened on their trip to Sláinte Ferries.

Agent Dove strode past Burns and sat down beside Wilson, who shifted nervously in his seat. As Burns closed the door, she noted that the woman also wore too much damn perfume. She'd have to open a window after this.

Burns walked behind her desk and sat down.

"OK, Agent Dove. Detective Wilson has brought me up to speed with what happened."

"Yes, and may I put it on record that he should be commended for his actions in performing CPR on the gentleman who collapsed. I believe his speedy response may have helped save a man's life."

Dove turned to Wilson and gave him one of her massive collection of wide smiles. Wilson nodded nervously, as though he wasn't sure if such a commendation was like winning a free trip on the *Titanic*.

"Noted," said Burns. "Although it does neatly bring us to the fact that you nearly killed a man."

"Excuse me?"

"I don't know how it works across the Atlantic, but here, we try not to induce heart attacks in interviewees. It's a health and safety thing."

"I don't think we can be held responsible for that."

Wilson didn't say anything, but his facial expression screamed that he felt he definitely shouldn't be part of the "we" here.

"You threatened an innocent man's family!"

"With all due respect, Superintendent, I did not."

"You told him—"

"I pointed out the powers of two US government agencies. That is merely information. By definition, an innocent person has nothing to fear from the law. Unless you are trying to cast aspersions on the integrity of American law enforcement? Or you are trying to suggest this gentleman's family is engaged in unlawful activity?"

DSI Burns rolled her eyes. "Cut the crap, Dove, that nonsense isn't going to work on me. You were strong-arming the man and you nearly killed him. Need I remind you that you have absolutely no legal jurisdiction here? We involved you in this investigation as a courtesy, a courtesy which you have abused."

"I fail to see how—"

"You went into the interview with extensive knowledge about the man's family."

"Fail to prepare, prepare to fail."

DSI Burns snatched up the stress ball from her desk so quickly, Wilson actually flinched. It gave a disconcerting squeak, like a distressed woodland creature, each time she squeezed it. She was not unaware of that fact. "So we're calling this a success then, are we?" Burns started squeezing the ball under the desk. It had been a long day, in a long week. "Dove, I want you on the first flight home. We will continue this investigation without your 'help'."

Agent Dove's face registered alarm – or at least the parts that were capable of doing so.

"But, you can't—"

"The hell I can't. I've already spoken to my bosses. Keen as they are to play nice with our American cousins, nobody wants the headlines if this man dies."

"Ehm..." Both women looked at Wilson in shock; they'd mostly forgotten he was there. To be fair, he looked more than a little surprised to find himself speaking. "The hospital did say he was expected to make a full recovery, guv."

"Yes," agreed Dove. "And it was the man's third heart attack. I mean, clearly he needs to look at his lifestyle."

"And how do you know that exactly?"

Dove didn't say anything.

"Wilson, did you know that?"

Wilson shifted about again. "No, boss, I didn't hear anyone mention it at the hospital, but then maybe I..."

Burns refocused her gaze on Dove. "Just to be clear, private information about Irish citizens is exactly that: private. If I get even the slightest hint that you're obtaining information illegally, then you will not be flying home. In fact, I'll be seeing to it that the state provides you with free room and board for one to three years."

"I heard that from one of the doctors at the hospital."

"Really?"

Burns glanced at Wilson, who shrugged. "She could have done, boss. I mean, they would've been checking records and stuff."

"Speaking of information," said Burns, "would it be fair to say, Agent Dove, that you haven't been sharing all of the information pertinent to this case with us?"

"There is confidential information that I am not at liberty to divulge."

"Bollocks."

Agent Dove looked confused. "I don't understand what—"

"Bullshit, does that make more sense? We are running a murder investigation here and it is absolutely not your job to decide what we do and do not need to know. In fact, withholding information pertinent to a murder investigation is called obstruction of justice in this funny little backwater, and we take a fierce dim view of it."

Dove said nothing.

"Apparently, right before he nearly joined the choir immortal, you started asking the interviewee questions about an individual that my officer had never even heard of. You expect our cooperation but you leave us in the dark."

Agent Dove reached into her bag and produced a copy of that day's *Herald*. She held it up to show the headline: "Wicklow Body is FBI Agent."

"The problem we have, Detective Superintendent, is that you are captain of a very leaky boat."

Burns's unseen stress ball let out a dying wail and went mysteriously silent. Wilson leaned back in his chair as far as he could go. On an instinctive level, every fibre of his body was telling him that now was a good time to run.

"You want to come in here and criticise *us*, after the day you've had? Right, that's it. Wilson, drop Agent Dove to Dublin Airport and sit there until she gets on the first available flight to America."

"You can't do that."

"Can't I? You watch me. Have fun explaining to your bosses why you got booted out of the country. Don't let the door hit you in the arse on the way out."

Dove gave one of those slow blinks. An iguana! That was it! She knew the woman reminded her of something, and it had finally popped into her head. She'd seen them when she'd brought her nephews to Dublin Zoo last month.

"I apologise," said Dove. "That was out of line."

"D'ye reckon?"

"I am sorry. Clearly, we have gotten off on the wrong foot here. I appreciate all of the assistance and I should have been more forthcoming regarding the nature of our investigation. How about we start afresh?"

"OK," said Burns. "Who is Simone Delamere?"

Agent Dove's left eye started to twitch and wink rapidly. She opened her mouth and closed it again.

DSI Burns turned to Wilson. "Keep your receipts for the parking at the airport, it can be expensive. Wave the badge, I want you to walk her all the way to the gate and onto the plane."

"I..."

"And ask one of the stewardesses if you can get one of those tiny packets of peanuts for me, I bloody love those."

"Ehm, yes, boss."

"Alright." The tone of Dove's voice suddenly changed, as if something had finally cracked. "But it doesn't leave this room."

Burns looked back at Wilson. "And one of those tiny cans of Coke they have. I think they remind me of going on holidays."

"Fine." Dove threw the newspaper she had been holding into her bag and then uncrossed and re-crossed her legs. "Simone Delamere is wanted for the murder of Alex Woolstencroft, a former partner of Agent Zayas, in New York back in 1998."

"And what makes you think she was in Ireland? I've already run the name; she doesn't appear on any database."

"Zayas was here. We assume he came looking for her."

"If he was here on an investigation, then—"

"He wasn't." Agent Dove shifted nervously. "We believe he was out for revenge. He had no interest in bringing Miss Delamere to justice. You can appreciate how agents turning vigilante isn't an optic the Bureau's wild about."

"And you think this Delamere woman killed Zayas and the other unidentified body we found?"

"We don't know," said Dove. "That's what I'm here to find out."

As the silence stretched out between them, Dove's left eye twitched out a staccato rhythm – and then she did another iguana blink. Burns wondered if she was trying to send secret Morse code messages. It might be her face begging for help to get out from under the make-up.

"Any and all information you have from here on out..."

"You'll be the first to know," said Dove.

"And for the love of God, try not to kill anybody."

CHAPTER TWENTY-EIGHT

Brigit shook the rain off her umbrella and pushed open the door of O'Hagan's pub. For a Wednesday night, it was reasonably busy. A screen on the back wall was showing some football match or other. From Brigit's limited experience, there was always football on.

As she walked in, she caught the eye of Tara Flynn, the owner, who raised her eyebrows and nodded her over.

"Brigit, right?"

"You've a great memory."

Tara smiled. "Ah, trick of the trade. The punters love it when you remember their names. Makes 'em think they're drinking in *Cheers* or something. One sec." Tara topped up a pint of Guinness that had been settling and walked it down the bar to a man in an ill-fitting grey suit. "There you go, Patrick. Four euros ninety-five, please."

The man smiled at her and handed over a five-euro note. "Cheers. Keep the change."

"Much obliged." Tara moved back down the bar towards Brigit and rang it up in the register, flipping the five-cent coin neatly into the tip jar beside the till. "At this rate, I'll be able to afford that dream holiday by 2045."

Brigit smiled back. "So, have you seen Bunny?"

Tara nodded. "I have. He's in his office." Tara noticed Brigit's confused expression. "By which I mean the snug in the back bar."

"Brilliant, thanks."

Tara raised her hand to stop Brigit from walking away. "Is he... alright?"

"How do you mean?"

"Well he's... he's not been himself."

Brigit could see the worry on Tara's face. "How so?"

Tara leaned in. "Well, look, I wouldn't say anything normally, but what with you working together and all and that business last year..."

O'Hagan's had been the last place Bunny had been seen before he'd been knocked out and kidnapped. To be fair, Brigit guessed O'Hagan's was the last place Bunny had been before almost everything happened to him. He appeared to be rather keen on the place.

"It's just..." Tara paused, trying to find the right words. "He's been really jumpy, if you know what I mean."

"Has this just been recently?"

"Mainly, yeah. Between you and me, I've known him a long time, and since the thing last year – and God knows that would've killed most men – he's been a bit... different. I mean, you wouldn't know it unless you knew him well. He's still bigger than life and twice as bad, but I think it's more for show. It's like he's doing what's expected."

"Right." Brigit felt awkward, not least because she once again realised that for all they'd been through, she didn't know that much about Bunny.

"Everyone has their ups and downs," continued Tara. "I remember back when I'd only started here, around the time his partner died, that was tough."

Brigit nodded. She didn't want to admit that she had no idea what Tara was talking about.

"It's just that now, well..." She looked pained, like she was crossing some line she didn't want to cross. "He's, y'know... talking to himself a bit. Maybe just talking out loud. I mean, I do that too, it's not a big deal, only…"

A man in a leather jacket walked up to the bar, waiting expectantly.

Tara stopped, seemingly running out of road. "Ahh, d'ye know what, don't mind me. I'm probably overreacting."

"No. Thanks. I appreciate the heads-up. Is it around this way?"

Tara nodded. "Yep." She moved off to serve the man in the leather jacket and Brigit made her way around the bar. On the other side, about a dozen high tables with similarly high stools were dotted around, mostly occupied. At the back of the room, boisterous laughter erupted from a group of seven or so men in suits.

Brigit looked around; she couldn't see Bunny anywhere. There were a few booths over by the wall and she glanced into them: a canoodling couple; three lads playing a board game; no Bunny.

"Are you alright there, darling?"

Brigit glanced briefly at the man with the goatee who had addressed her. "I'm fine, just looking for someone."

"You're in luck, so am I!"

Brigit gave him a tight smile. The corner booth appeared to be empty, save for a couple of dead pint glasses. She turned to head back the way she'd come.

"C'mon, let me buy you a drink?"

"No, thanks."

The goatee bounced into her path, a smile on his face. "I won't take no for answer."

"Yes, ye feckin' will!"

Brigit turned at the voice. There at the door of the gents' stood Bunny, still in the process of doing up his fly.

"What business is it of yours?"

Brigit moved quickly to intercept Bunny, putting her hands out. "Bunny, there you are. I've been looking for you."

He looked over her shoulder. "That gobshite bothering you, Conroy?"

She gave a laugh. "Nothing I can't handle."

Behind her, a voice made a remark that sounded a lot like "Mad old fucker".

"What was that?!" Bunny asked in a tone of voice that was very keen for an answer.

Brigit moved directly in front of him. "Don't mind those eejits. You go sit down, I'll grab us a drink."

She gave him a smile and a gentle push back towards the corner booth. "Go on, I'll be over in a second."

With a grumble, Bunny turned and started walking away. Brigit turned back to the bar, giving the group of suits a dirty look as she did so. She noticed Tara had now moved around to this side of the bar, her eyes flickering between the group and Brigit.

Brigit gave her an "everything is fine" smile as she walked over. "Can I get a white wine, please, and Bunny's usual."

"No problem."

Tara disappeared to go and get the drinks.

"If ye like, you can buy me a drink."

Brigit glanced up to see the goatee standing beside her, grinning.

"I'll pass."

"Bit tight, are ye?"

"If you like, I'll see if they have mints."

Out of the corner of her eye, Brigit could see the wattage on the grin being turned down considerably. "Alright, just having a bit of banter. No need to be a bitch about it."

Brigit turned at him and smiled. "OK, dipshit, here's the thing. First time was fine, nobody minds that, but if a woman doesn't respond to your first attempt at 'banter' then leave it alone as it means she is not interested."

The goatee went to speak.

"No, shut up and listen. I do not want to talk to you, I've made that pretty clear. Yet here you are, while your gormless mates look on, getting in my personal space again, and now you just referred to me as a bitch. I'm not one, but I can be, so listen to me very carefully: either turn around and piss off back over there right now or we're going to have a problem. Believe me when I say I would be more than happy to deal with you, but the thing is, if I do that, it'll escalate. You remember that gentleman I'm with? You're probably thinking he's some old duffer, and you'd be right. He's a lovely, sweet man, albeit one with a spectacular penchant for violence and an incredibly low tolerance for people being rude. So, if I dealt with you, he'd get involved, even though I wouldn't want him to. Then, you and the rest of the accounts department over there are suddenly in the kind of situation you're not prepared for. You might think you're handy, maybe you've been in a couple of fights before. Believe me, that's like thinking that having lifted a couple of rocks will prepare you for being right in the centre of a meteor shower. You'll spend the next few months trying to figure out what happened. It'll haunt your thoughts. It'll give you nightmares. So, for your sake, don't speak, don't even look in my direction again, just turn around and piss off like a good lad. Alright?"

He went to speak.

"Shush."

She waved him away. With an expression on his face like he'd just been given an unexpected rectal exam, the goatee departed.

Brigit turned back to the bar, surprised to see Tara standing there. "Well, you just earned these on the house."

Brigit walked towards the snug, trying not to notice that Bunny seemed to be talking to someone who wasn't there. She placed the drinks down on the table, plonked her bag down and started taking off her coat.

"Here we are."

"Everything alright, Conroy?"

"Yeah, course," she replied with a smile. "You know me, Bunny, well able to take care of myself." She sat down and picked up her glass. "Cheers."

Bunny clinked his against hers in response and they both took a sip. While doing so, she had the chance to take a proper look at him. He looked old. Old in a way he hadn't before. It wasn't like he'd ever been a picture of rude health, but this was something else. As long as she'd known him, Bunny McGarry had always been overflowing with life. Suddenly, he was starting to look like a bad reproduction of himself.

Brigit put her glass down. "So how've you been?"

"Grand."

"You sleeping OK?"

Bunny shrugged. "Y'know, as well as ever. Man of my age, I have to pee at odd hours."

"Ah, that's just God's way of getting you some exercise."

They smiled awkwardly at each other.

"I've been trying to ring you."

"Ah, yeah," Bunny ran a hand through his hair. "Sorry about that, not been paying much attention to the phone." Bunny looked over her shoulder. "D'ye see that bloke in the leather jacket?"

Brigit turned around to see the man Tara had been serving at the far side of the bar. "Yes."

"He's been following me."

"Has he?"

"Yeah, he's one of them. I clocked him this morning, only he had shorter hair and a beard."

Brigit turned to look back at Bunny. "Shorter hair?"

Bunny nodded, still watching the man as he took a seat facing away from them and pulled out a book.

"Maybe you're mistaken. He looks like he's just looking for somewhere quiet to read his book away from the interminable soccer."

"Ha, right, yeah. That's what they want you to think."

Brigit looked back at Bunny. There was an edginess to him that she didn't recognise. Bunny was a lot of things, but never edgy. He was the person that made other people nervous.

"Are you... are you alright in yourself, Bunny?"

He turned his eyes to her again. "Yeah, why wouldn't I be?"

"Just with the thing that happened last week."

Bunny gave her a panicky look. "What about it?"

"We're in a spot of trouble. Jacob Harrison is suing us."

Bunny's expression turned to one of genuine confusion.

"Jacob Harrison? You dangled him off a balcony?"

"Oh, that prick. I was just teaching him a lesson."

"Well, I'm afraid he's suing us, and it's not great, to be honest."

Bunny's eyes lit up. "Is that this thing?"

He rummaged around in the pocket of his ever-present long black sheepskin coat, which was bundled up on the seat beside him, and produced a crumpled letter. He handed it to Brigit. "Is this to do with that?"

She flattened it out on the table. It was essentially the same summons the company had received but addressed personally to Bunny. "Oh, for God's sake, Bunny, yes. Why didn't you talk to me about this?"

"Ah sure, it's only a load of old bollocks."

"It's not, Bunny, it really isn't. We're in the shit here. This could take down the whole company."

Brigit instantly felt bad for the harshness of her tone. Bunny looked down at the table, suddenly seeming smaller and older. "Sorry. I didn't think. I was... y'know. A lot going on."

Brigit placed her hand on top of his. "It's OK. The thing is, you've got to be careful now. I had a meeting with Nora Stokes about it. She reckons the Kelleher brothers might try and follow you, get evidence of you having, well, a tendency to be violent."

"Right."

"Look, we'll sort it out. Harrison is full of crap and we'll get proof. I just need you to lay low. Can you stay home for a couple of days?"

"I'm not staying there. They've been there. It's not safe."

Bunny again looked past her into the bar. He was really starting to freak her out. "Who are they?"

Bunny looked back at her. "Never mind, Conroy. 'Tis all ancient history."

"You seem really stressed, Bunny. Maybe you should have a chat with someone."

Bunny barked a humourless laugh. "Oh, believe me, I've plenty of people to talk to. Too many, in fact."

As his eyes were drawn once again to the bar behind her, Brigit moved her head to get into his field of vision. "Hey there, Bunny. This is me, remember. We've been through a lot together. I'll..." She stopped talking for a moment as a wave of emotion welled up inside her. She took a deep breath. "I'll always remember, you and me, in that room. That nightmare of a room. I was there for a few minutes, you were there for ten days. Nobody could come out of that unscarred, Bunny. There's no shame in admitting it."

Bunny pulled his hand away from under hers. He seemed agitated now. "Leave it, Conroy. I'm alright. It's just... I'm having a bad week. Don't worry about me. I'll stay away from you, don't worry."

"No, I didn't mean that, Bunny. I just meant lay low while we sort this Harrison thing out."

"Right, right. Yeah, good, yeah."

Bunny grabbed his coat. As he went to leave, Brigit stood up.

"Jesus, Bunny. Sit down and talk to me, would ye? Whatever's wrong, whatever problem you have, you know I'll always be there for you. We've been through a lot. Let me help you."

Bunny quickly put his coat on then placed his hands on Brigit's shoulders. "Conroy, you're a great girl. Can you do something for me?"

"Anything, Bunny. You know that."

"You and Paul, take care of each other and stay well away from me, alright?"

"Don't be—"

"Please, Conroy. It's the only thing I ask. Whatever happens, just know, I had good reasons and I did what I thought was right."

"You're scaring me now, Bunny."

Then he did something he had never done before. He hugged her, hard.

"I've got to go."

"Bunny. Wait."

He rushed past and was out the door before she could say another word.

She looked around the bar again. Goatee and his friends had departed and only a few tables were occupied. Brigit watched as the guy in the leather jacket was joined by a female friend. As they kissed hello, Brigit stared at the door Bunny had disappeared through, into a bitter Dublin night.

CHAPTER TWENTY-NINE

Detective Wilson pulled the car up in front of the hotel and put on the handbrakes.

"Right so, I'll pick you up at seven thirty in the morning."

"Great," said Agent Dove. "And Donnacha…" She'd never used his first name before; it sounded weird in her accent. "I want to thank you for your help today. I know I put you in an awkward position with your boss."

"No problem." He turned to look at her. She appeared to want to talk and it would be rude not to.

"No, you were really great. And thank you for not mentioning the gun."

"Wait, you really have a gun?"

"No." Then she winked. It could have been a 'wink' wink, or one of her array of 'twitchy' winks. Wilson had no idea.

"Seriously though, if you have a gun, I am going to have to—"

"The restaurant in the hotel is pretty good, how about I buy you a thank you dinner?"

If she was trying to throw him off balance to make him forget the gun thing, it was working. She was now beaming a disconcerting smile at him. She really did have enormous eyes. It was like looking into the eyes of one of those bunny rabbits that had make-up tested on it.

"Ehm, no, thanks. I've got a microwaveable dinner in the fridge and it goes off tonight." Even as he said it, he was aware it sounded weird.

"Right. How about you just come up for a drink?"

"Ahh, I'm driving and y'know..."

"Just a quickie then."

"Ah, I'd love to but, y'know, I'm a police officer. Wouldn't look good, me sitting around in a hotel bar, drinking." Again, that sounded odd – 'Eskimo freaks out at the sight of snow' odd.

Dove moved a little closer. "Well, you could come up to my room."

Wilson licked his lips. He wasn't trying to be sexy; his mouth was just very, very dry suddenly.

"Alcoholic!" He said it with the kind of fervour you'd normally expect from a shipwreck survivor who had spotted a plane. "Alcoholic," he repeated, and then realised that he might need to say more than that. "I'm a recovering alcoholic, so, y'know, I have to stay away from the booze. The demon drink. The Devil's thingy. I'm on those ten steps."

"Twelve."

"Yeah, not made the last two yet. One day at a time. Straight and narrow. Just say no. Like yer man on *Grange Hill*. Did you have that in America? Probably not. Doesn't matter. Anyway, no drinkies for me. But thanks all the same."

Wilson was aware he was babbling.

"OK," said Dove. "How about you come up and don't have a drink then?"

"Ehm. Like, y'mean..."

She placed her hand – her prosthetic hand – on his knee. "To be clear, Detective Wilson, I am offering you full-on, no-strings-attached, no-holds-barred, anything-goes, sweaty, dirty sex."

"I have a girlfriend," said a high reedy voice that Wilson was only dimly aware had come from him.

"That's OK."

"OK," said Wilson, before adding, "Thank you," because his mother had brought him up properly. The thought that Dove was about her age popped into his head and he really wished it hadn't.

Dove's face formed into a frown, which was a bit like watching a slow motion landslide. "I see. It's the arm, isn't it?"

Wilson didn't think he could have felt more embarrassed, but there it was. "Oh God, no, definitely not. No, no, no. Love the arm, it's a great arm. Dead sexy. Always, always been a big fan of technology. I have the latest iPhone." His mouth now seemed to be working entirely independently to the rest of him. "I've also got one of those Alexa things in the bedroom, you can tell it what to do for you. Y'know, voice activated. Great bit of kit."

"Do you like to be in control in the bedroom?"

He tried to laugh. It came out like a duck choking.

"Well then, you'll be pleased to hear that this little beauty" – her left hand stroked the prosthetic right – "actually comes with a couple of attachments that'll rock your world." The prosthetic hand had now moved off his knee and was slowly making its way up his inner thigh.

Agent Dove started to blink. By the time she was halfway through it, Wilson was out the door of the car. He threw a wave over his shoulder and walked across the road, nearly getting run over by an irate cyclist for his trouble.

It was only when he was a good couple of hundred yards away that it occurred to him that he'd been driving the car he had just abandoned. He considered leaving it. The hotel would probably get upset. He could call a friend? Maybe he could report it stolen?

He took a deep breath and tried to calm himself.

After a minute, he returned to find the car empty, surrounded by three hotel employees.

"Sorry, lads," said Wilson, producing his ID. "I was just, y'know, chasing a suspect." Then he hopped in and drove quickly away. He had a long night of cringing in embarrassment ahead of him and he wanted to get going on it as quickly as possible.

CHAPTER THIRTY

DSI Burns slurped a mouthful of tea and flipped over to page forty-six of an eighty-seven-page document that had seemingly been written with the express wish of breaking the reader's will to live. She had the monthly budget meeting in an hour and she had long since realised the finance department's penchant for burying significant budget alterations in the weeds of a report. Burns couldn't categorically decide what it was that had pushed her into a career in law enforcement, but she was damn sure it hadn't been a desire to see more spreadsheets.

There was a knock on the door.

"Come in."

DS Moira Clarke popped her head around the door. "Got a second, boss?"

"Not really, but..." DSI Burns stopped herself and looked up properly. "Christ, sorry. Let's start this conversation again and I'll pretend to be an actual human being. How was your... niece's wedding?"

"Aunt's funeral."

"Shit. Sorry."

"It's alright, you didn't kill her."

"Sorry for your loss."

"Yeah. It's tough. No idea what we'll do for a source of casual racism at Christmas dinner this year."

"Ah."

"In her defence, she always made a fruitcake."

"Oh, well that's nice."

"You didn't have to eat it. Even harder to stomach than her politics. The dog got it out of the bin two years ago, ninety per cent sure that's what killed him. I don't know if you've ever had to cook a turkey while simultaneously digging a grave, but it is quite the festive treat, let me tell you."

"OK. Well..." Burns looked down at her report.

"Right. Sorry, boss. I'm rambling. I just wanted a word about the Zayas case."

"OK."

"I had an idea yesterday, y'know, when we found out about this Simone Delamere woman."

"Right."

DS Moira Clarke looked embarrassed. Technically, she didn't actually work cases. What she did was run the incident room, and she did so brilliantly. Unglamorous as it was, modern police work was all about resources and nobody handled them better than Moira Clarke. Apparently, there was some story behind why she didn't go out into the field anymore, but Burns had never considered it her place to ask.

"Any ideas you have, Moira, fire away. I'm all ears."

"Well, I thought that, y'know – my daughter, Vanya – big singer. Loves singing. Cannot stop the kid singing."

"Right."

"Drives her brother mad. Even when she's doing her homework, she just can't stop herself."

Burns tried to remain patient. Clearly this was heading somewhere, although she couldn't see where just yet. "And?"

"Well, if this woman was a singer in the States, even if she was trying to keep a low profile, she might still, y'know, get the urge."

"Makes sense."

"So I put up a thing on this jazz forum, y'know, where anoraks argue the toss with each other for hours on end about everything and anything."

"And?"

"Someone remembered her. At least, I think so. Says a black woman called Simone used to sing in a bar called Charlie's. The guy doesn't know when, exactly, or—"

"Moira, you're a bloody genius." DSI Burns snatched up her phone. "Come in and sit down."

CHAPTER THIRTY-ONE

Wilson eased the car back into the space and turned off the engine. It had been an awkward drive over, although thankfully it had been mercifully short. This morning was the first time Agent Dove had been in his car since "the incident", as neither of them was referring to it, because they both appeared to be denying anything had happened, or rather hadn't. Dove had texted the next morning to say she was getting a cab into the office as she wanted to get an early start, and for the two days since then, there had always been some other reason for them to not need to travel together.

Wilson felt bad. He was a good-looking guy, after all, and he knew women went mental for the Irish accent. She may have misinterpreted his natural charisma for signals that he definitely hadn't been sending.

Dove, for her part, had carried on like nothing had happened. One of the advantages of her plastic fantastic face was that it probably made hiding emotions easy, seeing as it severely limited the capacity to express them in the first place.

"OK then," said Wilson, "just to remind you, as agreed, I take the lead here."

Dove nodded. "Okey-dokey."

Prior to their departure, DSI Burns had issued some very clear directives in this regard. Thankfully, Donal Martyn, the ferry guy, was recovering well, but she had been very clear that if another interviewee ended up in the hospital, there would be hell to pay. Agent Dove would only be allowed to attend the interview on the strict understanding that she did not speak. Dove had agreed to it – in that overly cheerful way she had that felt like sarcasm. It was impossible to be sure.

Wilson was nervous, as the investigation had spent the last few days on wild goose chases. Dove had followed up on the US side to see if they could get a DNA match on the unknown male who was buried with Zayas, but they had come up with nothing so far. They had tried all the big hotels in Dublin and Wicklow, hoping to find where Daniel Zayas might have stayed, under whatever pseudonym he had been using. It had proven impossible. The records were basic and the few members of staff who had been working at the same hotel eighteen years ago had, unsurprisingly, no recollection of a particular guest checking in or out. Similarly, all searches for Simone Delamere had proven fruitless. Black women may not be the norm in Ireland, but they were hardly so unprecedented an occurrence that people would remember her nearly two decades later.

That was until DS Moira Clarke had her brainwave. Wilson was slightly embarrassed; he should have thought of that.

It took them a few minutes to locate Charlie's. The neon sign that pointed down the cobbled alleyway was turned off, making it almost unnoticeable. They descended down a few steps to an old battered door with three Chubb locks. It was closed but Wilson could hear music, incongruous upbeat dance music to be exact, blaring out.

He knocked on the door.

Then he knocked louder.

Then he pounded.

A tall blonde woman in a tracksuit, her hair pulled back in a bun so tight it looked painful, flung the door open and glowered at them. "What? We are closed. Can't you see the sign?"

She pointed to a window where there was no sign and then wrinkled up her nose. "Who stole the fucking sign?"

Wilson took out his ID. "I'm Detective Donnacha Wilson, National Criminal Bureau of Investigation."

The woman pulled a face like he had just exposed himself. "Ah, fuck this bullshit. That guy grabbed my ass, motherfucker. I gave him slap, no big deal. His nose was broken before he come in. I have witness."

"We're actually here to speak to the owner, a Mr Noel Graffoe."

"Oh. You have search warrant?"

Wilson raised an eyebrow. "We don't need a search warrant. We're not searching the place. We just want to ask Mr Graffoe a few questions."

She thought about it for a second and then stepped back. "Come in. I get Noel."

Wilson took a seat at a table in the centre of the room. The whole place smelled heavily of disinfectant, but not enough that it felt clean. The furniture was mismatched and worn, the tiled floor stained in so many places that its original colour was tough to ascertain with any certainty. Beside the small bar was a tiny stage, almost entirely occupied by an immaculately well-maintained piano. You could see yourself in its shiny surface. It was the only thing that shone in the whole place. It probably looked even nicer with some mood lighting and when the music wasn't what sounded like the Venga Boys having a mental breakdown.

As Wilson sat, Dove wandered around, looking at the various pictures of what Wilson assumed were famous jazz musicians. She didn't strike Wilson as a natural jazz fan, but then, the idea of Dove doing anything "normal" was hard to fathom.

An elderly, white-haired man, wearing a cardigan, appeared from the door behind the bar, followed by the blonde in the tracksuit. As he walked towards them he twitched violently. "Yada, bollocks."

Wilson wasn't caught off guard by the Tourette's. They had spent several hours that morning trying to find out as much as was humanly possible about the bar and its owner.

"Svetlana, turn that crap off will you?"

The blonde woman stood behind the bar and pouted. "I listen to your music."

"Yada!" Twitch. "I pay you to."

She reached across and begrudgingly silenced a phone that had been sitting on a set of speakers on the bar. She then proceeded to do a very unconvincing attempt at cleaning the bar while earwigging.

Wilson stood and extended his hand. "Detective Donnacha Wilson, and this is FBI Special Agent Alana Dove."

Dove waved as she continued to move around the room, admiring the photographs.

"FBI? Really? Yada. You're a long way from home."

Dove said nothing in response. Noel and Wilson sat down on opposite sides of the table.

"Does she speak?"

Wilson gave him a smile. "I do most of the talking."

"How enlightened. Yada! Mother! Mother! Motherfucker! What can I help you with?"

Wilson looked around. "This is a great place you've got. How long have you owned it?"

"Best part of thirty years. If you and the FBI are looking for somewhere to have your Christmas party, you've left it late."

"Ha, no. We actually wanted to—"

"Yada. Sorry, does she sit down at all?"

Noel turned and looked pointedly at Dove, who smiled and moved across to sit beside Wilson.

"So," continued Wilson. "I was wondering if you knew a woman called Simone Delamere?"

Noel's face twitched vigorously, whatever that might mean. "Yada. No."

"You sure? Black lady? American?"

Noel twitched again and then shook his head. "Nah. I've a terrible memory and I don't normally work the bar."

"Maybe this will help." Wilson took the photograph of Simone Delamere out of his inside pocket and passed it across the table. Noel glanced at it. "Yada. Nope. Nothing."

"Right."

Noel slid the picture back.

"The thing is, we have it on good authority that she worked here about eighteen years ago."

"Nope."

Wilson paused meaningfully as he looked at Graffoe. "Technically, I appreciate she might not have been 'on the books', as they say. We're not worried about that."

"What are you worried about?"

Wilson paused. "This is a murder investigation."

"Yada. F— fff— fuck. Fuck. This woman is dead?"

Wilson paused. Graffoe was difficult to read for the exact opposite reason to Dove. Usually, micro-expressions could be interpreted to see if someone was lying or under undue stress. Dove had none; Graffoe had far too many.

"No. We have no reason to believe that Miss Delamere is dead. We just need to talk to her."

"Sorry. Can't help you."

Wilson left another gap. "Mr Graffoe, do you want to take a few moments to reconsider your answers? I think you do know this woman. Like I said, this is part of a murder investigation. The sentences that can potentially be imposed for perverting the course of justice in this country are frankly draconian."

Graffoe laughed. "Fuck off, sonny."

"Also, using insulting language to a Garda office—"

"Yeah," said Graffoe standing up. "Good luck making that stick on a Tourette's sufferer. Membership has its privileges. Asshole! Asshole!" After he barked the last two words, Graffoe smiled. "I'm almost eighty with a prostate the size of your head and blood pressure that you normally only find in a fire hose. Don't try and intimidate me, sunshine..."

"I wasn't."

"Sure you were. You want to talk to me, my lawyer is Louie Dockery. I assume you know the name?"

Wilson did. Everybody in law enforcement did.

"Lucky for me, he's a big jazz fan. Word of advice, don't try and intimidate somebody my age with prison. The idea of being in a small room with a toilet beside the bed is frankly heavenly. Now off you pop."

Wilson and Dove walked up the alleyway in silence.

"Well," said Wilson, "that went well."

"Oh, I don't know," replied Dove. "While you were having your chat, I was enjoying the decor. Especially the picture of Simone Delamere that was in that collage above the bar.

"Right. Well, I guess we'd better go and give Mr Graffoe's barrister a call then."

CHAPTER THIRTY-TWO

Bunny took a nip from his hip flask and placed it back in his coat pocket. It was a cold night now; it felt like it might snow. He needed gloves. He'd had gloves. What had happened to his gloves?

Zayas sat on the garden wall outside the row of redbrick Georgian houses. "Out for a walk, Detective?"

"Ara shut up, ye dead prick."

Bunny looked at the garden path leading up to the steps. His foot was killing him now, and he leaned on his hurling stick for support. The walk here had been filled with memories. They had made it together many times, he and Simone. He had come here on a few occasions since Simone had left – or, rather, he'd been summoned. Sister Bernadette was not someone you said no to. It had been several years since the last time, though. They had not left things in the best of states. Still, they needed to know.

"Ah yes, Detective, coming to warn your co-conspirators. Very wise."

"Would you ever fuck off!" He said it with real venom and then turned at the exclamation from an elderly lady who had been walking one of those tiny little dogs down the pavement. "Oh God, sorry, I didn't mean to..."

She rushed by, pulling the dog away from Bunny as she went.

Zayas clicked his tongue in disapproval. "Drunk and disorderly. How unbecoming, Detective."

Bunny rubbed a hand across his face. Since the call from Noel, he had gone to the pub to find some peace. A few drinks to steady his nerves, give him time to think. The Gardaí had been in Charlie's, asking questions about Simone. Noel had said there'd been an FBI agent too. Said they'd been talking about murder. So he'd decided to walk out here, to the home of the Sisters of the Saint. It had seemed like a better idea at the time; he wasn't so sure about it now.

He steadied himself and took a deep breath. Sister Bernadette did not approve of drinking. Bernadette did not approve of many things.

He opened the gate and started to walk down the path. They'd put a load more flowers in since he had last been here. Repainted the door too. He rang the bell and waited.

"Are you going to ask them to hide you, Detective? They have a history of protecting murderers, after all."

"I'm getting royally fucking sick of you, y'know? Just piss off."

"You can't get rid of me, Detective, and you know why. Your own mind isn't on your side anymore."

"I wish you weren't dead. I'd fecking love to kill you again."

"Hello?" The voice came from behind the door. Female. Nervous.

"Howerya. I was looking for Bernadette, please."

"There is no one here of that name."

Bunny took a step back and looked around. He hadn't gone to the wrong house, had he? He looked in both directions. No, this was it. This was definitely it.

"Is Sister Assumpta there then?"

"No. I don't know that person either. It's just me. I mean, it's just me and my husband. He's here as well. You have the wrong address."

Bunny moved towards the peephole. "Look, it's OK. It's me. I'm Bunny McGarry. Ask the sisters. I'm OK. I've helped with a few things. I'm – I'm one of the good guys."

Bunny tried to ignore the sound of Zayas's laughter.

"Why've you got a weapon?"

Bunny held up the hurling stick. "It's not a... I just carry a hurley about. It's..."

"Look, go away, or I'm calling the guards."

"I am the..." Bunny stopped himself. He wasn't. Not any more.

"You sound drunk. Go home."

"No, look... You're one of the Sisters of the Saint. I know it's all..." Bunny put his fingers to his lips. "It's all hush-hush. That's fine. I get that."

Bunny turned at the sound of a throat being cleared behind him. An elderly man was standing there, eyeing him suspiciously. "Is there a problem here?"

"No," said Bunny. "No problem. I've just come to talk to the sisters. I'm not... I'm not..."

"A couple of old nuns used to live there, but they moved out about seven years ago." "But... sure, I was..." Bunny thought about it. Could it really have been that long? "D'ye know where they went?"

The man shook his head. "No. I think you'd best be off now, don't you?"

Bunny nodded, feeling embarrassed. "Right, yeah, sorry." He stopped and turned back towards the door. "Sorry about... Sorry."

The older man stood to the side and waved him down the path. Bunny limped away.

"Oh dear, Detective. Are you embarrassing yourself?"

"Feck off, ye..."

"What was that?" asked the man.

"Nothing," said Bunny. "Sorry. Merry Christmas."

"Yes. Goodbye."

Bunny limped off down the pavement, back towards town. Once he'd gone about a hundred yards, he dipped his hand into his pocket without conscious thought and withdrew the flask. It was nearly empty. He unscrewed it and, with a swift jerk of his head, knocked back the last of it. He grimaced as the whiskey burned through him. He belched and got a sting of heartburn.

Then he saw it again. The motorbike. He'd noticed it more and more over the last few days. It seemed like it was there every time he turned around. The rider would pretend not to be watching him, but he was always there.

Bunny started hurrying towards it. "Come 'ere, you."

The rider was holding his phone in his hand and looked like he was texting – or pretending to. He was parked outside a row of three shops just down the road, beside the traffic lights. This time, he was in a leather jacket and leather biker trousers or whatever you called them. Yesterday he'd been dressed as a courier.

Bunny stepped between the parked cars, jumping back as a vehicle swerved to avoid him as it headed down the Rathmines Road. There was a plaintive honk as the driver drove on.

Bunny looked both ways and then hurried across. He could see the biker looking at him now.

"Come 'ere, you. I want to talk to ye."

The biker put his phone into his jacket and placed his hands on the handlebars. Bunny was maybe thirty yards from him now. He tried to run towards him. A loose paving stone snagged at his foot and he stumbled forward, but managed to right himself without falling.

Then he looked up to see the rider kicking the bike into life.

"No! Wait!"

The bike was onto the road, speeding past him. Bunny tried to get in front of it, flag it down, but it went by too quick. The biker didn't even look in his direction.

Bunny stood on the road behind it, waving his hurley.

"Come back, ye fucker, come back. Face me!"

A horn honked loudly.

Bunny turned to see a shaven-headed man with his head out the window of his car. "Get out of the road, ye mad old bastard."

"Yeah, alright. Alright!"

Bunny moved aside. There were people looking at him now. A couple on the far side of the street. A man putting his bins out just down the road. And there. There she was. The woman.

He'd seen them all over the last few days. The tall man. The short man. The woman. They always looked different, of course. They'd have goatees sometimes, different coloured hair. She'd been pregnant once, after having a pram the day before. Now she had neither the bump nor the buggy. She was wrapped up in a thick brown winter coat and a bobble hat, but it was her. She was coming out of the takeaway on the corner. He hurried towards her.

"You. It's you."

She stopped to look at him and then started to hurry away.

"Wait. No. Who are you? Why don't you just talk to me? I know you know. I know you know."

CHAPTER THIRTY-THREE

"Wakey, wakey."

The first thing he noticed was the stale taste in his mouth.

The second thing was the pounding in his head.

The third thing was the smell. That was different.

The first two things were old friends, but the smell... It was a mixture of body odour, piss and disinfectant. That was the new part, the disinfectant.

He clenched his eyelids tightly closed against the harsh light.

"C'mon, get up ta fuck!"

A boot pushed against his back.

Bunny tried to turn his body, but the moulded plastic bench he was sleeping on wasn't exactly spacious. With a yelp, he fell the eighteen inches onto the lino floor. His coat, which had been bunched under his head for a pillow, fell on top of him.

"Good God, man, look at the state of ye."

Bunny pushed the coat off himself and opened his eyes to see a familiar figure leaning casually against the wall. He looked around and realised where he was. Oh dear.

Taighe Fitzgerald had been a desk sergeant at Pearse Street for as long as anyone could remember. So long, in fact, that it was quite possible he'd always been standing there and they'd simply built the station around him. It had been a few years since Bunny had seen him, and the time hadn't been that kind to Taighe. But then, seeing as Bunny was in a heap on the floor, he was in no position to judge. Taighe's black hair had thinned in some places and greyed in others, and his paunch had expanded. There were a few more lines around his eyes too. You'd have called them laughter lines if anyone had ever seen him laugh.

It had been a while since Bunny's last visit, but the holding cells hadn't changed much. Previously, if he had slept in one, it had always been with the door open. He had also, no matter how much he'd had to drink, remembered how he got there.

"Howerya, Taighe, good to see ye."

"I wish I could say the same."

"I love what you've done with the place."

"Oh yeah, we're all mod cons now. Wi-Fi access and lattes. It's like Starbucks."

"Thanks for having me."

"Get up off the floor, would ye?" There was an unmistakable look of disgust on Taighe's face as he said it.

With difficulty Bunny dragged his bulk back up onto the bench. He had to pull his trousers up too. His belt was gone. His shoes also sat in the corner, laceless.

Bunny rubbed his hands up and down his face, then scratched at his beard, trying to will himself back into some form of life.

"Sorry if I was any trouble."

"Trouble? Trouble, he says. Do you remember much of last night?"

Bunny stared at the linoleum floor for a few seconds. "I'm a bit vague on a few of the finer points."

"Well, let me fill you in. Two uniforms responded to a call of a mad man ranting and raving up on the Rathmines Road. Chasing after some poor terrified French tourist, here for a bit of Christmas shopping. Accusing her of following him. From what I hear, she was actively trying to get away from him."

Bunny tried to recall it, but no memories came back, save for a flash of a woman's terrified expression as she looked at him in horror.

"I can…"

"Then, when the two Gardaí tried to calm the man down, he assaulted them."

Bunny closed his eyes and leaned back, feeling the cool of the wall against his back. "Oh shite."

"Yes. A broken nose and a sprained wrist."

Bunny looked up at the ceiling and immediately regretted doing so. He was betting the cleaners hadn't looked up there in quite some time.

"Bunny, look at me."

Bunny turned his head back down and looked at Taighe.

"No bullshit. Are you OK?"

"I…" Bunny looked over at the metal toilet in the corner, considering how best to answer the question. "I'm going through a bit of a rough patch."

"Rough patch? They were all set to have you sectioned. They were looking for a doctor willing to take the call when someone recognised you and I got the shout. I told them to hold off." The volume of his voice dropped a notch. "I'm not sure that was the right thing."

Bunny looked back at him. "Honestly, I'll be OK. I just overindulged in a few Christmas drinks. Lost the run of myself."

"Are you sure you don't want to go somewhere for a few days? Rest up? There's no shame in it. I can have a word. Make sure you're taken care of. You know we mind our own."

"Honestly, I'll be fine. A shower and a bit of proper kip and I'll be right as rain."

"Anyone else did what you've just done, they'd be up on charges."

Bunny opened his mouth and closed it again. He lowered his eyes to the floor, the smell of sweat and shame coming off him filling his nostrils.

"As it happens, the broken nose belonged to John Doyle Junior, son of John Doyle, aka Ditty Doyle."

"Christ, I walloped Ditty's young fella?" The memory of a young kid sitting on his lap at a Christmas party many moons ago flashed into his mind. Bunny had been Santa Claus for the kids' parties for several years in a row. It had been great craic.

"You did," replied Taighe. "He's none too pleased with you, but nobody's going to press charges."

"Tell him I said sorry."

"Which one?"

"Both of them, I guess. Everyone."

Taighe placed a cardboard cup of tea down on the bench beside Bunny. "Who can I call to come get you?"

"No need," said Bunny, picking up the tea.

"There is." Taighe said it in such a firm voice that it stopped the tea on its way to Bunny's lips. "To be honest, Bunny, the way you were carrying on – it's touch and go me letting you walk out of here as it is. I'm not doing it unless you give me the name of someone who can come and pick you up."

"Gringo."

"What?"

"G..." The word died in Bunny's mouth.

Taighe leaned in and placed a hand on Bunny's shoulder. "Bunny, Gringo is gone. You know that, right?"

Bunny nodded quickly. "Course I do, don't be daft. I was only, y'know, messing."

"Right. Yeah." Taighe gave him a long, hard look.

Bunny gave him the only name and number he could think of and Taighe left him alone with a weak cup of tea and a strong sense of shame.

"Oh dear, Detective. This is a bad look for you."

Bunny closed his eyes and lowered his chin to his chest. "Oh, for... Could we not do this now?"

Zayas laughed. "Ah, don't you want to play anymore? You were so much more fun last night. And besides, this is excellent practice for you. Incarceration is undoubtedly in your future."

Bunny tried to hum to himself.

"They know who I am now, and they know about Simone. They were at Charlie's bar. It's just a matter of time before they find out about you."

"Just piss off."

"A few people know about your little gun, don't they? The murder weapon. Who did you show it to? All those nights drinking, you probably told a lot of people."

"You're not real." Bunny opened his eyes to see Zayas leaning against the wall, in the same spot Taighe had been.

"No, I'm not. I'm just your mind's way of telling you what you refuse to think about, Detective. Forget the gun. What did Gringo do with my wallet after he left you that night? That's the first big question, isn't it?"

Bunny hummed more loudly to himself. He hadn't realised it until now, but he was humming "Auld Lang Syne".

"That's not the really big question though, is it? No. That's not the one that scares you. In all of this, you've never really cared much about yourself. So noble in that way."

Should auld acquaintance be forgot?

"You know what they're after, don't you? Those shadows just out of reach. They're not coming for you, are they? They're coming for her. Maybe they think that if – ha, sorry, *when* – you get arrested, she'll come back. Explain what happened. Then she'll go to jail, or... Well, whatever was chasing her will find her, won't it? Eighteen years running and she gives herself up, to save you."

And never brought to mind...

"That's your thing, isn't it, Detective? Being that knight in shining armour. But you'll have failed. Failed utterly to protect her. Your one job. The one woman you ever truly loved."

We'll take a cup...

"Then there's the even worse option: they arrest you and she doesn't come back. You were just convenient. A useful idiot to protect her. She left you so easily back then, and it'll be just like she's doing it again, only worse. It'll be like it's happening every day. Every day in that cell, you will know, know for certain, that she never loved you. That will be your real punishment."

Of kindness yet...

"That's why you can't keep me out. Because to close me out is to close out that whole time. Getting rid of me means getting rid of her. And all she left you with is your sad little memory."

"Shut up, shut up, shut up, shut up!"

Bunny's right fist flailed out and punched the wall where the dead man stood. He felt the crack of bone as it thumped into the plaster.

He let out a yelp of pain.

"Are you alright in there?"

Bunny cupped his hand to his chest and tried to regain control of himself. "Yeah, I'm fine. Just stubbed my toe."

The mocking laughter cascaded around him.

CHAPTER THIRTY-FOUR

Paul felt like crap.

Last night, the boiler in his flat had packed in. After leaving several messages on the letting agency's emergency number, which nobody seemed to be picking up, he had put on a couple of layers of clothing and huddled up under his duvet.

That had lasted all of fifteen minutes before a German Shepherd, who didn't like the cold any more than he did, had dragged the duvet off the bed. After something that could be described as a negotiation-cum-fight, they had both slept under the duvet. Or rather, one of them had slept while the other spent the night dreading the next funky eruption from the other one's arse.

Paul had called the letting agent; they had been both insincere in their apologies and half-arsed in the assertion that something would be done about it as soon as possible. He had then popped in to see them in person, with Maggie in tow. They had suddenly become very sincere in their apology and entirely arsed about their desire to get the boiler fixed. Maggie may have been a massive pain, but she did have her uses.

When she had eventually come back from chasing off Kevin and Vincent Kelleher after their ill-judged attempt at flooding the van, she had proudly presented him with what looked a lot like the arse out of a pinstriped suit. He was guessing the Kellehers would be giving Maggie a wide berth from now on.

After their trip to the letting agents, Paul had intended to drop into Phelan's for a pint and to enjoy their heating. He and Maggie had been just outside the door when he'd received the text from Phil, saying he needed to see Paul at the office right away. Paul had texted back that he wasn't allowed in the office, but Phil had assured him that "the boss", as he annoyingly called Brigit, wasn't there. Phil had been very insistent, and Paul had the inkling that he might have had an idea. Phil's ideas were a lot like children: they could be wonderful or a nightmare, but regardless, you couldn't leave them on their own for very long, or bad things would happen. Despite the biting cold, and over Maggie's protestations, Paul had diverted to the offices of MCM Investigations.

As Paul reached the door, Mr Wilkes from the architect's office downstairs gave him a dirty look. The reason for this wasn't hard to figure out. The theme tune to *Titanic* appeared to be blaring from the upstairs windows. Paul gave him an apologetic shrug as he pushed through the door and headed up.

Phil Nellis was standing in the middle of the room, which looked as though a tornado had just passed through it. Furniture was turned upside down, filing cabinets were emptied out and all of the computer equipment was piled in the corner. In the centre of the room, the AI flipchart so beloved by Brigit stood on its easel.

"Jesus, Phil," said Paul, loudly enough so that he could be heard over Celine Dion warbling away. "What on earth are you up to?"

"Hello, Paul. Just doing a bit of spring-cleaning. Rocking out to some tunes. You know how I love my music."

Phil flipped over the first page to reveal a sheet on which he had scrawled, in big red pen, "PLAY ALONG. BOSS SAID TO SEND BACK SECURITY SYSTEM."

"Right. Yeah," said Paul. "Celine Dion is dreadful though."

The boxes that had contained the six-grand security system,

which Paul had to grudgingly admit may have been a mistake, were piled up in the opposite corner to the computers.

"I think Celine Dion is very underrated," continued Phil, before flipping to the next page.

"MAN SAID I COULDN'T SEND BACK IF NOT BROKEN – SO I WAS IN PROCESS OF BREAKING IT."

"I think she sounds like a goose being played like a set of bagpipes." Phil flipped the page again.

"BOSS SAID YOU WERE AN IDIOT FOR BUYING IT."

Paul rolled his eyes. Only Phil would take the time to write that out. He rolled his finger to indicate Phil could move this along.

"That is very unfair," said Phil, probably in defence of Celine.

Phil flipped the page again.

"ONE BOX HAD THIS IN IT."

Phil reached his hand back onto the desk and picked up a Dictaphone. Paul looked at it, then down at Maggie, before looking back at Phil and shrugging.

Phil looked at the Dictaphone and then rolled his eyes. He put it down and picked up something else, holding it out for Paul to see. It was a piece of kit only slightly bigger than a Dictaphone, but a tad more sophisticated. The name on the side told him it was a Federation RX46 Surveillance Detector. To be honest, Paul didn't actually remember buying it but, while he would never admit this, he had ordered the whole security system while a tad drunk.

"No!" said Paul, as the realisation hit. Then he tried to remember the last thing Phil had said in the fake conversation. "Bryan Adams is also from Canada."

"Yes," said Phil. "He is." As he spoke, he held the RX46 up to the light in the ceiling. Paul could see the bar of lights on the front stretch from green to red. Phil nodded his head. He then moved across the room and put it down beside a plug socket. Again the lights filled up.

"Canada is home to over fifty-five thousand species of insects," continued Phil.

Paul reached across for the marker and flipped onto the next page, which was blank. "WHY DID YOU NOT JUST TEXT ME THIS??"

Phil read it and took the pen out of Paul's hand.

"Ehm, that's a lot of insects," said Paul, because he had to say something.

"Yes. Yes it is."

Phil wrote under Paul's note: "GOOD POINT!"

Paul resisted the urge to wallop him. Instead, he grabbed the pen back and scrawled another note. "THERE COULD BE CAMERAS TOO?!!"

Phil looked around the room, as if seeing it for the first time, his mouth gawping open. He then pointed at the flipchart, where he had already written "GOOD POINT!"

"Right," said Paul. "I'm going around the corner for a bacon sandwich."

Maggie barked, the conversation having finally moved onto something that interested her.

"I should probably stay here. The boss wanted me to do some filing."

Paul clinched his fist and pointed at the door emphatically.

"But I can finish that later."

Celine Dion finished singing about her heart going on, and the song restarted again. Paul guessed Phil must have had it on a loop. From the floor below, Paul heard the previously mild-mannered Mr Wilkes hit breaking point. "TURN THAT SHITE OFF!!!"

CHAPTER THIRTY-FIVE

Bunny raised his face to the bright winter sun, low on the horizon, and took in a long, deep breath.

"Are you alright?" asked Paul.

"I'm grand, Paulie, thanks for coming to get me out. Sorry for the hassle."

"No problem. So where are you off to now?"

He looked around them and then locked onto Neary's pub opposite the station. "Pint?"

It had the same down-in-the-mouth decor that you could find in a hundred other places. It was a proper old fellas' pub, with a telly up in the corner for the football and the implication of cigarette smoke hanging in the air, even though the ban meant smoking indoors hadn't been a reality for years now. Two men in their seventies sat at opposite ends of the bar, both reading the same newspaper, in a race to see who could make it last longer.

Paul took his change and then walked back to the table, laying down his Heineken and Bunny's Guinness. Bunny was engrossed in watching a wind-up toy chicken jerkily walk its way across the table.

"What's that?" asked Paul.

"I found it in a box of cornflakes there a few weeks ago. I've had it in my pocket ever since. Keep meaning to give it to some kid but never managed to."

Bunny lowered his head down to table level to watch the chicken moving towards him. "Look at the determined look on the little fella's face though."

"OK."

Bunny sat back up. "Feel a bit sorry for him. He can't sense the inevitability of his fate." The wind-up chicken walked itself straight off the side of the table, snatched up by Bunny before it could fall to the ground. "Bit of a metaphor for life really, isn't it?"

"Well, you've managed to make that child's toy pretty depressing."

"Sorry," said Bunny, shoving the toy back into his coat pocket with an embarrassed smile before raising his pint glass with a slow reverence. "Cheers, Paulie. Down your leg."

Paul took a sip of his own drink and placed it down. He fidgeted nervously. "So, ehm, what happened last night then, Bunny?"

"Ah, it was nothing. I had a few too many is all."

"Right, course." Paul picked up a beer mat and started slowly twirling it around in his hands. "Only, that sergeant fella said you were, y'know..."

"No, I don't. What did he say?"

Paul rubbed his left hand around the back of his neck. "Well, just that you were a bit, ehm... well, 'unhinged' was the word he used."

Bunny shrugged. "Sure, you'd know better than anyone, Paulie, I was never the most hinged to begin with."

"Yeah, but..."

"How're things with you and Brigit?"

Paul took another sip of his pint, trying to catch up with the change of direction. "Well, y'know, it's complicated."

"Do ye love her?"

Paul nearly spilled his pint. "What? That's a bit of a personal question, Bunny."

"Do you love her?" he repeated.

"It's not that simple."

Bunny clamped his hand onto Paul's upper arm, his eyes filled with an intensity that Paul had never seen. "Listen to me now, ye cloth-eared gobshite. It is exactly that simple. Take it from one who knows, it's the only thing that matters. Everything else is just bullshit."

"Jesus, Bunny, calm down."

Bunny's grip on his arm tightened. "I'm telling you, sort yourself out. Stop being an idiot and talk to the girl. Life gives you very few chances and, believe you me, if you mess this one up, you'll spend the rest of your life regretting it."

"Relax, would ye? You're hurting me."

Bunny looked down at his hand and then immediately pulled it back, as if surprised to discover what it was up to. "Sorry, Paulie, sorry. It's been a bit of a long night."

Paul rubbed his arm. "Don't worry about it. Although, seeing as we're being brutally honest here – seriously, what the hell happened? Yer man said you lost the plot at some French woman."

Bunny picked up his pint with one hand and scratched at his beard with the other. "Ah, it's not... it's not what it sounds like. I think, maybe... somebody might have been following me."

"They probably were," said Paul. "It'll be the fecking Kelleher brothers, trying to get evidence of your... behaviour... for the case."

"It's not those eejits."

"Seriously, I bet it is."

"Is this the same Kellehers we're talking about? I remember them as kids. They come from the Clanavale Estate. It was one of my first beats in Dublin. I remember young Vinny getting his head caught in the railings outside the post office one time and they'd to call the fire brigade to get him out. When they turned up, Kevin has his head stuck in the railings too. Apparently, he was taking the piss out of his brother and got stuck as well. Those Kellehers?"

"They've grown up now, Bunny. That Kevin Kelleher is a devious prick. They were involved in that thing, y'know, when Brigit's arsehole of an ex took those pictures of me. They were the ones he hired to help him what that."

"That was them?"

Paul realised he had never filled Bunny in on this. Bringing Bunny into a situation was very much the nuclear option and, angry as he had been, he'd tried to avoid it.

"Yes. That's the reason for this ongoing thing between us."

"Ah, right. Brigit mentioned something. I've not really been paying much attention. D'ye want me to go and sort them out?"

Paul's face flushed. "Oh God, no – definitely don't do that, Bunny. Promise me."

"Alright, fair enough."

"I was just saying, they'll be trying to get evidence on you for this Harrison fella's case, so them following you would make sense."

Bunny finished taking a long swig of his pint and put it down. He looked around the bar and then lowered his voice. "I'm telling you, it's not them. The Kellehers wouldn't be smart enough."

"You say that, but Phil just discovered they're bugging our offices." "What?"

Paul nodded vigorously. "We've got this gizmo that checks for listening devices and that. Phil did a sweep and discovered the whole office is bugged."

"Seriously?"

Paul nodded again. "I'm just trying to figure out if we can use it against them."

"Hmmm. Yeah." Bunny looked over Paul's shoulder towards the frosted glass window.

"You alright?"

Bunny stood up suddenly. "I've to get a move on, Paulie. Thanks for your help with... y'know."

"Sit down and relax, would ye? You've only had half your pint."

Bunny shook his head. "No, I can't. I've to..." He took two steps towards the door and stopped, then turned back. He extended his right hand towards Paul in a handshake.

Paul took it with a look of confusion. He noticed the swelling on the middle knuckle. "What happened to your—"

Bunny placed his hand on Paul's shoulder and lowered his voice. "Paulie, I need you to promise me something."

"Alright."

"From here on out, whatever happens, I need you to stay away from me."

"What?! Don't be daft."

He squeezed Paul's shoulder.

"Please, promise me. Just know that, whatever happens, I did what I thought was right."

"You're scaring me now, Bunny."

"Don't worry about me. I need you to sort out this thing with the Kellehers, alright? Show 'em they've messed with the wrong company."

"Don't worry, Bunny, I'll handle it."

"Good man. I knew I could count on you." Bunny gave Paul a pat on the shoulder. "You take care of yourself, and remember what I said about that girl. Sort it out."

"Right. Yeah."

Before Paul could think of anything else to say, Bunny had disappeared through the door and into the mid-morning hustle and bustle.

CHAPTER THIRTY-SIX

Brigit took a sip of her water and placed the glass back down. She looked around, checked nobody was looking and gave her blouse a quick scan. Italian had been a brave choice for lunch. As far as she was concerned, it was an entire national cuisine designed with the explicit intention of causing droppages. She had a quick scan of her boobs. *No spaghetti, well done me.* She had maintained the air of glamorous aloofness she was going for.

She felt guilty, nervous and annoyed. The reason she was annoyed was that she had no reason to feel guilty or nervous.

She was just out to lunch with a friend. Lunch was lunch. People ate lunch all the time. Dinner was the meal of flirtation and seduction, everyone knew that. Lunch was the meal of the casual catch-up. You had to eat something during the middle of the workday anyway – you might as well do it with someone else. It was essentially multitasking. Breakfast – well, if you were eating breakfast with an adult member of the opposite sex, it was one of three things: you had a tremendously high-powered job where the breakfast meeting was a thing; you were in a long-term relationship with that person and your schedules happen to match up; or you'd just had sex with that person. Having sex and not having breakfast seemed somehow vaguely slutty. Shit! Brigit noticed that her date – no, definitely not date, lunch partner – had just come out of the gents and was heading back to their table. She needed to stop thinking about sexy breakfast. She also needed to stop feeling guilty. She was single. There was no reason she couldn't have lunch with a man. Again, lunch was only lunch and Anto Kelleher was just somebody she knew. Alright, he wouldn't get kicked out of sexy breakfast in bed for leaving crumbs but that didn't mean anything. Why on earth should she feel guilty about Paul? How long were you supposed to wait for a grown man to grow up?

Anto smiled at her. "Miss me?"

"That depends. Did you wash your hands? If not, I'm sending you back."

"I did."

"Then sit down."

He did and he gave her a smile.

"You smile a lot. I don't trust it."

"Sorry, can't I just be happy?"

She picked up her glass of water. "You're unemployed. You shouldn't be that happy about anything."

"Oh, I dunno. I'm thinking of becoming a tramp – like one of the good ones. You know, the ones with the tied hanky on a stick who go around whistling."

"Well, you've got the beard for it."

"Thanks. They always look so happy though, don't they?"

"That's because they don't exist. You only ever see them on telly. You try wandering about Dublin whistling a happy tune at near freezing, you'll quickly lose your hanky."

Anto picked up his glass of water. "Ahhh, why've you got to go and step on my dreams? You heartless cow!"

He said it with a twinkle in his eye. He was very good at the twinkle.

Brigit cleared her throat and leaned forward slightly. "What are you going to do for work now?"

"I was thinking gigolo."

"Is that one of those Italian string instruments?"

"No, it's..." Anto stopped when he saw Brigit's grin. "Oh, ha ha! Actually, I was just talking to a buddy of mine out in Clontarf. He's got a painting business. Might be looking for somebody."

"Would you be happy doing that?"

Anto shrugged. "Anything is better than working with my brothers. I couldn't take another minute of that. Kevin has taken to leaving me threatening voicemails."

"Really? Are you worried?"

Anto shrugged again. He wasn't half bad at the shrugging either. "Ah, not really. It's not like I was any good at the private detective business, and I'd no interest in any of their dodgier activities." Anto leaned in closer. "Actually... I wanted to talk to you about that. I've been thinking. Kevin has a safe in his apartment. I know because I was there when he got it installed. He keeps certain files there. I think it's where all the stuff about their dodgier clients is kept."

"What are you suggesting?"

Anto glanced around. "I'm just saying, they're not playing fair, so why should you? It'd be the simplest way to get them off your back."

"So, what? I break in and steal it?"

"No." He gave her a cheeky smile. "I'm saying we break in and steal it. You get rid of my brothers and I get a little revenge. What's not to like?"

Brigit shook her head. "I'm not a criminal."

"No," said Anto, "but they are. When in Rome."

Brigit gave him an appraising look and then decided to throw him a curveball. "So, what are your plans for Christmas?"

He shrugged again and picked up his water glass. "I don't know. Can't go home for it, so... not much. What about you?"

"I'll be back to Leitrim but possibly not until the morning of."

Usually, she would have been home for longer, especially in the last couple of years. Since her mum was gone, Brigit hated the idea of her dad being alone at this time of year. Then, earlier this year, something truly unexpected had happened. The widower Conroy had found himself a lady friend. Her name was Deirdre; she was from a town a few miles away and a widow herself. Brigit had gradually noticed how more and more of Deirdre's stuff seemed to be in their house now. Brigit was happy, because her dad seemed happy and that was all that counted. Still, although she would never admit as much, it felt weird – another woman being there in Ma's place. They had never discussed it; her dad just wasn't set up for the big emotional explanation. It wasn't in the DNA of the Irish male of his generation. All that mattered was that he was happy. And Brigit would still be there for the dinner and a couple of nights after.

Through all of this, with MCM Investigations crumbling around her ears, it had dawned on Brigit that now Dad was fine and looked after, there was precious little holding her here. Maybe she could finally head off and see the world? Get a fresh start.

Anto cupped his hands around his mouth. "Earth to Conroy."

Brigit came back from staring at the future. "Sorry, I was miles away."

"I was just saying – how's about you come over to mine on Christmas Eve then and I'll cook you dinner?"

"Sure."

Brigit gave Anto a wave and headed up the stairs towards the office. As he'd walked her back, he'd mentioned his brother Kevin's safe again, but Brigit had moved the conversation on. Breaking and entering in order to get evidence against the man trying to bring them down felt like crossing a line.

Speaking of crossing lines, she had agreed to dinner – the meal of seduction – and not just any dinner either, dinner at his place, where presumably there would be a bed. Not that its use was on the cards, but it would be there.

She opened the door of the office to find Phil standing in reception, his hands on his hips, looking at her like a disapproving maiden aunt. Behind him stood her flipchart.

"What are you up to?" asked Brigit.

"What am I up to? What am *I* up to? What are *you* up to?"

Despite herself, Brigit blushed. "Mind your own business, Phil."

"Do you know who he is?"

"Yes. He's Anto Kelleher."

Much to Brigit's confusion, Phil looked horrified. "He is?"

"What's it to you, Phil? He doesn't work with his brother anymore. He's on our side now. Have you ever even met him?"

"No, but I recognise him."

"Look, I'm not talking about this. It's none of your business."

Phil looked around furtively. "Alright, yeah. Fair enough. But there's something else."

"What now?"

Phil leaned across and pressed a button on his keyboard. The unmistakable opening bars of the theme tune to *Titanic* started up.

He stood beside the flip chart and said in a deliberate voice, "Have I ever told you how much I enjoy the music of Celine Dion?"

Before she could respond, they were interrupted by a broom handle thumping against the ceiling downstairs. "Seriously, turn that shit off!!!"

Phil turned over the first sheet on the flipchart.

CHAPTER THIRTY-SEVEN

DSI Burns looked up from the report she was reading as there was a knock on her office door.

"Come in."

The door opened and Wilson leaned in. "You wanted to see us, boss?"

"Oh yes, come on in. Take a seat."

Wilson came in, with Agent Alana Dove following in his wake.

"Before I forget, Wilson, seeing as you've got that university education we're all so proud of, can I ask you to do me a favour?"

"Of course, boss."

"Could you explain to Detective Gilsenan the difference between the words 'rouse' and 'arouse'. It's only one letter but it really is crucial." She held up the document she had been reading. "He's inadvertently made his report on that assault in Maynooth into soft porn. I'd explain it to him myself, only, technically, that'd be an inappropriate conversation in the workplace."

"Yes, boss."

Burns looked over at Agent Dove. She was wearing the same disconcerting smile as always. No matter how many times Burns found herself in a room with her, it didn't become any less unsettling.

She would probably be an excellent interrogator, assuming she didn't induce a heart attack, of course.

"Speaking of a bit of word play. Agent Dove, are you familiar with the phrase deus ex machina?"

Dove shook her head. "No."

Wilson leaned forward. "It is a phrase taken from the Greeks. Attributed to Aristotle, it denotes…" Wilson stopped when he noticed the look on his boss's face. "Oh, sorry, chief. You meant that as more of a sort of a rhetorical thing, didn't you?"

"What does mansplaining mean, Wilson?"

"It means I'm going to shut up and only speak when spoken to, chief."

"That sounds like a very good idea." Burns returned her gaze to Agent Dove. "So, where was I? Oh yes, deus ex machina. As Aristotle here was about to point out, it means a solution appearing out of nowhere to resolve a problem. You know the sort of thing: Superman flies around the world so fast that he manages to turn back time. Doctor Who realises his sonic screwdriver has another setting he forgot about. A squad of marines just show up out of nowhere. You get the idea."

Dove nodded. She was good. She knew enough to let somebody get where they were going. Wilson could learn a lot.

"Or, say, if you're investigating an eighteen-year-old murder case and then suddenly, magically, out of nowhere…" Burns opened her drawer and pulled out the evidence bag contained within. "The victim's wallet turns up in the post."

She had received it that morning. Sergeant Moira Clarke was tasked with opening the NBCI's post. While it seemed like a job beneath her rank, it never ceased to amaze how much potentially useful stuff there could be in the mountain of crap. Amidst all the death threats, random abuse and letters from nutters claiming their cat was stealing from them, there would be the occasional badly spelled account of what really happened in some murder. A lot of your hardcore criminals wouldn't be seen dead talking to the Gardaí, but they'd be more than happy to anonymously rat out a rival or colleague in a letter. Often the spelling and penmanship were appalling, but then, a lot of the criminal fraternity hadn't paid that much attention in school. The last letter they'd written had probably been to Santa.

Burns placed the bag on the desk. It contained a brown leather wallet that was remarkably well preserved for its age.

"Said wallet contained six hundred and forty quid in old Irish punts, two hundred dollars and four credit cards in three different names, which is rather interesting in itself, don't you think?"

Dove finally spoke. "Yes, yes it is."

Burns pulled a piece of paper from her drawer, written in the meticulous hand of Moira Clarke, who had documented the wallet's contents, being careful not to interfere with any forensic evidence.

"There was also a card for a plumber in New York, a picture of a woman wearing frankly not enough clothing, three receipts and a membership card to the 'Golden Triangle' gentleman's club, which I'm guessing isn't filled with many true gentlemen. It also contained a small key – oh, and three condoms, flavours multiple, ribbed for her pleasure. Thoughts?"

"That is unexpected."

"Yes," agreed Burns, "it most certainly is. Oh, I forgot one thing."

Burns picked up the other evidence bag from her drawer and held it up in front of Agent Dove. "To confirm, does that appear to be Agent Zayas's FBI ID?"

Agent Dove leaned forward and stared at the card. "It certainly seems to be. If you like, I can get it and the wallet overnighted to our lab in—"

"No, thank you. It's evidence in an Irish murder enquiry. It'll be staying here."

"But with all due respect, our lab has some of the most sophisticated techniques in the world."

Burns put both of the evidence bags back into her drawer. "I'm sure. Well, while our labs consist of two lads with a bottle of talcum powder and a magnifying glass, they're still getting first crack."

"I didn't mean to imply..."

"Yes," said Burns. "I'm sure. I think we're missing the bigger picture though, don't you? Do you know in my twenty-one years in the Gardaí how many times a perfectly preserved piece of evidence – in an evidence bag – has turned up in the post?"

"I can't imagine…"

"None. Zero. Zilch. It has never happened. And in that time I've received several anonymous confessions, a couple of non-anonymous confessions and not one but three pictures of a gentleman's special little friend. One of which, by the way, we successfully IDed as part of an investigation. My point is, seeing as this investigation has taken yet another unusual turn, I'd like to revisit our earlier conversation. Have you told me everything I need to know regarding this case?"

"Absolutely."

"No offence, Agent Dove, but I don't believe a word that comes out of your mouth."

"I'm sorry to hear that, Detective Superintendent. I have nothing but the highest respect for you."

Burns gave Dove a stern look. If she was attempting to take the piss, she had an impeccable poker face.

"OK."

"In the unlikely event that your lab doesn't come up with anything from the wallet…"

"Then yes, we will discuss other options. However, I've got a sneaking suspicion that we will get a result. Somebody has gone to what appears to be a great deal of trouble to preserve this wallet for eighteen years. Assuming it isn't from some serial killer who's living with his mammy with an attic full of skulls, the sender is either taunting us or trying to point us in somebody's direction. I'm not wild about any of those options. Could you give me a moment to speak with my detective, please?"

Dove nodded. "Of course."

Burns stood and watched Dove through her office window as she walked back across the office to the desk opposite Wilson's.

"I wouldn't trust her as far as I could throw her."

"Yes, boss."

"Has she done anything unusual?"

Burns watched as Wilson shifted nervously in his seat. "I mean, not as such, no boss."

"What does that mean?"

"It's just, well... she's weird, isn't she? I mean with the arm, and the face not really moving thing. Everything the woman does is a bit weird."

Burns looked down at Wilson and then opened the drawer and took the two evidence bags out. "I want you to take this over to Doakes at the Technical Bureau, alone. Tell him it's from me and I want it treated as highly sensitive. Explain what's going on and that I would like this ASAP, and I really do mean ASAP."

"Yes, boss."

"And he only talks to you or to me. Nobody else."

"Yes, boss."

"We are going to give this gift horse a long, hard look in the mouth – and then we're going to look up its arse too, because I neither like nor trust this."

"Yes, boss."

CHAPTER THIRTY-EIGHT

In his dream, Paul was standing on a cliff side looking down at the waves as they crashed against the rocks. The wind fired raindrops like tiny bullets into his face.

Bunny sat beside him on a deckchair. He was wearing a one-piece swimming costume and sipping a pink cocktail with an umbrella in it.

"Ye should've talked to the girl."

The wind whipped viciously around Paul. As he looked down, he noticed he was naked. Of course he was.

"I did," shouted Paul.

"My hole ye did. Not really. It's easier to fight someone you hate than say something to someone you love."

Paul knew he was in a dream. Paul almost always knew, every time he dreamed, that he was dreaming. Unfortunately, it never meant he could control the dream or force himself to wake up from it.

"It's not like that."

"It's exactly like that."

The ground started to give way beneath his feet.

"You've been too busy thinking only of yourself," shouted Bunny, as the wind howled. "What about her? And me? And that Nellis eejit, come to think of it?"

"I'm just... I was..."

"Yeah – doing everything by yourself. You don't need anyone."

The mud sucked at his feet as the cliff began crumbling into the sea. Paul tried to grab at the ground behind him, but his fingers couldn't gain purchase. As the ground tumbled away, the waves and the rocks rushed up to meet him.

The last thought in his head was how foul the sea breeze smelled.

Then he awoke, in a different kind of nightmare. Beside him in the bed lay Maggie, her foul breath wafting into his face.

"Oh Jesus," said Paul, sitting up with a start. "What have we discussed? No dogs in the bed."

Maggie gave a low growl. She had agreed to no such thing.

"You are, you are..." Paul looked at the bedside clock: 1:12 am. He was having a hard time forming a sentence. Somewhere in the background, there was a pinging noise. "Seriously, get out of my bed." Paul stood up, and then tugged at the duvet. Maggie stayed resolutely on the bed. "That's it, no more drink for you after 6 pm. It makes you feisty."

She barked. In the background, there was another pinging noise.

"What the hell is that?"

It wasn't the notification noise for a text message, and his laptop was set up to give a Homer Simpson belch when an e-mail arrived.

Ping. There it was again.

Various parts of Paul's brain were gradually beginning to wake up. The part that held extremely important facts sprang into life, somewhere between the bit that wanted to go back to sleep and the bit that wanted to take a pee. It alerted him to what website he had left open before going to bed.

Paul rushed from the bedroom, or at least tried to. What he actually did was walk two steps and then wallop his left big toe into the side of the bed at an agonising velocity.

Two minutes and a considerable amount of high-grade and ultra-sincere swearing later, he hobbled to the laptop on the sofa. He tapped the space bar and the screen came alive. The messages appeared in a chat box in the right hand corner of the screen.

"Hello sexy."

"Great to hear from you."

"You look like just my type!"

Yes! thought Paul. It was past 1 am and he'd finally got a man horny.

Two days ago, a thought had struck him. For most of the previous week, he had been going over the same questions in his head. How on earth were they going to prove that Jacob Harrison, the scuzzy, philandering piece of crap who Bunny had dangled off a balcony, had not lost his ability to be a scuzzy, philandering piece of crap? That's what this lawsuit came down to, after all. They had to prove that Harrison hadn't been left permanently psychologically scarred, unable to get his end away – not to mention his supposed fear of water and heights. The problem was, Harrison and the Kellehers would have to be complete morons not to realise that Paul and Co. were looking for just such a way to catch Harrison out. It was like trying to rob a bank in broad daylight when they knew you were coming.

That was when Paul had had his big idea.

After a bit of digging around, he had found a way to contact Samantha Parkes, the woman with whom Harrison had been having an affair. She had been initially very frosty – until she had realised that Paul's interest was primarily in causing Harrison pain. Then she had warmed up considerably. It was her who introduced Paul to the Beautiful Unicorn dating site. Its tagline was "Where the elite come out to play" – although from a quick scan, it seemed fairly clear that "Horny horses sow their wild oats" would've worked equally well. You could put up pictures of yourself or have an "incognito" profile – the trick being that the incognito ones cost fifty euros a month, while the ones with pics were free. But first you had to make it past the "gatekeepers of gorgeous". That's right, they only let the best-looking people in. He assumed they went with the name "Beautiful Unicorn" because "Third Reich Singles" was already taken. Every time he looked at the website, Paul felt like he needed a shower.

Still, he had been accepted in an hour. Or rather, "Rebecca" had. To be accepted in this age of so many Photoshop fakers, you had to submit a ten-second video of yourself saying hi while holding up a recent newspaper. For this, Paul had called in a rather big favour. Rebecca was real alright, in the sense that she was Tina, the niece of Jacinta, the landlady of Phelan's pub. Seeing as she was studying acting, Paul had managed to pitch the whole idea as an acting job of sorts. And a paid one at that. He had then had a very careful conversation with Jacinta about exactly what her niece would be helping him with. It was made exceedingly clear to him that, should he upset her in any way, Paul's body would never be found. While this wasn't ideal, he had limited options when it came to hot women in their twenties who would do him a favour.

So Rebecca had been born – and accepted into Beautiful Unicorn about an hour later. Paul had then spent a couple of days receiving e-mails from men that, frankly, made him want to become a lesbian.

You could send out winks, but Rebecca had been very selective. She had sent out only one.

It was 1:12am and Cyrano deCaddyshack, the incognito profile that Paul knew belonged to Jacob Harrison, had messaged him back. Harrison must have not have been able to sleep. He had checked in on Beautiful Unicorn and, lo and behold, he seemed keen on the lovely Rebecca. No doubt flattered by her wink.

Now the fish was on the hook, Paul had to slowly reel him in – using all of his feminine wiles.

CHAPTER THIRTY-NINE

DSI Susan Burns prised open a couple of the slats on the Venetian blinds in her office and looked out. "They say it might snow later on."

"Yes, so I hear," said Dr Denise Devane, who was sitting on the opposite side of her desk. "That will no doubt cause chaos on the roads."

Burns turned away from the window and pulled out her own chair. "Have you got far to go this evening?"

"No. I'm staying in Dublin. I'm on call."

Burns raised an eyebrow. "Really? I thought seniority would get you out of that."

Devane shrugged. "All of the others have young families, so…"

"Right, yeah." Burns felt suddenly awkward. Devane wasn't known for being terribly forthcoming and it was starting to feel like they had strayed into uncomfortable territory. "I'm supposed to be heading out to Maynooth. My brother and his wife have this Christmas Eve party every year. For reasons beyond my understanding, I've had to go out and buy a deliberately awful Christmas jumper. The roads will no doubt be a nightmare, between snow and idiots trying to set the land-speed record to get home for last orders."

"Yes. Do be careful, Superintendent."

It was the kind of thing everyone said in conversation, but when the person saying it was the primary point of contact for road fatalities in the country, it did send a shiver down the spine. You could see how Dr Devane didn't get invited to many children's birthday parties.

"So," said Burns, turning to the pad in front of her. "How are we set prior to the holiday shutdown?"

"Well, the autopsy has been completed on that Finglas shooting, as requested."

"Yes, I saw that. Thank you."

"The thing in Galway will be done for the twenty-ninth."

Burns nodded. "That's fine. I got an update from the local team this morning. They think that could be wrapped up today anyway. The alibi has holes you could drive Santa's sleigh through."

Devane nodded. "As for your bodies in the mountains, the records the FBI sent us seem to confirm it is indeed Agent Zayas. We've still had absolutely no luck identifying the other one, I'm afraid. We sent the shot to my associate at NABIS, the specialist ballistics lab in the UK, and they confirmed that it is consistent with a derringer, of an older design."

"Right. I don't suppose it is possible to narrow it down any more than that, is it?"

Devane shook her head. "From what they've said, it is essentially an antique. Most of what are known as derringers haven't actually been made by a specific company. The name essentially denotes a type of gun that in the late nineteenth century any gunsmith with a bit of knowhow was making. They're all individual pieces."

"Great."

"Well, on the upside, if you do acquire a potential murder weapon, they'd have a good chance of matching it up, despite all of the time that has passed, because the weapons are so individual. Of course, I'm sure the chance of you getting hold of a murder weapon so long after the fact would no doubt be slim."

Burns twirled a biro in her fingers. "Oh, you'd be surprised. The victim's wallet just appeared out of nowhere yesterday."

"Really?"

"Yes."

"It wasn't buried in the plot. My team dug eight feet to either side in line with procedure."

"No, nothing like that. I got it in the post. It came in an evidence bag, in pristine condition."

Devane looked confused.

"Exactly," said Burns. "In all your years, have you ever known evidence to fall from the sky like that?"

"It does seem a tad suspicious."

"To say the least. I don't like—"

The phone on Burns's desk started to ring. She recognised the number. It was the Technical Bureau.

"Speak of the Devil. Let's see what Doakes has come up with." He was the best of the techs, so much so that his boss, DSI O'Brien, had brought up repeatedly how Burns should not request him in preference to other staff. She always agreed, but did it anyway.

She picked up the phone. "DSI Burns."

Devane gestured towards the door to ask if she should leave, but Burns shook her head.

"Susan, it's Mark O'Brien here."

"Oh, hello, Mark." Crap. Looked like she was in for another earful for playing favourites.

"Is this some kind of a joke?" He sounded really pissed.

"Sorry, I know I shouldn't put things directly to Doakes but—"

"What? No, I mean that's correct, you should not, but that isn't why I'm ringing. Is this your idea of, I don't know, some kind of a Christmas wind-up?"

"Mark, I honestly have no idea what you are talking about."

"Because if it is, I think it is in very poor taste. Never mind the waste of resources, there's also the—"

Burns cut him off. "Mark. Could you explain what you're actually angry about? Believe me, if anyone from my team has been wasting your teams' time, rest assured, I will deal with it severely."

When he spoke again, O'Brien at least sounded mollified. "This wallet we received yesterday?"

"Yes."

"Well, it does have prints. Between the plastic pane and a few of the cards, we have been able to recover one full and two partial sets of prints."

"OK," said Burns, waiting for the other shoe to drop.

"The full set matches the prints for Agent Daniel Zayas that the FBI sent us. The other two appear in our elimination file."

Burns started to get a sinking feeling in her stomach. "I'm getting a weird sense of déjà vu here."

"Yes," said O'Brien, "As am I. If this is someone's idea of a joke, can I remind you how long we spent giving evidence for the enquiry into—"

"Mark, just tell me what you found."

The edge in her voice stopped him dead.

"Very well. One set of partials matched up to DS Tim Spain, who died in 1999."

"Right."

"And the other set belong to his then partner, retired Detective Sergeant Bernard 'Bunny' McGarry."

"You are shitting me. Bunny McGarry?"

Burns looked across the table at the shocked face of Dr Denise Devane.

It wasn't much more than a year ago that McGarry's fingerprint had been found on a note in the pocket of a murder victim. He had briefly been public enemy number one, until, much to the Garda Síochána's embarrassment, it had emerged that he was being set up and had in fact been kidnapped and kept captive for ten days.

Two minutes later, after a rather terse phone call wherein each side assured the other that this wasn't some sick joke, Burns slammed the phone down.

She closed her eyes and rubbed her fingers into her temples. She could feel the mother of all migraines coming on.

"Merry fucking Christmas."

Devane flinched as Burns let out a roar.

"Moira, get me Wilson, now!"

CHAPTER FORTY

Bunny sat down heavily on the bench. A white and brown pigeon, uniquely coloured amongst its primarily black and blue brethren, strode purposefully towards him and gave an inquiring look.

"I've nothing for ye."

This earned Bunny a side-eyed glower.

He opened the carrier bag. "Well, unless you fancy half a stale baguette?"

The pigeons swarmed before he'd even ripped off the first chunk. While it was always nice to be popular, it helped to be the only game in town. St Stephen's Green was always thronged in the summer, but on a Christmas Eve barely above freezing, anyone that was there was only using it as the shortest distance between two points. Well, apart from the mad old one who was dancing around to no music on the far side of the park. She was doing it for no audience but God, which was just as well, because passers-by were pointedly ignoring her and all the pigeons were entirely focused on Bunny. He tossed out the last few chunks of bread and showed them his empty hands, like a blackjack dealer leaving the table.

"What is it with pigeons and stale bread? They're mad for it. Them and the French. Of all I've seen in this world, nothing confuses me more than the feckin' crouton. It's a square of stale bread. Feckin' lunatics."

He glanced to his left. Simone was sitting on the bench beside him, as he knew she would be. A great plus of feeding the pigeons was that talking to them was one of the few socially acceptable ways of talking to yourself.

He leaned back on the bench. "D'ye remember that day we walked through here, arm in arm under an umbrella while it bucketed down with rain? Everyone else rushing by, us the only two people strolling."

She said nothing.

"You said how you wanted to see it in the sun. We never did get our sunny day, did we?"

He leaned forward and rubbed his hands together. "D'ye know what pisses me off? After all these years, I never hear your voice. Even now, with all this. Zayas never shuts up, Gringo yaps away, yet your voice isn't up here." He tapped his finger against his temple. "And I don't know why. Eighteen years now. Eighteen years. I can't forget your face but for some damn reason I can't hear your voice. Where's the justice in that?"

He watched as a woman with long brown hair walked her poodle over the bridge. He recognised her gait. It was the same woman who'd had the pram, who'd been pregnant, who'd been French. Part of his mind was sure of it. Other parts of his mind didn't want to engage with how that sounded. How did they get the dogs? The different hair and stuff, he got that, but how did they always have so many different dogs to walk? She didn't look directly at him; they never did. They were very good at this, whoever they were.

Bunny looked down again at the pigeons, now in three clusters around the main chunks of bread, with the odd small one trying to catch crumbs on the fringes. He watched as they ripped through it. "Have ye ever really looked at pigeons? I mean close up? Everyone thinks they're these harmless things, but look at 'em go, ripping into that. All I'm saying is, if they were six feet tall instead of six inches, people would be running away screaming, in fear of their lives."

The phone in Bunny's pocket vibrated. He took it out and looked at the number, then pressed the button to send it to voicemail. "Brigit – again. Herself and Paulie are trying to get hold of me all the time. Keep leaving voicemails pretending they're not worried about me. I need to keep this away from them, whatever happens."

He put his hand into the inside pocket of his sheepskin coat and pulled out his wallet. At the back, in its own little pocket, was the note. Her note.

My dearest Bunny,

This is the hardest letter I have ever had to write. I'm so sorry about Tim. I know you will have done everything in your power to try and save him, just as you did for me. Please don't beat yourself up about it. You can't save everybody, but I do so love that you try.

I have tried and tried to think of a way around it, but the reality is that my past is always going to keep coming after me. I'm sorry I dragged you into it, and I can't in all good conscience continue to do that. With every fiber of my being, I'd love to stay with you here for the rest of my days, but it wouldn't be fair. You're a good man and you deserve better than this.

Please don't try and find me. I hope you get what you truly deserve in this life. Thank you for giving me the happiest time in mine, at a time when I thought I could never be truly happy again.

I love you,
Your Simone

He looked over at Simone and saw those eyes that made his heart ache. He looked away again, rubbing a finger into his own eye as the cold wind tugged at his coat. "D'ye know what? D'ye know what hurts the most? If you'd asked, I'd have gone with you. Y'know? I'd have gone anywhere with you. You could've just... But instead, I got a note." He folded it carefully and put it back in his wallet. "It doesn't matter now, I suppose. Water under the bridge."

He watched in silence for a minute as the pigeons squabbled over the last of the bread. Once it had gone, they slowly began to disperse, still keeping a wary eye on him in case he was holding out on them.

"I keep going over it in my head. I could run, but I'm too old to start over. I could try and get ahead of it, but I wouldn't even know where to start." He raised his voice into a mocking lilt. "Oh yeah, them bodies, Your Honour, I killed them alright, but I'd good reasons. No, can't really say more than that, you'll just have to take my word on it. Scout's honour, dib, dib, dib."

He kicked his left foot out at a stone lying in front of the bench, sending it skittering across the path and earning him an admonishing look from one of the pigeons.

He looked around him again. The woman with the poodle was walking back the other way now.

"Besides, it's not just the law, is it? Either I'm losing my mind or there's something else going on here." He nodded his head towards the woman with the dog. "They're not after me. They're after you."

Bunny was distracted from the dog walker by a large black crow landing on the opposite side of the path. It tilted its head and gave him an appraising look.

Bunny was suddenly possessed of the urge to try and hold Simone, the woman who wasn't really sitting beside him. He knew it was stupid. He was aware it would be crossing another line, allowing his mind to fracture that incremental inch further. He had to hold on to what was real for as long as he could.

"I want you to know, whatever happens, I don't blame you. What happened in New York wasn't your fault. You got forced into doing something you didn't want to in order to save somebody else. You didn't know that sleazy ex of yours would make a tape, and you did what you had to. You had to defend yourself from those monsters when they came for you. I don't blame you for running, I... I just wish you'd have let me come with you."

He watched the dog walker striding purposefully away, dog by her side, bag of shite held at arm's length, swaying back and forth. "I keep thinking of this old Peter O'Toole film I saw years ago, *The Lion in Winter*, I think it's called. He's the King of England in it – one of the

Henrys, I forget which one. There's loads of them bastards. Anyway, speaking of bastards, he's got all these sons because he's been sowing the royal oats. Proper randy bollocks. He needs to get shot of them so he can marry this French bird and have new sons and heirs. So, the existing sons, they're all locked in prison and Henry is coming to kill them. They know he's coming. One of them says, 'Don't let him see you cry. Stiff upper lip and that.' Then the other says, 'You fool! How does it matter how a man falls?' And the other fella says, 'When all that's left is the fall, the fall is everything.'" Bunny looked up at the heavy clouds hanging ominously overhead. "When all that's left is the fall, the fall is everything."

Bunny felt his phone vibrate in his pocket again. He took it out, about to send it to voicemail, when he stopped and looked at the number. It was a local Dublin number he didn't know. He'd received a lot of calls in the last week, but it'd either been Brigit, Paulie or that lawyer woman, Nora, who was leaving increasingly annoyed-sounding messages. This wasn't any of them. He answered it.

"Hello?"

"Hello. Hi, Bernard, ehm... Bunny. It's, ehm, Denise, Denise Devane here."

"Howerya, Doc, is everything OK? You sound a bit stressed out."

"Yes, sorry. I'm... I'd sort of assumed in my head I'd get your voicemail. I'd not really thought through what I was going to say."

"Are you alright? Do you need a hand with something?"

"No, I... Not this time. Thank you again for..."

He could feel her struggling for words. Most people who had worked with Dr Denise Devane would be surprised to hear her like this. She was always so assured.

"Look, Doc, don't be worrying about that. Long time ago now. You've nothing to be thanking me for. Happy to help. Merry Christmas."

"Right. Yes. Well... I want to help you, Bernard because... Sorry, this is hard for me. I'm making rather a mess of it. I had to walk all the way to Capel Street to find a phone box. You wouldn't believe how hard they are to find these days."

"I can imagine."

"You need to watch out. You are in trouble. They... I mean, when the bodies came in, when it was determined that a derringer..."

"Ah right. You've seen mine, of course. Right."

"I didn't... say anything. It could have been anyone's. Lots of them about. Well, enough to be..."

"Sure."

"There's something else."

"Don't, Doc. Don't say anything. I know what the job means to you. You're about to cross a line and I don't want to put that on you."

"But Bernard – Bunny – you need to know."

"I'll tell you what, how about you tell me nothing? How about I guess, and if I'm right, you just hang up the phone? OK?"

Silence for a couple of seconds. "Alright."

Bunny took a deep breath. "A wallet has turned up..."

Silence.

He scratched at his beard. "And my fingerprints are on it."

He listened to a couple of breaths, as if she wanted to say something – then the line went dead.

He held the phone in his hand and looked at the screen.

"When all that's left is the fall, the fall is everything."

CHAPTER FORTY-ONE

"There's no need to be nervous," said Paul.

The three of them were standing awkwardly in the back of the ice cream van-cum-mobile surveillance unit of MCM Investigations. The three of them being Paul, Phil and Tina Phelan. Tina looked at Paul.

"I'm not bleedin' nervous. You're bleedin' nervous. You'd want to calm the fuck down. And what the fuck is that smell?"

Tina was twenty-five, five-foot-six and had the kind of look you could easily see in a Hollywood film pretending to be improbably attracted to pensioner Tom Cruise. She was drop-dead gorgeous. She had the face of an angel, the physique of an athlete and the mouth of an offshore oil rig worker. Being trapped in close proximity with her would make any hot-blooded male nervous. Her being the niece of Jacinta Phelan, landlady of Phelan's pub, would make any sensible male's blood run cold again.

Tina's outfit consisted of high heels, a tight pair of leather trousers, a red leather jacket and a cream blouse. It was, in short, designed to be very distracting. The fact that it wasn't distracting Paul in the least was an indication of just how nervous he was.

"That smell," said Paul, "is damp. This van was flooded a few days ago." They had only just finished drying it out, or at least getting it as dry as it was going to get.

"Well it's absolutely fecking manky. Smells like somebody shat the bed. And what is the deal with your dog?"

Maggie was sitting in the corner, her nose about a half an inch away from the wall. She seemed to be having a staring contest with it.

"We don't have that kind of time. Right, Phil, have you got the mic?"

"Yep," he replied, holding up a small microphone attached to a battery pack.

"As long as you're wearing that, Tina, we can hear and record everything you say," said Paul.

"And where am I supposed to bleedin' shove that?"

Paul and Phil both looked at her, then hesitated, trying to find a way to suggest an answer to that question without appearing to be two men leering at a woman's cleavage. It involved a lot of blinking.

Tina laughed. "I'm only joking. Youse two are priceless." She took the mic from Phil and then stopped and looked at them both. "Well, turn around then."

"Oh God."

"Right, yeah."

"Sorry."

"Sorry."

They turned around.

When they turned back thirty seconds later, the mic and battery pack had completely disappeared and there was no trace of them about Tina's person. It was the closest thing Paul had seen to actual magic in real life.

"Right, let's go over it again."

"Ah Jaysus no, fuck that," said Tina. "We've been over it all three times already. I've read through the chats you had with this knob-jockey on the website – ye little prick tease, Paulie." Paul blushed. He had done what needed to be done to reel Harrison in. He had also felt like cleaning his eyes with a scouring pad afterwards. Tina gave him a playful slap on the cheek. "I'm supposed to woo him and get him talking about what he'd like to do to me and all that, so that you can prove he's still a randy bollocks in court."

"But don't let him touch you."

"No shit, Sherlock. My ma gave me that part of the talk about a decade ago, ye muppet. This arse-muncher aint getting his hands on the merchandise."

"Right. OK. Good."

This brought Paul to the tricky part. He had been unsuccessfully trying to find a way to say it for an hour now, and this was his last chance.

"Also, Tina, ehm – just a little note. This guy is from like Blackrock or somewhere equally posh so, y'know, you might need to – not that this is a criticism or anything – but if you could just, y'know, maybe tone down the, ehm, y'know..."

Tina took a step forward, so that she was inches from Paul's face, and then she softly pressed her finger to his lips. The voice that then came out of her made Paul realise that he'd had no idea what the term "soft and sultry" had meant up to this point in his sheltered life.

"Shush, Paulie. If what you're trying to say is that I need to personify a different approach, then I can do that." She batted her eyelashes in a way that could undoubtedly cause car accidents. "Don't you worry, I know how to make a man putty in my hands."

There was a long moment of silence, eventually broken by Maggie farting.

Tina's voice then reverted back to being Tina's voice. She punched Paul playfully on the arm. "Or in other words, ye cock-trumpet, I'm an actress, I know how to bleedin' act, don't I? Now, if youse don't mind, I've a date."

With that, she turned smartly and exited the van.

Phil and Paul stared at the door she had just slammed.

"Bloody hell," said Phil. "Did you ever wonder how women aren't running the world?"

"Maybe they are and we're too stupid to notice."

"Do you think this'll work?"

Paul sighed. "How do you rob a bank in broad daylight when they know you're coming?"

"There's no need to be nervous," said Jacob Harrison. He was talking to his own reflection in the toilets of La Rochelle wine bar on Leeson Street. It being Christmas Eve, it was busy. The place was filled with people having a few scoops with the work crew prior to shooting off home to the relatives. It was so crowded, in fact, that he was currently using the disabled toilets, as it was the only place where he could get a bit of space. It was time to get his game face on. He checked his suit one last time, making sure everything was perfect. He pointed at himself in the mirror. "You're a good-looking, charming guy and you deserve this. It's been a shitty couple of weeks. It's about time you got yourself a little Christmas present."

He'd reserved a booth at the back for him and his hot date. Antoine, the manager, was an old friend. At least he was when the odd fifty-euro note was slipped his way.

Jacob gave himself one more appreciative look in the mirror and strode out of the disabled toilet.

He quickly turned his swagger into a limp as he saw the woman in a wheelchair waiting outside, giving him the evil eye.

"There's no need to be nervous," said Vincent Kelleher, "but…"

"But what? I don't like 'but'. You know how I feel about 'but'." Kevin was in one of his moods, Vinny could tell.

He took a deep breath. "Look, Harrison has disappeared."

"What the hell do you mean? I gave you one job."

"It was just…"

"Forget it, I'll handle it. You are utterly useless. Seriously, what the fuck are you good for?"

The phone went dead. Vinny put it down and looked at the various scraps of notepaper strewn about on the passenger seat beside him. The first flakes of snow tumbling down had been inspirational, giving him the germ of the idea that would form the centrepiece of his new collection. He'd show Kevin. He'd show them all. They'd all be laughing on the other sides of their faces when he was a rich, successful poet.

"There's no need to be nervous." Brigit looked at the big red door. Warm light was spilling out from the windows and onto the street. "Christ," she said. "When did I start talking to myself? Like we haven't got enough people doing that."

Brigit had been trying to ring Bunny for the last couple of days but she had got no response. She had even dropped over to his house on the way home yesterday but there had been nobody in. It was starting to really worry her. It probably should have been worrying her more, but she had so much else to worry about these days, it was hard to fit it all in.

Still, she was about to scratch one big itch that she had had for a very long time. By the end of tonight, a lot of things would be different, one way or another. She was all in.

She took a deep breath and reached up for the doorbell.

Before she could reach it, the door flew open to reveal Anto Kelleher, in a Santa hat and an honest-to-God apron with "Kiss the Cook" emblazoned across it.

Brigit smiled nervously. "Hey, good looking, what ye got cooking?"

Anto wiggled his eyebrows and bowed low, a tea towel draped over his arm. "Well, m'lady, come into my boudoir and discover that for yourself."

CHAPTER FORTY-TWO

Nora Stokes pushed open the downstairs door to MCM Investigations.

"Hello?"

"Howerya." A voice carried down the stairs. "C'mon up."

Nora sighed. While she'd agreed to this, she had been half hoping he wouldn't be here. She had better things to be doing on Christmas Eve, but work was work, and this had proven a difficult meeting to set up. She needed to get it done and dusted once and for all.

Nora trudged up the stairs, her large bag of last-minute shopping whacking awkwardly against her shins as she did so.

When she reached the top and pushed open the door, Bunny McGarry was sitting behind the desk in the reception area, his feet up on the table. His large black sheepskin coat was bunched around him against the chill.

As he saw Nora walk in, he quickly stood up. "Sorry, can I give you a hand with that?"

She waved him away and dumped the bag beside the door. "It's fine. It's nice to finally meet you, Mr McGarry. I've been trying to do it for quite some time."

"Yeah, sorry about that, I've been very busy. And sorry it's so cold.

I've not been here much. Can't figure out how to turn on the central heating – or, for that matter, why the walls are covered in yellow paint."

"If you like, we could do this around the corner at my office?"

Bunny looked around him in a way Nora found peculiar. "No, it has to be here."

"Fair enough."

Bunny indicated the chair opposite. "Please, take a seat. And thanks again for coming in, I know it's a bad night for it."

Nora sat down. "Ah, don't worry about it. My mother is taking care of my demon child for a few hours. We're having to keep a special watch on him as he threatened to try and capture Santa. We are concerned about potential booby traps."

"Right. Yeah. Of course."

Nora could tell when someone wasn't paying any attention to her. "OK then, let's get down to it. I need to run you through the accusations and then you can give me your version of events."

"What?!"

Nora looked across the table. She had only briefly met Bunny once before, but there was a worn-out look to the man that she didn't remember. His eyes sagged and his beard looked unkempt. He looked tired in a way that no night's sleep, however good, could fix.

"The accusations made by Jacob Harrison against you."

Bunny waved his hand in a dismissive gesture. "Oh that? No, forget about that."

"But, that's why I'm here."

"I actually need your help with another thing. Did you bring the doo-dah?"

Nora gave him an exasperated look and then dipped her hand into her handbag and came out with her Dictaphone. "The recorder? Yes, I did, but I don't understand why you—"

Bunny cut across her. "Press record. Please."

Nora looked from Bunny to the recorder and then back again. "Could you—"

"Just. Please."

Nora shrugged and pressed the red button.

"Has it got enough tape?"

"It doesn't use tape. It's digital."

"Oh, right."

Bunny looked around again and then cleared his throat. "My name is Bernard McGarry. Last week, the Gardaí found two bodies in the Wicklow Mountains that had been killed and buried there eighteen years ago. I killed them."

"Fuck." Nora reached forward and stopped the recording. "Are you out of your tiny mind? What the hell are you doing?"

"I'm making a confession. I want to leave a record."

"No. No. No. I'm going to assume this is a joke as, if it isn't... Oh God, let's just call it a joke and—"

"No, it is no joke. I know what I'm doing. I just want to lay it all out now."

"Seriously, Mr McGarry, we can't do it now, but after the Christmas break, I can put you in touch with an excellent criminal lawyer. If you voluntarily go to the Gardaí and there's extenuating circumstances, that'll all go in your favour. But you need to handle this in the right way. You need—"

Bunny raised his hand for her to stop. "Look. I know what I'm doing. Believe me, the chances of this ever making court are slim-to-feck all. I just need to set out the facts and I need you to be a witness for me."

"But..."

"Please."

Against her better judgement, Nora leaned forward and pressed record again.

As Bunny spoke, he splayed his fingers out on the tabletop in front of him and spoke in a calm tone.

"One of the men was, I believe, called Daniel Zayas – although he had previously told me to refer to him as Mr Lopez. His ID said he was an FBI agent but I didn't know that until after. The other lad was hired muscle, an English guy. Zayas called him Mr Frock but feck knows if that was his real name."

Bunny paused. Nora wasn't sure what to do, but after he glanced up at her, she decided to fill the silence.

"Why did... why did you kill them?"

"Because they had kidnapped a lady called Simone. Ehm, I knew her as Simone Watson but I believe her real name was Simone Delamere."

"Was this a Garda matter?"

Bunny shook his head. "No. No other Gardaí but myself were involved. Well, my then partner, Gringo – sorry, Tim Spain – helped me, after the fact, but it was me who did all of the... y'know."

"If this woman was kidnapped, why didn't you go to the Gardaí?"

Bunny didn't look up as he spoke. "Because she was wanted for murder in New York. We couldn't... I couldn't... This was the only way I could protect her."

Nora lowered her voice. "What was she to you?"

Bunny glanced up briefly, his eyes wet. "We were together."

"I see. Where is she now?"

"I won't answer that."

"Alright then."

Bunny sat back and raised his voice. "The man Simone killed, it was self-defence. She got caught up in a thing..."

"What kind of thing?"

"It's best not to go into that. She got caught up, through no fault of her own, and she was forced to defend herself. Then she had to run and she ended up here. In Dublin."

"How did she get here?"

"I won't answer that either."

"Mr McGarry, if you really want to do this, it is important you're as honest as you can be, straight off the bat."

Bunny cleared his throat again. "I arranged an exchange with Lopez or Zayas or whatever the feck you want to call him. Simone for the tape."

"Wait, sorry – what tape?"

Bunny shifted around in the seat again. "There was a videotape that Simone gave me for safe keeping. If it fell into the wrong hands, it'd be bad news for some powerful arsehole."

"I see."

"But before we could do the exchange, Zayas tried to kill me."

"And you defended yourself?"

Bunny nodded. "I did, with what the Yanks would call 'extreme prejudice'. I shot Zayas in the eye and the other fella, Frock or whatever, I stabbed him in the chest."

"Right. Were they armed?"

"Oh God, yeah. They'd both got handguns. All I had was a knife, and this…"

Bunny shoved his hand in his pocket and came out holding something. Nora pulled away when she saw that it was a gun. A small, rather dainty affair, but a gun nonetheless.

"Jesus Christ."

"Sorry, sorry," said Bunny, quickly shoving it back into his pocket. "I didn't mean to scare you. It's just my derringer, a little one-shot thing."

"And you held on to the murder weapon?"

Bunny shrugged. "Ah, it's like a family heirloom."

"Right."

"I also still have the tape." Bunny leaned back in the seat again and looked around. "Not here, like. I've stored it somewhere safe. Those two men were willing to kill for it, and I'm pretty sure others will be too. They're coming for me. It's a matter of time."

"Why do you say that?"

"Call it a hunch. I'm going to go get it tonight, the tape. I think it's about time that the whole truth came out. It's time all the people standing in the shadows came into the light."

Nora gave him a firm look. "Mister McGarry – Bunny. Are you sure you're OK?"

Bunny gave her a sad little smile. "Define 'OK'."

"Maybe you should talk to someone about all this? I mean, y'know, like a…"

He stood up suddenly. "Anyway, thanks very much for your time."

"Wait, where are you going?"

Bunny slapped his palm into his forehead. "Sorry, of course, I didn't say. Eejit that I am. The tape is stored in a very safe location. Outside a town called Bandon in Sligo."

"Right. Wait, hang on – isn't that where?"

He nodded. "That's right, yeah. That's where all the stuff with the Fallons happened a couple of years ago. I moved it there."

"Why on earth would you do that?"

"Ah, 'tis the arsehole of nowhere, nobody would go looking there. Besides, everything has to end somewhere, I figured it was as good a place as any."

Nora stood. "Ok, can you just hang on for a few minutes? How about I call Brigit or Paul and we can talk all this through?"

"No, absolutely not. Whatever you do, don't do that. They're to be kept well out of this and they know nothing about it. I want to make that very clear."

"OK, but look... Alright. Come on, sit down."

Bunny opened the door. "I can't, I'm afraid. I've to get going."

"Right now?"

"That's right."

"But it's Christmas Eve!"

"Sure don't I know. I've to go visit an old friend, tell him he's on the naughty list."

Before Nora could think of anything else to say, he was out the door. She reached the top of the stairs just in time to see the front door close.

She leaned back against the wall and looked up at the ceiling. "Merry bloody Christmas!"

CHAPTER FORTY-THREE

"I don't understand," said Agent Dove, looking between DSI Burns and Detective Wilson. "Why can't we bring this man in for questioning?"

"Because," said Burns, "this isn't the first time Bunny McGarry's fingerprints have mysteriously appeared on a key piece of evidence in a murder investigation, and frankly this whole thing stinks to high heaven."

"It's déjà vu all over again," said Wilson, to nobody in particular.

"So, you're going to do nothing?"

"No," replied Burns. "We – and I emphasise the 'we' here – are going to do nothing until Wednesday."

"That's in three days' time!"

"I can't fault your maths, Agent Dove. On Wednesday, I will ring my boss, who will ring his boss, and there will be some discussions, because this is a bloody minefield. There are only so many times you can announce someone as being public enemy number one and be wrong. I like my job, Agent Dove, and I intend to still have it by New Year's."

"Two people are dead!"

"Yes, and they've been so for eighteen years. Three days either way isn't going to make that big a difference. To be clear, nobody is saying this lead will not be followed up, but it'll be done carefully and by the book. Please pass that on to your bosses when you ring them to lodge your latest complaint. And by the way, I happen to know the commissioner takes a very dim view of anyone disturbing her Christmas. You should remember that when you start trying to shake this particular tree."

"And what are we going to do in the meantime?"

"Honestly, Dove, that's up to you. Personally, I'm already late for a party where I have to arrive wearing a hideous Christmas jumper, as otherwise I will be labelled as someone who is 'no craic'. It's hard to explain to a foreigner the social stigma attached to that label. Now, I would like to storm out, but seeing as we're in my office and I need to lock it, could the two of you please bugger off and, y'know, have yourselves a merry little Christmas. I'll see you both on Wednesday."

Wilson shifted nervously. "Ehm, guv, I'm actually on leave until Sunday. Me and a few of the guys..."

He stopped talking when he noticed his boss's facial expression.

"I'll see you on Wednesday."

CHAPTER FORTY-FOUR

Jacob Harrison stood at the bar, trying to not look impatient as he waited to be served. They only seemed to have two staff on, which was nowhere near enough to keep the drink flowing for this amount of customers.

Jacob's date was already ten minutes late. He glanced in the direction of the door again while trying not to look like he was looking. The problem with something that seemed too good to be true was that it often was.

At the bar beside him, a woman with long red hair had her phone strapped to her ear and a face like thunder.

She spoke in an urgent whisper. "For Christ's sake, Brian, where the fuck are you? You're over thirty minutes late. You said you were coming. You said you'd made your choice."

Harrison got caught looking at her and diverted his gaze quickly. When he looked back again, the redhead was off the phone, but she shot him a dirty look. Then she raised her hand with her empty wine glass in it. "Cheryl, same again, please, sweetheart."

She was an attractive woman, Harrison thought – for her age, that was. He'd never been one to be attracted to the older woman. At a guess, she was four or five years older than him, but then, most women her age weren't quite so well maintained. Even allowing for the kind of sucking in and propping up that seemed to be the mainstays of the older woman's wardrobe, she was in very good shape. She had an arse you could bounce coins off, although the scowl on her face said she'd not give you change for a tenner.

Shit. She turned to catch him looking again.

She was opening her mouth to say something when Rebecca appeared beside her. "Hi, Jacob – or should I say Cyrano." She giggled. "Sorry I'm late. Traffic was a totes mare."

Damn. She was even fitter in person than her pictures had suggested. Jacob had learned to take twenty-five per cent off the hotness score, as everyone's online pics were some form of lie. Not Rebecca.

"No problem, hon. Lovely to meet you in person, finally. I've reserved us a booth just back there." He casually waved behind him. "If you like, you can head back and I'll get some drinks in?"

"Sure."

"What would you like?"

"Anything bubbly."

"Champagne it is."

Rebecca giggled and walked by, giving his arm a little squeeze on her way past.

Harrison turned back to the bar. The redhead threw him a disgusted glance and then picked up the large glass of white wine that had just arrived.

Harrison turned to watch Rebecca make her way back to the booth. Yes! Get in! This was going to be a big night, he could feel it. Merry Christmas!

CHAPTER FORTY-FIVE

"Ahem!"

Brigit looked up guiltily from her phone to see Anto standing behind the kitchen counter looking pointedly at her.

"Oh God, sorry, I was being rude."

"Yes, yes you were. The man who is currently cooking you dinner – coq au vin, no less – was telling a hilarious story about his friend's stag do and a duck, and you entirely failed to politely laugh at the supposed punchline."

"Sorry, sorry, sorry. I'm a bit distracted." She shoved her phone back into her bag.

"Well, it's your own loss. You'll never know what happened now, and I'll be honest, I have been saving my A-grade material especially for tonight."

"I'm a tough crowd. Think of me as a challenge."

He gave her a big smile. "Oh, don't worry, Ms Conroy, I already do."

She smiled and pushed her hair back behind her ear. "Your place is very nice."

And it was. Unusually for a guy living on his own, it actually felt like he'd put a lot of thought into the decor, beyond "I need to get chairs". It was simply decorated, but there were some nice pictures of skylines from around the world on the walls. New York, London, Dublin, Sydney and what she guessed was San Francisco.

"Thank you very much. I have spent many a lonely night on that sofa watching property porn, so I've figured out a few tricks: warm earthy tones, throw cushions, somewhere to hide your PlayStation for when company drops around."

"Impressive."

"Speaking of which," he said, indicating the barely touched glass of white in front of her. "I don't want to brag, but I've actually got more than one bottle of wine in the joint."

"I'm sure, but I'm pacing myself. I'm driving and all, so..."

"Of course." Anto took a lid off a pot and poked something with a fork, before turning a dial down on the hob. "Well, as you can see, I have an exceptionally comfortable sofa, so you are more than welcome to stay over."

He said it casually. When he looked up, he saw Brigit with her phone in her hand again. "Right, that is it. Me and my exquisitely prepared coq are now officially offended. Are you expecting a booty call or something?"

"Sorry, sorry. Alright, well... look, I didn't want to say anything, but fingers crossed, we might have found a way out of our Harrison problem."

"Really?" Anto came around and leaned against the near side of the kitchen counter, snatching up his own wineglass. "How so?"

"Well, Phil has been keeping me in the loop. Do you know Phil? Phil Nellis?"

Anto shook his head. "I don't think so."

"Sorry. That's classic country girl that, assuming everyone from Dublin knows each other. He's Paul's oldest mate, sort of works for us now. He's a nice lad, but a bit, well... I don't want to say dim, that's unfair. Odd? He has a very odd sense of logic to him but he's a lovely fella. Has an incredible memory. Never forgets a face."

"That'd be handy for an investigator, I suppose."

"Anyway, long story short, Paul had a brainwave and he found the website Harrison was using. Like, the dating website."

"Don't tell me the horny cretin is still on it?"

Brigit nodded. "Apparently so. He's out on a date right now with a girl Paul hired."

"Really? Oh, that's brilliant."

"Hopefully. If they can get him saying stuff that indicates his 'fear of sex' might be cured."

"Genius. Absolute genius."

Brigit shrugged. "I'm trying not to get my hopes up. I mean, your brothers must be keeping an eye on Harrison. So the chances of this little ruse working…"

"Oh, you never know. Fingers crossed they've taken Christmas Eve off from being arseholes."

"Hopefully. I sat down with our accountant again today. Between legal fees and the complaint Harrison put in to the Private Security Authority, trying to get our licence suspended, and how much that's going to cost to fight, it's looking like MCM Investigations might not be opening up again after Christmas."

"Christ, it can't really be that bad?"

Brigit nodded. "It really is. I feel like I'm captaining a sinking ship, where everybody else jumped overboard ages ago."

"So, if this plan has to work, it'll work. It's Christmas. Miracles always happen at Christmas!"

"I hope you're right."

"I always am. Right you, come over here."

Brigit stood up.

"I am just going to nip to the little boy's room and I need you to keep an eye on my coq for a minute."

Brigit shook her head and smiled. "Did you pick this menu entirely so you could make that joke all night?"

"I'm not going to lie, that was a big part of it, yes."

CHAPTER FORTY-SIX

Phil and Paul sat in the van, looking at Phil's laptop screen, which was perched on the dash in front of them. The only movement on it was the graphic rendering of the sound wave as it recorded the conversation between Tina and Harrison. They were parked up around the corner in a loading bay on Hatch Street, opposite Cafe Sol. Near enough if needed, but far enough out of sight that Harrison wouldn't see the van unless he really went looking for it.

"Have you ever been to St Tropez?" they heard Harrison ask.

"No, I haven't."

"Oh my God, you simply must go."

"I'm waiting for someone to take me." Tina, aka Rebecca, giggled.

"Say no more. What are you doing for New Year's?"

"Christ," said Paul, "how many different ways in the last twenty-five minutes has this plank found to point out he's got money?"

"Ah, at least a dozen. I wouldn't mind if he actually did, but he's unemployed and suing us. There's no justice in the world."

"No justice."

"You're not wrong."

"I just repeated what you said."

"Well, when you're right, you're right."

"Excuse me a sec, J, I'm going to go powder my nose," said Tina.

"Hurry right back, I'll be waiting."

"You'd better be." She giggled again.

"Ah Christ, Paulie!"

"What?"

"We can't listen to the girl go to the toilet, that wouldn't be decent."

"Relax." Paul leaned forward and turned the volume down a couple of notches. "So how's the missus?"

"Ready to pop. She's due in four days. I just hope she doesn't have it tomorrow."

"Why?"

"Have you ever met somebody whose birthday is on Christmas Day? They're always bitter about it. Only one present."

"Well, it worked out alright for Jesus."

"Did it? Going around turning water into wine all the time, dude clearly had a problem."

"He only did that the once."

"How come they're always banging on about it then?"

Paul looked out the window as two blotto men in suits passed by, attempting to carry each other home. They were of an age to know better. One was singing, the other was crying.

"I think it was his first big miracle, wasn't it? That and the loaves and fishes thing. The lad should've gone into catering. He would've cleaned up."

"Loaves and fishes," said Phil. "Is that not just basically fish fingers?"

On the laptop, they could hear a murmur of background conversation and what sounded like a stall door being closed.

"I've always wondered what goes on in the ladies' toilets," said Paul.

"Well you're not finding out now, ye pervert." Phil leaned forward and turned the sound down a couple more notches. "Do you think we've enough so far?"

Paul shrugged his shoulders. "I doubt it. I'm only guessing, but I think we need to get him specifically saying stuff about shagging. Offers and what not."

"On a first date? Jesus. Who are these people?"

"Well, Phil, not everyone meets their missus over the Internet like you did."

Phil pointed at the laptop. "These two met over the Internet."

"Very different area of the Internet though. You were on the nicer end."

Paul felt the phone in his pocket vibrate. He pulled it out and looked at the unknown number.

"Who is it?"

"I don't know." Paul answered the call. "Hello?"

"Paul. Merry Christmas. Kevin Kelleher here, I just wanted to pass on season's greetings to you and yours."

"Ah, Kevin," Paul said, while looking at Phil pointedly. "Lovely to hear from you. I hope you're not bearing a grudge from my dog ripping the arse out of one of your lovely suits when she ran you off."

"Oh not at all, Paul. I've got plenty of suits. In fact, I've a lovely new one on now. If you look out the right-hand window of your shitheap of a van, you can see for yourself."

Paul looked over. There on the far side of the road stood Kevin Kelleher, a wide grin on his lips. He waved. "It was a nice try and all, but did you really expect this to work?"

"I don't know what you're talking about."

"Ha, sure you don't. So when I go into La Rochelle around the corner, I won't find our friend Mr Harrison with some floozy you've paid to throw herself at him. You were clever to find him through that website though, I'll give you that."

"How do you know that?"

"Lucky guess. Anyway, I've got old Jacob and his wandering libido on this tracking app I installed on his phone. He can't go missing from me. Now if you'll excuse me, I've to go inside and break up the happy couple."

Having polished off the champagne, Jacob Harrison had moved on to the cognac, always his tipple of choice. He looked around the bar. The crowd had started to thin out as people drifted off home for the festivities. The redhead still sat at the bar, staring at her phone. Poor bitch. Looked like she was destined to be alone at Christmas.

He watched Rebecca walking towards him, smiling as she sashayed around the tables. He noticed eyes following her. Who could blame them; she was stunning. He was going to have a very merry Christmas indeed.

She slid back into their booth, moving herself closer to him.

"So," Jacob said, with a playful waggle of his eyebrows, "I have had a very naughty idea."

"Yeah," said a male voice, "I bleedin' bet you have."

Jacob whipped his head around. Kevin Kelleher was standing beside them. "Christ, Kevin. I wasn't expecting to see you here."

"Yeah, no kidding." He turned to Rebecca. "The game's up, love, grab your stuff and fuck off."

"Excuse me?" said Rebecca.

"Jesus, Kevin, that was uncalled for."

"Uncalled for? You fucking idiot." Kelleher pointed an accusing finger at Rebecca. "You've been set up, you moron. She works for MCM. Didn't I tell you that we'd be fine as long as you kept it in your pants for a few weeks? You weak little—"

"Jacob, I don't know what he's talking about. Who is this guy?"

"Drop the act, love. To be fair, as whores go, you're a cute one, but that's all you are."

"What did you call me, ye knob gobbler? I'll shove your teeth down your throat, ye shiny-faced bag of shite."

Jacob looked at Rebecca in shock as her accent suddenly changed.

"Charming," said Kelleher. "C'mon." He reached across to grab her arm but stopped as the phone in his hand started to vibrate. "Ah, speak of the Devil." He thumbed the answer button and raised the phone to his ear. "Mr Mulchrone, what can I do for you?"

"Before you put a finger on that girl, do yourself a favour and ask her who her auntie is."

Kelleher stopped and looked at the girl.

"Why would I give two shits who her auntie is?"

"Because it's Jacinta Phelan," said Paul.

Kelleher withdrew his hand as if "Rebecca" were on fire. He looked at her for a long second. "OK. No harm done. Off you pop."

Rebecca glared at him and then slowly slid back out of the booth and headed straight for the door.

"What the hell, dude?" said Harrison, in full-on huff mode.

Kelleher hung up the phone. "Relax, Jacob. Seeing as we're here, let's have a drink. Looks like you've suddenly got some free time."

CHAPTER FORTY-SEVEN

Brigit groaned appreciatively.

"Say it."

She let out a slow gasp of air and then fanned her face with her hand. "Oh. My. God."

"Say it," Anto repeated.

"I am not saying it."

"Say it!"

Brigit looked across the table into his eyes. "Alright. This is a spectacular coq."

Anto punched the air with delight. "Yes! C'mon! In your face, Jamie Oliver."

"Seriously, you've got some mad culinary skills going on there. I am impressed."

"Oh, you have only just begun to appreciate my talents."

Brigit grinned. "Oh really?" Her bag started buzzing and she looked across at Anto.

"It's OK, take it."

She took her phone out and answered it. "Hi, Phil, how's everything going?"

As she listened to Phil, Anto watched the hope drain from her face.

"Crap. How did he know?"

There was more indistinguishable talk from the other end of the line.

"Damn it. Alright. Well, thanks for trying."

Brigit glanced at Anto and then turned away. "Don't worry about it, Phil, it'll be alright. We'll think of something... Yeah, Merry Christmas to you too."

Brigit hung up the phone, then she tossed it onto the sofa.

"Shit."

Anto stood up, not exactly sure what to do with himself. "I take it the plan didn't work then?"

Brigit shook her head and walked over to the sofa. "No." She sat down. Anto could see tears in the corners of her eyes. "I suppose it was a long shot. I mean, your brothers knew we were going to try something. How do you rob a bank in broad daylight when they know you're coming?"

Anto moved towards her.

Brigit looked around the room. "I don't suppose you have such a thing as a tissue?"

"Ehm, sure, I think I might have some in the bathroom."

"Failing that, a bit of loo roll. I'm not feeling too proud."

"I'll be back in a minute."

Anto left the room and nipped into the bathroom. He quickly fished his phone out of his pocket and saw the message from Kevin: "Got there in plenty of time. Dealt with!"

Anto had known Kev and Vinny were keeping tabs on Harrison to make sure he didn't mess anything up, but he had still texted them when Brigit had let slip their little plan, just be sure nothing went awry.

Anto typed out a quick response: "Excellent. I'm moving in for the kill. It's going to be a damn good Xmas!"

He grabbed the box of tissues from the shelf, took a moment to compose himself and came back into the front room.

Brigit was still sitting on the sofa, looking forlorn. He moved across and wordlessly presented the box of tissues.

"Thanks. Grab us my drink there, would you, please?"

"Sure."

Anto picked up both glasses from the table and brought them over. Brigit blew her nose loudly on a tissue. Not the most graceful thing Anto had ever seen.

He handed her wine to her and sat down close to her on the sofa, placing a comforting arm around her.

"There now. C'mon, it'll be alright. Look, I've been thinking. I can try and get into Kevin's flat, see if I can't get into his safe. That might give you the ammunition you need to get this stupid thing called off."

She looked up at him, hope in her teary eyes. "You'd do that for us?"

"I'd do that for you."

Brigit nervously took a gulp of her wine.

Anto drained his near-full glass too; he didn't want it spilling and staining his carpet. He put it on the back of the sofa, and then he reached across and gently put his fingers under Brigit's chin, softly raising her face towards his as he moved forward and then...

She stood up suddenly. So suddenly that Anto nearly fell off the sofa. Brigit moved across to the table.

"You see, the thing about Phil – you remember I told you about Phil? Friend of Paul's – actually, no, friend of ours. I really like him. Sure he's a bit daft, but he has a great heart and a cracking memory."

Anto looked up at Brigit. Suddenly he was getting a funny feeling that the earth had shifted in a way he didn't really understand.

"For example, he remembers you. He saw you last week when you walked me back to the office after lunch, and he remembered seeing you before."

"Small world." Only two words, but as he said them, Anto's mouth had a peculiar feeling, like his tongue was no longer entirely under his control.

"It is that. Thing is, Phil remembers where and when he'd seen you before. The night that Paul got spiked and your brothers took those horrible pictures. You know, when they generally messed up his life and mine."

Anto opened his mouth to speak but it seemed he had lost the facility.

"Phil remembers passing you on his way out of the pub that night. Imagine having that good a memory?"

Anto put his hands down on the sofa; the room was starting to spin now. "What d… did…"

"What did I put in your drink when you were in the bathroom?" She was smiling down at him now. "Oh, just a little something for the pain. For mine and Paul's, I mean. Your pain hasn't started yet."

"Ahhh… wahhh."

"Sorry you went to all this trouble, but your little double-agent ruse has been rumbled. Thanks for passing on that message to your brother though – you actually got him right where we wanted him. And I'm afraid what you thought was going to happen tonight definitely isn't. If I look in your bedroom, would I find a little concealed camera? I bet I would, you sleazy piece of crap."

Anto looked down in confusion as he felt something drip onto his pants. He realised it was drool coming from his own mouth.

"Actually," continued Brigit, "that's not true because you see, though not in the way you intended, rest assured…"

Anto tried to stand. The world tilted on its axis.

Then nothing.

He lay unconscious on the floor.

"You're definitely getting screwed."

CHAPTER FORTY-EIGHT

DSI Susan Burns – or, as her older brother Keith still insisted on calling her, Little Suzie – parked her car up on the side of the cul-de-sac. It'd been a predictably hellish ninety-minute drive out to Maynooth. She had counted forty-seven instances of reckless driving. She could have filled every cell in a five-mile area with people who thought the rules of the road only applied to other people.

She could hear the music pumping out of her brother's house from here. His was the semi-detached with enough Christmas lights on it to be seen from space. She took a deep breath. She was about to be forced into polite conversation with men who were four drinks ahead of her. Her sister-in-law had made some tremendously unsubtle hints about friends of Keith's from work being there. They were all engineers at Intel. Invariably she would have to smile at the same tedious gags about bringing handcuffs home with her. Maybe this year would finally be the year where she informed her family that she was a lesbian.

She wasn't, but the temptation to go with that as a way of knocking this kind of stuff on the head was occasionally overwhelming. She had a theory that more than a few lesbians were just straight and happily-single women who couldn't face another awkward shove towards Nigel who once went skiing and supports Everton.

She reached into the back seat and grabbed the jumper. She'd found it in a second-hand shop. She couldn't face buying one of these monstrosities new. This particular monstrosity featured a reindeer wearing a demented grin. If she met such a creature in real life, she would be pulling it over on suspicion of massive cocaine use.

She was halfway through pulling it on when her phone started to ring. "Oh, for fuck's sake. Hang on, Keith, I'm coming!"

She pulled her head through. It wasn't Keith. Another name flashed up on the car's control screen.

She pressed the button to answer. "Wilson, if this is about your holiday plans, then I'm sorry, but—"

"No, boss."

"OK."

"I just got a call from O'Mara at Pearse Street. Svetlana Mannis is a woman who works at Charlie's jazz bar. It was closed today but she went in to surprise Noel Graffoe, the owner, with a birthday cake."

"Christ, don't tell me..."

"Dead, guv. They rang me because he had my card on him."

DSI Burns ran her hand over her furrowed brow. "Natural causes?"

"I'm afraid not, boss. Initially, they were thinking robbery that went wrong but... I'm heading there now, but O'Mara said it looked like the guy had been slapped around a lot. Tied to a chair."

"Crap. It could be a coincidence."

There was silence on the other end.

"But," continued Burns, "when have we ever been that lucky." She pulled the ridiculous jumper off. "I'll start making some calls. Let me know what you find at the scene."

"Yes, guv."

"I'm going to send a unit to Mr McGarry's house too, see if he'd like to come in for a late-night chat and some mulled wine."

"Yes, guv."

She pressed the button to disconnect the call and then looked at her brother's house again. With a sigh she restarted the car.

CHAPTER FORTY-NINE

His eyelids flickered open and registered light. Distant light.

It was a road, flanked by streetlights, traffic travelling slowly down it.

Then he noticed the flakes of snow that were meandering to the ground before his eyes.

Then, belatedly, his mind registered the message his body was screaming at him. *Cold. Cold. Cold.*

His body was shivering.

His teeth rattled in his head, which felt like it was filled with cotton wool.

Come to that, his head felt very weird. Freezing. His skin was...

None of this made any sense.

Then a pair of legs appeared in his field of vision and a head bent down to smile at him. Brigit Conroy.

"There he is. Wakey wakey, rise and shine. You're missing the magical Christmas wonderland. Don't you love the snow? It makes the whole place look so clean, doesn't it? I mean, initially, before it ends up a shitty pile of sludge by the side of the road. There's probably a metaphor in there but I can't be arsed."

Anto's body was gradually gathering information. The reason it was so cold was because he was naked. Bollock naked. "Where am I?"

"Call yourself a true Dub? You should recognise the Phoenix Park. Although, admittedly, this is one of the less well-travelled parts."

He was sitting on the ground, the uncomfortable ground. His back seemed to be resting on the trunk of a tree. Things were poking into his arse, his naked arse. Twigs. Pinecones.

"What's going..." Anto stopped speaking. He had moved his hands to his face. His truly naked face. His beard was gone. He moved his hands to his head. His hair – all of his hair – was gone. He felt something soft on his otherwise bald scalp. He pulled it off and looked at it. It was his Santa hat.

"What the... You shaved me? You mad bitch!"

"Now now. Language."

"What the fuck are you doing? This is assault." The rage and the cold were finally clearing his foggy mind. "And you... you drugged me!"

"Really? You're going to go for the moral high ground on that point, are you?"

He tried to stand. "Give me my clothes. This isn't funny."

"Well, that's a matter of perspective. It's hilarious from where I'm standing."

"You mad—"

"Keep in mind, I'm your only way out of your current predicament, so go ahead – use the word bitch again and see what happens."

"Give me my clothes. You've no right to do this!"

"Really? Like you'd the right to try and set me up as your sick little conquest. Like you'd the right to drug Paul and fuck with our lives. Like you've the right to try and destroy our business?"

"I'm calling the guards. You're going to jail."

Brigit pulled a face. "Oh dear, that'll really ruin Christmas. Anyway, have a nice time getting in touch with nature."

Brigit turned and started to walk away. Anto now saw that her car was sitting about twenty feet away in the darkness.

"Wait. Please. I'm sorry!"

He leaned a hand on the tree trunk and managed to stand on his unsteady legs.

She threw a wave over her shoulder. "You most certainly are. A really sorry piece of shit."

"Look. Can we talk about this? I've made some mistakes."

Brigit opened the front door of her car, which creaked a little in protest. "It's wonderful that you're starting to see that. A real Christmas miracle."

"You can't just leave me here."

"Can't I? Watch me."

"You bitch!"

"Oh dear, there's that word again. Just when you were making such good progress."

He ran towards her, his anger and desperation propelling him forward on his aching legs.

When he'd travelled about six feet, his foggy mind registered the sensation of something attached to his left ankle just a fraction too late. The rope caught his leg and his momentum sent him sprawling to the ground.

Brigit lowered the window. "Ouch! Not a good landing. Your leg is tied to the tree. Sorry, should've mentioned that. My bad."

Brigit started the engine of her car. "You'll untie it eventually, but it'll take you some time. I was a Girl Guide."

With a grinding noise, she released the handbrake of her car and put it in gear.

Anto spat the dirt from his mouth. "Wait. Please. I'm sorry. I can explain."

"Oh please. Bit late for that. In fact..."

With a thunk, an object landed in the snow beside him.

"There's your phone. Go ring somebody who cares."

CHAPTER FIFTY

Jacob Harrison stared mournfully into his drink. Kevin Kelleher slapped him on the shoulder.

"Oh, for Christ's sake, Harrison, cheer up. You're wrecking my buzz here. Today has been a great day."

"How so?"

"How so?" Kelleher held his drink up triumphantly. "We have vanquished our foe. Foiled their nefarious scheme. Made Paulie Mulchrone look like a clueless dipshit. It's all good."

Over at the bar, the redhead was talking too loudly into her phone. "Yeah well, fuck you, Brian. Go back to her, but don't think I'll be waiting for you when she kicks you out again. I had plans for tonight, big plans. You are missing out!"

She slammed her phone down on the bar and held up her glass again. "Cheryl, fill this fucker up." There was now a distinct slur to her voice.

Kelleher nodded in the redhead's direction. "At least you're not that sad sack. Nice arse, to be fair to her. Why is it the mental ones are always the best in bed?"

Harrison mumbled something under his breath.

"Oh, for Christ's sake, cheer the fuck up!"

"That's easy for you to say," snapped Harrison. "I'm the one who was on to a sure thing, until you messed it up."

"Jesus, man, you seriously do have a problem."

"Fuck you, what do you know about it? The wife won't let me near the house or the kids. My own parents won't speak to me. You're not the one that's going to be all alone at Christmas."

"Christ, what I wouldn't give to be alone at Christmas! No kids screaming at each other, wife nagging me, my ma complaining about every bloody thing. You can relax, put your feet up, eat something nicer than dry-as-a-desert turkey. You're a lucky man. You should come around mine for Christmas dinner."

Harrison looked up, his face full of hope. "Really?"

"Eh no, not really. I've got a sixteen-year-old niece, Jacob, and frankly, you're a sex pest. But, on the upside, once we own MCM Investigations, you'll have a bit of money again. And then you're not a sex pest, you're a player."

"You're really fucking rude, do you know that?"

Kelleher reached below the table and, with a quick glance around to make sure they were unobserved, grabbed Harrison's nuts and hence his undivided attention.

"Listen to me, you little creep. You nearly just fucked this whole thing up, something me and my brothers have put a lot of work into. Be very, very happy I'm in a Christmas mood, because otherwise you'd be lying in a pool of your own blood somewhere. Do we understand each other?"

Harrison nodded.

"Good lad. You're lucky it's me you're having this chat with. I'm the softie in the family. One of my brothers would have..."

Kelleher's phone started to ring and he released his grip. "Oh, speak of the Devil."

He placed the phone to his ear. "Mission accomplished, Anto?"

Harrison watched as the smile crumbled from Kelleher's lips.

"What? Where? Hang on, I'm on my way."

Without another word, Kelleher stood up and rushed towards the doors.

Harrison raised his glass in toast at his back. "Merry bloody Christmas."

CHAPTER FIFTY-ONE

Jacob Harrison threw back the last of his cognac and belched. He was starting to get heartburn. Of course he was. What a perfect evening. It was time to go home. Not "home" home – his future ex-wife had made it very clear that he was not welcome there. Even his own parents had backed her up. They always took everyone else's side. Throughout his childhood they had invariably backed his two older siblings against him. He had never enjoyed their support. He was a truly self-made man. Fuck the lot of 'em!

And fuck Kevin Kelleher too. Wherever he'd gone, it seemed pretty clear he wasn't coming back. Not that Jacob liked him. Kelleher was a tasteless oik who wore what money he had in a gauche manner, but at least his presence had meant he had someone to drink with.

The two young couples in the corner, all of them looking like they'd just walked out of a Christmas TV ad, laughed uproariously. Jacob noticed one of the women glance in his direction and then look away. Were they laughing at him? The fuckers were laughing at him. Christ, could this day get any worse? Time to go back to his shitty flat and see what immigrants were willing to deliver a takeaway on Christmas Eve.

He stood on unsteady feet, bumping against the table in the

booth. He was feeling a little woozy now. Maybe he'd had too much to drink. He'd hardly eaten anything before he left the flat.

He walked over to the bar and signalled to the brunette chatting at the other end that he wished to settle his bill. She nodded and walked over towards the register.

Shit, his coat. As he turned back towards the booth to retrieve his forgotten grand's worth of Louis Vuitton, he collided with someone walking the other way. Perfume filled his nostrils, white wine splashed on his shirt. He took a step back as the redhead glared at him.

"Oh, for shit's sake, you clumsy idiot. Why don't you watch where you're going?"

"Sorry, sorry."

The woman brushed at the large white wine stain spreading across her cream blouse. "Sorry don't do shit for me. Look at the state of this."

He reached forward to try and assist and got slapped away.

"Keep your hands to yourself, you creepy little weasel."

Harrison's face reddened. "I was only trying to help."

"I think you've done more than enough."

The manager, Antoine, leaned over the bar. "Is there a problem here?"

"No problem," said Jacob, forcing a smile. "Just a little accident. Can I buy the lady another one?"

"Sure," said Antoine, giving them a tight smile. Jacob knew he was being assessed. Was his presence lowering the tone of the establishment? Tonight just got better and better.

"A large," said the redhead. "And some tissues, if you've got them."

They both stood at the bar, side by side, watching as Antoine had a quick word with the brunette, who eyed them and then nodded.

The redhead looked at her blouse again. "Look at the state of this. It's ruined."

"I'll pay for the dry cleaning."

"Too right you will. I've no time to go home. I'm meeting someone, you clumsy drunken idiot."

Jacob had taken enough insults for one night. "No, you're not. I think Brian decided to spend Christmas with his wife."

She turned and glowered at him through squinted eyes. Jacob smiled back. "The whole bar heard your phone calls, you weren't exactly quiet."

"Yeah, well, he was one of many options. He can go spend Christmas with his family. He's got a daughter about the same age as your date was. Y'know, the one that stormed out?"

"That's not what that was."

"Sure." She smiled venom. "Course not. What is it with men like you that you're so terrified of women your own age? You'd rather bang some airhead who's barely out of school." She slurred the last word.

"Probably because most women of your age are bitter old hags."

She gave a humourless laugh. "That's what you call a woman who won't put up with your shit anymore, is it? Who isn't cowed enough to lie there and fake it? Who isn't interested in mentally rearranging her shoe collection while you wheeze and chug away, like a clapped-out motor trying to get up a hill?"

"What would you know about it?"

"Just a hunch. I bet a real woman would have you shaking in your boots."

"Oh really?"

She looked him up and down. "Without a doubt."

Jacob hated this woman. He hated her smug grin, her fine figure and the mocking scorn that dripped from her every word. Why, then, could he feel more than his anger rising?

"What's your name?"

She stopped and looked at him again. "Do you care?"

"No."

CHAPTER FIFTY-TWO

Tina sat in the back of the van. From the front seat, Phil Nellis was taking an ill-advised stab at becoming a motivational speaker.

"Ye shouldn't feel bad about this, Tina. You're a lovely girl. I'm sure, given time, you'd be able to convince any man to go to bed with you."

She patted Maggie on the head and laughed. "Thanks a bleedin' bunch, Romeo."

Phil reddened. "I mean not me, obviously. I'm a happily married man, with a baby on the way. But other men, y'know."

Tina pointed at Paul as he sat in the driving seat. "Like him?"

"Yeah, I mean. He's sort of, well he's not – well, he's sort of in a relationship, but it's complicated."

"Is that right?" said Tina, in a teasing voice.

Phil nodded. "I mean, he keeps messing it up and that, but if he ever sorts himself out. You see—"

"OK," said Paul loudly, "that's enough of this line of conversation, I think." He pulled the van over to the side of the road. They were just off Eustace Street. Paul took some notes out of his wallet. "As agreed, two hundred euros."

Tina took it. "Cheers. Sorry it didn't work out."

"Oh, I wouldn't say that. We're going to have to stay here for a bit. I'll call you a taxi if you like?"

Phil turned to look at Paul. "What do you mean we need to stay here?"

"We've got work to do."

"What?"

"Remember how I asked you how you rob a bank in broad daylight when they know you're coming?"

Phil looked around. "We're robbing a bank?"

Paul sighed. "No, Phil. Remember how last week we talked about metaphors?"

"What you're doing is talking in riddles."

Paul took out his phone. "So, will I call you a taxi?"

Actually," replied Tina, "if I hang about, will I see that Harrison cock-muppet make a proper idiot of himself?"

"You just might do."

Phil looked from Paul to Tina and then back again – as if watching a tennis rally. "How in the hell is she going to see that?"

There was a knock on the back door of the van.

Paul nodded back at it. "Tina, would you mind?"

Tina opened the door and Brigit climbed in.

"Hiya. You must be Tina?"

"I am."

They shook hands.

"Ah for..." Phil walloped the dashboard. "Brigit is involved now? Seriously, what in the hell is going on?"

I'll explain in a second," said Paul. "Did everything go alright at your end?"

Brigit nodded. "Yep. And on yours?"

Paul nodded. "Kevin Kelleher legged it out of there like something was on fire."

"Well, Anto was certainly feeling the cold when I left him, so I'd imagine he needed big brother to come save him."

"Seriously," said Phil, "you two are working together again?"

They both looked sheepish.

"Sort of," said Paul.

"In a manner of speaking," said Brigit.

"This is doing my head in."

"Look," said Paul, "we didn't tell you everything because, well, you aren't going to like part of the plan."

"I'm not currently liking any of the plan."

"Can I take your dog for a walk?" This was Tina.

"Really?"

"Yeah. I like dogs and she's got a nice vibe going on."

Paul looked down at Maggie. Previously, her "vibe" had not been something that people had commented positively upon.

"Sure," said Paul.

"Oh no," said Phil, causing the other occupants of the van to look at him in surprise. "I mean, as a soon-to-be father of a daughter, no disrespect, but I don't want you wandering around this kind of area at this time of night. There are a lot of drunken men around."

There was a moment of embarrassed silence before Brigit stepped in.

"Ehm, Phil, I'm sure Tina here is well able to take care of herself."

"I know, no disrespect meant to you at all now, Tina. Just, y'know, in this job you see how badly men behave."

"It's not like that comes as a shock."

"And," continued Brigit, pointing down at the dog, "she is taking Maggie – as in *Maggie* – for a walk."

Phil nodded. "Right. Yeah. Point taken. Still though, somebody needs to explain what the plan is, as apparently what I thought was the plan isn't the plan."

Paul looked at Brigit. "He's going to hate this."

Brigit grinned. "Don't look at me! You tell him."

"Somebody better tell me something soon or my head is going to explode!"

"OK, Phil. Seeing as Kelleher was watching Harrison like a hawk, we figured there was a good chance he'd catch Tina here in her attempts to... y'know."

"Right," said Phil.

Brigit pointed over Paul's shoulder, to alert him to the taxi that was pulling up outside of the Phoenix Apartments building opposite.

"So, how you rob a bank when they know you're coming is that you pretend to rob it..."

They all watched as Jacob Harrison exited the taxi.

"And then when they think they've caught you..."

"You rob it for real," finished Brigit.

Phil watched as someone else got out of the taxi behind Harrison.

"Ah no."

Brigit nodded. "Yep."

CHAPTER FIFTY-THREE

As the lift doors closed, Jacob Harrison attempted to push himself against her.

The redhead slapped him in the face and pushed him back. "No. Not yet."

Harrison rubbed his jaw. "You're a crazy bitch, you know that?"

"Shut up. When I want to hear you talk, I'll tell you. To be clear, when we're doing it, I don't want to look at your stupid face, and when we're done, I want you to get the hell out."

"Fine by me. I don't even know your name."

She gave him a humourless smile. "I know."

The doors opened on the top floor.

"You're in the penthouse?"

She walked out of the lift, not looking back. "Well spotted. The ladies must go wild for your keen mind."

She took a key out of her bag and quickly unlocked the door. She pushed it open and stood to the side. "Get in."

"I love it when—"

"Shut up. I've no interest in what you think is charm."

Harrison moved inside. He really hated this woman.

She closed the door behind them and leaned against it. He moved towards her only to be kneed in the knackers.

"Jesus." Harrison collapsed onto the carpet.

"That's for the crack about woman my age back in the bar. I'm going to change into something that is frankly far too good to be wasted on the likes of you. Get yourself up. There's a jacuzzi out on the balcony. If you're not in it naked in two minutes, this whole sick affair is over and I'll call security and have you thrown out."

Harrison stared at her high heels as she walked away, disappearing through a door at the far side of the suite. With difficulty, he gradually pulled himself off the floor. The room was incredible: a sunken lounge area, a kitchen behind a glass wall, tasteful furnishings in red and cream, a TV that was bigger than his car. He picked himself up and staggered towards the balcony, dropping his jacket on a sofa and unbuttoning his trousers.

Her mocking voice carried behind him. "So, tell me what you're going to do to me, big boy."

Harrison opened the balcony door, and a cold breeze ripped into him. He quickly slipped out of his shirt. He looked down at Dublin stretching away beneath them. God, he felt so damn alive.

"I'm going to..."

Over the next three minutes or so, Jacob Harrison proceeded to tell her exactly what he was going to do, as he undressed and plunged into the bubbling hot waters of the jacuzzi that sat on the balcony, enjoying the relief from the biting December chill. This place was bloody amazing.

He was talking, a stream-of-dirty-consciousness, making promises that even a part of his drunken, lust-filled brain realised were very probably impossible, both to him and quite possibly to any man. Still. He was angry, he was horny, he was...

She appeared at the door, wearing a robe, her arm stretched above her head as she leaned against the doorway.

He growled at her.

"OK, that's enough. Is that enough?"

The last question wasn't directed at him. It was directed at the four figures who had appeared behind her.

He recognised the man who had appeared at the window when he'd been having his massage. Kelleher had later told him it was Paul Mulchrone. Beside him was a woman, holding a camcorder. "Oh yeah," she said. "I'd imagine between this, and the cameras there, there and there..."

Numb, Harrison watched as she pointed at a small red light in the corner of the balcony and a couple more dotted around the room behind her.

"We have very detailed coverage of Mr Harrison's recovery from his fears of – what was it? Oh yes, sex, heights and water. Quite miraculous."

Beside her stood the girl Harrison had known as Rebecca. She waved at him. She was also holding a German Shepherd on a lead. It was so incongruous, he'd later wonder if he'd imagined it. Behind her stood a lanky bloke, holding his hand over his eyes.

The redheaded woman pulled off a wig to reveal that she actually had a short auburn bob. "OK, that's a wrap, kids. Can someone get this idiot out of my hot tub."

"Ehm," said Mulchrone, "you know it's not actually yours."

"You've rented this place for the night, Paulie, and I intend to make full use of it. Abdul is coming over as soon as you're gone." She looked back at Harrison. "I guess we'll have to change the water."

The lanky bloke finally spoke. "Ah Jesus, Auntie Lynn, would you stop embarrassing me?"

"Embarrassing you? This is the thanks I get?"

A dim distant part of Harrison's brain noticed that the redhead also now sounded a lot less drunk, and had a lot more Dublin in her accent.

She turned back to Harrison and threw him a towel. "Seriously, bugger off, there's a good lad. Oh, and just as an FYI..." She pulled open her robe. "No man has ever turned this down!"

"JESUS!" That was the lanky one again.

She closed her robe again. "Oh calm down, Phil, I'm allowed to have a bit of fun."

"Not that." He held his phone up. "I got a message. There's a message. I have received a message. Oh Jesus, oh Jesus, oh Jesus."

Paul looked him up and down. "I think you finally broke Phil's brain, Auntie Lynn."

"I'm not your auntie."

"Sorry, I keep forgetting."

Brigit stepped forward and took Phil's phone out of his hand. "Oh crap."

"What?"

"It's from Da Xin. Her contractions have started."

For the first time, the redhead looked panicked. "For Christ's sake, get my clothes!"

CHAPTER FIFTY-FOUR

Brigit and Paul stood side by side on the balcony, watching the snow. It was falling gently, the flakes dancing down towards the street below.

Brigit watched on as Phil and Auntie Lynn rushed across the street beneath them towards the van, Tina and Maggie scampering to keep up.

"Why is that Tina girl going?"

Paul shrugged. "I think because she's attached to Maggie and Maggie decided she was going."

"Ah," said Brigit. "At least she can drive the van. I don't think either Phil or Lynn are in the best state to do so."

"Should you be criticising other people's driving?"

Brigit shot him a look.

He gave her a nervous smile.

Then they watched as Jacob Harrison emerged onto the street and skulked away like a beaten dog.

"Now there goes a man who is not having a great Christmas," said Paul.

"Oh, I dunno. I think he's getting exactly the Christmas he

deserves. By the way, do I want to know how much this room is costing the company?" asked Brigit.

Paul winced. "I seriously doubt it. To be fair, the options of places with a jacuzzi were pretty limited."

"I can imagine. We don't really have the climate for it."

As they watched on, the MCM ice cream van made a phenomenally illegal U-turn that was greeted by a cacophony of car horns.

A familiar voice carried up on the cold winter's breeze. "We're having a baby!"

"So..." said Brigit.

"So..." said Paul.

"I should get going. I need to get back to Leitrim for Christmas and I should get moving before this snow starts messing up the roads."

"Right, yeah. How's your da?"

"Grand. Loved up, weird as that is to say. Him and the new girlfriend are going great guns."

"Are you alright with that?"

Brigit thought about it. "Yeah, yeah, I suppose I am. I mean, it's weird, but it's good weird. Life's too short to spend it regretting stuff or moping about and..."

She stopped talking as he leaned across and kissed her.

She kissed him back.

Then she pushed him away. "And what was that for?"

"Life being too short." He gave her a nervous smile. "So here's the thing – I'm an idiot."

"Tell me something I don't know."

"I'm an idiot who loves you and I'm an idiot who is truly sorry for, well, y'know..."

"Being an idiot?" finished Brigit.

"Yeah. That. I almost messed everything up and..."

"Keep going."

"And... and if you'll let me, I'd like to spend the rest of my life being less of an idiot."

"Is this your way of asking for your job back?"

Paul shrugged. "I guess."

"Well, you can't have it."

"Really?"

"Really."

"OK." Paul nodded. "No, that's fair. I did mess up badly."

"You did, but that isn't the reason. You see, as your boss, which I basically would be, there are strict rules on what I can and can't ask you to do."

Paul gave her a confused look.

"But as a woman you do not work for, I can mostly say whatever I like."

"I suppose."

"Like, for example, get your clothes off and get into that hot tub right now."

"Yes, boss."

CHAPTER FIFTY-FIVE

Fintan O'Rourke awoke with a start, his heart racing. On impulse, he reached out to the other side of the bed, before remembering that there was nobody there. He dragged in a deep breath before slowly releasing it. A nightmare, just another nightmare.

He closed his eyes again for an instant before sitting bolt upright.

If he was alone in the house, why could he hear music?

He stopped and listened, trying to settle his breathing. There was definitely music – Ella Fitzgerald, unless he was very much mistaken.

He sat on the side of the bed and slid his feet into his slippers, simultaneously picking up the golf club that sat by the nightstand.

He limped slowly towards the bedroom door. When he had been thrown off the balcony of his own study two years ago by a man he had considered a friend, he had broken both of his legs, among many other injuries. Despite the left one being a worse break, the right hadn't healed as well. He now suffered from stabbing pains, particularly in the mornings, or if for some reason he had to get out of bed in the middle of the night.

He glanced at the bedside table: 11:46 pm. He'd gone to bed early because he hadn't been able to think of a damn thing else to do.

He slowly opened the bedroom door.

The music was coming from his study, one floor up. A shiver of déjà vu ran down his spine. It couldn't be. Could it?

He walked up the stairs slowly, the golf club clutched in his sweaty grip, his heartbeat pounding in his ears, giving an unwanted driving rhythm to Ella Fitzgerald crooning "They Can't Take That Away from Me". A murmur of conversation mingled below the music.

He took a deep breath and pushed open the door. He had known what to expect, yet at the same time, he couldn't quite believe his eyes.

Bunny McGarry sat in the leather easy chair in front of the TV, his hurley sitting on his lap, his sheepskin overcoat slung over the arm of the chair. He raised a tumbler of O'Rourke's own whiskey at him in toast. "Commissioner, up your arse."

"What in the hell are you doing here?"

Bunny took a sip of the whiskey and looked at the glass as he spoke. "Oh, I think you know the answer to that."

O'Rourke looked around the room. "Who were you talking to?"

Bunny shrugged. "Nobody."

"First sign of madness."

"Oh, I don't think it was the first sign in my case."

O'Rourke moved quickly across the room and snatched the half-empty bottle of whiskey from the table.

"I have to say, I'm not enjoying this dram as much as the last one I had here."

"Tough. I've had to make some economies, what with not having a job anymore, thanks to you." O'Rourke poured himself a generous measure and then put the bottle back on the drinks cabinet where it belonged.

"Oh, I think you're giving me too much credit, Commissioner."

O'Rourke threw back most of his drink in one gulp and felt it burn in his chest. "Stop calling me that."

"Do they not let you keep the title after you retire?"

"Not when you retire like I did. How the fuck did you manage to get in here again? The supposedly sophisticated alarm system this house has was upgraded after your last visit."

Bunny nodded. "Yeah, it was alright. I had to hit it several more times with my sophisticated stick to get by it this time." Bunny patted the hurley on his lap.

O'Rourke seethed. He was going to string that yappy little sod from the security company up by the knackers this time.

Bunny took another sip of his whiskey as O'Rourke sat down behind his desk, taking the weight off his aching legs.

"I hope my visit won't be disturbing your good lady wife?"

O'Rourke shook his head. "She's moved out. Gone down to Kerry. The kids are spending Christmas with her."

"Is that right? 'Twas the night before Christmas and all through the house, nothing was stirring, feck all."

"Most amusing, Bunny. I'm sure you'll be the belle of the ball in prison when I have you arrested for breaking and entering."

"Ha, that'd be the least of my worries."

O'Rourke leaned back in his chair. "Got yourself some other troubles, have you?"

"I think you know I do, Fintan. They dug up a couple of bodies in the Wicklow Mountains there last week."

"I saw it on the news."

"I'm sure you did. That's when you sent that wallet into the Gardaí – anonymously, of course. You wouldn't have been keen on explaining how you got hold of it."

O'Rourke smirked. "For the record, I've no idea what you're talking about."

"Save it. Like I'd really be wearing a wire for this. You can spare me listening to ye denying you were Gerry Fallon's performing monkey for twenty years too."

"None of that was ever proven." O'Rourke's smirk fell away, leaving only a bitter snarl.

"Thanks to Gerry Fallon not waking up from his coma yet, no, it hasn't. Fingers crossed for a Christmas miracle on that score. Still, though, we had our little chat down on your lawn that night. I don't know if you remember it? You weren't at your best."

"You nearly killed me. You should be in prison for that."

"We could've been cellmates. Unfortunately, it was tricky for you to press charges without talking about the Fallon stuff in court, and your brief wasn't too keen on that, I believe. They'd not enough evidence to convict you on the Fallon thing, but they obviously had more than enough for the Garda Síochána to be in a mad rush to find a window to shove you out of." Bunny looked pointedly towards the door that led onto the balcony behind O'Rourke. "Sorry, Fintan, bad choice of words."

"So, they're after you for a double murder, are they? I hope you're enjoying your last ever Christmas of freedom."

"D'ye know," said Bunny, ignoring O'Rourke's last statement, "in a way, I always knew. Not about the Fallon thing, but when Gringo and those two other poor fools had the idea of ripping off Tommy Carter all those years ago, it never made that much sense to me. I mean, how were they going to get away with it? They had to have someone higher up, covering their tracks."

"I have no idea what you're talking about, Bunny. DS Tim Spain was buried in 1999 as a hero, gunned down in the line of duty while assisting in the biggest drugs bust in the history of the state. I distinctly remember speaking at his funeral."

Bunny's hand flexed around the hurley. "Yeah, Fintan, you always talked a good game."

O'Rourke leaned forward, warming to his subject. "This wallet you speak of though. Assuming that Gringo had it because he was with you up in the mountains where these two individuals were killed, I don't know how you think I would have got hold of it. I mean, unless your closest, dearest friend betrayed you?"

Bunny gave O'Rourke a long look. "Gringo wasn't a perfect man, not by any means, but he did the right thing in the end. More than can be said for you."

"For a man wanted for a double murder, you're rather preachy this evening."

"Here's the thing though, Fintan. You wanted your revenge on me, fine, I don't really mind, but d'ye know what bothers me about you? For a smart man, you're blind to collateral damage. Through your toadying for Gerry Fallon, innocent people got killed. I mean directly, not accounting for the death toll of the drugs he brought into the country."

"Gerry Fallon has been out of the picture for quite some time, Bunny. I don't know if you've seen the papers, but the drugs are still there. It's like holding back the sea."

Bunny shrugged. "That's as may be. Perhaps that's the difference between you and me, Fintan. You fought the fights you thought you could win; I fought the fights that needed to be fought."

"Oh, spare me."

"No, I won't. When I leave here, d'ye know where I'm going? The Rock. Yeah, the place where we found Fallon had stashed his psycho little brother away. Do you know why? Because of Simone, a woman you never met. She was on the run from some gold-plated evil bastards. We killed two of them. I'm sure when the bodies turned up, it really was Christmas for you. On its own, the wallet was feck all – but with the bodies, jackpot!"

O'Rourke nodded as he held up his glass in a mock toast. "It's the most wonderful time of the year."

"And now that you've used that wallet to get me, you're going to hurt her too. Another innocent for that list etched upon your dirty soul. Forces you don't understand, I don't understand, are moving now. They think they can get to her through me. I have to do whatever it takes to prevent that from happening."

A moment of silence stretched out between them as O'Rourke knocked back the last of his drink.

"You're wrong, you know. I did meet her. Simone. Nice girl. Gringo explained it all to me, you see. After the mess you'd made and then all that business on the beach, there was too much crap. Too many loose ends, waiting to trip us up. I knew I had to get her away from here. It was too dangerous. Something would come out and take us all down. I was protecting you, believe it or not."

"My hole."

"Alright." O'Rourke gave a sad smile. "I was protecting myself too, of course. I spoke to her that night you were in the hospital, when she came to see you. I told her that I knew she was wanted for murder in the States and that you'd buried two bodies in the mountains. I said the only way I could protect you was if she was gone. Just so you know, she cried when she wrote that note."

Bunny said nothing, staring at O'Rourke with unnerving intensity.

"She wanted me to give it to you – the note, I mean, but I said I couldn't. I said you couldn't know I knew, it would just further complicate things. I asked her if she wanted help to get out of the country but she didn't. I dropped her back to a street in Rathmines and she disappeared. I still don't know how. Do you?"

When Bunny spoke again, his voice was different. There was an icy cold to it. "You sent her away?"

O'Rourke pounded on the desk with his fist. "Wake up, you moron! I protected you! What? Did you think you could set up house together and play happy families? That nobody else would come looking for her? Or did you think you could ride off into the sunset? She was a murderer! Gringo was dead and I needed you here to help cover up the shit. And you did."

"You ruined my life."

"Oh, grow up. I saved it. For all the thanks it got me. We were friends."

Bunny stood up. "The fuck we were. You used me, just like you use everybody."

O'Rourke stood. "Screw you, you ingrate muck savage. Life isn't as ludicrously simple as you seem to think it is. I tried to help you – now look at me! My wife wants to divorce me, my kids won't speak to me. I'm a pariah. People I've known for years – decades – cross the street to avoid me. All because of you. You ruined my life!"

"Ara feck off, Fintan. *You* ruined your life. *You* took the money, *you* sold your soul. I've done a lot wrong, Christ knows, but I never did that. I never took money to look the other way."

"Oh, so noble. Is that what you'd like carved on your gravestone?"

O'Rourke raised his right hand, in which was held a handgun.

"Interesting fact for you, Bunny, if you reach assistant commissioner level and you retire, even if you retire in disgrace while they're still trying to figure a way to throw you in jail, you have the right to hold a firearm in the house for your personal protection. There's a lot of bad people with grudges knocking about."

"You going to shoot an unarmed man, Fintan?"

"No. I'm going to shoot a trespasser with a history of violence. Any last words?"

Bunny laughed. "D'ye know, Fintan, that's something else that's different between you and me. I don't think I ever prized my own life as highly as you prize your fecking ego. Honestly, I'm not expecting to live through the night. You see, I'm the one route that anyone has to get to Simone. So I'm going to The Rock of all places, to finish this, because it has to happen somewhere and I want there to be no innocent parties around."

"So you picked there for your elephant's graveyard, did you?"

Bunny shrugged. "We've all got to go some time, somewhere. There. Here. What difference does it make? Ultimately, it's all the same."

O'Rourke tutted. "So defeatist, Bunny. You really have lost your edge. That, and letting me catch you cold like this."

"Yeah, I've lost my edge." Bunny looked down at the floor, as if saying a final prayer.

Then he looked back up. "Of course, I'm not the one who doesn't know the difference between the weight of a loaded gun and an empty one."

"What?"

Bunny reached his hand into his pocket and pulled something out.

He extended it before him and one by one let the bullets fall onto the wooden floorboards, each one thunking in turn.

"I just wanted to see you. Let you know that I know it was you. I also wanted you to know that by trying to get your revenge on me, you've put an innocent woman in danger. A good woman. That's you though, isn't it, Fintan? Not giving two shites about collateral damage."

O'Rourke opened his mouth to say something but no words would come.

"Do you even remember why you became a guard? I mean, at some point you must have had some higher ideals, before your own greed and ambition ate you alive."

O'Rourke stared at the tabletop in front of him, his teeth biting into his lower lip hard enough to draw blood.

He didn't look up as, with a thunk, a final bullet landed on the table in front of him.

"That should be all you need."

O'Rourke placed the gun down on the table and collapsed into the chair behind him.

He watched in silence as Bunny picked up his hurley and coat and left.

He also watched in silence as Bunny re-entered the room a few moments later, walked across to the drinks cabinet and snatched up the bottle of whiskey.

"And I'm taking this. Merry Christmas."

CHAPTER FIFTY-SIX

"Jingle bells... snow is falling... something something... had a very shiny doo-dah... walking in a winter funderland."

Brigit Conroy was a woman of many talents, but even she would admit that remembering song lyrics was not one of them. However, the radio in her car was broken, and all it got now was the fuzzy signal of a dance music station that sounded like roadworks, so she was entertaining herself with badly-remembered lyrics and butchered melodies. She was an absolute nightmare in a sing-song. In school, that old biddy Sister Riordan had made her stand at the back of the choir and mouth along so she wouldn't put off the other girls. She actually had a decent singing voice, it just couldn't stay on the straight and narrow of what the song was. In a way, it was not dissimilar to her driving.

She was on the N17. A car that had been behind her for a couple of miles overtook, the driver honking and gesturing. She waved happily. She was in too good a mood to have some impatient arsehole ruin it for her. The snow was coming down steadily now. It was going to be a white Christmas, something that was magical – as long as you were inside when it happened. The roads out this way weren't great at the best of times and she couldn't imagine roadside assistance would be that easy to come by. Still, she was less than an hour from Leitrim. All going well, she'd be in front of a blazing fire by 3am with a mulled wine in hand. So far tonight everything had gone bloody brilliantly, and she was fully expecting her run of luck to continue.

"Christmas tree, you and me... ehm, K I S S I N G." Brigit giggled to herself.

Just then her phone rang. She could see on the screen that it was Nora Stokes. The most valuable thing in Brigit's car was the Bluetooth hands-free kit that she had installed last year because, although it may've come as a shock to other road users, she took safety very seriously.

She pressed the button.

"Nora, Nora, Nora. Merry Christmas! And a very merry Christmas it has been!"

"Yeah, hi, Bridge."

"What are you doing ringing this late? Actually, forget that. Ask me what I've been up to tonight."

"What?"

"I said, ask me what I've been up to tonight. There have been developments. Several developments. One of them happened in a hot tub."

"Right. Glad to hear it. Thing is..."

Brigit started singing again. "When I get that feeling—"

"Brigit. Shut up."

The tone of Nora's voice stopped her stone dead. "OK."

"I met with Bunny tonight. Well, last night now."

"OK."

"No, no, it isn't. Nothing is OK."

"Actually it is. The whole thing with Harrison has been—"

"Brigit!" Nora sounded really irritated now. "You need to shut up and listen to me, alright?"

"OK, sorry."

"What I'm... I'm technically breaking attorney-client privilege here, alright. I've been going back and forward on this all night, so just shut up and listen."

Brigit nodded at the phone, then realised that was stupid. "Right. Of course."

"Bunny... confessed."

"To the Harrison thing?"

"No, not that. Those two bodies they found up in the Wicklow Mountains last week. He confessed to killing them."

"What?!"

"Yes. That's not all though..."

CHAPTER FIFTY-SEVEN

Bunny poked the ashes of the makeshift fire with the last piece of wood before sticking it on. The smoke was thick but the natural air current carried it up the tunnel and out into the night. Everything had been cleared out, leaving the bunker more like the cavern it would have originally been. The steel doors were gone, as were all the furnishings, bar the milk crate he was currently sitting on. Ragged scraps of carpeting were the only sign that it had ever been any more than a cave.

The fire had maybe another hour in it, at best, then he'd be cold and alone. The only piece of wood he had left was the hurley, but he'd rather die than burn that. That would be sacrilege. There was a dodgy torch he'd found in the back of Jesus Malone's loaner car, but it needed a hard wallop on the side to do anything. He kept it off for the moment, trying to conserve the batteries.

It had taken him quite a while to find the place, isolated as it was. He had headed for the town of Bandon and then eventually found it after a few false starts. It would've been reasonably straightforward in the daytime, but at night, with snow falling, it had been quite a challenge. As he'd driven, he'd passed houses covered in Christmas lights, with smoking chimneys. He'd caught the occasional glimpse through a front window of another kind of life. He felt like a ghost, passing through a world he'd only vaguely known.

Eventually, he'd nearly hit a sign covered in snow that was actually advertising The Rock. Someone had tried to turn it into a tourist attraction. The official pitch had been that you could come and see an honest-to-God nuclear bunker, built by a loony old farmer in the sixties who thought the Russians were coming to Sligo. That's what they pretended, but the poorly disguised real pitch had been, "Come see the dungeon under an ordinary-looking farmhouse where the monster Fiachra Fallon was kept for thirty years." He had read about it in the papers last year. It had opened to the public and closed three weeks later. Whatever people's morbid fascination with murder, there hadn't actually been that much to see. Apparently, the TripAdvisor reviews had been scathing.

Since then, it had seemingly lain empty, although the scrawls on the walls indicated the local youth occasionally hung out there. From what he could see as the flames flickered against the stone, the place was now an impromptu monument to the fact that country kids really couldn't do graffiti properly. The house above it stood more or less intact but empty. Nobody wanted to live somewhere that so much evil had occurred. Bunny had taken a quick look inside but then rejected it. He needed somewhere with one way in and one way out. He needed what lay beneath.

The shed that had stood outside the bunker's entrance was gone, as indeed was the actual entrance. The big steel door had been ripped out, presumably sold for scrap. Whatever was about to happen tonight, if the bombs started dropping, Bunny would not survive it.

He blew into his hands and pulled his sheepskin coat tighter around him. He may be alone but he wasn't lonely. He had ghosts for company.

Zayas: "So this is it, Detective? This is where you come to die? Where you have chosen to come and face the shadows that have been stalking you?"

Gringo: "Amigo, are you sure this is the best way to be spending the Crimbo? While I appreciate your sense of style, are you positive the Butch and Sundance ending is how you want to go?"

He ignored them. He wasn't in a talkative mood. Instead, he took the note that he kept in the back of his wallet out and read it again.

He had read it countless times before, but it felt very different now. Now he knew that Rigger O'Rourke had been standing over Simone, telling her she had no choice. That she had to leave to save him. All those long nights spent wondering if he had been a damn fool to think the relationship had been more than it was. Now he knew that he had been a lot of things, but he hadn't been wrong.

Across the fire, Simone sat looking back at him.

"I know what you're thinking. Not very Christmassy? The trick is not to think of it as a bunker. Think of it as a stable and it becomes a lot more festive." Bunny looked into the flames and watched them dance. "Maybe I'm right, maybe I'm wrong. Maybe there aren't shadows chasing me, trying to get to you. Maybe it is all just my mind running away on me. Either way, something is coming, whether I like it or not." Bunny hesitated. "Maybe if you could speak you'd tell me it's never too late."

He looked up as he heard a sound coming from the tunnel to his right and noticed the beam of a torch bouncing against the walls.

"But I think it might be."

Brigit prided herself on being a very practical woman. She'd been a nurse, for God's sake. You can't have ideas above your station when you regularly have to change bedpans. She'd also grown up on a farm, so she had never been the fairy princess type.

Still, that night, she had made an effort and worn heels. She'd been on a date, after all. Yes, it had been with a man she had known was lying to her, and whom she had been intending to drug – in order to exact a suitable vengeance on the despicable little shite – but still, a date was a date and she had wanted to look nice. Admittedly, she had regretted wearing heels when she had been dragging the unconscious Anto Kelleher into and out of her car, but you couldn't plan for every eventuality. Given the complexity of the plan – which they had executed to near-perfection – her inappropriate footwear had been a minor quibble.

Then, she and Paul had "made up their differences" – twice, in fact! Once in a hot tub. After that, she had got into the car to drive home. Then the phone call from Nora Stokes had rather blown what had been a previously excellent evening all to hell. Bandon, as it happened, had only been an hour out of her way. She had debated several other courses of action, but nothing else made sense. Bunny had saved her before; she owed it to him to try and save him, even if it was from himself.

What he had told Nora perhaps gave some context to how he had been acting. She didn't know what to think, but she knew she had to do something. So here she was, walking down a tunnel in inappropriate footwear. The last time she had been here, she had been with Paul and Bunny, and there had been a monster at the other end. That time, she had at least been wearing sensible shoes. This time, she had the torch from her car in one hand and a tyre iron in the other, because she was a practical woman.

As she approached the bottom of the tunnel, she could see flames flickering dimly against the far wall.

The shoes, impractical though they were, turned out to be a godsend. As she reached the bottom of the tunnel, she slipped and lost her balance. So she was already falling when a madman with a hurley wheeled around the corner, in a practised motion designed to take somebody's head off. The beast roared as the stick clattered into the rock wall above her head.

The torch in Brigit's hand shone upwards, into the demented visage of Bunny McGarry.

"Fucking hell!"

He looked down in confusion. "Conroy? What the bloody hell are you doing here?"

"Thankfully falling on my arse, otherwise you'd have decapitated me, ye mad old bastard."

He reached a hand down to help her up. "Jesus, girl, you shouldn't be here."

With Bunny's assistance, Brigit was able to ungraciously get her wounded pride and bruised arse back on her impractically-shoed feet. "I shouldn't be here? Neither should you. For Christ's sake, Bunny, what the hell are you thinking?"

She glanced behind him and saw the small campfire in the centre of the room.

"I'm..." He glanced up the tunnel behind her. "It's complicated. How did you even know I was here?"

"You told Nora where you were heading. She said you made a big deal out of it."

Bunny whacked the hurley off the wall in frustration. "Of course I did. I was doing it so they would hear."

"What? Who?"

"The people who've been following me for the last few days, since those bodies were discovered. They bugged our offices."

"Oh, for God's sake! Bugged? Did you get that off Phil?"

"Paulie told me."

"Jesus, Phil Nellis – the man who still believes the moon landings were faked and filmed on the Arran Islands – thinks our offices are bugged. Even if him and the dodgy bit of kit Paul bought off the Internet are right, it'll have been the Kelleher brothers."

Bunny shook his head. "I don't think so."

Brigit tried to soften her tone. She'd come here to reason with a man who was clearly losing his mind. The shock of nearly losing her head had made her forget that. "Look, Bunny, I know you're worried. You're involved with those bodies, but I'm sure you had your reasons. We can explain it. Work something out."

Bunny shook his head. "It's too late for that, and it's not the Gardaí I'm worried about."

"The people? The ones following you?"

He nodded.

"Bunny, there's nobody following you."

"Think about it. They had that picture of me and Simone. Gringo had given it to the fella at the US Embassy. That's how Zayas found Simone in the first place. So, when his body showed up, they must've thought that I know where she is. I got a lad I know to stick Zayas on a ferry manifest at the time, throw them off the scent. Over the years, I've been suspicious that somebody might have come looking, but nothing like now."

In the half-light of the beam of her torch, she looked at Bunny's face. He couldn't look directly at her. His breath was coming in pants; his cheeks were flushed.

She rubbed her hand along his arm. "You need to calm down. None of this is making any sense."

He put his hand on her shoulder. "Seriously, Conroy, you need to get out of here, right feckin' now. They're coming. This is where I make my stand."

"With what? A hurley?"

"Well, that. And this…" Bunny pulled what looked to Brigit a lot like a small toy gun out of his pocket. "To be honest, I should've got myself a proper gun. I wasn't really thinking straight. I don't suppose you've got one?"

"No."

"Well, no harm in asking. Now, you need to get out of here."

"I'll leave if you come with me."

"I can't."

"Then I'm staying."

Bunny turned around and paced back into the cave. He tossed the hurley on the ground and ran his fingers through his hair. "Jesus, Conroy, it's not what you think."

"Bunny, it's nearly 3 am on Christmas morning, nobody is coming. Listen to yourself, would you? I've just been outside. There's nobody around for miles."

He stared down at the fire.

"I'm telling you, they're coming."

Brigit moved across and stood behind him. When she spoke, it was as softly and calmly as she could. "Look, how's about you come home to Leitrim with me, hey? We've got a nice spare room. You can get a good night's sleep and a good meal inside you and things will look a lot different." She reached forward and put his hand in hers. She could feel it trembling in her grasp. "Come on, let's get out of here. I'm doing my goose-fat roast potatoes for dinner, they'll blow your mind."

He stood there looking into the flames for what felt like a very long time, before finally nodding.

They made their way back up the tunnel, still hand in hand. Brigit's powerful torch lighting the way. Damn it! She'd left her tyre iron at the bottom of the tunnel. She couldn't go back; she needed to get Bunny into her car and out of here as fast as possible. In the back of her mind, the thought that perhaps she should take him straight to a hospital kept poking at her conscience, but she couldn't do it. At least not yet. She'd see how he was after a night's sleep.

They reached the mouth of the cave. Bunny pulled her back.

"Wait. Hang on."

"Come on, Bunny, it'll be OK. Let's just get to the car."

Brigit stepped out into the night. The snow was falling thick and fast and she could see her breath. She started to walk back up the slope that led to the deserted farmhouse, where their cars were parked. They'd have to leave Bunny's here; he was clearly in no state to drive. She kept the torch's beam on the ground in front of them, so they could see where they were going.

A sound to her right drew her attention and on instinct she turned the light towards it. She was just quick enough to catch sight of a figure diving behind a rock.

Then several things happened at once.

Someone shouted, 'Freeze!'

Bunny heaved her back by the arm, sending her spinning back towards the entrance of the cave. She lost her footing and slammed into the wall.

Bunny hit the ground in front of her as she heard a deadened thunk.

Then something sparked and pinged on the rock beside her and ricocheted down the tunnel. Bunny rolled back into the tunnel behind her, taking her feet from under her and sending them both tumbling into a heap on the ground as something else whistled past above their heads.

Brigit lost her grip on her torch. It landed on the ground with a clunk, its beam shining out into the night.

Bunny regained his footing and dragged her back down the tunnel into the darkness.

Brigit tasted something on her lip. Blood. Somewhere in all of that she must have bitten it.

"What the fuck? I mean, what the actual fuck? People are shooting at us?!"

"Well," said Bunny, "the good news is, I'm not fecking mental!"

CHAPTER FIFTY-EIGHT

"I do not believe this!"

Brigit was pacing up and down in the cavern, the light from the fire throwing her shadow up against the wall. "I mean seriously, I don't believe this."

Bunny was sitting down on the milk crate beside the fire again. In front of him he had laid out his hurley, a box of matches, his small antique gun, a half bottle of whiskey, a pair of handcuffs, Brigit's tyre iron and both of their torches.

"Why are you so calm?"

Bunny said nothing.

"Bunny!"

He looked up.

"I said, why are you so calm? People are trying to kill us!"

Bunny shrugged. "Well, to be fair, I think they're mainly trying to kill me. You're an unfortunate bystander in all of this."

"Oh great, I'm your plus one. That makes me feel so much better."

"And to be honest, when the choices are you're completely losing your fecking mind or that people really are following you, it's kind of a relief to know it's the latter. That gives me someone to fight – more in my field of expertise."

Brigit looked down at the pathetic collection in front of Bunny. "You're going to fight? With this lot? Against armed attackers?"

"I didn't say I thought I'd win."

Brigit pointed at the gun. "Is that an actual gun?"

"Oh, God yeah. It's a derringer. It only has one shot, mind, at best."

"At best? You don't know if it even works?"

"Well, it worked once before. Kind of got us into this whole mess."

Brigit threw her hands up. "Brilliant. This gets better and better. How many of them are there?"

Bunny scratched at his beard. "I'm not sure. At least one woman, a tall guy, a shorter lad. I'd say three minimum. Could be more."

"Against just us two?"

Bunny gave her a look that Brigit couldn't read. "Don't worry about it."

Brigit looked around again. "Why of all places did you come here? We almost died here once before!"

Bunny pulled his shirt out from under his jumper and started ripping strips off the end of it.

"I needed somewhere isolated with only one way in. If you're outnumbered, you don't want to give them a way of sneaking up on you."

Brigit clicked her fingers excitedly. "But no, hang on, there's the other way out, in the roof of the store room. Remember, whatshisname, the little rat-like fella, he escaped up through it."

"Sorry to be the bearer of bad news, but the ladder is gone. Somebody ripped it out. There's no way up there now. First thing I checked."

Brigit slapped the stone wall in consternation. "What kind of a monumental prick takes the ladder out of a nuclear bunker?"

Bunny shrugged his shoulders and opened the bottle of whiskey. He took a deep slug from it and held it out towards Brigit.

"No, thanks, I'm driving."

"I've always admired your sense of civic responsibility."

Bunny doused some of the strips from his shirt in the whiskey and shoved them into the top of the bottle. "Do you have any idea how well whiskey burns?"

"Ehm, I dunno. It usually takes me a few goes to get it going on a Christmas pudding, but I've never used it as a Molotov cocktail."

Bunny looked at the bottle and shrugged. "Well, we'll soon find out, I suppose."

Brigit held her mobile in her hand. "No signal, of course. This is all feeling eerily familiar."

"Well look on the bright side, Conroy, last time we were locked in here. This time, there's no doors."

"Which means they can come in." She lowered her voice to a whisper. "Do you think they're coming in?"

He shook his head. "Not yet. They don't know we aren't armed yet, so we've got that going for us. I mean, they will be coming in, but at a guess, they might try and smoke us out first or something like that. That's what I'd do. Plus, they'll be careful about not destroying the tape. Although maybe not. Maybe they just want to destroy it. Hard to know."

"What tape?"

"Oh yeah, they think I have a tape that I don't have. That's what they've come to get. Well, that, and they probably think I know where Simone is."

"Simone. Is that the woman I saw in the picture beside your bed?"

Bunny looked offended. "When were you in my bedroom?"

"Last year. Remember when you'd disappeared and I was the only one actually looking for you?"

"Oh yeah. Thanks again for that. You're a great girl."

"You're welcome. I'll say this for you: life is never boring with you around."

Brigit moved closer to the exit of the cavern and listened to see if she could hear anything.

"So, have yourself and Paulie sorted yourselves out yet?"

She closed her eyes, trying to adjust to the darkness, then quickly peeked around the corner. She could see nothing in the tunnel as it rose up, bar the faintest of lights at the far end, where just around the bend an overcast night and God knows what else awaited them.

She looked back at Bunny. "Is now really the time to discuss this?"

Bunny stood up. "Trust me, Conroy, there is no time like the present."

"Well, alright then. If you must know, we have, actually. Just tonight. We also sorted that thing with the Kellehers, by the way, although it's starting to feel like something of a hollow victory now that we're going to actually die. Saving the company seems somehow redundant."

"That's fantastic news, Conroy – about you and Paulie, I mean. 'Tis great. He can be an eejit but he's a good lad. I'm glad he has you."

"Well, we'll see how things go."

"Take it from one who knows, don't waste time. There are no second chances."

Brigit held Bunny's wonky-eyed gaze for a moment and then he looked away.

"Of course, my love life is fairly dependent on not dying in the next twenty or so minutes."

"You'll be fine. I'm going to take care of this. You just stay out of the way. This isn't your fight."

She turned to Bunny, full of outrage. "Now that's a shitty thing to say. We're in this together. I'm not going to stand on the sideline like some helpless damsel in distress. Screw you and your kamikaze bollocks, McGarry, we will sort this out together."

Bunny held his hands up. "Alright, alright. Relax, would you?"

"'Relax,' he says. You can be really annoying sometimes, you know that?"

"No, to be honest, you're the first person to mention it. Come here and give me a hand with this, would you?"

Brigit followed Bunny over to the far wall. There was a metal bar firmly attached to it, about six inches off the ground. "I think this is where they had Fiachra's chain attached for all those years."

"Christ."

"Yeah. Grab a hold of it there, would you please?"

Brigit grabbed it with both hands. "I don't think we'll be able to shift this, Bunny. It's really sturdy."

"It'll be fine, just get a good grip there."

"OK, but..."

"One... two..."

Then she heard the click. She looked down at the metal bracelet wrapped around her wrist. The handcuffs. The other end was fastened to the bar.

Bunny stepped smartly away.

"What in the hell?"

"Sorry, Conroy. Can't have you getting yourself hurt. Like I said, this isn't your fight."

Brigit ran the handcuffs up and down the metre-long bar of metal. "Are you out of your damn mind?! Let me out of this right this minute."

He pulled something out of his coat pocket and held it out. It appeared to be a wind-up toy chicken.

"I'll attach the key to this little fella. He'll walk it over to you in a couple of minutes and you can release yourself. That should be enough time."

"Time for what?"

Bunny bent down and picked up the hurley in one hand and the Molotov cocktail in the other. "I'm going to rush them. They won't be expecting that. I'll catch them by surprise."

"They're armed, Bunny. That's suicide."

He shrugged. "You never know, Conroy. I've probably lived longer than I should've already. At least this way, I get to go out swinging."

Tears of frustration were now streaming down Brigit's face. She heaved at the handcuffs again.

"Look, just let me out and I promise I'll do what you say."

Bunny shook his head sadly. "You won't, Conroy. You'll try and help. It's in your DNA. You couldn't stop yourself if you wanted to."

"Let me out!"

As he spoke, Bunny moved back over to the fire, placing the tiny gun in one pocket, the improvised Molotov cocktail in the other. "Soon enough. Sorry about all this, Conroy. Now, in a few minutes, hopefully there'll be a fair bit of confusion outside. You sneak up to the exit and then you run. Don't head for the cars, they'll have disabled them. Just run as fast as you can. No matter what you see or what you hear, you run as far as you can and you don't look back. Have your phone in your hand with 999 in it and call when you get a signal, but keep running."

"Please don't do this."

Bunny wound the toy and went to place it on the ground, the key to the handcuffs dangling off the little plastic winding arm on its side. As he was about to put it down, he stopped and looked behind him. Then he looked at Brigit. "There's one more thing."

"What?"

He stood back up. "Do you know why Paulie and me didn't speak for all those years?"

"Really? You want to discuss that now?"

"Humour me."

Brigit sighed heavily. "Of course I do. He was playing on your hurling team and he was God's gift to whacking a ball with a stick. A couple from down the country somewhere, lecturers or something, wanted to adopt him and you... you messed it up because you wanted him to stay on the team and win some championship."

Bunny nodded. "Yeah, that."

"Look, he's forgiven you for all of that. Long time ago."

"Nah, he hasn't. Not really. Thing is..." A peculiar look passed across his face. "It's not true."

"OK."

"Nobody would've been happier to see Paulie get a chance like that than me. I would've been over the moon, only..." Bunny shifted the hurley around in his hand, his eyes firmly fixed on it as he spoke. "I looked into them, to be certain, y'know, that everything was on the up and up. Took some digging but it turned out the husband was a grade A fucking scumbag."

Brigit watched as Bunny's face reddened at the memory. He pursed his lips and tightened his grip on the hurley.

"D'you mean…"

He nodded. "Yeah. So I couldn't let Paulie, y'know…"

There was a crack in his voice as he spoke.

"So I stopped it. Killed it dead. I didn't have proof – I mean legal proof. Not yet. But I knew. A friend of mine was helping me out with it. Then the husband, he died the next year in a car crash."

"Was that… ?"

Bunny looked up into Brigit's eyes. "Me? No. Actual car crash. Sometimes God beats you to the punchline. There were rumours by then, but it hadn't properly come out."

"I don't… why didn't you tell Paul? Why leave him hating you all those years?"

"His da left when he was a baby. His ma, God rest her, died. His Aunt Fidelma and the rest of her bloody family wanted nothing to do with him. I couldn't have the lad thinking the only people who seemed to actually want him were… I couldn't have that. Him hating me was easier. I could still keep an eye on him, even if he thought I was only doing so to try and get my own back in some way."

"Christ. All this time…"

Bunny puffed out his cheeks. "So, up to you. Tell him, don't tell him. I was never going to say anything but, well, he has you now. Somebody who wants him for the right reasons. That's a good thing. The best thing. Maybe he doesn't need to go to his grave thinking ill of me. At least, not for that."

"Jesus, Bunny…"

He quickly wound the toy chicken and placed it down on the ground.

"Please don't…"

He watched it for a couple of seconds, making sure it was heading in the right direction, and then turned and walked away.

"Please, Bunny, don't do this."

He stopped, the light of the fire throwing his giant shadow against the tunnel wall.

"Remember," said Bunny, "don't look back."

Then he was gone.

She wanted to call out after him, scream, but she knew she couldn't. Whatever element of surprise he might have, she couldn't take that away. She got onto the floor and stretched her legs out – straining every fibre of her being to reach for the chicken as it slowly, painfully slowly, marched its way towards her. She kept her eyes focused on it as if was the centre of her world, which, in a way, it was now.

In the background, she heard a roar – Bunny.

Then a scream.

Then a series of rapid-fire shots.

Then another shot.

Then nothing. Nothing but the steady whirr of the little robot chicken, diligently making its way towards her.

Four inches...

Three inches...

Two more shots rang out.

Two inches...

She flinched as a final shot rang out.

Then nothing.

One inch...

CHAPTER FIFTY-NINE

Christmas Morning, 3:15am

Bunny watched the flakes of snow flutter down from the sky. It was like they just appeared out of thin air a few feet above his head. Magical. Dawn had only started to touch the sky in the east, the light of a new day creeping up on the night of the old one. As ways to die went, there were worse.

All around the country, parents would be silently swearing as they assembled toys they hadn't realised would require assembling. Kids would be lying in their beds, counting the seconds, waiting for whatever was the agreed upon acceptable time for morning to start. Everywhere, life would be proceeding as it should. Memories would be made, the kind of memories a life was supposed to be made up of.

Not his. His life was filled with the dead and departed. Even now, they swirled around him.

Zayas: "Oh dear, Detective, things have not gone well for you. This is most unfortunate."

"Yeah, well, you still died first, so one–nil to me, ye flabby-arsed goat-humper."

He moved his hand down to his stomach area. Pain greeted his slightest touch. He could feel his blood soaking through his jumper, sticky and clinging. He also had a wound on his neck where a knife had almost ended him. He felt cold. It was a different kind of cold to the way you usually felt from lying in the snow.

As suicide missions went, it had not gone badly. Two out of three ain't bad. Meatloaf had said that, although he had not been referring to the dispatching of trained killers at the time. At least, Bunny didn't think so, but then he had never paid a great deal of attention to the lyrics. The problem with two out of three was the third.

The tall man stood over him. "Mr McGarry, nice to finally meet you properly."

"Likewise, I'm sure."

This was the man Bunny had seen outside the flats in a baseball cap and then elsewhere in a coat with a goatee. He was clean-shaven again now. Looking at him, it seemed that the man had spent forever in the corner of Bunny's eye.

"You'll forgive me if I don't get up."

The man looked down at him, a calm expression on his face. His accent was a hard–to-place, generic American. "You are quite the tricky individual. We have been following you for some time now – since the bodies were discovered, in fact. I reasoned you weren't the type to respond favourably to interrogation."

"Ah, you'd be right on that front. I'm not much of a talker."

"I thought, given your erratic behaviour, that you might be tempted to contact Ms Delamere, to warn her. We were up on your phone, house, office. We covered you 24/7, but nothing."

"That must've been awful disappointing for you."

He nodded. "Yes. I'm inclined to think you don't know where she is."

"You'd be right."

"We pursued a couple of other lines of enquiry while here, but sadly they came to a dead end too. We were about to take you, before the authorities did, when you announced you were going to retrieve the tape."

Bunny coughed. He felt something thick and wet catch in his

throat. He spat it out. "Yeah, well, I figured if you were looking for her, you were probably ultimately looking for that."

"Correct. Do you have it?"

"Afraid not."

"That is unfortunate. If you have any information, I will promise to dispatch your lady friend quickly."

"Simone?"

"The one in the cave."

"You're too late on that front. When you shot at us the first time, you got her right in the head. You'll just find a dead body in there, ye prick."

"We'll see."

"Sorry about your two buddies though."

He shrugged. "Merely employees. Frankly, they weren't very good at their jobs to have been taken so easily, especially as you appear to have been mostly unarmed."

"Ah, I've got my devastating looks at least."

"Incidentally, whiskey doesn't burn well enough to make a Molotov cocktail."

"I thought that. Luckily, your employee didn't."

Bunny had charged the short fella and hurled the dud Molotov. It had at least forced him to duck, putting his head at the perfect height to taste Mabel's kiss. A brief struggle over the hurley had followed and then Bunny had snapped the man's neck.

"In their defence, they had been told to try and take you alive."

"Ah, right."

The man nudged the derringer, which lay on the ground, with his foot. "I presume this is the murder weapon that dispatched Agent Zayas. How interesting."

There was a groan somewhere in the darkness to their left.

"Oh good," said Bunny. "I'm glad she isn't dead."

He had managed to take the woman's gun out with a swing of Mabel, but not before she had shot him in the leg. Then she had come at him with the knife. She had sliced his neck and made a deep wound in his arm before he'd managed to reach his derringer and fire a shot into her midsection.

"To be honest with you, I wasn't comfortable at all with fighting a woman. I mean, she did have a gun and a knife. 'Tis a minefield isn't it – is it more sexist to hit her or not hit her in that situation?"

"Personally, I am an equal opportunity employer."

Bunny winced as the man casually fired two shots towards the source of the groaning, which abruptly ceased.

"I can't afford to carry passengers."

"Did anyone ever tell you you're a shit-stain on the soul of humanity?"

"It really is nothing personal. In an ideal situation, I'd try and patch you up and take you with me, so we could have a much longer and detailed chat, but sadly this operation is blown." The man looked down at Bunny's midsection. "You also don't look like you have long left."

"Ah, I made it longer than I'd any right to."

"Luckily, you were kind enough to choose a location so remote that I'll be out of the country by the time your bodies are discovered." He looked up at the sky. "Still, I must get on. I need to check the cave before the sun comes up, just in case you actually did have the tape, and of course to kill your friend."

Bunny looked up at the sky and smiled.

"Mr McGarry, are you listening to me?"

No reaction, just the same smile.

"Is there anything you'd like to offer in an attempt to save your life?"

Nothing.

"Mr—"

"Shush." With blood staining his lips, he gave a broad smile. "I can hear her singing."

He closed his eyes.

The man pointed the gun at Bunny's head.

A final shot rang out.

CHAPTER SIXTY

January 2018

Brigit held Paul's hands, which were wrapped around the handle of an umbrella, held over both their heads. The rain had started to come down steadily now.

The priest was doing his best to be heard but there were far more people than he could ever reach, regardless of how hard he shouted. Brigit looked around her. There were umbrellas as far as the eye could see. Most of the people under them couldn't hope to hear proceedings but still they stood in silence, paying their respects.

Everywhere she looked, people were crying. Kids, women, men.

Beside them, little Lynn Chen Bernard Nellis, all of nine days old, sat in her buggy, under the watchful eyes of her parents. They had felt it was important to bring her. Phil Nellis stood hand in hand with his wife, tears streaming down his face.

That made Brigit feel awkward.

As if on cue, the baby started to wail.

Phil bent down and picked her up and her cries instantly ceased. It was quite the extraordinary thing. As soon as he picked her up, without fail, little Lynn stopped crying. Babies that young can't see, and yet she seemed to look at her daddy with a kind of wonder.

Brigit gave a little smile and then scanned the rest of the crowd. Most people had their eyes on the ground, some on the priest, some looking at the coffin. Brigit stopped with a jolt as she made eye contact with a face she recognised. DI Jimmy Stewart (retired) was looking right at her.

She nodded at him.

He nodded back.

Brigit blushed and turned back towards the grave. They had started to lower the coffin.

In the absence of family – a proper family, at least – people had felt the need to come and express their condolences to Paul, Brigit and Phil. They'd shaken countless hands over the last hour. Paul and Phil had appeared to know at least some of them, Brigit only a small percentage. It seemed like half of Dublin was there.

Just as things were finishing, Jimmy Stewart appeared. He grasped Brigit's hand in a firm shake and leaned in to whisper, "I don't believe this."

Odd choice of words – it had mostly been variations on "sorry for your loss" up until this point, with more than a few "great man" and "he'll be missed" thrown in.

"Yes," replied Brigit, "it came as a big shock to us all."

"No. I mean I think this whole thing is nonsense. He's not dead."

Brigit and Paul looked at each other.

"I don't know what you mean."

"I think you do. I'll be at the afters at O'Hagan's. I'll give you a chance to explain this to me, or I could just go looking. Maybe I'm wrong, of course, in which case, sorry for your trouble."

He said it with a smile, one that said he knew he wasn't wrong.

It took them a while to get there, to the back stairs of O'Hagan's. The entire place was rammed with mourners in the midst of a traditional Irish funeral. The drink had started to flow and stories were being swapped. It was only a matter of time before someone started singing.

Paul and Brigit followed Tara Flynn as she brought them through. "I put him in my office like you asked. Is everything OK?"

"Course it is," said Brigit. "It's just... the Gardaí were asking about a memorial fund. They just wanted to talk to us about it."

"Oh right. That'd make sense. Seems like a good thing to do."

Tara led them up the stairs and through a "Staff Only" door into an office. Jimmy Stewart was leaning against the table.

He nodded as they both entered and Paul closed the door behind them.

"OK," said Brigit, "we'll keep this short. I don't know what you think you know, Jimmy, but you're wrong. Bunny is dead."

"A heart attack."

Brigit nodded.

"Why the closed coffin?"

Brigit looked at Paul, who stepped forward. "For Christ's sake. Not a heart attack. He..." Paul was unable to look up. "He took his own life."

"Bollocks, he's not the sort."

"What would you know about it?" Paul sounded angry now. Brigit took his hand.

"Jesus, Jimmy," said Brigit, "have you considered working for the Samaritans?"

"Maybe I'm way off – maybe. But here's why I think I'm not. Couple of things really, closed coffin aside. Firstly, you two. I've been to a lot of funerals – too many, in fact. I went to every damn murder I worked on, so I've seen a lot of grief. You two aren't grieving."

"I don't know what you—"

"To be fair," continued Stewart, "hardly anyone would know. I mean, you're doing most of the right things, but that's just it. The whole thing is very controlled. I watched you very closely and, more than anything, you looked like you felt guilty."

"Guilty?"

"Oh, not like that. Unless I'm way off, you've not killed the man.

You looked guilty because everyone was going to all this trouble."

"Seriously, Jimmy," said Paul. "Get a grip, would you? Do you have any idea how ridiculous you sound? This is incredibly inappropriate."

Jimmy shrugged. "Do either of you know Dr Denise Devane?"

They gave him blank looks.

"There's no reason you would. She's the state pathologist. Very good at her job. Almost nobody would know this, mind you, but way back in the day, Bunny and I were involved in a case with her. You would never guess from meeting her, but she has, well... I don't know if soft spot is the right word, but she holds Bunny in very high regard, for reasons I can't really go into."

"OK."

"She wasn't at the funeral."

"And?"

Again, Jimmy shrugged. "It's highly unusual. I mean, given the circumstances."

"People are busy."

"Maybe so, but I bet her name is on the death certificate. Finally, there's your reaction when I said this was nonsense. The more I see, the more I smell a rat. Of course, if I'm wrong, I sincerely apologise but, fair warning, I'm going to go looking. I've a lot of spare time on my hands these days. Retirement is not exactly agreeing with me."

"Oh, for Christ's sake." Brigit ran her hand over her brow. "This is bloody ridiculous." She raised her voice. "You can come in."

After a second, the door opened and Detective Superintendent Susan Burns entered the room, followed by a very sheepish Detective Donnacha Wilson.

"Ah, Wilson," said Stewart. "Merry Christmas."

Wilson blushed. "Jimmy, this is DSI Burns."

Stewart extended his hand to Burns, who took it begrudgingly. "Nice to make your acquaintance, Superintendent. I was gone by the time you took over at the NBCI but I've heard a lot about you. Wilson here speaks very highly of you."

"Yes; he doesn't mention you at all, although I have noticed that he occasionally comes in after a long lunch and suddenly he has a few new ideas on a case. By any chance, have you been working as an unofficial consultant?"

Stewart shook his head. "I don't know what you're talking about. That would be against the law."

Burns nodded. "Yes, technically it would."

"Can you keep a secret, Superintendent?"

"Of course."

"Good. So can I." Stewart smiled at her. The mad old bastard was enjoying himself. He turned to Wilson. "Well, Donnacha, at least this explains why you've been dodging my calls. You're part of some far-reaching conspiracy. I thought you'd just got the hump because I didn't send you a Christmas card."

Wilson's face reddened again. "Fuck's sake, Jimmy."

Burns looked between the two of them. "So, did Wilson tip you off?"

"No!" blurted out Wilson.

Stewart locked eyes with Burns. "He genuinely did not. Do you think I'd be here if I thought I'd be dropping him in it?"

She looked between the two of them again. "Fair enough. You really got all this from Devane being a no-show and watching people at a funeral?"

"Call it a lucky guess."

Burns sighed heavily again. "I'm beginning to think our rules on retirement are a joke. You should really still be in the tent, pissing out."

"I'll take that as a compliment. So, is somebody going to tell me what is actually going on here?"

"I assume we can rely on your discretion?"

"Of course."

Burns looked at Wilson. "Guv, he's a pain in the arse but I'd trust him with my life."

"Good. Because rest assured, you are."

Stewart looked around the assembled foursome.

Finally, it was Brigit who spoke. "Alright then…"

CHAPTER SIXTY-ONE

Christmas Morning, 3:17am

Bunny looked up at the sky and smiled.

"Mr McGarry, are you listening to me?"

No reaction, just the same smile.

"Is there anything you'd like to offer in an attempt to save your life?"

Nothing.

"Mr—"

"Shush." With blood staining his lips, he gave a broad smile. "I can hear her singing."

He closed his eyes.

The man pointed the gun at Bunny's head.

A final shot rang out.

Bunny began to lose consciousness... He was dimly aware of the man slumping to the ground beside him.

Then there was another figure standing above him.

"Wake up."

Bunny's eyes flickered open to see Fintan O'Rourke.

"You were right, ye Cork arsehole, I did only need one bullet. Now wake up, you're not going to die tonight. You and your bullshit martyrdom routine."

O'Rourke raised his gun at the sound of rushing footsteps through the snow. "What the—"

"Don't shoot!"

"Jesus," said O'Rourke. "What in the hell are you doing here?"

Brigit held her hands up. "Me? You're a bit of a surprise. Can I?"

She indicated Bunny and, as he nodded, she dived onto the ground beside him. "Christ, Bunny, look at the state of you."

"You should see the other fella. Actually..." He pointed at the body lying face down on the ground beside him. "There he is."

She had her phone in her hand. "Ambulance, please. Emergency. Gunshot wound."

"I told you to run."

"Like you've ever done what anyone told you to do." Brigit pulled her coat off and put it under Bunny's head. Then she pulled his hands away from his stomach and bent down to look at the damage. "This isn't great. Can you..."

When she looked up at where Fintan O'Rourke had been standing, he was gone.

When she looked back at Bunny, he was unconscious.

CHAPTER SIXTY-TWO

Bunny awoke to whiteness.

It wasn't a pure white. A heavenly white. A 'clouds upon which fat-arsed cherubs, constipated for all eternity, sit around strumming harps' white.

No. It was an institutional white. The kind of not-quite-white white that'll do because you have twenty other things to spend the money on that are more important than a coat of paint and you barely have enough money to pay for two of them.

It was the kind of white you woke up to when you were fairly sure that it was going to hurt like hell when the morphine wore off. Right now, his head was fuzzy and his mouth felt like a Care Bear had shat in it.

A face appeared above him. It was human, sort of. Female, at least. It had an unnaturally smooth and shiny quality to it. He saw red hair, big blue eyes and a wide grin.

"Jesus. Is this hell?"

The grin disappeared. It seemed to be an unnaturally slow process.

When the woman spoke, she had an American accent. "No, it's a hospital, Mr McGarry."

"Close enough."

The face disappeared from view and the bed started to rise, moving him up into an almost sitting position.

Bunny watched as the woman slowly came into full view. "Who are you?"

"I am FBI Special Agent Alana Dove."

"Is there a doctor about?"

"No."

"Anybody else?"

"Not right now. Is everything OK?"

"That depends. No offence, but the last Yank I was alone with was trying to execute me." Bunny squinted his eyes and looked back up at the ceiling. "Come to that, I'm not entirely sure how he didn't."

"It's a long story. Can we move this along? We don't have much time."

"I'm not going anywhere."

"Actually, I'm afraid you are. The Irish police have a great deal of evidence linking you to the two bodies in the Wicklow Mountains. And the reason they have that is because you murdered them."

"No comment."

"It was not a question. That's not to mention the three dead bodies you left in a field in Sligo."

"If you're here to exact vengeance, could you come back tomorrow? It's been a hell of a day."

Agent Dove sat down on the visitor's chair. "Actually, it has been two days. You've been in a coma. The doctors seem very impressed with themselves that you're not dead."

"Don't hold it against them. They've not met me."

"This will go faster if you stop interrupting."

"If you wanted to do a monologue, love, you'd the two days when I was asleep."

"You're a very rude man."

"If I was, I'd have mentioned the metal arm by now."

Agent Dove shifted forward in her seat, the calm tone of her voice slipping. "I am trying to help you, Mr McGarry."

"Call me Bunny."

"I'd rather not."

"Your bedside manner needs a little work."

Agent Dove stood up. "Just listen. Here are your options. One, I walk out of this room and disappear, leaving you and the Irish authorities to sort out this unholy mess. You can try to explain how you have left quite so many dead bodies in your wake—"

A part of Bunny's brain suddenly kicked in. "Is Conroy alright?"

"If you let me—"

"Is Conroy alright?" he repeated, a hard edge to his voice.

"She is fine. She's waiting outside."

"I want to see her."

"Not until I've explained your options. My God, you are the most difficult man. I am trying to help you."

"Bollocks."

"OK, I am trying to see if we can help each other. Do you want to go to prison for a very long time?"

"I've got a solicitor. She seemed pretty good in the brief chat we had."

"OK then, good luck with that."

Agent Dove turned towards the door.

"Out of curiosity, what was the second option?"

She turned back. "It involves helping Simone Delamere, before the people who sent your would-be killers find her."

"Nobody knows where she is."

"Yet, Mr McGarry. Yet. To be honest, nobody was really looking for several years but, for obvious reasons, recent events have changed that."

"What are you talking about? What obvious reasons?"

Agent Dove looked at him for a long moment. "Oh my God, you don't know, do you?"

"Know what?"

"Who is on the tape."

"I do. Simone was—"

"Not her. The other person on the tape."

Silence descended on the room again. Agent Dove shook her head and spoke as if not really speaking to Bunny. "You went through all of this and you don't even know why?"

"I knew people were trying to hurt Simone."

Agent Dove moved closer. "The man on the tape has recently achieved a position of some influence. Let's leave it at that. Whoever has that tape controls that influence. When Agent Zayas's body turned up, it fired the starting gun on a treasure hunt. One that goes through Simone Delamere."

"She'll be fine. She's been fine for, what, eighteen years now?"

Agent Dove shook her head. "You really don't get it. Nobody was looking for her before. Zayas was a small-time, corrupt piece of crap. Nobody cared he was dead. Hell, several people shared a few drinks to celebrate it. Now though, people have realised that Simone Delamere is still out there somewhere and so too, presumably, is that tape, and they will stop at nothing to get it. I think you've already seen that."

Bunny moved his tongue around his mouth, trying to find some moisture.

"We want to find her," continued Agent Dove, "before the other side does."

"So? Maybe you're an even bigger shower of pricks than they are."

Agent Dove nodded. "It is a fair point. I also expect you won't tell us anything that might help us find her, will you?"

"Spot on."

"Which brings me right back to option two: the deal I have been instructed to offer you. You leave here, in an ambulance meant to take you to hospital back in Dublin. You don't make it. You die of a heart attack enroute. Hardly implausible, given your condition."

"You're going to fake my death? Bollocks."

Dove wrinkled her nose in disapproval. "It is not without its challenges, but we believe we can. Luckily the holidays, the weather and the location all help. You don't need to know the how, just that we can, and my bosses believe we should."

"But you don't agree?"

"No. I've read your file."

"In my defence, I was drunk when a lot of those things happened."

"I don't doubt it."

"So, let me guess, all I need to do is find Simone Delamere and hand her over to you?"

Agent Dove shook her head. "No, because we know you won't. If the trail of bodies you've left behind you proves anything, it is the lengths you will apparently go to in order to protect her."

"And why the feck should I trust you?"

"We don't need you to. We just want you to not trust *them* – the people who sent a squad to track and ultimately attempt to kill you. All we want is for you to realise Simone Delamere is in grave danger and then do what it is you do. I'll be honest, Mr McGarry, your friend finds herself slap bang in the middle of a war, and frankly, my side is losing. We're outnumbered, outgunned... Call it what you will, but we can't hope to match them for resources. We have looked into you. Against my advice, my superiors believe that you might just be the wild card we need. A dead man the opposition don't see coming. Someone who, I'm guessing, has at least a couple of ideas on how to find Simone if he really had to. We will drop you anywhere in the world and give you what assistance we can. Maybe, over time, you might grow to trust us enough to let us assist you and Ms Delamere in bringing down those that are hunting her. At the very least, we imagine you will at least find a way to cause them pain."

"Oh, ye can bet your arm on that."

Dove pulled a disapproving face. "If you get in trouble, we will of course have complete deniability."

"Yeah? How many Agent Doves can there be in the FBI?"

"None. That's why we chose the name."

"Can I think about it?"

"No. In fact, we need you to make a phone call. Reluctantly, but under instructions from her bosses, DSI Susan Burns is willing to assist us in organising your death, but there is one problem."

"Is it my mobile phone contract? Those bastards won't let anyone go."

Agent Dove did what Bunny was fairly sure was meant to be an eye roll.

"We need you to be dead. Despite any pressure that we can apply, the state pathologist has point-blank refused to countenance being part of this. Not unless she speaks directly to you."

Dr Denise Devane.

Bunny looked back at the not-quite-white ceiling for a long few moments. In all honesty, it wasn't like he had many options. "Give me the phone."

CHAPTER SIXTY-THREE

Jimmy Stewart looked slowly around the room. "So you're telling me that Bunny's death has been faked to allow him to disappear off the radar?"

They all nodded in turn.

"And that's all you know?"

Brigit shrugged. "Pretty much. I mean, I think this woman he was in a relationship with is in trouble and Bunny can help. We don't know anything more than that. This Agent Dove woman went into the room to speak to him and when they called us in, it was a done deal."

Stewart looked at DSI Burns. "And you're happy with this?"

"Christ, no. Of course I'm not. There's not a damn thing I don't hate about it, but what were the options? As it was explained to me by Agent Dove, Bunny almost certainly killed those men in self-defence, but she made it very clear that the US government would be publicly sticking to that ridiculous story that Zayas was here to find his roots. Do I want to push for a trial when I know the accused isn't going to get a fair defence? Then I got two phone calls that made it very clear that the Irish government was going to give the Yanks what they wanted."

Jimmy Stewart looked at Conroy and Mulchrone. "And you two are willing to go along with this?"

Mulchrone shrugged. "It's what Bunny wants. You know him – has he ever backed away from what he thought was the right thing to do?"

Stewart looked down at the floor for quite some time before nodding to himself. "OK."

The others looked at each other in confusion.

"OK what?" asked Burns.

"OK, I won't say anything. OK, I'll leave this room and forget all about this."

Conroy looked shocked. "Really?"

Stewart shrugged. "Mr Mulchrone here said it himself, it's what Bunny wants. He's a lunatic and I wouldn't get into a car with him behind the wheel, but I know him well enough to know that if he sets his mind on something, that's it, and generally, he means to do good, even if it all ends up disastrously."

"So you won't say anything?"

Stewart shook his head. "None of my business."

A couple of minutes later, they were all heading down the stairs again.

"So..." said Paul. "Ehm, sorry I don't know what to call you now. Mr Stewart? Retired DI..."

"Jimmy is fine."

"Can I buy you a drink?"

He shook his head. "No, thanks. I don't."

"What? Ever?"

Stewart didn't respond beyond a look.

"Sorry, I didn't mean to..." Paul looked suitably embarrassed. "I'd better get back in there. Put in an appearance."

They shook hands and Paul re-entered the lounge bar. Someone was on the second verse of "The Fields of Athenry".

Burns and Wilson made their excuses and left. Stewart was about to do the same when Brigit took him by the arm. "Jimmy, can I have a word?"

"Sure."

She opened the fire door at the bottom of the stairs and they stepped out into a dank Dublin day. The rain hadn't stopped, but the wind was at least blowing it in a new direction.

They stood there, awkwardly huddled together.

"So here's an idea," said Conroy.

"What?"

"You clearly have too much time on your hands, and we've got a detective agency..."

Stewart barked a laugh. "I don't know if chasing adulterers around Dublin would suit me."

"There's more to it than that."

"Really?"

She shrugged. "We could make sure there is."

"I'll think about it." He nodded, pulled his coat around him and headed off into the kind of sideways rain that was always blowing in the wrong direction.

EPILOGUE 1

"Mickey Marsh, what are you doing, fella? We gave you a stick for a good reason – use that to hit the ball!"

The manager of St Jude's under 12s was red in the face and sweating. Johnny Canning did his best to hide a smile.

"I don't know, I don't know. Is anyone listening to me out there at all?"

They were. Since Paul Mulchrone had taken over as manager, they were on a streak of four wins. Beating the previous record for the last decade by three.

"We're six points up, Paulie."

"I know, but it should be about twelve by now."

It wasn't just Paul, of course: Johnny Canning was now only a quarter of the new management team that was in place. Phil Nellis, possibly the only man to attempt to coach defence with a baby strapped to his chest, stood three feet behind Paul. In truth, he spent most of the game looking at the baby, who in turn stared up adoringly at him. He held his hands over the baby's ears during the swearier parts of the half-time team talk.

Paul hopped up and down the sideline some more. "Come on, lads, keep the shape. Remember what we talked about. Theo

Murphy, so help me God, if you are texting, I will boot you so far off this team you'll be texting from space."

The third new member of the management team sighed dramatically from his deckchair beside Johnny. He was a self-styled tactical guru of the game. He had played on the team with Paul and Phil back when they were youngsters, and he'd agreed to come along when they had a ring around their former teammates.

"D'ye know what his problem is, boss? He has no appreciation of the fundamentals of the game."

"You're not wrong, Deccie, you're not wrong."

EPILOGUE 2

Several weeks later

He stood on the bow and let the sea breeze freshen his face. After all those weeks indoors, it felt good to be out in the fresh air again, even if most of what he could see was fog. The hulking bulk of a bridge passed overhead.

The ship had the finest buffet he had ever seen, and he'd managed to pile back on the weight he'd lost from hospital food. He had walked the decks to improve his mobility. Between that and his morning dips in the pool, he was almost back to his old self, at least as far as anyone else knew. He had also been surprised to discover how much he enjoyed bingo.

He had been keen to get going, but Agent Dove had explained that he couldn't go anywhere until he had managed to heal up. So he had spent several weeks in a private room in an unidentified hospital overlooking the Mediterranean, where the staff were under strict instructions not to speak to him. Still, he had noticed the lack of bacon on the menu.

He was a dead man now. Instead of giving him a passport, they had agreed to provide him with some cash and passage to wherever he wanted to go. When they docked, he was to stay in his cabin and someone would come and get him to assist him with his circumnavigation of border control. Dove's bosses clearly didn't want it to be too easy for him to disappear. They were about to be disappointed on that front.

A familiar voice spoke beside him. "Christ, amigo, it's colder than a witch's tit out here."

"You're not wrong, Gringo. I've not seen you for a while."

"Yeah. If I didn't know better, I'd say you were relatively sane these days."

"Ha, everything is relative."

Bunny drummed his hand along the guard rail. On the deck below, he could just make out a couple walking hand in hand. They saw him and waved up. He waved back. They were on their honeymoon. The hubby was terrified of flying, so here they were.

"Are you ready for this?"

Bunny breathed in deeply, filling his lungs with the sea air.

Looming out of the fog above them was what he had come out to see. A sight that thousands, if not millions, had seen before him. First he saw her head, then the hand reaching up, holding the torch aloft.

"Ah sure, feck it, I'll give it a lash."

FREE STUFF

Hi there reader-person,
I hope you enjoyed *Last Orders*. If you did, you'll be pleased to hear that Bunny McGarry will return in early 2019(probably) in the provisionally titled *Dead Man's Drop*. if you don't want to miss it, then sign up for my monthly newsletter to receive updates and you'll get the e-book of *How to Send a Message* – my short story collection FOR FREE. A couple of the stories even feature Bunny McGarry at his belligerent best. Just go to my website WhiteHairedIrishman.com to sign up.
And if you're feeling helpful, a review of my books on Amazon or elsewhere is always greatly appreciated.

Cheers muchly,

Caimh

ALSO BY CAIMH MCDONNELL

THE DUBLIN TRILOGY (FEATURING BUNNY MCGARRY)

A Man With One of Those Faces (Book 1)

The Day That Never Comes (Book 2)

Angels in the Moonlight (A prequel to the trilogy that should be read before Book 3)

Last Orders (Book 3)

Lightning Source UK Ltd.
Milton Keynes UK
UKHW010558130519
342540UK00001B/184/P